A Twin Flame For Fae

Magic of Maypoleton Book Two

Dawn Bramwell

Copyright © 2025 Dawn Bramwell

All rights reserved, including the right to reproduce this book, or portions thereof in any form. No part of this text may be reproduced, transmitted, downloaded, decompiled, reverse engineered, or stored, in any form or introduced into any information storage and retrieval system, in any form or by any means, whether electronic or mechanical without the express written permission of the author.

This is a work of fiction. Names and characters are the product of the author's imagination and any resemblance to actual persons, living or dead, is entirely coincidental.

The views expressed in this work are solely those of the author and do not necessarily reflect the views of the publisher, and the publisher hereby disclaims any responsibility for them.

ISBN: 978-1-917778-05-3

Social media links: www: http://dawnbramwellauthor.com

Instagram: @dawnbramwellauthor

Facebook: www.facebook.com/dawnbramwellauthor

*This book is dedicated with love
to anyone who has lost themselves
in the heat of a twin flame passion,
and burnt within those fires.
It is also dedicated to the countless
innocent women, who in past times were
persecuted and executed as witches,
especially those I may call kin,
amongst the Lancashire witches.
May they rest in peace.*

CHAPTER ONE

I was looking for trouble.
Rattling the chains that throttled more life out of me with each passing year, to the point where I doubted my very existence. Nobody saw it, I was sure of this. I was an expert at creating the persona I wanted them all to see. I was playing a role worthy of an award. Performing daily though was wearying to the bones, and I was heartily sick of it.
"You alright Angel?"
I hadn't realised I had sighed out loud.
"I'm fine, just a little tired that's all. That sick bug I had knocked me flat." I gave Neil Hennessey the benefit of my full wattage smile and then wished I had dampened it down a little.
He blushed as he said, "I hope you won't be too tired to join us tonight after work. You know it's Miriam's birthday. We're all meeting at Papa Luigi's for a meal and then going on somewhere afterwards."
That was the last thing I wanted to do, especially tonight of all nights. "I'm not sure. Look I must go. Mr Carlisle needs his meds."
"How is he today?"
Neil was the owner of the nursing home where I worked, and he genuinely cared about the people under his roof. I had a lot of respect for him. Too much respect to get involved with him. He was far too nice for me.
"Not too good," I said thinking about the elderly gentleman in room 65.
"Really? I thought he was in fine spirits this morning when I spoke to him? Has anything happened?"
Immediately I could see the concern in his face, worry in his warm brown eyes that perhaps he had missed something.

He hadn't of course. To everyone else who worked at Sharwood House Mr Carlisle was indeed in fine spirits. But I couldn't tell Neil that he did not have long to live. I couldn't explain how I knew this. I just knew that I knew, if that makes sense. Which was why I was going to sit with him for as long as it took that night.

Besides I was rather glad to have the excuse to miss out on the meal. I might join them all later for drinks but sit round a table singing happy birthday to Miriam the deputy manager, no thank you.

It was a clear- cut case of jealousy. She fancied Neil and he fancied me. In any environment which is predominantly female, this was never going to make for a good working relationship. Miriam went out of her way to assign me the worst shifts, the most difficult residents and hardest jobs.

The funny thing was the joke was on her. I liked the unsociable hours. I had the knack of getting the best out of the crankiest of souls. They loved the attitude I showed them beneath my pristine exterior and neat as a pin uniform. They especially loved the jokes I would tell them, the filthier the better at times.

It was on hearing such raucous laughter one day that I caught the attention of Neil as he followed the sound to see what was so funny. Mavis Bagshawe, notorious for her imperious demands and rudeness was crying with laughter.

"Oh, it's you," she said sitting up a little straighter when she spotted him. "Thank goodness you've finally employed someone with a bit of life in them. This girl's got more spirit than the rest of them put together. This place is like a morgue at times with all those dreary faces I usually see. Make sure that Angel is down to look after me more often."

Angel is not my name.

But it had quickly come to be how I was known at Sharwood House. It wasn't just that I could make the residents laugh, I was also the one they chose to have sit with them if they were poorly.

I suppose it helped that I looked like an angel, or at least that was their description of me and another reason why Miriam disliked me so much. I am petite both in stature and bone structure and I have the sort of face that could be described as angelic. Symmetrical features, a neat little nose, pert mouth and eyes a pale aquamarine blue fringed with dark lashes and naturally ash blonde hair.

Mother nature had been in a generous mood when she passed on the gift of looks to me. I was aware of this and sometimes, it must be said, I would use it to my advantage. I never thought it made me special in anyway though and for this reason I easily made female friends.

I was simply me.

Well, not quite true.

I was the version of me that I wanted them to see.

Friendly, pleasant, kind, always the first to offer to help and volunteer, no problem I would shy away from trying to solve. So yes, I was popular and had many good friends. Good but not close. I kept them at a distance, just as I maintained a certain amiable reserve towards my work colleagues. It was easier that way.

"Are you still here?" Kelsey the manager smiled as she passed me in the corridor much later. "I thought you started at seven today?"

"I did. But Shannon is off sick with that bug I had, so I offered to cover her hours this evening."

"You're an angel, Angel," Kelsey laughed as she said it. "And I don't suppose you were overly keen on going to Miriam's do either?"

There was a conspiratorial light in her eyes as she smiled at me. Kelsey, an attractively curvaceous woman my age, around thirty, had been the one to interview me for the position six months previously. We had instantly hit it off and I was glad that she was the manager and not Miriam.

"I said I would join them for some drinks later," I commented.

"See that you do. All work and no play," chided Kelsey gently.

"Oh, don't worry, I do play," I reassured her, thinking that she would have a fit if she knew how I liked to play.

"Okay. Well, take the light duties this evening until you finish, you've clocked up goodness knows how much over time already this month."

"I'm going to sit with Mr Carlisle," I said repeating my earlier conversation. "He just wants a little company so I said I would read to him for a while."

"Not one of those bodice rippers you've got Mavis hooked on, I hope? I couldn't believe it when she told me what you had been reading to her."

"She enjoyed it," I protested with a laugh.

"I am sure she did. I suppose we assume that because they are old, they have never lost themselves in erotic passion, which is rather insulting when you think about it. As long as you don't go and give one of them a heart attack with the choice of literary entertainment."

"I won't," I reassured her, although later, this was precisely the first of the accusations that came my way from Miriam.

"Oh, bless you love, have you come to read to me?" Mr Carlisle beamed at me as I entered his room. I was genuinely fond of the old man. He was a gentleman in the truest sense of the word, and I loved to hear his army tales.

"Bulldog Drummond?" I said as I went to pick up the well-worn book that lay on his bedside table.

It had been written a hundred years ago and was in some ways the precursor to the James Bond novels. These stories were based in the nineteen twenties and had a charm and innocence to them as well as a sharp wit and humour that appealed to me. Bulldog Drummond was my kind of bloke. Manly, ex-army, happy to break the rules, which he did all the time, and prepared to fight for his woman. No political correctness there.

"We're at the bit where Carl Peterson has him tied up and his thugs are giving him a bashing, remember."

"I do. Are you comfortable? Good, then I shall begin."

I was happy to read for an hour or so, the old-fashioned style of writing a pleasant change from modern novels. One of the other members of staff popped her head round the door with a cup of coffee for me, some hot milk for Mr Carlisle, and a message from Kelsey that it was quiet elsewhere so I could leave whenever I wanted.

"Tell her thanks but I am happy to stay for now," I said quietly as I took the drinks from her.

Mr Carlisle had drifted off to sleep during the last chapter.

"Are you going to wake him for his meds?"

I shook my head. "Not just yet. I'll let him doze a little."

When she went, I sat back down, closed the book and placed it gently on the bedside table. I knew he would hear no more of Bulldog Drummond's exploits. He was going on the final adventure there was. It would be a little while, but it would be peaceful and more importantly he would not be alone. I sat with him, drinking my coffee and when that was finished, I opened my mind and let the thoughts come.

This was not something I ever included on my job applications.

Qualified nursing assistant and oh yes, I can sense when someone is close to dying and see the images in their minds as they do so. At twenty minutes past ten, over fifteen hours since I had begun my shift, Mr Carlisle passed over. He took with him memories of loved ones long since lost, dreadful images of war and suffering intermingled with joyful scenes from a childhood that would fit with Bulldog Drummonds'.

I wiped the tears from my face. This was one facet of my life that was not a lie. I did care every time. It was impossible not to when you have just shared someone's last and most precious moments along with their hidden memories. Making a note of the time, I rose and went in search of Kelsey who understandably expressed her shock and concern at the sudden unexplained death.

"But he looked so well at supper time."

I shrugged. "He did. But he just went to sleep. Must have been my reading." I said lightly but Kelsey for once did not respond with a smile.

I couldn't blame her. Having worked in the care sector all my adult life I knew there would now be rigorous procedures to follow. It was nearly midnight when everything had been taken care of, and Kelsey shooed me out of the door.

"Go home and get some sleep. You've been here since seven. Don't bother about joining the others, they have probably all gone home themselves anyway. I'll see you on Sunday."

Tonight was Friday and unusually for me I was having a day off tomorrow. So no, I did not fancy just going home and crawling into bed.

I felt wired.
Jumpy.
Uncomfortable in my skin.
Uncomfortable in the skin I was pretending to live in.
Time to shed it, just for a little while.
Time to be a little more me.

"Neil messaged me ten minutes ago," I said to her as I grabbed my coat and car keys. "They've ended up in Number 10. Miriam insisted they all went for cocktails apparently."

"Oh well rather you than me. Enjoy."

That was the intention as I drove the short trip home, just ten minutes in the car. I went straight to the tiny kitchen in my ground floor flat where I ripped off my uniform and the functional underwear I wore beneath, tossing it straight in the washing machine.

Fifteen minutes later I was in a taxi and on my way to Number 10, a smart and ridiculously expensive cocktail bar that people with more money than sense chose to frequent. In normal circumstances I would have given it a miss, but I needed to let off steam a little. More than that, I needed to rid myself of the energy that seemed to cling to me following a death.

I also was desperate to forget what night it was.

In the small, crowded bar, with shiny granite counters, leather stools and glass tables, I felt the buzz of life and conversation as I pushed open the door. I paused, the cold night air I was letting in making people look up and glance over. Most of the male gazes lingered.

Including Neil's. He stood up from where he was sitting, squashed up tight next to the birthday girl and I hid my smile at the way his jaw dropped. But as he offered to go and get me a drink, a madly expensive dark rum cocktail otherwise known as a Zombie, I allowed myself to grin openly at Miriam.

"Happy birthday Miriam, sorry I missed the meal, is there room for me?"

The others shuffled up but Miriam, sour faced and scowling darkly, remained where she was.

"Oh thanks, that's so sweet of you," I beamed a smile at Neil, and then pulled over a stool that had just become empty. "Don't worry I can perch on here." I wriggled onto the stool, my short, barely there, black dress riding up even higher on my thighs. "Gosh it's hot in here, isn't it?" I shed my black leather biker jacket that looked so good against my long light blond hair and passed it to Neil. "Would you mind just putting that on the bench next to you, I'd hate to lose it."

He took it from me wordlessly, his eyes glued to my body. I wore no bra, having tiny breasts in keeping with the rest of my frame and I could see that he had clocked this notable lack of underwear.

Yes, this was me not being angelic at all.

This was me being me.

Fae.

Fae by name, Fae by nature.

Which no doubt would cause a lot of comment and speculation next time I turned up at work, but I was just so exhausted from pretending. I knew I could not keep this up much longer.

Mr Carlisle's death had shaken me more than I cared to admit. Not just that he had died, but that my ability to tune into death seemed to be getting stronger. That other part of me that I had tried so long to bury was screaming at me to get out.

So, I drank the Zombie.

I flirted with Neil.

I drank another Zombie.

I flirted some more with Neil.

I ignored the killer looks from Miriam.

I drank another Zombie.

Time passed with growing laughter and noisy conversation. I told jokes that had them splitting their sides and gasping in shocked delight. I was the life and soul of the party, Miriam's birthday party which by now had been long forgotten. With each round of drinks, I felt a little more like me, and a little less like the person I was trying so hard to be. Eventually it was time for us all to leave. Two o'clock in the morning and a mad rush to call taxis.

"Do you want to share a taxi with me? We go the same way?" Neil asked me as we brushed close together in the muddle of people getting coats and jackets and searching for phones that had been carelessly misplaced.

He had that look about him, one I knew very well. An infatuated male who had consumed the right, or wrong, depending on your viewpoint, amount of alcohol to risk abandoning common sense. He was up for it and work relationships be damned. Right there in that dimly lit, hot stuffy cocktail bar, he was looking at me like a man in need of the next drink with a thirst that only I could quench.

So much for Miriam and her birthday wishes I thought as I caught her glaring at me from behind him. But as much as it would have been fun to accept, if only to see her face scrunch into an even tighter knot of displeasure, I had to decline.

"I am going to get a bit of fresh air first," I said as I pulled my leather jacket back on. "I fancy a walk on the prom."

"At this time of night, morning, whatever it is. Angel that's not safe."

My name is not Angel, and I don't want to be safe!

I kept the thoughts in my head but remained adamant that I would get myself a taxi home once I had had a blast of sea air.

Not surprisingly by the time I had got to the sea front and begun to walk along the promenade, there was no one around. It was the end of January. The thirty first to be precise. A date that was etched into my soul with agonising guilt.

"I'm not the angel!" I shouted up to the clear starry sky. "It was you. Always you. It should be you down here, not me!"

"Talking to yourself darling? Come over here and talk to us, we can keep you company."

Coarse laughter along with foul language accompanied the comment.

I had thought I was alone on the promenade, but it appeared not. Clustered around one of the Victorian shelters was a group of men, drinking from cans and by the look of things exchanging drugs.

"You look like a fucking angel to me," called one of them and began to swagger over to me. "I've never fucked an angel. What do you reckon lads, any of you ever fucked an angel?"

"Nah. But I reckon tonight I might."

A this point I was mostly angry. How dare they intrude on my private moment. "Not interested," I snapped and began to walk away.

"You fucking will be!" My arm was grabbed from behind and I was pulled into a rough beery embrace.

My reactions were slow. Countless Zombies and the sea air, not to mention the overwhelming guilt I carried in my heart combined to make me clumsy. The knee aimed at his groin simply collided with his thigh and he laughed.

"Ooh feisty, nice. Come on lads, we've got ourselves a live wire here."

"Fuck off!" I yelled, perhaps not the best choice of word given the circumstances. Again, blame this on the Zombies.

"Don't worry love, I'm going to fuck you, and then he is and then him and him and all of us. Besides what are you complaining about, you're dressed for it, you want it."

I was surrounded now by a black clad pack of hooded hyenas who had moved fast to hem me in tight. I could hear the roaring ebb and flow of the tide against the sea wall. I could hear the thick heavy breathing of men anticipating primal pleasure. I could hear my own breathing light, shallow, fearful now. I could hear all of this, but what I could not hear was the sound of anyone else around.

The one who had spoken to me had pulled at the hem of my dress exposing my bare thighs and black skimpy thong.

"Get off me!" There was panic in my voice and a thudding realisation that I was in trouble.

Not the sort of trouble I had been looking for.

Real trouble.

Stupid. Stupid. Stupid.

I screamed for help. I wriggled, kicked, tried to bite but there were too many hands grabbing at me, holding my arms and legs and pulling me roughly towards to the bench under the cover of the shelter.

Not on the agenda.

Gang raped in a shelter most definitely not on the agenda.

I thought back to a few hours earlier and the peace of reading to Mr Carlisle. I thought of Bulldog Drummond, the ex-army captain who never failed to pull his punches and protect his woman. I felt tears beginning to swim in my eyes as dress was pushed up and my thong ripped from me.

Where was a hero when you really needed him?

CHAPTER TWO

"For fuck's sake hold her still, will you?"
"We are doing, she's wriggling like a fucking eel! Keep still bitch."
"Ow fuck, she bit me!"
Wriggling like an eel, yes, biting at the hand clamped over my mouth, yes, kicking against the hands that held my legs, doing anything I could to avoid the moment when the man who had his jeans unzipped would force himself into me. I may have been stupid enough to get myself into this situation, but I was not going to take it without a fight. In the second my mouth was free I screamed like a banshee despite having no real hope of anyone hearing.
"Shut the fuck….."
He didn't get chance to finish. Just as he was about to push himself inside me, his head cracked sideways, and he went flying into the wall of the shelter. A cacophony of swearing, grunts, sharp snapping noises followed amidst a whirlwind of dark movement.
  Let loose from the men who held my ankles and wrists I tumbled from the bench to the cold hard floor with a thud that jarred every vertebra in my back. There were legs and arms flying everywhere. In the dim light of the promenade I watched as the five men who had been about to rape me were sent slamming into each other, being kicked in the groin, head butted, punched in the face and knocked from their feet.
  They fell like skittles one by one.
  Drunken predators no more. Five men lying in a heap with discarded beer cans rolling around beside them. One of them, on the receiving end of a brutal kick to his stomach, curled into a ball and vomited. A couple were out cold.
  "Can you stand?"

The words were sharp, clipped. Not are you okay? Can you stand? Almost an order.

"Yes. Yes, I can." At least I thought I could. Truth be told my legs had suddenly developed a most unusual wobble and that had nothing to do with the zombies.

"Get up then."

"Yes, yes, sorry." I suddenly realised I was curled up like the ball in the middle of all the fallen skittles. I also realised that he, whoever he was must have been treated to an eyeful of my exposed naked nether regions.

Nice one Fae. Go and flash yourself at your rescuer why don't you?

ABandoning any attempt to find my discarded thong, I scrambled to my feet, tugging down my dress as far as I could. My feet wobbled in my high heeled ankle boots as I gingerly stepped over the prone bodies.

Had he actually killed any of them?

Shamefully I experienced a tiny thrill of excitement at this thought and had to mentally slap myself across the face. He was not Bulldog Drummond and this was not a bloody 1920's novel!

"Do you want to go to the police?" Snapped out again with a sharp sense of impatience behind the words.

I looked at the cluster of bodies on the floor. They were beginning to groan and stir. I thought of the aggravation and processing it would involve. I thought of my own stupid recklessness that had brought this on myself. I thought what my parents, particularly Mum would say. I thought of how much trouble my rescuer would no doubt get into.

We were not living in the twenties.

Well, we were, but another century on from when it would have been considered quite the done thing for a man to completely batter senseless a group of males about to rape a defenceless, if stupid, woman. Back in those times he would have been hailed a hero.

These days my rescuer would probably be given a prison sentence and the drunken, drug taking thugs compensation for their 'suffering'.

Screw that. "No. Let's go."

Let's go?

Let's go where exactly?

I looked at him then and could see the thought reflected on his face.

And then I thought, wow. I mean really wow. My tongue seemed to grow in size and make it impossible to speak. He must have thought me even more lacking in intelligence and he suddenly exhaled a stifled swear word and grabbed hold of my arm.

His footsteps were hardly audible next to my boots tapping along the sea front as he marched me quick time until we were well away from the shelter and in a much brighter spot, closer to the shops and bars that I had left not all that long ago. I was cold now, the wintry sea air nipping around my bare legs, and I hunched my shoulders up within my biker's jacket.

Briefly I thought of Neil and the others. By now they would all be safely tucked up in their beds. And here I was, side by side with this mystery man who had saved me from a brutal assault, not by calling the police like any ordinary person would have done, but by knocking them all unconscious.

I decided then that I was beyond stupid, I was bordering on the insane.

Because only an absolute lunatic would be feeling how I did right now.

Alive!

Really alive in a way I had not done in years.

It may have been adrenaline.

Shock.

Relief after fear.

Whatever it was I felt as though every sense in me had just gone into overdrive. I was surprised he couldn't hear my heart beating because to me it seemed as though it was exploding in my chest.

It was.

I couldn't breathe properly, and I heard him swear again.

"For fuck's sake, here, sit down."

Another bench, but this time not one hidden in a shelter, one directly under a cast iron Victorian streetlamp. Didn't he realise he was making it even harder for me to breathe with him standing over me like that? He must have done because he sighed impatiently and sat down next to me.

I caught a whiff of pleasant woody after shave and male scent, most welcome after the sweaty beer aromas that had clogged my nostrils as the men had attacked me. I focused on this and gradually my breathing calmed, and my heart rate slowed. The stars in the clear sky that had begun to blur slightly, dazzled once more in their clarity.

"What the hell were you doing out by yourself at this time of night? Were you looking for trouble?"

"Yes."

He wasn't expecting that. I could see it in the tiny flicker that altered the stony expression on his face. No doubt he had been expecting a drunken rambling apology and an admission that I had been a total fool.

"Yes?" Interrogative. Demanding that I expand.

"Yes," I said and looked him in the eyes.

My breath caught again.

I was bold enough to hold his stare, but only for a second. Blue eyes as cold as the sea defeated me. I was looking into the eyes of a killer; I thought with a shiver. Yet as I dropped my gaze, I didn't feel afraid. If anything, I felt safer than I had ever done.

Safe enough to be honest?

"I was looking for trouble." I said slowly as I moved my head, so I did not have to feel that probing stare upon me. I turned my eyes heavenwards and thought of her. I thought of what kind of trouble I had gone looking for. I had come close to finding it this time. Tears formed in my eyes. Not tears of sorrow for what I had narrowly avoided. Tears of guilt and shame that I had once more cheated fate.

I was still here.

I was still alive.

And she wasn't.

I waited for the barrage of accusations to come my way. How reckless and stupid, that kind of comment.

Instead, he said in a slightly different tone of voice, "Where do you live?"

Of course, he was going to see I now got home safely. He was a hero. Hero's do not rescue damsels in distress and then leave them to get a taxi. That would not be in the hero's code. Beat men up, knock them senseless, then deliver stupid female back to her door in one piece, job done. I had some pride left. Not much, but enough to at least think about arguing. Then I looked at his face and left the words unspoken. I quietly told him my address.

"It's not far, about ten minutes, probably less now with no traffic."

Without speaking he stood up and began walking. "Well, are you coming then?" Again, the implication that he was dealing with an idiot resounding in his voice.

"Sorry." Bloody hell, when did I ever trail after a man? But look at me now, I thought to myself as I did my best to keep up with him. Which wasn't easy considering he must have been all of six foot four and me a mere elf in comparison. I needed at least three strides to match one of his.

He didn't seem to notice though or consider his pace. Coming down now from my own rush of shock and adrenaline, I felt the power of the energy he was giving off. Not too surprising given what he had just done, and I supposed he would not wish to linger in the vicinity just in case the police did turn up.

Parked in a side street nearby, just in front of the town's homeless shelter, was a very ordinary looking car. Not what I had in mind for my hero. Surely, he drove a supercharged Porsche or a Jaguar something like that, or even a great beast of a jeep? Not a bloody Volvo!

Bulldog Drummond drove a Bentley for Christ's sake!

Not Bulldog Drummond girl.

"Get in," he said curtly just as I was about to ask him what his name was.

The tone of his voice was enough to clamp my lips together and I reminded myself that this was a man who had just battered five others single handedly. He was not someone to provoke. I pulled the seat belt across me, but it was an old car, and it stuck awkwardly.

"I can't get it in," I said needlessly as it was blindingly obvious this was the case.

Another stifled sigh, and he leant across. There was a moment, just a moment, as his hand briefly brushed against me, not on purpose, I knew that he couldn't avoid it. But a moment, nevertheless. His face was close to mine. Cold blue-grey eyes flicked to my face then dropped for the merest of a second to my thighs, bare even though it was January.

A second can be all it takes.

Again, I felt the breath slam from my lungs, and I was glad when his hands were on the steering wheel and the car was pulling away from the kerb. I was not surprised to see that he drove sharply and efficiently. But not fast. His eyes were quick to keep checking his mirrors and again I thought that he might be keeping an eye out for police cars. It wouldn't do to get done for speeding and then be logged down for the time and location just in case one of those thugs decided to go to the police themselves.

Ten minutes later we had left the popular area of the seaside town behind and were in the far less alluring suburb that I called home. Parking was always something of a problem around here. I had a small car parking space as a resident of the flats but for visitors it was often tricky, especially at the weekend and this was a Friday night.

He made do with a spot two hundred yards from my home and I had to swallow my admiration for the quick way he squeezed the vehicle into the space. I would have taken about ten attempts to get my much smaller car in between the others and even then, I probably would have ended up banging one of them. Or both.

"Thank you." I had not uttered these words so far and realising that I was about to go safely back into my flat unharmed it was I knew, very remiss of me.

Was I surprised when he got out of the car as well?

Not really.

He was a 'see you to the door', kind of man, not trusting that more misadventure might come my way in the two hundred yards between the car and my flat. I felt peculiarly vulnerable as we walked the short distance. How many times had I brought men to my door? Countless. Often strangers I had picked up in bars. Never did I feel I wasn't in control of what I was doing. Tonight, everything had changed. This was not a man who I was about to ask in to stay the night with me.

But as he stood impatiently by my side whilst I rooted in my leather jacket pockets for my key, I was swamped with longing to do exactly that. I was a jumbled cocktail of emotions and feelings far more lethal than any rum based drink. And as I had carelessly knocked back the drinks in the bar, knowing that they would barely touch the pain I wanted to numb, I was all too aware that there would be nothing careless in the outcome if I did ask him in.

Not that he was giving me the remotest hint that he was waiting for me to do that. There had been that moment in the car, but other than that I got the impression he was viewing me as a total inconvenience. More than that perhaps, as I sensed an underlying hostility brewing in him as he waited for me to open the door.

"I can't find my key," I stuttered awkwardly. Since when did I stutter?

He swore succinctly. "Did you drop your bag?"

"No. I never take a bag with me, it makes you too much of a target," I explained and realised the absurdity of my words as soon as they had left my mouth.

There was another stifled sigh. I had the feeling his patience was running out. "Move."

I jumped sideways at his command no pert retort finding its way to my lips. I watched in silence as he dug into his own pockets, pulled out a small folding tool object, and with a couple of quick certain movements my front door was open. So much for my security I thought as he looked at me with ever growing impatience in his eyes whilst I stood rooted to the spot.

This was it then.

Time to say goodbye.

I had not even asked his name, nor given him mine.

It had been an encounter of barely an hour but somehow, I felt my life had changed because he had come into it and the thought that he would just as quickly depart was terrifyingly devastating.

What on earth was happening to me?

This was not merely a matter of me wanting a man to have sex with, this was far more than that. I had never felt so vulnerable and in need as I did right then. I did something I had never done before, nor would I have even imagined myself capable of doing.

I begged him to stay. "Please don't go."

He didn't speak.

We stood in the doorway of my flat, the open plan living, dining and kitchen area dimly lit by the table lamps I always left on so I wouldn't be coming home to the dark. I wondered perhaps if he had not heard me. Maybe I had not actually spoken the words. Surely there should have been some reaction?

I stared at him and saw there was.

It was faint, just the tiniest twitch of a muscle in his cheek giving away the control he was exerting over himself. Hard to say at this point whether it was impatience, anger, or something else. Unlike all the men I had been with, I couldn't read him at all.

I just knew that I was drowning in the dark pools of his blue-grey eyes and that I longed to have the well sculpted mouth press against mine, to be crushed in an embrace with his powerfully built arms, to feel the hardness of his thighs moving with me, to wipe out the memory and fear of such a short while ago. All I could think, was that I could not possibly survive this night unless I had him with me.

I begged him once more. "Please, stay with me."

There was a moment's indecision and a tightening of his lips as though he was fighting a battle within himself. In that instant I knew I had the fraction of a chance to sway his mind. But only if I was honest. Truly honest. This was a man who would not compromise. I knew that much about him.

"I don't want to be alone tonight." I dropped my guard, lowered my defences and let him see the pain I hid from everyone else. "Just for tonight, please. Just until the morning."

"Oh shit," he ground out with a clenched jaw. Then he bundled me further into the room and slammed the door behind us.

CHAPTER THREE

I was lifted off my feet as he pulled me up to kiss me.

It was a bruising angry kiss that evoked a whimpering of stunned response from me. He moved in close with an urgency that had me stumbling backwards until I bumped into the sofa. My jacket was slid from my shoulders, my boots kicked from my feet. Those hands that had punched, beaten and bruised, not to mention so skilfully broken into my house made short work of my ridiculously short dress.

Naked now, I was scooped up into his arms and within seconds I would be on the sofa, and he would be on me, and inside me. And that would normally be fine. It wasn't like I hadn't often had sex right there on the sofa with men I had just met.

But he was not just any man.

And tonight was not just any night.

"Bedroom please?"

"Didn't have you down for the romantic sort?" He spoke softly against my ear as he kissed my neck bitingly, hands giving my body a quick but thorough once over, before he scooped me up properly this time and carried me through to the bedroom.

This was more like it.

Bulldog Drummond would carry his woman into the bedroom.

But I don't think Bulldog Drummond would have tossed me quite so unceremoniously on the bed like an unwanted parcel, a throw away gift. There was an element of anger still running through him as though part of him really did not want to be here. Not very flattering to my ego, despite how he had kissed me so urgently.

I could see the battle going on in his mind as he stood at the edge of the bed looking down at me. As in the living room, I had left my small bedside table light on and I watched as his eyes scanned me from head to toe, lingering on every inch in a way that had me squirming with need.

And fear.

Was he going to reject me?

It had never happened with any of my other men. But then I already knew he was far from being like my other men. I would not have been surprised if he had just turned and walked away, cold contempt blistering me from his eyes.

I was spared this indignity.

"Fucking hell," he muttered under his breath as though he realised he was actually going to do this.

Again, not so flattering for me.

But what was flattering was the way he then tore off his own clothes and within seconds was completely naked before me letting me see how aroused he was. He stood still for a second so I could look at him. I knew he watched as my eyes left his face and trailed down his body. I couldn't prevent the small exclamation from escaping.

"Oh."

A cold, hard questioning look in his eyes as mine met his once more.

Wordlessly I moved on the bed and opened my legs slightly, inviting him in.

He needed no further encouragement and from that point I was under no illusion that he wanted me.

Me?

Or anybody?

Just a need to burn off the adrenaline he must have stirred up in the fight?

It didn't really matter.

All that mattered was the way I felt as soon as his body touched mine. The skin-to-skin contact as he lay full length on top of me. The deep plundering kisses that grew more feverish with every breath we took. The way his hands moulded and shaped every line and curve of my body as though he couldn't quite believe he was touching me. A need entwined with a lack of control in contrast to what I had seen of him so far.

When he had had enough of kissing me, he latched his mouth onto one nipple and then the other, lapping with his tongue and then tugging and grazing with his teeth in a way that had me clutching at his head to hold him in place there. His hair was cropped to his skull, black, shot with grey, so short the feel of it was rough against my skin.

The feel of his body was rough against mine. Hard muscles with not an ounce of fat. Rippled patterns of skin.

Scars I explored with trembling fingers, feeling him tense beneath my touch.

There was a moment when our eyes met as though he was waiting for some comment. I wondered if a woman had ever said anything to add to the wounds on his body. For every scar on the outside there must be more on the inside.

They didn't put me off.

As ugly as they were, they didn't stop the desire he was stirring in me.

Once more I was begging.

"Please," as his hands found their way down to my thighs.

"Please," as he opened me up with his fingers as easily as he had unpicked my lock.

"Oh shit," he groaned and pulled away suddenly.

"What?"

"I've nothing with me."

Comprehension dawned. "I'm on the pill."

He raised his eyebrows at me, and I knew with an embarrassing certainty what he was thinking. I may well be on the pill, but if my behaviour tonight was anything to go by, and it was, I slept around, and he could catch anything from me.

Ouch. That was a shower of freezing cold water over my head.

Stung, I said. "I'm clean. I mean, I always, usually that is, even though I am on the pill, I always make them, you know…"

"Them? There's that many?" Hard, cynical, world weary.

Tears filled my eyes. "Yes, there's that many. You can go if you want. It doesn't matter. I shouldn't have asked you in, I'm sorry."

Once more I was behaving completely out of character. I shifted back slightly on the bed and turned my head away from his punishing gaze. My eyes fell on the photo. The two of us together. I bit my lip wondering what she would say if she could see me right now.

I never cried. I hadn't done since I was a teenager anyway.
I absolutely never cried in front of any man.
Not even one who had rescued me.
Yet there were tears sliding rebelliously down my cheeks as hard as I tried to stop them from spilling over from my eyes. Brusquely I wiped them away and hunched up my knees to my chest.

"It's okay, just go."

He had pulled back himself, lying slightly to one side now, propped up on his elbows. He hadn't missed a thing though and his eyes went from the photograph back to my face.

"Oh, fucking hell, come here." With a resignation in his voice now as though he was saying to himself, he may as well be hung for a sheep as for a lamb, he shifted quickly on the bed and before I could think any further, he had me full length underneath him.

And then the full length of him within me.

I should have realised he would not hesitate or be tentative.

His hands slid quickly beneath my bottom to lift my hips up to his and in one swift and sure movement I was entered, filled, possessed.

The sureness of his actions drove a startled gasp from my lips. He looked at me mockingly. I had exclaimed as loudly and with as much surprise as a coy virgin.

I wasn't acting.

I really hadn't felt like this before.

I was used to being the seducer, taking the lead, always the one in control.

I wasn't in control of anything with him.

From the moment his body entered mine I was flying off a cliff with a dangerous crash landing awaiting me. It was thrilling and terrifying in equal measures. I had no idea what he was thinking or feeling. Apart from that one mocking look, the face that hovered above mine, so close to me, was completely unreadable in his expressions.

Yet there was an intensity there that was compelling.

His eyes were locked onto mine and we didn't kiss as he moved within me. It was though he was forcing himself to look at me, to register what he was doing. And what he was doing was so good all the men I had ever had sex with faded away into ghosts of my past.

Deep, powerful strokes, driven with purpose and energy, just as he had been with the men he had attacked. No waste of movement. Every withdrawal, every following thrust given with intent. I am not sure what that intent was. There was a lack of sensuality and seductiveness about this. More a feeling of pain and punishment as with every thrust of his hips, and every answering cry from my lips, he was somehow fighting demons that were chasing him. It grew in intensity, not just with the spiralling pleasure of the climax that was building, but with the fierceness that began to burn in his eyes.

The sea blue had turned stormy grey, and a grim line had tightened around his mouth. The softer and more pliant I became, the more rigid and determined he appeared to be. And with this an increasing pace to his thrusts that were slamming into me so fully I could feel him bruising the tender flesh between my legs.

I would be sore in the morning.

I would be lost without him in the morning.

A thought out of nowhere that had me crying out with a pain that was not physical but came from my soul. The cry turned into tortured gasps of pleasure as that cliff I had approached so carelessly, fell away behind me. I tumbled fast into the dizzying spirals of a climax that had me staring wide eyed at this stranger above me, unable to believe what I was feeling.

Coldly, dispassionately he watched my face as I crumpled beneath him.

Then, when I was about to land on the rocks, shattered with passion, he finally closed that distance of a mouth's breath between us, and pressed his mouth over mine. His kiss breathed new life into me, and I flew once more on a rising crest of pleasure. With his eyes at last closed, mine too, our mouths as fiercely engaged as our bodies, he finally let himself go.

I say that because all along there had been the sense that he was battling with himself to not lose control. To not give way to this passion. To not even enjoy it somehow. There was no denying though that whatever thoughts may have gone on in his head, his body was now in charge. He pounded into me, kissed me deeply, then groaned as though in hell, as his body went taut, and I felt him pulse deep within me.

For a moment he lay there heavily upon me.

He was a big man, well built with muscle and I was tiny in comparison. A part of my brain registered the fact that I liked this difference between us. I liked feeling small and fragile beneath him. I liked feeling protected.

Protected?

Then he moved, as swiftly and surely as he had entered me and rolled over to lie beside me on the bed. I could breathe and yet I felt starved now of oxygen. How was that possible? How could I just feel as though I had lost a limb as he pulled himself out of me? How could I feel as though my body had only just come alive?

"Wow, oh my God, that was fucking amazing!"

I waited for this to be said into the silence that hung between us. Or at least a comment of similar content. That was usually what happened. The men I brought back here were normally as vocal in their appreciation afterwards as during the event.

Silence?

I was almost afraid to turn my head and look at him I was so out of my depth. That sensation of falling off a cliff came back only this time not with pleasure but of uncertainty. I dared to risk a look. He had his eyes focused on the ceiling and I took the opportunity to let my gaze drift over the body that had just taken me to the heights of ecstasy.

I had felt the muscles and the scars, but looking at them was something else. Never one to shy from probing questions, here I was, tongue tied and unable to frame a sentence at all. This was not a man to casually ask what had happened to cause such damage to his body.

Had he been in a fire? Some kind of chemical accident?

My mind went a little into overdrive then and thoughts of fantasy films and mutant heroes sprang to mind. Wolverine, Spider Man, changed from a normal man to a being with superpowers. Be honest, what woman would not want a superhero in her life at some point and the way he had handled those men was far from average.

"What happened to her?"

"Sorry?" I was so lost down this train of thought that he took me by surprise in speaking.

He turned his gaze from the ceiling to look at me and I felt even more exposed and naked under his stare than when we had been locked together in passion.

"Your twin. What happened to her?"
I sat up then, reaching suddenly for the duvet to cover myself. Totally exposed.

Was he a mind reader or something?

Back to the idea of a superhero.

He dashed this theory then by adding in a cool and no-nonsense voice. "You were in tears when you looked at the photo earlier. Something must have happened to her."

Not a superhero then. Just extraordinarily observant. More a Sherlock Holmes.

"She died."

He continued to look at me, and I think that was the first hint of a human being I saw in his eyes, not some kind of machine. It was an unrelenting look. Helplessly, I gave away another part of my soul.

"Tonight is her anniversary. She died on the 31st of January."

"How old was she?"

God he was good at this. He asked in a way that demanded I tell him.

"Fifteen." My eyes left his and went to the photograph, the two of us together, identical, laughing at Dad who had held the camera. I felt the constriction in my chest, the lump in my throat, the pain like a knife ever twisting in my gut.

An imaginary pain.

Imaginary to me.

Real to her.

He didn't ask anything more then. I think he must have realised I had gone as far as I could. The way I had wrapped my arms around me was telling enough. I had begun to rock myself as a child does when in need of comfort. Only I was not a child I was a thirty-year-old woman. I was a thirty-year-old woman who had lived half her life, without the other half of herself.

I was not aware I had moaned out loud until he moved and drew me down alongside him.

I was not aware I was crying until he wiped the tears from my eyes with a gentle thumb.

I was not aware that I had been searching for love until he began kissing me once more.

CHAPTER FOUR

Hailstones woke me, battering against the window like bullets.

There was a tiny hint of daylight poking through the gap in the curtains which meant it was at least after eight. So that meant today was not a workday then, as usually my alarm would wake me, and it would still be dark.

So, I could roll over and …..

I got that far and sat bolt upright.

My bed was empty. That is to say I was in it, but nobody else was. I actually patted the other side of the bed and lifted the edge of the duvet up to make sure. Then I strained my ears to listen to the sounds of the shower running, or the toilet flushing. Nothing. The only sound I could hear was that of the hailstones.

Maybe he was in the kitchen making a brew.

I scrambled to find the over- sized t-shirt I usually slept in and pulling it over my head I went into the open plan living room and kitchen area. It was empty. I spotted my leather jacket and the skimpy black dress I had worn last night. They had been placed neatly on the back of the sofa.

Maybe, I thought, he had gone to get milk for a coffee? I frequently ran out and there was a shop just across the road which was clearly visible from the front window. I walked into the kitchen area and opened the fridge. There was plenty of milk which put a stop to that idea.

Perhaps I wondered, he had gone to buy croissants?

Perhaps I had lost my marbles completely?

Because that was the only excuse for me thinking this way.

What exactly was I thinking? That this was the start of some wonderful romance in my life? Bloody hell Fae, get a grip. Angry with myself I filled the kettle and switched it on. I would make a coffee, have some toast, enjoy the fact that I did not have to go to work, and I absolutely would not give him another thought.

Him.

I didn't even know his name and I was pretty sure he had not asked mine. Again, all par for the course with me. Very often I didn't want to know their names, although they usually told me and usually asked mine. Very often I would tell them the name I was known by at work, Angel, and they would say how much it suited me. Somehow, I knew if I had told this to my stranger last night, I would have received a much different response.

The kettle was taking forever to boil; I must have filled it to the brim, stupidly hoping that he, whoever he was, would be returning from the shops to join me for breakfast.

Muttering under my breath, I had never, ever considered myself to be the sort of woman who dangled after a man, I went to get dressed. Really, I should have showered, I know that. I was about to as I usually did in the morning. But I caught a trace of his scent on me, I could still smell him in the room.

My bedroom was only small, and I liked to keep it simple. My tastes ran to the uncluttered, neutral colours and natural fabrics where possible. The whole flat was like that revealing little if any of my personality. The few pictures I had on the walls were of the generic type you could find in any run of the mill supermarket. A few of my friends had commented how much it looked like a hotel at times, so clean, tidy, and unfussy.

Like a hotel my flat did not offer the visitor the sense of being a home and that was exactly how I liked it. A home indicated permanence. More than that. A home was where a person created a family and memories. The photo by my bed was a constant reminder, not that I needed it, of the person who should have been filling a home with love, laughter, and children. All those precious gifts of life denied her.

And if Fliss could not have them, well then neither could I.

Which meant that the men I invited back here would never be the kind to leave any imprint at all on my flat, my life, on me. Visitors merely passing through like the many guests one could expect in a hotel. Yet as my eyes went to the crumpled bed and my thoughts back to last night, I had the strongest sense that I was kidding myself.

He had left an imprint on my bed.

I swallowed at the images in my head, the way his lovemaking had made me feel.

He had made an imprint on more than my bed.

The reason I was shying from taking a shower was that I was reluctant to wash away the imprint he had left upon my body. If I shut my eyes, I could still feel the touch of his hands, the melting pressure of his lips, the throbbing, pulsing heat of him. The more I thought of this, the more I felt something deeper, the more I feared he had made an imprint beyond the physical. I heard the kettle switching off in the kitchen but right now I didn't want coffee.

I wanted to be back in bed.

With him.

Him of no name.

Despising the weakness, I felt as I did this, I crawled back into the bed, lamely telling myself it was a day off and I deserved a lie in, all the while ignoring the voice that was screaming in my mind that I never had lie ins, I never dreamt about men who had left without even telling me their name.

I was always the one who told them when to go. Either the morning after, sometimes even during the night if they had not come up to standard, or at the very latest a few weeks down the line when they were on the point of declaring themselves in love with me. Cocooning myself into the folds of my duvet I had to acknowledge that the tables had most definitely been turned.

My eyes turned to meet Fliss's in the photo. What would she have thought of him? Would she have seen that he was different from all the rest? Because he was. I knew that for a certainty. Even without the heroics of his rescue, he was way, way different to all the rest. Then of course my thoughts spun back to what had happened just before he came and I shivered into a ball, thinking how bloody lucky I had been for him to come along like he had.

Luck?

I didn't believe in luck.

I didn't believe in anything these days, so I just lay there in the haven of my duvet and allowed my mind to replay the previous night. From brutal assault to wild passion.

That second time he had made love to me I told myself, it had not been just sex. Hell no, it had been way more than that. Most definitely not just sex. So, it must have been making love. Making love? Love Fae? I struggled at this point. Okay at least if not love because really that was a nonsensical word to apply to two people who had literally just met and fallen into bed, it was something a little deeper than the first round of sex had been.

Healing?

The word popped into my head, and I dismissed it with a snort of disgust.

That would imply that he could mend me, and he couldn't. No one could. No one short of the Universe bringing my sister back down to this earth could do that. So no, best not to call it healing.

But it had been powerful.

Erotic.

Gloriously so.

It was as though once he had crossed whatever barrier had been holding him back, he had to release everything inside him in one go. Which made for a very satisfied woman indeed. He had never stopped kissing me that second time. Sometimes light quick kisses in between dropping his mouth lower down my body to explore more, then back up to my mouth. Sometimes deep, really deep demanding kisses that hinted he was as desperately in need of something in the same way I was.

Searching for redemption in the arms of another.

And if his kisses had been all the more seductive second time around, the way he had moved within me had been equally sensuous. Less of an angry energy from him this time. More a sense that he was reading my responses, no, better than that, anticipating my needs and desires. Completely in tune with me in a way I had never felt with any man before. As though we were literally one being.

I moaned now at the memory of how he had slowly, lightly, teased his way into me, then picked up the pace according to my cries and moans. When I had wrapped my legs tightly around his waist, he had taken the hint to cradle my bottom up under his hands and pull me towards him as close as he could.

Then in as deep as he could with slow, deliberate strokes that had taken me to not one but two orgasms with him joining me on the second. Tangled tightly together, my arms around his neck, his hands firm on my waist, my lips brushing against the side of his head, his mouth nuzzling deep into the crook of my neck, it had been shattering in intensity.

Intimate too.

I wasn't used to that.

We had let something escape from ourselves and I think we had both known it.

A long drawn-out sigh had blown warm air across my breasts as he had lain against me, not moving straight away. Then aware as he must have been of the weight on top of me, he had rolled us over together so that I had sprawled across him, still joined. A film of sweat had covered us, but the heat between us kept us warm and a slumberous sense of relief had filled the room along with the heady scent of our bodies. Before I could fall asleep with him still inside me, he had gently moved my body but kept me close to his side. Spooning together we had fallen asleep.

I never spooned with anyone!

I wasn't a spooning kind of woman.

If a man did stay the night, it was on his side of the bed and me on mine.

But I had drifted off into a dreamy sleep so very content to have the weight of his arm falling over my body, and the warmth of his hips and long muscled thighs echoing the curve of mine, my bottom fitting snugly against him.

Nice.

Really nice.

So nice that when I had woken alone, I had felt cold and bereft.

Back to square one.

This time I did toss aside the duvet cover. As I usually would after such a night, I stripped the sheets and went to put them into the washing machine. Then into the shower, as cold as I could stand it, and plenty of shampoo, exfoliating scrub and body wash to restore order and balance.

A short while later, satisfied that I had eliminated all traces of him from my room, my body and my mind, I made a slice of toast and got round to having that coffee, ladling in three spoons of sugar because it felt like that kind of day.

I curled myself up on my sofa, flicking the television on and pondering how to spend my Saturday when my phone pinged beside me. For a fraction of a second, I wondered if it was him and swore at my phone for allowing the ridiculous thought to even consider entering my head.

"Hi Annie, what are you up to?" I greeted my best friend with a sense of relief that she was on the other end.

"Coffee at the café if you fancy it? Shane's had to go into work this morning so I was hoping you would be free."

"As a matter of fact, I am. I've got to pop round and see Dad later, but coffee and a catch up first would be good. How come Shane's working on a weekend again? I thought you did enough stupid shifts for the pair of you?" Like me, Annie worked as a nursing assistant, that was how we had met.

"He got asked to do some over time and well the money will be handy."

There was a note in her voice I had not heard before and I was immediately concerned. "Are things alright, Annie, I mean I can help you out if you are struggling at all, I've got a bit put by. God knows I never spend on myself, so just ask if you need anything."

She laughed down the phone. "Ah bless you Fae, no we are managing fine. You'll understand when I see you. I've got something to tell you, but I don't want to do it over the phone."

"Okay. Well, how about I meet you in half an hour?"

"Perfect, see you then."

I finished my toast and coffee and debated whether to walk or take my car. The hailstones had long since stopped their attack on my windows and looking at the sky it was going to be a bright day after all. I wasn't much of a gym person and much to the annoyance of my friends I never had a problem with my weight, but I did occasionally like to run, and more often got my exercise with brisk walks. Today looked a good day for just that.

I had dressed in jeans and a multi coloured stripey sweater that Annie herself had knitted me with a matching scarf and gloves from the wool she had left over. This was typical Annie. She loved making things for other people and usually there was always more than she intended.

I checked to see if my washing was ready to hang out, but it was still sloshing around the tub. Never mind, there was time for that later. I brushed my long hair that fell in a dead straight curtain of ash blonde silk down my back and quickly gave my lashes a coat of mascara and my lips a slick of gloss.

My hand trembled slightly as I outlined my mouth, remembering the way I had felt when he kissed me. I scowled at my reflection and then a few minutes later swore under my breath as I went to put my leather jacket on.

Deep in one of the pockets was the key I had been unable to find last night. It had been there all along, I must have been in such a muddle from the zombies, not to mention the attack, and him. A sudden flash of memory of him making short shift of picking my lock, bundling me inside and then slamming the door behind him.

Stop this now!

Get a grip.

Coffee with Annie.

My legs pumped double quick time down the streets towards the promenade. I was wearing my pink doc marten boots this morning, no teetering around on killer heels as I burnt off the energy that was bubbling inside of me. I should have been tired, exhausted even from the lack of sleep last night, and no doubt later this afternoon I would fall into a slump, but right now I had adrenaline to burn off.

One of the things I liked about the seaside town where I lived was the eclectic mix of people you would see on the promenade. It wasn't the poshest of places along the south coast, otherwise I wouldn't have been able to afford to live there, but at least the promenade was always bright and cheerful, looking out to sea with its Victorian railings and lamp posts.

And shelters with benches where gangs could gather in the early hours of the morning.

No, I wasn't thinking about that now.

That was done, over, forgotten.

I unclenched my hands from the fists I had not realised I was making in my gloves and cheerily said hello to as many dog walkers, cyclists, and runners that I could. I was not going to let one incident spoil my pleasure of this place. The café was an ideal meeting place for Annie and me as it was halfway between where we lived. I got there first, I usually did. Annie was practical in many ways but easily distracted. I knew what she always ordered though, so I went straight to the counter and joined the queue. Saturday mornings, particularly nice ones like this were understandably busy. I was musing on what kind of cake to treat myself to when I caught snippets of conversation from Doris who owned the café, and the lady two places ahead of me.

"Shocking what this place is coming to when you hear things like that. Gang warfare, I mean we're not safe on the streets."

"I don't think you have to worry." Doris was seventy if she was a day and nothing, I mean nothing ever phased her. "Not unless you are going to start taking a walk in the early hours of the morning. It was three am I was told that the police found them."

I stiffened and slid further along as the lady she had been speaking to paid and went to find her table.

"What happened?" I asked her lightly when it was my turn. "One large Cappuccino and a slice of coffee and walnut cake, and a pot of tea and a toasted tea cake please, with a pot of strawberry jam."

"Oh, a bunch of druggies were found beaten up underneath one of the shelters. The police were fussing about here earlier, well a pair of those community support officers, you know the ones. Asking if we had heard of any rival gangs cropping up cos from the sound of it, there must have been one hell of a fight to have laid five of them out like that."

No.

Only one man.

I smiled at her and paid for my order just as the door opened and in walked Annie.

"Perfect timing," she grinned at me. Bagging one of the best tables by the window I carried the tray over and placed it on the table.

"My treat," I said as she rummaged in her oversized bag for her purse.

"Don't be silly, Fae, you bought the last one."

"No, you did."

"No, it was definitely you."

We had this argument most times. It was a bit of a game between us to see who could pick up the bill and treat the other one. As I was usually first there it was most often me. But I told myself this was my way of paying her back for the dozens of favours and small kindnesses she showed me.

Annie Lomond was as close to a best friend as I could have. Where I was petite and small boned, she was also small in height but deliciously curvy with breasts that had men dropping their jaws in longing. She also had the most infectious laugh, bright shining dark eyes, and dusky skin offset by her lustrous dark hair.

We were the perfect foil for each other, not just in looks. She was a natural home bird, having married Shane three years ago, I was resolutely single. Annie loved to surround herself with family and friends. I was a lone wolf. She was intent on finding me Mr Right. I was determined that would not happen. I liked things just the way they were, and I liked the comfort blanket that having Annie in my life provided me with.

But it appeared things were about to change.

"So, go on then," I said once we had shed our outer layers, and taken a couple of mouthfuls of our coffees, "what have you got to tell me? Let me guess, Shane has finally agreed to you painting the kitchen pink? No. Alright, he's agreed to get you a hot tub, which is why he is working the over time? No to that either? Well, go on then, spit it out, I can see you are about to burst."

She was.

The bubble that was our easy friendship was going to pop.

"I'm pregnant."

I should have known. Of course, Annie and Shane would want to have children. They had been married three years and like me they had both turned thirty last year. It seemed that everyone around me of a similar age was succumbing to that ticking biological clock.

"Wow."

"I'm so excited!" Her joy was spilling over, and I was being a cow for not immediately sharing it.

"Yes, yes of course you are. I am so happy for you. So go on then, tell me everything, when is it due, do you know the sex, do you want to?"

She laughed some more and began to tell me all there was to know at this stage. I listened and smiled and hoped to God that my face was hiding my true emotions. The last person I would wish to hurt was Annie, she was one of the few people I genuinely liked, maybe even loved. After a while she popped the last piece of tea cake into her mouth and when she had swallowed it, asked me what I had done last night. "Wasn't it Miriam's birthday meal?"

I pulled a face. "Yes, but I managed to avoid that. I joined them later at Number 10."

"Anyone interesting there? Is Neil still after you?"

"No to the first and yes to the second."

"And…..are you going to give him a chance?"

I scowled at her.

"Fae, he is nice! You could do a lot worse you know."

I scowled some more, and she poked me good naturedly. "Honestly Fae, you're your own worst enemy."

She was right on target there.

"So did you just go home afterwards?" Her dark brown eyes were regarding me under her fringe with a query in them.

"Yes," I lied. "Just had a quiet night in afterwards."

What kind of woman doesn't share those sorts of details with her best friend I hear you wonder?

The kind of woman who is not who she should be.

CHAPTER FIVE

I walked more slowly on my way back from the café. Annie had wanted to chat non-stop and who could blame her. We had stayed for a couple of hours, re-ordering with a second round. Annie had opted for herbal tea, the first of many changes no doubt in her new life as an expectant mum. I went for another cappuccino, loaded with sugar and a chocolate brownie, ignoring that I had already eaten the walnut cake.

Full of sugar now, I would have benefited from a run, but I knew that I really ought to go and see Dad. I usually loved spending time with him, but not today. Today was always that day when I was so painfully aware that the wrong twin had died. He never said this, and maybe he didn't feel it. But I did and Mum certainly let me know.

So, despite the energy rush I had given my body in the café, I was trudging slowly now, avoiding the cheery faces of the people I had been happy to say hello to earlier. It seemed that every other group was a young family, a buggy and toddler in tow. By the end of this year, that would be Annie and Shane.

Fuck.

Was it possible to hate myself even more?

"What kind of a miserable cow are you, Fae?" I muttered to myself under the snuggly folds of the scarf that Annie had knitted for me. What normal woman resents a friend for getting pregnant?

It wasn't as though I was jealous. Not in that sense. The idea of being pregnant horrified me. Absolutely no way did I envisage motherhood anywhere in my future, either near or anytime distant. It was not a case of my biological clock ticking and me not being able to heed it. I rounded my shoulders against the wind that was whipping up, creating white horses out at sea. Lost for a moment, I stared at the waves. What was it that was causing me to feel this way?

Maybe it was that with Annie becoming a mother, I was once more faced with how life was moving on and that for Fliss, it never would. I knew as soon as the thought entered my mind that this was the truth of it. My stomach felt that sharp imagined pain and my hands clutched at the place my mind's eye told me the knife had gone in.

"Shit." I swore into my scarf, conscious of two children approaching on their small bikes. "Shit, shit, shit, shit, shit." It was all a huge mountain of shit, and I was buried beneath it.

I heard my phone ringing in my pocket. Grateful for some intrusion into my thoughts I took off my gloves to dig it out. By the time I had done this it had stopped ringing, but a message had been left.

Neil. Had I got home safely last night?

Another hit to the stomach, only this time not thoughts of Fliss. Thoughts of him.

I briefly considered throwing my phone into the sea as I stared at the screen wishing that it would ring again and somehow, impossibly, he would be on the other end. He had wiped out all those men, he had unpicked my lock. He was some kind of superhero, spy guy, right? He must have a way of getting hold of my number even though I not given it to him. I quickly replied to Neil's message then angrily shoved my phone back in my pocket.

Fuck him!

Whoever he was.

Fuck him!

No more wasting thoughts on him. Home, sort the laundry, then round to my parents. I picked up my pace and was soon back at my flat. Another stupid moment as I let myself in and hoped that he would be there.

Really Fae?

Tutting in self-disgust, I tossed my jacket on the back of the sofa, unravelled myself from Annie's scarf, and went into the kitchen to pull out my washing. It was windy enough now, despite the chilly air to stand a chance of drying outside. That done, I made a quick shopping list of food, thinking I could call in at the supermarket on the way to my parents.

It was as I was making my list, that I spotted the money. It was folded neatly between the salt and pepper pots. Puzzled I reached for it and unfolded the notes. There were five crisp twenties. A hundred pounds. There was also one of the coloured notes that I used at times to remind me if I needed to do anything. I felt a burning sense of shame and rage as I read the words that were neatly written on the pink paper.

For last night.

He had paid me!

The bastard had paid me as though as I was a prostitute.

I swallowed this thought which landed in my stomach like a jagged lump of rock. My fingers trembled as they fingered the notes and for a second, I was tempted to tear them up. Then practicality took over, as much as that rock of shame churned bile in my gut. A hundred pounds was a hundred pounds.

I would, I told myself fiercely, buy something special for Annie's baby. They were short of money, and it would help them out. Satisfied with this solution, because there was no way on this earth could I spend it on myself, I stuffed the money in my jacket pocket and snatched up my car keys.

It was forty minutes' drive to my parents' house and there was a supermarket on the way. I whizzed round with a small trolley, a demon in my in my head as I chundered over the insult that I been paid. I realised that this was no state to turn up at my parents in, certainly not today of all days.

Forced to wait in the queue, it was Saturday after all, I did my best to alter my mood. My eyes fell upon the display of flowers that were located near to the check out. I was used to receiving flowers, mostly red roses from the men I saw. Well, those that lasted longer than a night. Of course, this meant my thoughts went straight to him.

Bastard!

"Sorry love?"

I hadn't realised I had spoken out loud.

An elderly lady had joined the queue behind me. She didn't look very well dressed and the contents of her basket were pretty meagre. But she still had a lovely, sweet smile on her face.

"Sorry," I apologised for my language. "Here, you go before me, you don't have as much, and I am not in a rush."

"That is kind," she said shuffling past me.

I succumbed to my swirling thoughts as the conveyor belt moved inexorably forwards and was jolted out of them by the old woman's exclamation.

"Oh, what am I going to do?"

"What's the matter?"

"I've been so silly. I have come out without enough money. I shall have to put something back. I am so sorry. I am holding you all up now. Oh, dearie me, what a fool I am."

She was on the verge of tears, and I stepped forwards immediately. "Here, let me." I had my card out in a flash.

"Oh no I couldn't," she protested in a shaky voice.

I nodded at the check-out girl and then on impulse I reached for one of the large bunches of flowers from the display. "Yes. I can and here, have these as well."

"Thank you so much. Oh, wait till I tell my friends how kind you have been. You're an angel, and absolute angel. And thank you for the flowers. I can't remember when anyone last bought me flowers."

Really, I wasn't, but as it was my turn now to go through with my shopping, I had a sudden thought that maybe a second bunch of flowers might be a good idea today.

The nearer I got to my parents' home, the worse my jitters. I wished with all my heart that they would move. Every time I returned to the neat little village, with its thatched cottages and pretty gardens I was forced into confronting the past. Why couldn't they have moved? How could they possibly be happy staying here?

But apparently, they were and Mum for one had made it clear that she would never consider leaving the house that Fliss had grown up in.

"This was her home, and this is where I am staying. I will leave here when I die and not before." Her eyes had warned me it was not a subject to ever be mentioned again, when I had dared to broach it once I had moved out.

Dad had little or no say in it. He never did. But to be fair I don't think he cared either way. He and Mum were so different I often wondered how they managed to stay married. Perhaps it was because they were so different.

Mum was highly efficient, practical, a domestic goddess in every way. She was a member of every possible local committee and chairwoman of the village WI. Dad on the other hand was a dreamer. But that was okay because as well as being a dreamer, he was also a very successful writer.

He had written a series of children's adventure stories, based on the tales he used to tell Fliss and me when we were little. Coming from a highly educated background, he was a professor in English literature, he had been the most surprised of anyone when his, silly little tales, as he described them, had gone on to make lots and lots of money.

It had enabled them both to take early retirement, Dad from his position as lecturer at the local university and Mum from her role as deputy head at a private girls' school. They had both worked hard to buy Honeysuckle cottage, once a dilapidated wreck of a building dating back to the seventeenth century. Now they were able to enjoy the comforts that life had to offer them.

Which was lovely and I truly was happy for them. I couldn't fault how hard they had both worked to give Fliss and I a happy secure childhood, with a decent education and family holidays. I just hated the reminder that there was always someone missing when I came here.

"I thought you'd be here today."

Mum was in the front garden as I arrived, wrapped up against the cold in cord trousers, woolly sweater and padded jacket with a mauve cashmere scarf wrapped around her neck. She rarely wore a hat and declared with her thick mass of hair she never felt the cold on her head. Her wavy iron-grey hair was always kept trim in a jaw length bob that showed off her still fine bone structure. She was a handsome woman and when she smiled, she could be beautiful.

I rarely saw that smile. It was reserved for Dad, the vicar, and most of the other villagers she had close connections to. I told myself that I didn't mind, not even when I held out the flowers I had bought for her. She took them with a casual glance and then a pointed look around the garden.

Of course, she would have fresh flowers a plenty in a couple of months and of a much higher quality than the shop bought variety. I kicked myself for trying. And then I kicked myself for caring.

"I suppose you had better come in then."

I followed her up the garden path that led between the two neat flower beds and into the cosy warmth of Honeysuckle cottage. On the right of the entrance porch was the large sitting room with an open fire that I knew would be lit on a day like today, and to the left at the front of the house was the study where Dad created his stories. Adjacent to this was the dining room which a few years ago they had opened up to create an airy space leading into the kitchen which ran along that back of the house.

Mum had done this when she became chairwoman of the WI and had started hosting a number of events, many of which centred around cooking, or baking. I had made the mistake once of calling round in the middle of one of these evenings. Surrounded by these women, some of whom were my age, who were all married with children, or grandchildren, and yet able to run their own businesses, or have some kind of professional status, I was more than an oddity, I was an embarrassment.

I was everything they were not.

I was everything that Fliss would never have been.

Fliss would have fitted in perfectly.

"Your father's in the study," said Mum as my mind dwelt on this. At least she was gracious enough to carefully open the bunch of flowers and deftly arrange them in a cut glass vase.

"Shall I take him a cup of tea?" Knowing Dad he would be lost in his writing and not have surfaced for hours.

Mum glanced at the clock on the wall. "Yes. There's time for one before lunch. I take it you are staying?"

I hadn't really given any thought to the time that I had turned up but despite the walnut cake and chocolate brownie I was happy to have something to eat. Mum's cooking far surpassed my own and there was a delicious homey smell coming from the aga.

"If that's okay?"

"This is your home you know." Mum turned and looked at me reproachfully.

As ever she could mess with my head, on the one hand making me feel so damn uncomfortable here, and yet always with that suggestion that I didn't visit enough, or that I should have stayed more local and got a job in the village. I could never figure it out. I suppose she was torn between wanting me around as a reminder of Fliss and hating me for the fact that I was the one who had not been killed.

"I'll make Dad that tea then," I said and busied myself with the tea pot and china mugs, taking far more care than I would do for myself at home.

Whilst Mum checked the contents of the dish in the aga, a rich looking lasagne, I prepared a tea tray for Dad and gazed out of the window. At the far end of the long lawn was a small orchard of mixed fruit trees and hidden in between these was a wooden summer house that Fliss and I used to sleep in on hot summer nights.

My hand shook as I placed the tea pot and two china mugs onto the tray. I had not been in it in fifteen years, and I wondered if I went down there now, would I find her ghost? The tray rattled in my hands as a shiver ran through my entire body.

"Are you alright? You aren't sickening for something are you? All those old folk you work with, must be a positive germ factory." Already Mum's hand was opening the cupboard which was always well stocked with cold and flu remedies.

"No, I'm fine. I did have a sick bug, but that was a few days ago now. Don't worry, I wouldn't come here if I thought I was carrying anything infectious."

I took the tea tray down the hallway to the study, knocking before I entered. Usually, Dad would be engrossed in his writing, head bowed over the desk, fingers working feverishly at the keyboard, piles of paper to one side where he scribbled his notes. Today though he was sitting back in his leather chair, his glasses on the desk, a hand over his eyes.

"Oh Dad," I couldn't stop it from slipping out. It saddened me to see that he wiped his eyes as soon as he realised, he was not alone.

"Fae my darling, how lovely to see you." A soft quiet voice, never raised in anger in all my life, only ever coloured with love and sometimes pain. Or a pain filled love, like now.

"I am so sorry." I nearly dropped the tray in my haste to put it in the desk and kneel down beside him. "I'd bring her back if I could. I'd swap with her if I could…." I wished I had bitten off my tongue then as the sorrow deepened in his sad blue eyes.

Too late Fae. Far, far, far too late.

But still he took my hand and patted it. "She wouldn't want us to be crying like this," he said, and I saw that on his lap was the same photo of us that I had in my flat. The last one of us together.

Crying we were though.

I rested my head on his shoulders and felt his arm slide around me. A gesture of comfort that could never be enough. It didn't last long, just a few brief minutes and then Dad moved his arm and coughed. The moment had passed. He blew his nose on a snowy white handkerchief and restored the photo to its usual place on the windowsill. Wiping my eyes with the back of my hand I poured out the tea that I had miraculously managed not to spill.

"Mum said lunch will be ready soon."

"Is it that time already? Goodness."

A quick look at the screen as he sat back down and a frown that told me he had written nothing since he had come in here since breakfast. All his thoughts had been on Fliss and what had happened that dreadful night.

"So how is work?" He began as he always did, keen to know what I was doing and taking a genuine interest.

"Much the same," I answered as chirpily as I could. "I have been reading a fabulous book written in the nineteen twenties about a character called Bulldog Drummond. You'd love him, Dad, and the style of writing."

It was easy then to chat about the book and I neglected to mention that the owner of it had passed away last night. Was it only last night? I shut my mind quickly, slamming the door on what else had happened last night.

Then we heard Mum call for lunch. The lasagne was as delicious as ever and a million miles away from the packaged varieties I bought for myself. Every time I ate a meal Mum cooked; I wondered why I persisted in eating such rubbish. The answer of course was two-fold. I worked stupidly long hours and as much over time as I could manage to survive on my low wage, and there was no real pleasure to me in cooking just for one person.

Halfway through the meal Mum brought this up in a roundabout kind of way. "So, is there anyone new in your life Fae?"

I was momentarily taken aback. Mum didn't usually express an interest in my love life, for which I was extremely thankful. "No," I said quickly and then to my horror felt my cheeks actually heating with a blush.

Dad, as absent minded as he was, also had a writer's observational skills and noticed straight away. "Is there something you are not telling us, Fae. You know we would be happy for you to bring someone home with you?"

Thoughts of my nameless stranger, of wild, erotic sex were not what I wanted in my head right now. I choked down the rest of my lasagne and was quick to quash this notion. "Seriously there is no one. I am far too busy, Dad anyway at work. I simply don't have the time for a relationship."

Mum had to comment. "Mm. Well it's one thing to be dedicated to work, Fae, if you are in a proper profession, but even then, it is possible to juggle the two you know. I did after all with you two….."

And there it was that heavy moment of silence, the pained looks at the photos on the walls, the drowning sensation of guilt that pulled me under every time. I placed my knife and fork carefully on the empty plate.

"That was lovely, Mum, thank you," I said quietly.

"Susannah Curtis was telling me the other day she is going to be a grandmother again."

It seemed that now she was on a roll, and I may as well sink to the depths. I listened as Mum told me all about Shelly Stevens, nee Curtis who I had been at school with, now onto her second pregnancy.

"She's still working too; she's a sister now you know at the hospital. Susannah's ever so proud of her."

"I'm sure she is, Mum."

Just as you would have been proud of Fliss. My beloved twin who had been set on becoming a doctor. She had had the brains to do it as well. Top sets in all of her subjects. Whatever Shelly Stevens could have accomplished, Fliss would have easily outstripped her. She would have married and had two children, no doubt a boy and a girl by now.

I was never going to marry and have children, but I had tried in every other way to make up for Fliss not being there. I had done the best I could with my meagre exam results and taken the path closest to that that Fliss would have chosen. I had turned my back on the real essence of who I was and as I sat there, overwhelmed by Fliss's presence, or lack of I knew that I was failing even in this.

I thought of Mr Carlisle as he lay dying.

I thought of the knowledge that I hid from everyone else.

I wondered how much longer I could hide that side of me?

When I could reasonably make my goodbyes and leave, a tight hug from Dad, a sad smile from Mum, I felt as though I couldn't breathe. I sat in my car for a few moments, trying to steady the churning inside my mind, my body and my soul. I felt as though the merest thing could push me right over the edge and I would tumble into hell.

Or maybe I was already there.

Because living without Fliss for so long certainly felt like it.

Living with the guilt was a never- ending torment.

My phone rang insistently. I ignored it until stupidly I thought that it might be him. It was a number I didn't recognise. My heart rate shot up and I fumbled to answer it before it cut off.

"Hello?"

"Angel, sorry to ring you like this." I heard Kelsey's calm voice, sounding not quite so calm as usual, "but I wanted to give you a bit of warning before you come into work tomorrow. I shouldn't actually be doing this, but I like you and I know that Miriam can be less than altruistic at times in her motives."

"What do you mean?" My mind was not on the ball.

"It's Mr Carlisle. Miriam has made an accusation, or rather a suggestion that it seems very odd that since you joined us three residents have died, and you have been with them each at the time of death. I am sorry to tell you this, but she has gone so far as to suggest to the next of kin that it should be investigated."

"What?"

"She's calling you the Angel of death."

I closed my eyes and thought of Fliss. "She's not wrong there," I said softly.

"What did you say?"

"Nothing," I said in a louder voice to Kelsey. "Well thanks at least for letting me know and giving me the heads up. I'll see you in the morning." Then I switched off my phone, opened the car door and promptly threw up my lunch all over the grass verge.

CHAPTER SIX

Neil and Kelsey were both incredibly apologetic the following morning.

I turned up for work as usual. I was on a run of late starts which meant that by the time I arrived at Sharwood House the daily routine was already well on its way.

"Ah there you are Angel," Neil greeted me as I walked into the entrance hall. "Er Fae, rather." I think he struggled to remember what my real name was. I suppose calling me Angel right now would not be appropriate.

I squared my shoulders, plastered a smile on my face and tilted my neck back to look at him. Like most men he was a lot taller than me.

"Morning Neil, it's a lovely day."

"What? Yes. I suppose it is. Look Angel, I mean Fae, would you mind just popping in here for a moment. It's a bit awkward really."

Just behind him were two other members of staff. They were about to do the rounds with the mid-morning tea trolley. I caught them looking over and bending their heads to whisper something. It was going to be like that was it?

"Lead on," I said to Neil with a resigned sigh.

Kelsey was sitting behind her desk as I followed him into the main office. A busy lady at the best of times she was usually juggling any number of tasks in one go. Right now, she was typing something on her laptop, whilst cradling her phone to her ear and listening intently to whatever was being said.

Her face was creased into a frown which momentarily brightened when she saw me and then contorted into another expression. More of a wince I thought and wondered about the content of the call that was clearly adding to the stresses of the day.

"Sorry about that," she said indicating that I sit down. Neil had already done so. She flashed a look at him and then at me, and I gathered from this that she had not told him that she had already spoken to me. "Neil, would you like to explain to Fae what this is all about?"

Frankly no, judging from the look on his face. He would rather give her that bullet to fire, but he was the owner and in situations like these ultimately his name was the one that counted. In a rambling fashion that would make a politician proud he began to tell me what had occurred since I had left work on Friday night.

Eventually Kelsey cut across him. "The thing is Fae, we know that you had nothing to do with Mr Carlisle's death, or that of Elsie Broadshaw, or Flora Dunhelm, but as you know these allegations have been made. Obviously, we know that when the results of the postmortem are available your name will be fully cleared, but in the interim, I am going to have to ask that you take a leave of absence from work."

I sat there like a statue trying to not give anything away, hiding my anger as I hid everything else.

"It's Mr Carlisle's daughter really who has pushed for this," Kelsey continued with a deepening frown.

I could understand her displeasure and knew it was not directed at me. Mr Carlisle's daughter was a snooty uncaring bitch who had hardly ever visited her father, and I was one of Sharwood's hardest working employees.

"And we have to make allowances for her grief," interrupted Neil at this point although Kelsey and I were both probably thinking the same thing. He had to make sure that all fees owing were paid by the daughter.

"Also to muddy the water's further and to make matters worse for you, Fae, although in the long run I hope this is actually a benefit to you, that was her on the phone just now." A wicked smile flashed briefly across Kelsey's face, betraying the sense of fun in her personality behind the professional exterior. "It would appear that Mr Carlisle has made you a beneficiary in his will."

"Oh?" Neil sat up straight at this and shot a look at me. "Really?"

I echoed his comments, but I think mine held more delighted surprise than Neil's sharp suspicion. "I hope it's his books," I said with a genuine flush of warmth to my heart. "I really enjoyed reading them to him."

Kelsey's smile widened. "I think it's rather more than that judging by the way his daughter was exploding at me just now. Which Fae I am delighted at for your sake. Anyone with eyes in their head could see you were devoted to caring for him, as you are to all our other residents. Unfortunately, though......"

"It gives me a cracking motive for wanting to kill him," I said succinctly. It didn't take a detective to work this out.

"Precisely," said Neil looking more uncomfortable by the second. "You can see why...."

I cut him off as well. "I'll go. I really don't want to cause you any trouble." I stood up and looked at Kelsey. "How long do I need to be off work?"

"Hopefully just for the time it takes to get the postmortem through although Miss Carlisle was also insisting there was an inquest. And that my dear all depends on the police."

I must confess to feeling a shade uncomfortable at this point. Malicious gossip I could cope with. A police investigation was another matter. I knew I had done nothing wrong, but I also knew how the facts could be so easily twisted.

"And the press," said Neil with a slight cough. "We want to keep this as quiet as possible so maybe the longer the better."

"What about my wages?"

After much humming and ahhing, Neil did agree to pay me whilst I was off. But only half my salary. I could see that Kelsey wasn't happy about this, but Neil for all his wishy washiness, when it came to his money he was as certain as they come.

Kelsey walked with me to the front door. "Why don't you see it as a chance for a holiday? Go away somewhere nice. You hardly ever take any leave as it is, and you do look a little peaky from that sick bug you had last week. Book yourself somewhere in the sun or go and visit friends maybe in the countryside."

I thanked her for her support. "Hopping on a plane right now seems a very good idea."

My comment was overheard by two smartly dressed men who had just got out of a black BMW and were approaching the entrance.

"Not if your name is Fae Eliza Winters it isn't." The older of the two gentleman, bald, slightly overweight but with an energetic air about him, stopped just in front of me at the bottom of the steps. He showed me his ID card. "Detective Inspector Crankshaw, and this is DS Wilson. We've come to investigate some disturbing accusations. I take it you are Fae Eliza Winters?"

Puzzled I nodded and looked at Kelsey who shrugged.

DI Crankshaw then displayed a sense of humour surprising for someone with his rank. "Doesn't take a genius or detecting skills to fit you for the description of Angel, does it DI Wilson?"

The younger man, good looking with blond hair and blue eyes was obviously keen to progress in the ranks. "No sir, but as we know in this game, looks can be deceptive."

Crankshaw shot him a rather disappointed glance and I decided then that I might be in safe hands with the older detective.

"Do you need to speak to me here, or can it be done at home?" I may be small, I may look like an angel, I may be on the wrong side of a murder accusation, but that did not make me timid. "I was just leaving for there now."

"We can come to you. But as I said Miss Winters, no plane hopping or you will incur my wrath and that you do not wish to do."

I liked him and reassured him with a smile that I would be at home for the rest of the day. True to my word I went straight home, changed out of my uniform and into a pair of jeans, a bright pink hooded top and warm fluffy slippers that were made to look like hedgehogs, another present from Annie.

Then I wondered what I was going to do with myself for the next couple of weeks or however long it was going to take before I could go back to work. I hated being idle. Having time on my hands opened the doorway to trouble. If I didn't work myself to the bone, relying on physical exhaustion to dull my senses, I was open to that other side of me that I needed to keep buried.

My flat was spotless by the time DI Crankshaw and DS Wilson knocked on my door about an hour later, not because I was a clean freak, it just gave me something to do. I offered them both a tea or coffee but I was assured that they had been well supplied at Sharwood House.

Then after giving my flat the once over with his deceptively mild brown eyes, DI Crankshaw sat on the sofa whilst I curled up as casually as I could on the armchair. DI Wilson rejected the offer of sitting on one of the kitchen chairs and leant instead by the wall near to the window.

"Miss Winters, it appears you have ruffled rather a lot of feathers," began DI Crankshaw. "Since the initial telephone call, we have received complaints from relatives of a Mrs Elsie Broadshaw and a Miss Flora Dunhelm, both deceased whilst you were in the employment of Sharwood House and also it appears whilst you were present with them."

My casual pose was hard to maintain. "Is that what you think? That I killed them?"

"It is not what I think that counts, Miss Winters. I am telling you what has been suggested on the back of Miss Carlisle's accusation. It behoves us as public servants to look into this as a matter of course. If you have done nothing wrong, you have nothing to worry about."

"I've done plenty wrong but nothing to those lovely old souls," I said with a bite to my words that I couldn't help.

DI Crankshaw smiled. "Which I am sure will prove to be the case. So shall we get down to business."

There followed as to be expected a lengthy and thorough set of questions that I answered truthfully knowing I had nothing to hide. Well, apart from the fact that I had known all three elderly residents had been about to die because I sensed it and that when they did, I experienced their last memories with them.

Nope. Not sharing that one.

Finally, DI Crankshaw appeared satisfied that I had fulfilled his requirements for now but he did repeat what he had said earlier. "I would be most unhappy if you were to take off until this has all been cleared up."

I pulled a face wondering how I was going to stay sane without work to occupy me. Then in a flash from nowhere I had a name pop into my head. Maypoleton. Where on earth had that come from? I hadn't visited there for years. Not since.....

I sat upright in my chair, unfolded my legs and looked directly at him. "What about visiting relatives? I mean would it be okay if it was in this country?"

"That would depend on how far away they live?"

"Lancashire."

At least I could see he was considering it if only for a brief second. "I am afraid that would be too far. I will need to speak to you again no doubt numerous times until I get to the bottom of this. I am afraid Miss Winters you are going to have to run the gauntlet for the time being and sit it out."

"Oh bollocks!"

DS Wilson was not impressed by my exclamation, and I scowled at him. "I haven't done anything wrong, and I have to stay at home like billy no mates until this pack of lies is dealt with."

DI Crankshaw added to this wryly. "I'm afraid it will also mean it won't not be long before you are being hounded by the press. Miss Carlisle is on the warpath; it was she who stirred up the relatives of the other residents to put in a complaint. But that is what happens sadly when money is involved."

I shrugged. "Kelsey told me Mr Carlisle had left me something in the will, but I don't know what? I'm hoping it's his books."

DS Wilson gave a little snort at this which earned him a scowl from me, and I was pleased to see a small frown of disapproval from his superior.

"Well, I won't be the one to spoil that little surprise. Thank you for your time, Miss Winters, here's my card. Let me know if there is anything you may have forgotten to tell me."

"That would be tricky as I have not done anything," I smiled wide eyed at him.

They said goodbye and left me to wonder what to do next. It was a Sunday, and I was sure that Annie had said she was not working today. But with the news of her pregnancy, I didn't really feel like calling round for a brew and a chat. There was only one thing for it, I would go for a run and a blast of sea air along the promenade. I was fuelled with nervous energy and in no time at all I was passing by the shelter where the incident had happened on Friday night.

That was how I referred to it in my mind.

The incident.

I paused to catch my breath, having set a pace that was reserved for doing charity races and not just a Sunday run. Where had he come from? Who was he? How did a man like him appear out of the dark, have such an impact on my life, and then vanish? It was as crazy as anything I had read in fiction. Annie was a lover of wild romances, and I would tease her about the improbability of the plots when she told me about them.

"Don't be daft," I would scoff. "Things like that don't happen in real life. Real life is boring, mundane. Grim."

"Oh Fae, you're such a kill joy at times," she would laugh, and I would try and laugh in return.

If only she knew where my sense of fun had once led.

But stretching out my burning hamstrings on the bench where I had so nearly been raped, all I could think about was wanting to see him again. Wishing desperately that life was not boring, mundane, grim. Or complicated with a murder accusation! This was no good. I had come for a run to clear my head not to muddle it further. I completed the run back to my flat in record time, my lungs protesting and a stitch burning in my side.

"Angel Winters?" A glossy looking blonde woman, loads of make-up and fake tan was hanging around when I got back, a black mini cooper parked at the kerb.

I denied this with a shake of my head.

"Come on I know it's you. Or Fae Winters to give you your real name. How about an exclusive for the local paper before it hits the nationals. Get your side of the story in first."

"What?"

"Angel of death tells all, it'll make front page."

"Fuck off!" I brushed past her and hurried to get my key in the door.

"It would be better for you if you did. That way you won't get misrepresented." There was a sly look on her face that told me I was going to get written about and misrepresented anyway so she may as well be the one to do it.

"Seriously fuck off!"

She shrugged. "Oh well. I'll just have to speak to your neighbours then. See what they have to say about you?"

I thought of my neighbours and their disapproval of the many men they saw coming into my flat. Oh hell. That was going to go down a treat. Wincing at the thought of the headlines I let myself in my flat and slammed the door behind me.

My phone began ringing almost as soon as I had done so.

"If you are another bloody reporter, you can fuck off as well," I snarled into the phone not recognising the number.

"I do assure you Miss Winters I can think of nothing I would hate to be more." A calm and amused voice greeted my insult with humour.

"Who is this?" Not him, that was for sure. I would recognise his voice in an instant.

He introduced himself as Charles Seed, solicitor to the late Mr Carlisle. Then he asked me if I was sitting down. Sweaty and chilly now from my run, I ignored this minor discomfort to listen to what he had to say.

Charles explained that I would not be able to access the money whilst the investigation was underway, but he was sure it would soon be resolved and the matter dealt with. Meanwhile I could at least have the comfort of taking time off work and not having to worry about finances.

I had tears in my eyes when I put the phone down. "Oh, bless you," I said to my empty flat thinking of the kind old man.

He hadn't just left me his books, he had bequeathed the majority share of his estate to me, leaving his miserly daughter, a miserly ten percent. No wonder she was on the warpath! No wonder the reporter thought she had a juicy story and wasted no time in telling it. She also had a thorough rummage through my life, and it did not present a pretty picture at all.

"Fae what the hell is going on?"

Annie didn't bother phoning me she, just turned up on my doorstep on Monday teatime, still in her own uniform. A copy of the local paper was in her hands, and she held it out to me an expression of hurt, disappointment and anger in her face.

"Do you want a cup of tea? I've bought some herbal in for you. Now that you're pregnant. How are you feeling today?"

For once Annie was not her laughing smiling self. "For God's sake Fae, listen to yourself! No, I don't want a bloody cup of tea."

She tossed the paper down on the small coffee table near to the sofa and stared at me. "I want to know why I have to find out from the bloody newspaper that my so-called best friend is being accused of murder, a serial killer of old folk no less, and not only that she had a sister, a twin for crying out loud who was stabbed to death when she was fifteen! For fuck's sake Fae, what kind of friend are you? I thought I knew you."

Ouch, ouch and triple ouch.

I deserved every verbal blow.

I was a rubbish friend.

But you see, no one could ever compare to Fliss. She had been the other half of myself. The better half of myself. How could any friend ever match up to that? I suppose I always felt disloyal to Fliss if I allowed myself to get close to another female friend.

"I'm sorry," I said feeling completely worm like. She had every right to be angry.

Annie was too good natured to bear grudges. She gave a little shrug and sat down on the edge of the sofa.

"Go on then, make that herbal tea. And I'll have a couple of biscuits whilst you're at it."

I made us both a cup, grateful that she was giving me a chance and then sat down across from her, waiting in silence as she munched on the biscuits.

"Is there anything in your life you have told me that is true?"

"Most of it is." I answered her quietly. "I just don't like talking about Fliss that's all."

"But that's the sort of thing you tell your best friend Fae. You share the most important things in your life with them. The good, the bad, and the ugly."

I bit my lip.

Annie, sweet Annie. It was easy for her to say. The worst thing she had ever done in her life was to incur a parking fine. She felt guilty about that for days!

"I know. I am sorry. I promise to be more open in the future."

"Promise?"

"I promise," I lied.

How could I tell her? I had not even told Mum and Dad. Fliss dying had not been an accident. It had all been my fault.

I had killed my sister.

CHAPTER SEVEN

The newspapers had of course covered the story at the time. It made national headlines and why wouldn't it? The tragic stabbing of a fifteen-year-old girl especially one as pretty and angelic looking as Fliss, was always going to be a heart wrenching story.

The fact that Fliss had been killed because I had asked her to pretend to be me, was the burden I had carried since. Mum had never been able to forgive me and why should she? My guilt over that was so huge I had never confessed to the rest.

I tried to compensate.

I became as much like Fliss as I possibly could.

We all hoped in time that the pain would ease, that perhaps we could move on and be happy again. Something that was not going to be helped at all by this current situation. Following Annie's visit, I knew I would have to go and face my parents once more. I hated to see the look in Mum's face as for the second time in one week I turned up at their house.

She was in the kitchen, pummelling a mound of dough in a manner that made me think she wished the dough was me. Her hands were covered in flour, and I watched as she suddenly stopped her frantic hand movements, wiped them roughly on her apron and then raised them to her face.

Oh God she was crying.

"Mum." I had let myself in to the house and she had no idea I was standing behind her.

"Fae! Good grief girl did you have to creep up on me like that." She whirled around. Her eyes were red rimmed and puffy, so the tears had been coming for a while then.

The guilt I carried bowed me down further. "Sorry Mum. I didn't mean to startle you."

"You never mean to do anything Fae, do you. It just seems to happen doesn't it! Betty Chalmers couldn't wait to bring me last night's paper. Do you know what they are calling you?"

I stood there helplessly, no words at my defence.

"What are you going to do then?" Mum covered up her distress with briskness as she returned to her task of kneading. "I imagine you won't be able to work for a while, if ever again! At least not in a position like that. Even if it is all proved false," a sudden sharp look for a horrifying second, then she shook her head.

I was thankful that at least she was not going to pursue that line of thought. I don't think I could have coped if Mum had believed for one moment, I could actually be guilty.

She continued, "I doubt they will want you back, or any other nursing home for that matter. Mud sticks Fae. Look what they said about......"

The dough was pulverised, no other word for it. Mum belted it with the passion and anger she reserved for anything to do with Fliss's death. The mud that had stuck to my sister had been that she must have been looking for trouble that night, that somehow it was her fault, she had been asking for it.

No, no no. She hadn't. I had. All my fault.

But even though Mum had known this she still had to put up with the horrible village gossip on top of the despairing grief. Now I was bringing shame and gossip to her door once more, as well as a painful reminder of that time as the blood sucking reporter dug up all she could. No doubt there would be others too, following her example.

"I've got to take some time off," I said and watched as she put the dough in the fridge to rest.

With the same restless energy Mum wiped the counter clean and then went to put the kettle on. "I hope you aren't thinking of coming here to stay, this has hit your dad hard."

I winced. Dad was always the more gentle of them. As Fliss had been. A quiet soul. Never one to hurt another, easily wounded and as such should be protected.

"Don't worry, I'm going to stay home and keep my head down."

Mum passed me a mug of tea and unable to help herself opened a cake tin. However, she may feel, or whatever words she may speak, I knew that underneath she did still care. She was still Mum and always would be, even if it was served up with a side dish of resentment.

"That will be a challenge for you." She cut us both a slice of cake, sliding one to me, and then she went to call out of the back door. "Coffee and cake darling?"

A few minutes later Dad walked through the door, dressed in the clothes he wore for making a bonfire. He brought with him the woody smell of the outdoors and I longed to throw myself in his arms for a cuddle.

"Oh, hello Fae." He dropped a light kiss on my head and patted my shoulder. "In a bit of bother, lass aren't you."

Lass, a northern endearment, from Lancashire. From where I had been born.

"I'm so sorry Dad. It's not fair for either of you. It's this woman at work, she's jealous and she's caused all this by stirring things up. The police don't believe it, well I am pretty sure they don't, but they have to investigate it, and the daughter of the deceased gentleman has added to it all as well."

"She's got to take some time off work," said Mum as she fussed over Dad, handing him a clean towel to wash his hands and then passing him his drink in his favourite mug.

"Well, that's no bad thing surely? You always work far too many hours." Dad smiled at me.

Because I hated to be idle.

Idleness opened the doorway to memories.

I really wasn't sure how I was going to cope with the enforced time off especially if I was going to be hounded by the press. This was highlighted when one of Mum's neighbours kindly popped round, just in case they hadn't seen the news in the local paper.

I felt a choking need to escape. From the cosy warmth of Mum's kitchen where I didn't quite belong anymore, from the prying nosiness of people, from life itself. Blocking out the stilted conversation around me, I wondered if it was visible that I was cracking up inside? A longing to lose myself completely and be someone else threatened to suffocate me.

But who did I want to be?
That was the question.
The answer that rang like a knell of doom in my head, was that I wanted to be the real Fae. Whoever the hell she now was. And then I thought with a devastating clarity that I wanted to be the woman who had lost herself in the arms of a lover for just one night. A lover who had held her when she wept and made her feel whole once more.
Bullshit Fae!
I tuned back into the conversation around me. Mum was politely showing the neighbour the door and Dad, I realised, was asking me if I wanted to borrow any of his books to keep me occupied. It was as reasonable suggestion as any and I spent some time browsing through his vast collection of novels and factual books he refused to part with. Books, he declared to Mum whenever she threatened to parcel boxes of them up to the charity shop, were lifelong friends and you didn't throw them out.

Dad's taste in literature was extremely eclectic. I picked out a couple of French detective novels a fantasy novel about a world of dragons, and an autobiography of a female climber. Note I did not opt for anything of the romantic nature, of which Dad, bless him was a big fan.

"Have you got enough to be going on with then?" He asked a while later when I was still idly browsing.

"I think so."

"You can always pop back for more anytime."

I hugged him tightly. He had never uttered one word of reproach or recrimination in all these years. "Thanks Dad, but these should keep me occupied for now. I'd best be off."

Then as I made to go to the door of his study, a book fell off the top shelf which was nearly at ceiling height as Dad had made the shelves to fit. It hit me on the head and landed on the floor by my feet.

"Ow, that hurt."

"I'm not surprised; it's a big book. Let's have a look which one it is," said Dad bending down to pick it up. "Oh, my word, how odd."

"What?"

His face held a strange expression and when he spoke his voice was gruff.

"It's Mist Over Pendle. It was your mother's. I bought it for her in the shop in Pendle the day I asked her to marry me."

I felt a shiver running through me, more of a tingling maybe. Not unpleasant. "May I see it?"

He cleared his throat. "Yes, yes of course."

Strange to hold in my hands something that had belonged to my mother. It felt weighty in my hands, and I don't mean just from the size of it. It came with a presence. Gingerly I opened the front cover.

To my darling Rowan with all my love, Geoff.

My Dad's handwriting was on the inside front page. Tears filled my eyes and when I looked back to him, he had turned away and was staring out of the window. There was such a gulf of emptiness I suddenly felt unutterably lost. The book in my hands seemed to call me back from the dizzying edge of desolation.

"May I read it?"

"What?" He turned round, deep sadness in his eyes. "I rather think she wanted you to have it, don't you," he said with a smile at the way it had fallen from the shelf. "She always did have a certain way with her, Rowan, part of her ancestry. That's why I bought her the book."

"Are you going to be long in there Geoff, I could do to nip to the supermarket?"

Mum's voice carried along the hallway.

I clutched the book to me and nodded at Dad. I would not say anything.

"Be right with you, darling," he called out to her opening the study door. To me he added, "Maybe when all this mess at work is resolved you could go and visit your Aunty Ruth. Maybe that would do you good, Fae. I hate seeing you look so unhappy."

I was about to protest but he stopped me with a gentle smile. "Fae, I am a writer remember. Oh, I know you think I always have my head in my books, but you cannot be a writer and not be observant about people. I know you are not happy. You haven't been all these years without her. Maybe going back to your roots will bring you some peace."

If it hadn't been for Mum waiting outside the door, I would have lost it then and blubbed like a child. All I could do was to nod at him and smile, holding the book to my chest like a talisman. It sat beside me on the passenger seat of my car, and I was itching to get home and read it, yet at the same time partially dreading it.

Dad's words had disturbed me. What had he meant that Rowan had a certain way with her? The book mockingly gave me the answer as I kept glancing at it. I was both thrilled and terrified.

On the top of everything that had happened this last week it was beginning to make my head spin, and I decided as I drove home that I needed something grounding. Annie was the best person to do this, and I had royally upset her the other day. On impulse I took a quick detour and headed off to a retail centre where I knew there was a mother and baby shop.

"When are you due?" A smiling woman, with a bonny face and plump figure came over to me as soon as I set foot in the shop.

"Oh gosh not me!" I laughed at the thought. "I've got enough trouble managing my own life thank you, never mind contemplating being solely responsible for another. I am here to buy something for my friend."

I told her the budget. I was using the hundred pounds that He had left for me.

Paid me.

Bastard!

"Well, that would go a long way towards a buggy, or a cot you know if you want to help them out."

"I know, but I am guessing they will want to choose that kind of thing themselves, and I really want to give them, well, my friend in particular, a present right now."

The assistant nodded wisely and then guided me towards all manner of tiny outfits, blankets, and accessories that a newborn would need. It felt most odd to be considering baby Lomond as a person. I tried to picture Annie nursing an infant the size that would wear these little clothes. She would be the perfect mother. As would Fliss have been. Once more the sharp twist of guilt as it drove its blade into my stomach.

I knew that I had been a coward since that night in so many ways. For one thing, when my other friends had become pregnant, I had successfully managed to keep my distance and not get involved with the new life. I knew that with Annie this would be harder. I knew that had it not been for the bruising hurt she had shown me I would be pulling away even now.

Ashamed of my cowardice I stood there in the mother and baby shop and made a promise to myself that I would for once in my life do the right thing. I would be a good friend to Annie when her baby came.

I took my time over my purchases, again different to when I would buy a hastily chosen present for my other friends who had become mothers. My hands lingered over the soft fabrics, my mouth smiled at the pretty motifs, my cynicism melted at the delicate sizes of mittens and booties. Careful Fae, you could be accused of succumbing to a moment of broodiness and that would never do.

"I'm sure it will be you next," said the ever smiling assistant when I got to the till. "Don't worry, you aren't the only one it happens to."

I flashed her a look. "No, really. I don't want children."

She smiled annoyingly. "I hope to see you back here soon."

Virtually snatching the bag from her, I stopped myself from telling her to fuck off. Just.

Annie, I hope you appreciate the lengths I have gone to here; I thought to myself as I made my way home. There was another cluster of reporters around my door, and it was only the thought of how I had already made Mum and Dad suffer that prevented me from hurling abuse at them too.

I smiled as sweetly as I could. "It's all been a horrible misunderstanding and that is all I am prepared to say," I kept repeating this as I pushed my way past them and let myself into my flat.

I placed my bags of presents on the sofa and then took the books through to my bedroom. The detective novels and the others I had picked out, I stacked on my shelf. The one that had hit me on the head, I placed on the bedside table, next to the photograph.

The rest of the day dragged until it was time for Annie to be home from work. I checked to see if there were any reporters hanging around, but it seemed they were a fair-weather lot and it had begun to rain heavily mid-afternoon. Grateful for this, I made my way over to Annie and Shane's house, to make my peace offering. Annie, being the darling she was, took my bundle of carefully wrapped presents and burst into tears, hugging me effusively.

"Oh Fae, you are so kind. You really are lovely you know. And I am so sorry for all the hurtful things I said. Shane told me I was probably being overly emotional because of my hormones."

I wasn't good at hugs, but Annie had a way about her that penetrated my armour. "Don't be daft you had every right to be cross."

Over tea which they insisted I stay for, I told them that I was having to take some time off work and had to stay local in case the police wanted to speak to me.

Annie knew how much I hated being idle, even if she was clueless as to why. "What will you do with yourself, you'll get bored rotten?"

"I've picked up some books from Dad's," I said.

Shane asked me what books I had chosen. We both smiled with affection at Annie who offered to lend me some of her romances.

"Some French detective novels, Fred Vargas, you'd like them Shane, a couple of sci fi and one written by a female climber," I paused, "Oh, and one called Mist Over Pendle."

"That sounds romantic," enthused Annie.

I had briefly looked at the description of the book earlier. "Not exactly. It's the story of the Lancashire Witches. A true story. Most of them ended up hanging."

Annie grimaced. "What on earth do you want to read that for, sounds positively gruesome."

"Dad bought it for my mother on the day he asked her to marry him."

"Really? Well, that's sort of nice, but bit of a weird book to buy your fiancée. I wouldn't have thought that was your mum's cup of tea at all."

I twirled some strands of spaghetti carefully round my fork. "Apparently it was. Dad suggested that when I am allowed to, that is unless I get charged with murder, that I go and spend some time up there."

"What in Lancashire? Isn't it grim up North?" Shane grinned at me. "That's what they say."

I shook my head, feeling the stirrings of a strange emotion within me. "There is some lovely countryside up there, it's wild and untamed in parts, just not as well known as Yorkshire and the Lake District. It's a hidden gem."

"Fair enough," he smiled back at me.

"Why did your dad suggest there though?" Annie asked.

"It is where I was born."

"Oh. I never realised that. I thought you had always lived around here, down on the South coast."

"No. It is also where my mother is buried."

Annie dropped her fork onto her place. "Your mother is buried?"

"My birth mother."

Annie's eyes were on stalks.

Shane prompted ever so gently, "Go on."

"She died when I…..when Fliss and I were two. Dad married Mum a year later. So, Mum to me is Mum. I have no memories of my mother at all. But she lived in a village in Lancashire called Maypoleton, and that is where my Aunty Ruth still lives."

Aunty Ruth was also new to Annie. She leant back in her chair. "Fae this is like getting to know a whole new person."

Shane quietly got up and began clearing the pots giving me the chance to explain.

"I guess I shut down on so much of my life when I lost Fliss. It was the only way I could cope."

Annie took this with the sensitivity that she had in spades, and I totally lacked. "It must have been so difficult. And now it's all in the papers again. I am not surprised you feel like disappearing once you get the chance. So, tell us then, what it's like where your Aunty lives."

"It is in the middle of nowhere," I grinned. "The nearest large town, well city is Lancaster, but it's surrounded by miles of wild moorland, it's quite remote."

"I'm not sure I can see you enjoying being in the middle of nowhere," Shane teased.

"Don't forget I love being outdoors. Aunty Ruth has a horse and there is a riding school nearby. When we were little, she used to take us there for lessons." Memories came flooding back, bittersweet and sharp.

"Maybe you could take that up again," said Annie. "When do you think you will be able to go?"

"I really don't know. I can't go anywhere until this investigation is all cleared up but as soon as possible hopefully."

"I think it sounds like a cracking idea," said Shane, "although I still think you will get bored out of your skull up there."

"You never know," said Annie with a sly smile. "Maybe if Fae is away for a while and in a different environment, she might finally lose herself in a proper romance."

Shane gave a rather uncomplimentary snort. Although this did give an unflattering view on my relationships, or lack of them, I was quick to add to this myself.

"Annie, I am not looking for love, or a relationship, or marriage, or children, or any of the lovely stuff you have going on here with Shane. It's right for you, but trust me, it is not what I am after."

She persisted in giving me one of those looks.

"It's not," I insisted, my mind full suddenly of a tall dangerous man with sea-coloured eyes, a scarred body and killer bedroom moves. "And even if it was, Maypoleton is the last place on this earth I would be likely to find it."

CHAPTER EIGHT

Weeks of frustration later, I was finally able to put my plan into action. Despite the combined efforts of Mr Carlise's daughter and Miriam to blacken my name and drag my reputation through the mud, DI Crankshaw was able to tell me that there were no charges to answer.

The affable detective had come to visit me in person, alone this time, to put an end to my home-based incarceration. The weather which had been awful up to this point, all dark skies, showers, hail and wind, had briefly decided to play nicely. I had been getting myself ready to go for an early morning run along the promenade when his black BMW had pulled up outside my flat.

"Mind if I come in?"

"That depends if you are carrying handcuffs?"

Over the course of the investigation, we had developed an odd sort of rapport. Crankshaw held his hands out in an open gesture. "I won't keep you long, I can see you are ready to go out."

He stepped into my lounge his eyes alighting on the Fred Vargas novel on my coffee table. I had devoured Mist Over Pendle in the first two weeks off work.

"Any good?"

"Yes, it is. You can borrow it if you like, I've just finished it. I'm sure Dad won't mind. I am going there later to pick up some more books, unless of course you have come to tell me I am free to wander at will."

He picked up the novel with an appreciative smile. "Thank you, Miss Winters. I will see it gets returned. And yes, you will be pleased to know that is precisely why I am here. The results of the postmortem and inquest on Mr Carlisle have come through. Death due to a blood clot on the brain, which however clever you may be, so far, we have never come across a person who is capable of killing anyone by that method. So, in the clear. Also, the reports on the two other residents, Elsie Broadshaw and Flora Dunhelm have been thoroughly re-scrutinised by our pathologist and again there is no way you could have caused death by a pulmonary embolism or acute liver failure. The relatives concerned have been reassured that the accusations were born out of spite and malice."

"Good to know," I nodded at him, not wanting to betray for an instant the intense stress I had been under. I only needed an inconclusive postmortem and I would have been really in the mire. "I'm a free woman then?"

"You are indeed."

"Perhaps you can tell that to the local papers then, so they can all piss off and stop hounding me?"

He pulled a face. "I will do my best. I'm sorry you had to be subjected to that. Perhaps you can now go somewhere nice for a little while and try and put this behind you?"

I told him of my plans to visit my aunt. "I intend to do just that. I'm in no hurry to go back to work, not there anyway. Mud sticks Inspector, regardless of the truth."

Another wry expression, agreeing with me. "I wish you well Miss Winters. Have a safe trip and hopefully it will not be too long before you may enjoy your legacy from Mr Carlisle. I should imagine that will be some sort of balm." He made his way to the door and gave me a friendly wink.

As soon as I had completed my run, energised from this good news I had rung my Aunty Ruth to ask if I could visit. Her audible delight triggered more shame that I had so badly neglected my relationship with her.

"Come as soon as you want, love. Your bedroom is always ready for you."

Hearing her warm northern tones and picturing the bedroom I had shared with Fliss so long ago, had me on the point of tears. I told her I would drive up the next morning. I wanted to go and spend some time with my parents before I did this and tell them in person that there were no charges to be pressed.

I also wanted to reassure Mum in a weird kind of way. Ours was a fragile relationship at best and the fact that I was going back to Maypoleton would be another source of disturbance to her. I did understand that she hated any reminders that she was not my natural mother and in this, it was one area where her own vulnerability showed.

This done, I set off the following morning on my long journey north.

My ten-year-old car did not have a sat nav and I had to rely on my phone for directions as the last time I had been to Maypoleton I had been fifteen. The route itself was fairly straightforward. Once I had joined the M6 North I had blithely carried on until I got to turn off for the A6.

Shortly afterwards it all went to pot.

The roads led me on a windingly merry dance with signposts that jutted at confusing angles, and matters were not helped further by the rain that had begun to lash down, making visibility that much harder. Twice I had to slam on my brakes having shot past a turning, to then reverse dangerously hoping that no cars were coming in the same direction.

I passed small hamlets and farms, but these grew few and far between until I found myself in the middle of wildly open rolling moorland, the snaking tarmac road ahead the only evidence of human existence, past or present. This was when I checked my phone and saw that the screen had gone wonderfully blank.

"Oh, for fuck's sake," I muttered and tossed it onto the passenger seat. My concentration had momentarily lapsed and as my eyes refocused through the furious swishing of the wind screen wipers, I saw with horror that there was a huge sheep standing in the middle of the road.

I didn't have time to stop, I would hit it if I even attempted this. As much as I enjoy a lamb roast, I was pretty sure that my car would receive as much damage if not more in the collision and a hefty bill was the last thing I needed.

I yanked the steering wheel hard thinking surely, I would be okay to swerve just a little and venture off the road. Either side was just miles and miles of grass and heather, my little car could cope with that I told myself in the fraction of a second I had to react.

Grass and heather may be.

Bloody great ruts no.

There was a thrilling few seconds of rally style driving which I rather enjoyed and then an almighty couple of jolts as the left-hand wheels went one after another through a deep rut that jarred the whole car and my spine. My hands battled with the steering wheel to right the car back onto the road and I prayed that no damage had been caused.

As soon as I hit the tarmac, I knew that at least one of the tyres had burst. Groaning I braked and brought the car to a crawl. Stopping here to try and change it would be outright folly but just ahead I could see a passing place on the narrow road. Nursing my injured vehicle to this point I cursed the sheep, my useless sat nav, and then the weather.

But cursing never did anyone much use apart from letting off steam, so once I had done that, I reached for my coat which was on the back seat and braved the rain. I was right, the front left tyre was as flat as a pancake. Oh well, at least Dad had taught me how to change a wheel and a bit of rain never hurt anyone.

Pleased with my positive spin on this little hiccup which others may have viewed as a catastrophe, I pulled the hood up over my head and opened my boot. I had to unload my bags into the back of the car before I could get to the spare wheel and tools, and I was ready to get going.

Another minor irritation was that the tyre had only recently been fitted by my local garage for its MOT. How annoying was that? Then as I began to loosen the wheel nuts, I was swamped with further irritation and this time it threatened to really sour my mood.

Why was it, I wondered in frustration, that mechanics seemed to think they needed to tighten every nut to the last possible turn? I tried all the tricks Dad had shown me, which included belting the spanner with a rock and even trying to jam it down with my foot, but no, it was not for shifting and of course I tried swearing at it.

Just then the sheep who had caused all this came along and baaed really loudly.

"You are that close to being Sunday lunch," I warned it with a look from underneath my hood which was now dripping with rain.

It baaed in reply. "Am I bothered?"

"Piss off, you horrible creature!"

It continued to ignore me and tossing the heavy rock to the floor where it landed in the soggy ground with a squelch, I contemplated my options. My phone still had no signal. There had been no buildings of any sort for the last few miles in the direction I had come from. I wasn't sure at this point if I was even on the right road. The way I saw it I had two choices. I could sit in my car and wait for someone to pass by or start walking in the hope that I would come to some kind of civilisation.

I am not very good at sitting and waiting, for anything, and at least the rain had finally decided to stop. The brooding clouds still hung heavy and darkened the sky with this a reminder that the light would soon begin to fade, and I didn't fancy being stuck out here overnight with just the sheep for company.

I was about to start walking when I heard the sound of a car approaching. Soon enough one came into sight. Deciding it was my turn now to be like the sheep, I stood in the middle of the road making damn sure that they would have to stop or run me over.

"Need a hand?"

Luck it appeared was now most definitely on my side. The driver could have been a slightly built female like me and whilst I am the first to hate any form of sexism what I really needed right now was muscle, the sort that weight lifting females aside, usually only came in the male form.

"If you wouldn't mind?" I pushed back my hood, gave my hair a little shake and smiled. Well, it wouldn't hurt, would it?

"Always happy to help a damsel in distress," he said as he got out of his car with an answering smile.

It struck me that this was the second time in a matter of weeks that I had been rescued by a man. Only there the comparison ended. This time it had hardly been my fault, I could totally blame the bloody sheep, and my rescuer was not a dark clad figure who carried with him an air of violence as well as masses of sex appeal.

Alright amend that last point.

This guy was cute in a totally different way.

I don't usually go for blonds but there is always a first time for everything. Especially when it comes to tall hunky Viking looking blonds.

"I've changed loads of tyres before," I said to him as I would only allow myself to be treated like a helpless female so far, "but I just cannot loosen the bloody nut."

"Well let's see what I can do about that then, shall we? My name's Matt by the way."

"Nice to meet you Matt. I'm Fae. I was just about to start walking to get help."

He grinned and his appeal deepened. An easy open smile that went right up to his eyes which were a light hazel in colour, an interesting contrast to his blond hair.

"Well, if you were carrying on in the direction you are facing you would have had quite a walk. It's five miles till Maypoleton."

"Oh well at least I am on the right road then," I said as he followed me round to the side of the car to change my wheel.

"You're heading to Maypoleton? What takes you there?" He squatted down, displaying a nice amount of thigh muscle in his jeans as he did so and strong looking hands as he made light work of loosening the nuts.

"What?"

He grinned again and I reciprocated, letting him know that yes, I had been admiring his physique. The day was getting better by the second.

"I am going to visit my aunt, she lives there."

"She does? Who would that be then?" He rolled off the flat tyre and with the ease of someone who either works out or regularly plays sport, he hefted the spare one into place.

"Ruth Thorneby."

"I know Ruth and Eric, lovely couple."

"You know my aunt and uncle?" So, there will be a chance of seeing you again. Nice.

"Eric's in the same running club as I am. We're friendly rivals."

"You live in Maypoleton then?" Better and better.

"I'm the deputy head at the primary school."

Better just became perfect.

"Oh well, in that case then," I said with a swish of my hair, not that I needed to do this, I already had his interest, "I will be able to buy you a drink to say thank you for rescuing me."

Note the fact that I had not checked if he was wearing a ring or asked if he was involved with anyone. Annie would be shaking her head severely at this point and rightly so.

"Are you free to do that?" Matt clearly had higher standards than I did. He made short work of tightening up the nuts on the tyre and then stood up, wiping his hands carelessly on his jeans as he looked at me. "I only have drinks with ladies if they are unattached."

I wasn't altogether sure if I fitted in the category of lady, but I was not going to spoil his illusions on this score. "Absolutely. I agree," I lied, thinking of all the married men I had happily taken home to my flat.

There was a safety in sleeping with married men, they rarely pushed for anything more. And whilst I had protested to Annie that romance was the last thing on my mind in visiting Maypoleton, sampling the local fare, well that was different. That was allowed surely, and he certainly looked appetising.

"Right then, you can follow me if you like?"

I do like, I do indeed.

"Thank you, I have been having a bit of trouble with my sat nav on my phone."

"Reception is always useless up here. What made you swerve off the road?" He asked looking back at the obvious tracks my car had made.

"A suicidal sheep."

He laughed, a sound that was as easy and warm as his smile. "Yes, they are a bit like that round here. Don't worry you'll get used to them. Right then, let's get going." He started to walk back to his car and then paused. "You do know the way to your aunt's house once you get to Maypoleton don't you? Only I have lived there for the last five years, and I am pretty sure I haven't seen you around before." There was flattery in the comment, meaning he would have remembered if I had.

"It has been a long time," I explained, "but I think I can remember."

"Right then," he said again, and this time got into his car.

I set off after him feeling really quite happy with how things had turned out, even going so far as to mentally say thank you to the errant sheep. No doubt I would have bumped into Matt in the village anyway, but that was a good way to strike up a conversation and a reason to ask him for a drink. I liked to be the one doing the asking, no matter how attractive they were.

Again, a flash back to that horrible moment in the promenade shelter.

I pushed it firmly out of my mind along with the events that followed and looked ahead to arriving at Maypoleton.

It seemed that it wanted to welcome me

As I turned a bend and the high road dipped down into a valley, a rainbow appeared. The dazzling arc spanned the village that I could now see nestling in the sheltered spot with the river running through the centre of it.

Home.

I was coming home.

A lump formed in my throat, and it wasn't rain now that was making it difficult to see. It was the tears in my eyes. Unprepared for this reaction, I wiped them quickly away. I couldn't afford to go off road again.

Crying Fae, really?

At the sight of Maypoleton?

I sniffed back the tears and bit down on my lip that was persisting in wobbling. As I descended the hill that led into the village, I wondered what had provoked this response. The answer of course came quickly. The last time I had been here had been with Fliss. We had stayed with Aunty Ruth during the summer holidays.

"Woah, woah, woah," I muttered to myself to steady the rush of memories.

Such a happy time. Days spent mucking around with the horses at Farthing Hall livery yard with Aunty Ruth, tramping over the hills and moors with Uncle Eric, learning to kayak in the river that ran through the village, larking around in the grave yard with some of the other local teenagers, exploring that side of myself that burned so brightly and yet had been extinguished now for years.

It had not been long afterwards that Fliss had been killed. Aunty Ruth had repeatedly asked me to visit, and I know she must have been hurt at times with my absence. But I had been drowning in my sorrow, choking on my guilt, too poisoned by the hatred for myself that ran in my veins to consider anyone else's feelings.

And how could I possibly go there, to Fliss's favourite place which I remembered now it was with a clarity that outshone the rainbow for blinding brilliance. Fliss had absolutely loved it here, we both had. How could I have stayed away so long?

"Because Fae Eliza Winters you are a first-class fucking coward," I said to myself as I slowed my speed as I approached the village.

Ahead of me, Matt waved his arm out of the window, and I tooted to thank him once more and to let him know I was now fine with where I was. He drove on ahead and I watched the direction his car took. Along the main street with the pub, row of old-fashioned shops, passing by the village green complete with stocks and the huge, withered, ancient silver birch tree which gave the village its' name as it had stood for a maypole for centuries, and then over the arched stone bridge and the river.

On the other side of the flowing peaty brown water was the primary school and the village hall. So that was where Matt worked, I thought as his car then turned away from the school and towards a housing development that had not been there before.

At the top end of the village, in prime position, was the church and the vicarage, a gracious building that faced the green and duck pond. It was a quintessential English village scene, and I felt a moments pride for the place of my birth. Maypoleton was worthy of being a setting for a television drama, either historical or present day.

I thought of DI Crankshaw and the fictional detective he reminded me of. He would fit in here a treat I thought with a smile. I thought of Sharwood house and the job I had left behind. It didn't bother me in the slightest. I was back here.

Where I belonged.

The voice was loud and clear in my mind, and I wasn't sure whose it was.

Mine?

Fliss?

I liked to think it was my twin speaking to me as I nosed my car carefully down the main street with it's one row of shops that faced the green, and looked out for the side street where Aunty Ruth lived.

I passed Baker St, then Tanners Yard, Smithy Court and at last came to Cobblers Row. The cosy looking terraced cottages with their pretty little front gardens had been built at a time when cobbles were used for the roads. They were still in place here. As such it was a narrow street, and I saw as soon as I turned my car into it that parking would be a problem.

Aunty Ruth had mentioned this, but I had forgotten, or rather not paid it attention until now. But there was a large village car park a little way back down the main street past the vicarage. I reversed carefully back so that I could carry on until I found this. How sensible, I thought, and how community spirited I noted as I parked my car in the large and free space.

I did then have to walk a short distance with my bags but that was not a problem to me. I collected everything I had and then set off back to Cobblers Row. A police car passed me as I turned into the street. For a brief second, I stupidly thought it had come looking for me which just highlighted how unnerving the murder accusation had been. I let out the breath I had suddenly held in then watched with curiosity as it parked alongside the kerb next to number 3.

Curious, I dawdled slightly in my pace. Aunty Ruth lived at number one, the last house in the row on the left-hand side. What were her neighbours up to? A tall and well-built man got out of the car, and I noted with approval that he was good looking too in a rugged way. Hhhm. Maypoleton certainly seemed to have its' fair share of hunky men so far.

Things were looking up indeed.

I would have been quite happy to be interrogated by him I thought as he turned his head to glance in my direction, a typical copper's stare, cool and assessing. I flashed the bright beam of my smile, disappointed to only receive a nod of acknowledgment in return.

Then the door to number one opened and my disappointment lessened a little. The policeman was greeted by an attractive woman, older than myself I would say but looking trim and lovely, nevertheless. She threw her arms around his neck and gave him a passionate kiss the sort of which was usually reserved for lovers and not for married couples. I had to walk past, and she gave me a smile which was more of a cheeky grin that had me responding in kind.

"Sorry. Shameless of me snogging on the doorstep. You must be Fae, Ruth told me her niece was coming to stay. I'm Eve and this is my husband, Craig."

"Hi. Nice to meet you." Nice husband. I think I would be snogging him shamelessly on the doorstep if I was married to him.

Jealous Fae?

Then a figure at the window of number one caught my eye and the next moment the door was opened, as Eve and Craig disappeared inside. Straight to the bedroom I wondered briefly, again feeling that stab of envy before coming face to face with Aunty Ruth.

"Oh, my word. You're the image of your mother, child."

Aunty Ruth, mid-sixties, with short blonde hair, kind blue eyes and a smile as bonny as her face and personality, stared at me with an expression of such love and sadness that I felt my lip begin to tremble again.

"Hello Aunty Ruth." I felt fifteen again.

"Welcome home love," she said opening her arms to me.

I dropped my bags and burst into tears.

CHAPTER NINE

Oh, to be a child again.

That was how it felt stepping through the door into the cosy warmth of my aunt's cottage and into her care.

"There there, lass, there's nowt to cry about." Aunty Ruth was Lancashire born and bred and the endearment tripping off her tongue had me sobbing even more.

"I'm sorry Aunty Ruth."

"What on earth have you got to be sorry for?"

Plenty I thought but contented myself with saying, "For not coming sooner. For staying away. It's just that….." My eyes had strayed to the fireplace, logs burning brightly and above it on the mantel shelf a photo of Fliss and I on our very last visit here, in pride of place.

"I know," she patted me on the back as her eyes followed mine. "Oh dear, lass. Come on, sit down and I'll get the kettle one."

"It's already on." Uncle Eric, also in his mid-sixties, but you would never guess it he was so lean and fit with twinkling bright eyes behind silver framed glasses, neatly cut grey hair and trim moustache, came through from the kitchen. There were just the two rooms downstairs, the front lounge with the wooden staircase, and the kitchen which had been opened up from a small dining room and galley kitchen into the larger open space it was now.

"Now then, Fae," he said in that no nonsense manner that I remembered from being a teenager, "you're here now and that's all that matters. You've kept in touch with letters and by phone, and we would have come to visit you but well…."

Aunty Ruth sent him a quick warning look and I guessed he was about to say that Mum had not been too keen on the idea. I loved him for his blunt honesty but that's what you get from

Lancashire folk. They called a spade a spade and be damned with it.

"Your mum was never too keen on having the reminder that she isn't your natural mum and my Ruthie here, well, she is always going to be that reminder, isn't she?"

"Eric there's no need to go into that now," Aunty Ruth said softly.

"It's okay," I nodded at them both. "I get it, I really do."

"Mm. How about a nice slice of parkin with your tea?"

"Lovely. I hope you haven't just been baking on my account?"

Uncle Eric laughed. "Don't fret about that lass. Your aunt is far too busy looking after her latest rescue horse to be baking, every minute she is not working she's down at Farthing Hall with Treacle and Toffee."

"As are you." Aunty Ruth teased him as she went into the kitchen coming back a few minutes later with a tea tray fully laden.

"Here, let me," Uncle Eric, ever the gentleman took it from her.

"Maypoleton's bakery's finest," she said cutting me a thick slice of the rich, sticky, ginger tasting cake that filled my taste buds with satisfaction and my mind with childhood memories.

Then we talked and laughed, and it was as though the clock had turned back and everything was alright with the world. Apart from the empty chair. Fliss's presence was here as it was at Mum's house back home but somehow it had less power to hurt me here. Or maybe I felt her with me, telling me that this was where I should be. As I ate the cake, two slices, and drank more tea, I felt a peculiar sensation washing over me.

"Are you alright, love?" Aunty Ruth asked me when there was a lull in the conversation.

"I'm fine," I said but really, I was not at all sure that I was. There was a sense of weightlessness creeping into me and a tiredness that was suddenly overwhelming. It was only four o'clock in the afternoon, but I was struggling to keep my eyes open.

"You look ready for bed," Uncle Eric teased gently, and I had to nod at him.

"I'm sorry. I don't know what's come over me."

Aunty Ruth put down her teacup and leant over to pat my knee. "Come on love, let's get you into bed. You look fit to drop."

I protested as I rose from the chair, but my body had other ideas. Willingly I followed her up the narrow staircase and into the spare bedroom. I was grateful that it had been redecorated since Fliss and I had last slept here. The walls were painted a soft lemon shade and the matching duvets on the twin beds had a delicate floral pattern, buttercups and daisies, matching the curtains at the window that overlooked the street.

"You can unpack later, Fae, just get into bed for now love and sleep."

Staggered that I should need to sleep at such a time I pulled back the covers on the bed I always slept in and laid my head on the pillow shutting my eyes, aware as I did so that more tears were sliding silently down my cheeks. I heard the door closing softly and then drifted on into sleep.

Sunlight was streaming through the gap in the curtains when I awoke a while later. Although when I stirred from beneath the cosy duvet and checked my phone I had to look twice. It was seven o'clock but not in the evening as I expected, it was seven the following morning. I had slept right through.

I took a couple of moments to process that I was here in Maypoleton at Aunty Ruth's. Outside there was very little noise from the main street which was different to at home with a constant stream of traffic passing by my flat, the peace and quiet of a quaint rural village allowing far more room for thought.

Briskly I got out of bed realising I was still in my clothes from yesterday. Aunty Ruth and Uncle Eric had always been early risers and today was no exception. There was no sign of anyone in the house and I had a quick shower and dressed. In the kitchen there was a note telling me that they had both gone to work but I was to make myself at home and relax. Aunty Ruth worked in a cafe attached to a farm five miles away and Uncle Eric was counting down his days to retiring from his job as a senior civil servant in Lancaster which was even further away.

They were a hard-working couple, always had been, but they always made time for me and Fliss and their shared love of horses had been a substitute for not having children. As I made some breakfast and pottered around the cottage, I saw with fresh eyes the number of photos that highlighted this along with a multitude of horse related ornaments, and reading materials. I would join them later at the stables but for now I had a day to myself.

Never one to be idle I finished my breakfast and then grabbed my leather jacket deciding to go for a walk. My long sleep had energised me, and it would do me good to reconnect to my roots. I walked up Cobblers Row, giving number three a not so idle glance wondering about Eve and Craig who lived next door, and then onto the main street.

To the right of me was the church and vicarage and of course beyond that the graveyard. My mother was buried there. I had to go, of course I did, but I needed to summon up a little courage first and maybe buy some flowers. Yes, flowers that was a good idea. There had to be somewhere on the main street that sold flowers.

It wasn't nine o'clock yet so I doubted any of the shops would be open, apart from maybe the general store and bakery but I began to wander down the road anyway. Opposite the main street I could see a handful of women and children, together with the odd baby in a buggy walking along towards the bridge.

They were on their way to school, and I thought immediately of Matt. I had not got his number yesterday but that didn't bother me. This was a small enough place I was bound to catch up with him sooner or later.

I wandered leisurely along following their route so that I could walk over the stone bridge. From the middle of it you had a fabulous view. One way you looked back towards the church, and the green with the duck pond, stocks and maypole in the form of the ancient twisted tree.

Turning the other way, the eye followed the river out of Maypoleton, down the valley and into the wilderness of moorland, heather and bracken. The bridge itself was as ancient in origin as the village. It had been modified and strengthened over the years but many of the original stones remained.

Standing there with my hands leaning on the old stones and looking at the place of my birth I felt awash with feelings and sentiments that would have made Annie laugh. This was where I belonged, and I should never have stayed away. I listened to the water passing beneath me and the growing noise from the primary school in the distance. Both sounds had a merry musical note to them, the rippling water and children's laughter very easy on the ears.

People passed by. Most smiled and said hello. There was a look of curiosity in some of the faces, no doubt wondering who I was. Maypoleton got its' fair share of visitors in the summer, although it was a hidden place in many ways and there was a perverse sense amongst the locals that whilst tourists and walkers brought in money to the shops, Maypoleton was not to be widely shared.

The sound of a bell ringing cut through the murmur of water and children's voices. Over in the playground I could see the small figures lining up in neat rows. I could also see the blond head of Matt, his hair catching the sunlight. He had his back to me, and I willed him turn around.

He did so and I caught my breath in surprise.

Had that been co-incidence?

Or had that been something else?

Either way he raised his hand in a wave, and I returned the gesture with a smile on my face that he would not be able to see but I felt like smiling anyway. I watched as a very attractive woman went over to him to say something. She was wearing an eye-catching scarlet dress with a pattered woollen wrap around her shoulders and black boots with killer heels. Was that the head teacher? If so, I liked her style. From her clothing alone she looked far more glamourous than the rest of the women I had seen that morning, most of whom were in jeans and outdoor coats with flat boots. Pretty much like myself for that matter.

Turning my attention away from the school, I reasoned that by now the shops would be open and I would be able to buy some flowers. At the far end of the main street, there was a small florist which also doubled up as a cards and gift shop with delightful items on display from local artists and craftspeople. I thought of Annie. She would love all this and maybe I could invite her up some time as well. My thoughts tripped up over themselves in my head. How long was I thinking of staying?

"Do you need help with anything?" A woman in her fifties or thereabouts was busy with half a dozen buckets of fresh flowers.

"Some flowers for a grave."

She had grey hair tied up in a ponytail too young for her age and large tortoiseshell glasses that seemed too big for her face. The expression in her eyes was one of sharp curiosity. "Are you local?" I was born here, I felt like replying, her attitude instantly getting me bristling. "Something natural, not too fussy."

Ignoring her question, I was struck by a sense of sadness that I had no idea what my real mother's favourite flowers had been. By the time Fliss and I were old enough to stay with Aunty Ruth by ourselves, Mum was the Mum we knew, and I think she had made it very clear to my Aunty that if she crossed the line in that way, our visits would come to an end.

"It would help it I knew who they were for?"

In itself this was a reasonable question. I just didn't like her. She was being nosy for the sake of it I thought.

"I've changed my mind." I was not going to give her my money, flowers or not. There were plenty of grass verges along the green with daffodils a plenty. Grinning to myself at the tutting I could hear behind me, I turned around and left the shop.

I realised as I walked briskly back up the main street that I was angry with the woman. She had shone an unwelcome spotlight into an area of my life that I had not wanted to face. It wasn't right that I knew so little about my natural mother. Well, that was something I could put right whilst I was here, I determined, set now on going to her grave. First though a sugar rush was required never mind that I had just eaten breakfast.

This may have been a delaying tactic, I was very good at these, but I would defy anyone to walk past the window of the local bakery and not be drawn in by the goodies on offer. There was already a queue of people and a lively hum of conversation as I pushed open the door making the bell above it ring. All eyes turned to glance in my direction but the reaction of the lady behind the counter was not what I was expecting.

"Blessed be Rowan Pendleby!" Her blue eyes met mine for a second and then realisation shone in them. "I am sorry love, you must be Fae, of course. Ruth told me you were coming. I haven't seen you here since you were a youngster, but looking at you now, well it's like looking at your mother. Oh, my dearie me."

My mother had obviously meant something to her, and I couldn't wait to speak properly to her. I watched in amusement as the other customers were served as quickly as possible, their attempts to linger and talk cut short as she waved them away until there was only me left in the shop.

"Let me have a look at you. You won't remember me."

I smiled at her. "I do as a matter of fact. I remember coming in here with…..We always used to argue over who was going to have the choice of what cakes there would be for tea."

"And I always kept the peace by making up a box of everything," she nodded her head, her face showing that instant of understanding and sympathy for the gap in my words.

"It's lovely to see you again. What brings you back?"

Mabel was about the same age as Aunty Ruth. She was as plump as you would expect a baker to be with a kindly face, thick white hair piled up on her head in a bun and shrewd blue eyes that pierced right into you.

"I needed to get away from home for a while. There was a spot of bother where I was working, but please don't tell Aunty Ruth. I haven't had chance to mention it to her yet. I want to spend some time catching up with her here and then I will go back."

"No, my dear I don't think so."

"I beg your pardon?"

"Whatever reason you think brought you back to Maypoleton, I can tell you that you are here to stay." She smiled brightly and patted my arm. "Maypoleton has brought back one of her own. I am so glad. Now then, how about I make up a box of treats for you like I used to do?"

"That would be lovely, but what do you mean I am here to stay?"

She tilted her head in a bird like way and the smile grew more enigmatic. "There will be plenty of time to talk, Fae. You and I can get to know each other once you have had chance to catch up with your aunt."

I was drawn to the woman in complete contrast to how I had reacted to the owner of the florist, even though I was a little disturbed at some of what she had said.

"Thank you," I said as I took the box of carefully wrapped cakes from her and reached into the pocket of my leather jacket for my card.

"On no love, these are a treat from me." She positively beamed at me across the counter. "I am so happy to see you back. I was saying as much to Eve yesterday. It will be lovely to have another addition to our little group."

"Group?"

She waved a hand airily, "There's me running away with myself again. No rush for that either. But you will get to know Eve, she's another young friend of mine, she lives next door to your aunt."

I thought of the attractive lady, with the even more attractive husband. "Yes, I have already met her. She's seems nice."

"She is. Most of us in Maypoleton are my dear, although it does depend what side of the fence you are sitting on," she said this with a rather mischievous twinkle in her eyes.

I didn't have chance to ask about this as more customers came into the shop. Thanking Mabel once more for my box of goodies, I said goodbye and went back onto the main street. Although it was a cold day, I didn't want to be walking around the graveyard with a box of cream cakes so I did a quick detour back to Aunty Ruths', deposited them in the fridge and then set off again.

There was nobody around at the church or the vicarage but as it was mid-week, I didn't expect there to be. No doubt the vicar was out in the parish doing vicary things whatever that entailed, so there was no one to bother me as I pushed open the wrought iron gate that led into the graveyard.

Or so I thought.

I hadn't taken five steps down the path that led between neatly organised rows of headstone, before a female voice called to me. "And who would you be then?"

Thin, middle aged, wearing a tweed skirt, woollen sweater and sensible shoes, the lady was regarding me with a frosty expression. I don't think she approved of my ripped jeans, leather biker jacket and pink doc marten boots.

"What's it to do with you?" I thought I was being very well behaved, restraining myself from saying instead, "None of your fucking business." I didn't want to cause trouble for my aunt.

She pulled herself up rigidly, puffing out a meagre chest. "I am Mrs. Mannering, housekeeper for the Reverend Temple and he likes to know who is wandering around his graveyard."

"Does he indeed?"

I turned my back on her and carried on wanting to search out my mother's grave in peace although that was questionable. As soon as I had set foot in the graveyard, I had felt peculiar. It was similar to that feeling I got when I sensed that one of the people in my care was close to death.

Only magnified.

I was surrounded by death, and it was calling out to me.

Years ago, with Fliss, I had experienced something of this nature when I been dabbling in things I shouldn't have done. It had seemed something to giggle over at the time, although my twin had always been a little scared side of it all.

Now, as a grown woman I was feeling it far more intensely.

Be quiet!

I consciously had to speak to the voices that were calling out to me. Essentially, they were saying hello! Welcome into our midst stranger, how nice to be listened to after all this time. The echoes of the long departed simply wanted recognition that they had not been forgotten. Which was all very good and another time perhaps I would stay and chat but today was about my mother. Finally, I found her grave and seeing the name drove a blow to my stomach the same way a fist would.

Rowan Winters nee Pendleby beloved wife and mother.

Mother.

My mother.

I squatted down, realising that I had after all come without flowers. Damn.

"I'll bring some tomorrow," I said softly as I traced the outline of the word mother with my fingers.

"She shouldn't be here at all you know."

In my efforts to block out the voices of the dead I had not been aware that Mrs Mannering had followed me. I whirled around to see her standing a few feet away. There was a look of malicious satisfaction on her face.

"What do you mean? She shouldn't be here?"

I didn't like the way she smiled. "You don't know do you?"

I ground my teeth together. "Know what?"

"A churchyard is no place for suicides. She killed herself."

CHAPTER TEN

Asking your aunt if your mother had killed herself was, I discovered later that day, a very difficult question to put into words. I had had to physically restrain myself from slapping Mrs Mannering and shouting at her that this could not possibly be true.

But what if it was?

Was this the reason Mum disliked having her mentioned at all? Or why Dad for that matter hardly spoke of her?

I spent the rest of the day in some agitation, counting the hours until Aunty Ruth returned home from work. I got a text from her to say she was finishing at the cafe but would be going straight to Farthing Hall to bring the horses in from the field and did I want to meet her there?

Farthing Hall was situated half a mile outside of the village. It was an elegant manor house that dated back to the seventeenth century, if not earlier in some parts. The current owners, members of the family who had lived here for generations had created the equestrian centre there as a way of keeping the old building going.

I loved horses but not in quite the same way that Aunty Ruth did. For one thing I could never have the commitment it would take to look after one properly. But I enjoyed being around them, the smells and gentle noises they made, the simple pleasures of grooming them, combing manes and tails until they shone like silk.

As I parked my car in the livery side of the yard I was greeted by Sally Farthing, the owner.

"Hello, Fae how lovely to see you again. I remember when you used to visit with." She stopped abruptly, seeing perhaps the instant look of pain in my eyes. She gave me a motherly smile and carried on. "Ruth told me you would be coming down. Eric is in the stable mucking out, but your aunt is in the field bringing the girls in. Would you like me to show you the way?"

I remembered her too. Blonde, curvaceously bonny with super skin for an older lady and stunning blue eyes. And always that caring warmth. "Thank you."

As I walked alongside her past the outdoor school, I spotted my neighbour on a dark bay horse. She was doing her best to ask it to canter but all the horse wanted to do was trot at a million miles an hour. It didn't seem to be bothering Eve though. She was laughing and saying something to an elderly gentleman who was leaning on the fence and watching her progress.

"That's Eve and Sam," said Sally giving them a wave. "The horse I mean, he's Sam. The gentleman there is Seth. Sam's a rescue horse. Dear old soul has never cantered in his life, been too used to trotting with a cart, but Eve and Seth will get there with him."

"Looks like they're having fun anyway," I responded and returned Eve's friendly wave and the welcoming nod from Seth.

"That's what we aim to do here," said Sally with a grin. "Horse around with horses, having fun. Ruth, look who I've found!" She shouted over a five-bar gate down the length of a field. "There you go, Fae, I'll catch up with you later."

Aunty Ruth was walking up from the bottom of the field with a horse either side of her, no lead rope attached. I knew from her phone calls and cards that my aunt was a keen natural horsewoman, and I watched with admiration as the two animals walked in time with her.

"Now then," she said as she drew nearer. "This is Treacle, and this is Toffee, which would you like?" I knew Treacle was the love of her life, so I reached for the headcollar on the gate with Toffee's name embroidered on it.

"Hello beautiful," I said to the gentle looking palomino who did indeed look the colour of butterscotch toffee.

"How are you feeling then love? I didn't want to wake you this morning. We are always down here for six thirty mucking out before work and you sounded fast asleep."

"You mean I was snoring?"

"A little. Do you feel better for your sleep?"

"I do thanks."

I spent the next hour enjoying the company of the horses and everyone else down at the yard. It was easy to see why Aunty Ruth was so at home there. It was also therapeutic filling hay nets and water buckets, mindless tasks that I could do whilst those thoughts buzzed in my head.

Had my mother killed herself?

Why would she do that?

How had she done it?

"Penny for them, love?" Uncle Eric joined me over by the water tap. "You looked miles away."

"Sorry. Doesn't matter."

"Doesn't look like it doesn't matter," he said shrewdly, taking hold of one handle of the large water bucket so we could carry it together.

I looked at the people milling around here and there. This was not the time or place for that kind of conversation.

"I get it," he said straight away. "Let's wait until we're back home hey. It's always easier talking over a pot of tea and a slice of cake."

I couldn't agree more, but I found the words were sticking in my throat a couple of hours later. We had eaten a hearty casserole that had been slow cooking all day, and a couple of cakes from the bakery and talked about the horses and life in Maypoleton in general. Then, Aunty Ruth had refilled the tea pot and once more we were settled back in the cosy front room, only unlike last night I didn't feel the need to fall asleep just yet.

"Saying it can't be worse than thinking it," she said sitting next to me on the well-worn, sofa that was easy to sink into and very difficult to get out of. She patted my knee. "It's obvious something is troubling you. Is it to do with why you are here?"

I had completely forgotten about the murder accusation. Just a small omission Fae, nothing major at all. "No. That was just a misunderstanding. I went to the grave this morning."

"Oh yes love. Must have been strange."

Strange wasn't my word for it. "I met Mrs Mannering."

"Oh her. She's the vicar's housekeeper. You can't set foot on church property without her setting on you like a bleeding Rottweiler," snorted Eric from where had had settled himself on a chair by the fire.

"Now then, Eric. She can't help it," said Aunty Ruth, never having a bad word to say about anyone.

Uncle Eric gave me a look which in other circumstances would have made me smile. "Oh heck," he said at the serious expression on my face. "What has she said to upset you?"

Beside me I felt my aunt stiffen.

"She said my mother had killed herself."

The clocked ticked for all of twenty seconds. Then thirty. I had no idea half a minute could feel so long.

"I always believed it was an accident," said Aunty Ruth taking hold of my hand and squeezing it tightly. "She loved you so much. She loved the very bones of you, both of you. Oh God. So hard losing a sister as you know. Rowan was ten years older than me. Same age you are now in fact."

"What happened?" I could hardly speak, this all seemed unreal.

"She was badly depressed after you two were born. Postnatal depression. It just never seemed to leave her. And she was so tired all the time. Looking after twins must have been exhausting for her. I only saw it during the holidays when I came back home. I was away at university then. I still blame myself. Perhaps if I had stayed here and helped more, she wouldn't have been so low, so tired and worn out."

I knew that bitter blade of guilt, but my aunt had nothing to blame herself for compared to me. "It can't have been your fault," I said, hating to see her beginning to cry.

"It wasn't," Eric said staunchly, his face scrunching up at his wife's distress. "It was the bloody useless doctor who didn't realise how she was feeling and just prescribed a load of sleeping pills."

"Was that how she did it?"

Aunty Ruth nodded. "There was no note though, so I always told myself it was an accident. She never meant to do it. She just took too many so she could sleep. She wouldn't have left you and Fliss willingly, Fae. You must believe that."

"Mum… Mum and Dad always said it was cancer."

"Yes well," Aunty Ruth wiped her tears and was pragmatic once more, "We all agreed it would do more harm than good for you to grow up believing your mother had killed herself. And somehow as the years went by, well it was never something to talk about really. I'm sorry if you feel you have been lied to."

I thought of the lies I was hiding. "It doesn't matter. It was just hard hearing it like that from Mrs Mannering that's all."

"Bloody woman!" Eric grunted in disgust. "Calls herself a Christian. I'd throw her to the bloody lions I would."

His anger on my behalf was touching. "It's alright," I told him. "I have dealt with far worse."

"Even so, it was cruel. I shall have words with her myself," announced Aunty Ruth with an unusually flinty expression in her eyes. "She had no right telling you that, no right at all. That's my sister she is talking about don't forget."

I knew better than most the bond between sisters. I felt the headache that had been brewing since the morning begin to pound a little harder. It was a lot to take in, on top of the emotional hit of simply being here.

"You alright love?" Aunty Ruth was gentle again as she looked at me. "You've gone very peaky."

I nodded. "I just need some fresh air. I think I'll take myself for another walk."

"Do you want company lass, or would you rather be alone?" Eric asked.

"I think I need to be alone if you don't mind. I'm going back to the grave. I don't suppose Mrs Mannering will be stalking the place at this time?"

Aunty Ruth shook her head. "But it's dark."

I grinned at her. "Don't worry. I am used to being out after dark."

"Aye stop meithering her woman, she's not a child anymore." Eric teased her.

Knowing that they both kept early hours, and I was a night owl, I said to them both, "Please don't wait up for me. I may take myself to the pub for a drink afterwards, I am used to working till late don't forget."

I fetched my leather jacket, put on my boots and kissed them both on the cheek before letting myself out into the evening air. Fresh in a totally different way to at home. There of course there was always the sharp tang of salt from the sea. Here the breeze carried with it a far more earthy scent, just as pleasant in its' own way. I dug my hands in my jacket pocket and began walking.

"Hello Fae, do you want to join us at the pub? It's quiz night tonight, usually a good laugh which goes on till quite late."

I turned around to see Eve and Craig from next door just behind me. Close up I could see how pretty she was with wavy light brown hair and unusual eyes a mix of blue, green and brown. I was also aware of how attractive he was in jeans and a thick woolly jumper, cool grey eyes a little warmer now as he smiled and said hello.

Damp it down Fae.

Jump on it right now.

Rule number one, you do not shit on your own doorstep.

Or in this case you do not set your sights on your aunt's married neighbour. "Maybe later," I said acknowledging the friendly invitation with a smile. "I'm going for a walk round the graveyard first. I went there this morning but got interrupted by Mrs Mannering."

Eve echoed Eric's comments. "Bloody Rottweiler, can't stand the woman."

Craig spoke with an amused catch to his voice. "Yes, but you hate anything to do with the church darling."

A stab of longing drove into my heart at the way he spoke to her. Love and passion intermingled.

She replied with a teasing smile and a wink at me. "Apart from Reverend Temple. I don't hate him."

This earned a snort from Craig. "Control yourself woman." To me he added, "Our new vicar is causing something of a stir."

"You have to admit he is a vast improvement on Reverend Michael, mean old bugger," his wife replied snappily.

Craig shot me a look and said evenly. "Bit of history between my lovely wife and the previous custodian of our church. But take it from me, the Reverend Temple is far more amenable than his housekeeper so if you wish to take an evening wander through his churchyard, he will not mind at all."

"Not scared of ghosts then?" Eve said lightly as we reached the top of Cobblers Row.

"Eve," Craig said with a slight warning note in his voice, "behave."

Was I scared of ghosts?
Not at all.
Was I scared of what I would learn from my mother?
Absolutely.

"I might catch you later in the pub then," I said without responding to Eve's comment, "although I must warn you, I am not all that hot on quizzes."

Then I walked in the opposite direction, back towards the vicarage and churchyard. Dusk was falling now. It was quiet with only the sounds of the light breeze in the trees and my footsteps on the pavement to intrude on my thoughts. I cast a glance at the vicarage ready to do battle with Mrs Mannering if she dared to interfere once more. It was adjacent to the churchyard but separated by an old brick wall covered in ivy. I paused before opening the wrought iron gate.

Was I insane doing this?

Probably but I opened the gate anyway. As soon as my feet stepped onto the path, I had to consciously block out the pressure from the voices calling to me.

"Be quiet I have come to speak to my mother."

It felt both frightening and deliriously exhilarating to be feeling so connected. As though every cell in my body was waking up, almost intoxicating with the giddiness of it.

I realised just how damnably suppressed I had been working at the nursing home all these years. The only times to feel this way had been those moments when the elderly folk had died and then I had had to hide it, ram it tightly into a box, and even in doing that look what had happened with Mr Carlisle.

I was in a strangely joyous mood which warred with my apprehension as I made my way to my mother's grave once more. I checked to make sure I was alone this time and then knelt down. "What happened"?

I didn't know whether to call her Mother, Mum, or even Rowan so I kept it simple. I traced the carving of her name, my fingers taking their time over every letter.

"Rowan Pendleby, Rowan Pendleby, Rowan Pendleby," a whisper of a thought that became spoken words without realising it. Her maiden name, the name of her birth.

"*Forgive me.*"

It was in the wind softly blowing around my face. It was in the touch of the gravestone. It was in the vibration of the ground beneath me.

"Forgive me."

"What happened?" I asked again, closing my eyes.

She was the image of me.

But pale, so very pale. She was rocking a baby in her arms whilst another lay sleeping quietly. The crying was incessant. Tears of exhaustion rolling down her face as the baby would not settle. I knew the baby was me, screaming in a manner that would drive anyone insane.

Fast forward in time. A fractious baby now a toddler, crawling with a twin. Thinner than before, face drawn and haggard, I saw her sitting at a table, weeping. I saw a house in disarray, the paraphernalia of children everywhere, pots left unwashed, a pan spilling over on the cooker, spitting and hissing unheeded.

I saw a woman lost in motherhood and unable to cope.

Where was Dad in all of this?

Lost in his own world of academia, studying to become a professor of English Literature, no idea at all that his wife was on the edge. Hardly at home, absent minded in his love and attention, thinking that everything was fine in his world.

A day of none stop crying from me, a fever that had me scarlet faced and screaming. Fliss sleeping peacefully, whilst she sat with me, rocked me, cooled my brow, paced the bedroom with me in the early hours even though I must have weighed quite heavy by this time.

Quiet at last. Dad fast asleep, oblivious to the disturbance in the nursery. She stumbles wearily back into their bedroom. It is three o clock in the morning. There is a bottle of pills beside the bed. She picks it up, a frown on her face. Has she taken any earlier that evening? She can't remember. One or two more can't hurt surely? She swallows two.

The crying starts again.

Tears of exhaustion fill her eyes as she tries to wake Dad. He slumbers on, snoring loudly. Staggering now with fatigue she walks back in the nursery. Fliss this time but easily settled with a stroke of her hand and a teddy back in place.

Once more back to bed.
Sleep, precious sleep.
Just for a few hours please.
She looks at the bottle of pills.
No, she is certain she didn't take any before.
She swallows two more.
Sleep at last.
"Forgive me."
I am crying now in the graveyard. "There is nothing to forgive. Oh Mum, there is nothing to forgive."
I wrap my arms around the gravestone, my eyes shut tight, and I picture her in my mind. It is my mother I am holding, not the cold stone. Her scent is that of lavender orange blossom, her hair soft against my face, her body is fragile and thin, so painfully thin. Too tired to cook for herself, underweight and more susceptible to the pills because of it.
"I didn't want to leave you."
"I know. I'm sorry Mum, I cried too much. I wore you out. It was me."
"Hush now child, cry no more."
"I love you daughter of mine."
"I love you too Mum," I said softly, reluctant to let go of the stone, but there was someone else coming and already she was fading.
I whirled around to see whose presence it was that had disturbed the moment. Anger mixed with grief on top of a deep psychic connection makes for a potent drug. I needed to get wildly drunk, fight someone, or have sex.
"Oh sorry, I didn't realise anyone was here."
Getting to my feet, energy pulsing through me as though I had just plugged myself into the mains, I was face to face with the lovely form of Matt, dressed in running gear and panting slightly.
Alcohol, violence, or sex? "Hello Matt," I got to my feet and smiled at him.

CHAPTER ELEVEN

"Fae it's you. What the hell are you doing in the graveyard at this time of night?"

I didn't want to talk to him about my mother. I didn't want to talk to him at all. Why spoil the moment with words? There was an energy now charging through the air between us. I could see Matt's breathing alter and a confused expression come over his face. He knew he was feeling something, but I suspected he was too practical in nature to consider what it may be.

I knew though.

The psychic energy created from the bond between Rowan and I was swirling in the night air, mingling with the scent of damp earth, carried on the breeze. It would have been odd for it not to have had some kind of effect.

Admittedly what happened next was a little extreme even for me, but my actions were powered by more than just my own nature. Surrounded by the dead, the sorrow, the regret, there was an urgent need to feel alive.

It transmuted to Matt as I walked slowly towards him. "Fae?"

"Shush," I placed a finger on his lips and then clasped my hands around his neck to pull him closer to me.

I felt the startled jolt go through him as I kissed him. His hands were still loosely by his side, unsure what to do. My lips opened against his and his mouth had to obey, no other choice than to let my tongue enter and seek his.

A sudden movement of his hands as they grabbed at my waist and pulled me to him. Through the thin fabric of his running shorts, I could feel how quickly and deeply aroused he was. I knew some of that was down to the atmosphere around us, but that didn't matter to me.

Leaning into him, I raised myself a little on tip toes so that my hips were on a level with his, the writhing movements making him groan and harden further. He was kissing me back with passion now, his hands eagerly roaming my body, over my bottom, under my leather jacket, finding the way to the gap between my sweater and bare skin.

No shrinking violet myself, I had already let my hands travel down the muscular length of his back, trail over the breadth of his chest, and lower still.

"We're in the graveyard!" He yanked his mouth from mine at the same time my hands clasped around the full, naked length of him beneath his shorts.

"Point being," I murmured, stroking him lightly enough to tease, not hard enough to please.

"We... are... in... the... grave... yard, Fae," he said again as though I either had not heard him or was too stupid to realise what this meant.

Deaf? No.

Stupid? No.

High on a psychic overload, yes and graveyard be damned. Besides, there was a lovely old tree just a few feet away that was begging to have someone fucked against it. Taking hold of his hand tightly, I led, he followed.

"Fae, this is wrong. I'm the scout leader."

Bless him. "It's okay, Matt, trust me, it's okay. No one will ever know." I had unzipped my jeans and leant back against the tree. Reaching for his hand once more I guided him to feel what I was feeling.

Pulsing hot, wet desire.

He groaned as his fingers slid into my depths. "Oh Christ, Fae."

"Shush," I whispered softly into his neck as he bent to kiss me once more. "It's okay, honestly, it's okay. Yes, like that, oh yes like that."

His fingers inside me, the feel of his palm against me, his mouth greedy against mine, I let my hips dance to their own tune, the trunk of the tree hard against my back. As my body spasmed against his hand, mine went to his shorts to release him.

The feel of him inside me prolonged my orgasm with one intense wave after another. By now he had clearly lost all thoughts of being a scout leader. He was simply a red-blooded male, fired up on his own adrenaline from running, with a female body that was there to be enjoyed, pleasured, and taken.

Take me he did, with a satisfying zest and enthusiasm. Jeans, pants and boots efficiently removed and discarded. He was strong enough to lift me up by my hips so I could wrap my legs around his waist and then, he let go of any inhibitions or annoying little details like the fact we were in a graveyard. It was shamefully fast, hard, greedy fucking. Exactly what I needed. Hot breath on each of our necks, sweat forming despite the chilly air, moans that could not quite by stifled, cries of pleasure that could quite possibly wake the dead.

I did wonder as he collapsed against me, my back now welded into the bark of the tree, if we may have done that? But no. There were no shadowy figures drifting in between the gravestones. Just the two of us, coiled together like serpents around the tree.

"Christ Fae." He eased my legs down to the ground and shifted his position so he could withdraw from me, hastily tucking himself away.

I picked up my knickers and jeans from the floor, scrabbled back into them, put my boots back on and ran a hand through my hair to loosen the tangles. My body felt deliciously limp now and the wild energy that had been revving through me had thankfully subsided.

"Are you ok?" Not usual I know for the woman to ask the man this after such a rushed encounter.

He gave a shaky laugh. "Yeah, I think so. I mean bloody hell Fae, I only met you the other day, is this usual for you?"

I felt a little sorry for him. In the gentle light of the moon that was now making her appearance he looked like a boy who had just stolen some sweets and was frightened of getting found out.

"Not exactly," I said with a rueful shake of my head. "I must admit I have never done it in a graveyard before." I shrugged. "I needed sex, you were there, and I like you."

A long slow whistle escaped his lips. "Wow. I don't really know what to say to that."

"Don't tell me you have never felt the same way yourself?"

Here we go, I thought, time for the double standards. It was okay a man to behave like that but not a woman.

"Felt it maybe. Acted on it never. And certainly not in a graveyard for crying out loud. What if one of my scouts had seen us?"

I bit my lip to stop myself from laughing.

"It's not funny Fae, and I'm the deputy head at the school. Bloody hell we could have been seen by a parent!"

"I'm sorry." I took pity on his plight. I really did like him. He struck me as the sort of man that didn't have a bad bone in his body. He was genuinely mortified at his actions and that no doubt put him into the category of men with whom I really should not entangle myself. Far too nice for me. Annie would love him. Annie would be thinking about wedding dresses for me.

"Look, how about we go for that drink now. I promise I won't jump on you in the pub in front of everyone," I gave him my most winning smile and I could see him melt.

"Oh fuck."

"No, we've just done that."

"You're crazy you know that."

"I've been called worse."

"Alright. But I need to go home and change first. I'll see you there in about half an hour."

"Fair enough," I said pleased with myself. "Don't go standing me up now though will you."

"I wouldn't dare," he called over his shoulder as he began to jog out of the graveyard.

I followed him at a much more leisurely pace opting to go for a walk around the village rather than go straight to the pub. Away from the heavy atmosphere of the graveyard and its effect on me, I could think about what I had learnt from my mother. My footsteps took me around the green with the small duckpond. There was a bench there and I sat on it, wondering if my mother had sat here once herself.

I knew so little about her. Had she always lived here? Had she been born here like Fliss and I were? Had she had a happy childhood? My heart felt utterly broken at the scenes I had witnessed from beyond the grave. I had no doubts at all that Dad had loved her, and she him. She had just been so damnably lost in postnatal depression and exhaustion. He had been so absorbed in his studies and his work.

Mum, the Mum I knew, always joked that a bomb could go off in the house and he wouldn't notice. It never seemed to bother her, but then we had been a little older when she had married Dad, and she had not been subjected to the devastating effects of hormones out of control.

"I wish I had known you, Rowan" I said quietly to the wind that whispered in the trees. "I have a feeling you would have understood me more than Mum." It struck me then to wonder if Fliss was now with her. That was too sorrowful for me to contemplate. What would my mother have thought over Fliss's death?

Time for that drink.

Sitting here brooding was a dangerous game and now that the sun had gone down it was distinctly chilly. I looked down the road to see if there was any sign of Matt coming, but I was not one to wait for a man, so I walked off in the direction of the Maypoleton Arms.

Along with the rest of the buildings on this side of the village, the pub was at least a few hundred years old. Most people would need to duck their heads to avoid hitting the beam, black with age over the doorway. I didn't and I pushed open the door to walk into what was clearly the last round of the weekly pub quiz. It was like one of those scenes from a television programme where a stranger walks into a pub and every goes silent and turns to stare.

"Evening," I announced myself with a cheery grin and a smile at Eve and Craig who were sitting at a table with the glamourous looking lady I had spotted from a distance in the school yard.

"Fae come and join us; there's two more questions to go." Aunty Ruth's neighbour beckoned.

"Oy that's cheating that is, you can't have outsiders just joining in," someone called out.

"I'm not an outsider I was born here," I retorted with a cool stare. "Don't worry, I will let you all finish your little game. Pint of stout please," I said to the landlord who was wiping a glass and watching with interest.

"You'll be Fae Pendleby then," he said as he slid it across the bar to me. "Mabel said you had arrived."

I let it slide that Pendleby was my mother's maiden name. It seemed to be the name most people here knew her by. "Did you know my mother?"

He nodded with a smile. "Aye. Bonny lass that she was. We were all half in love with her you know in the village. I certainly was from the day I sat next to her at the primary school. She was a bit special was our Rowan." He waved aside my attempts to pay him. "A real gentle soul would never harm a fly. You've certainly got her looks."

But not her character I thought to myself as I smiled my thanks for the drink and made my way through the tables to sit in the space Eve had made for me. Craig was leaning back against his chair with a disinterested air as the last of the quiz questions was put forward. I smiled at him in welcome, but I got the impression his wife was the far more sociable of the two.

The other lady with them was extremely pretty with a sleek chin length bob the colour of dark chocolate, brown eyes and gorgeous smooth skin. I received a flash of a smile from her, bold scarlet lipstick outlining her mouth.

"Hi, I'm Laura," she said earning a look of disapproval from the quiz master as the last question was read out.

"Thank goodness that's over," said Craig with a loud yawn a couple of minutes later. "Ladies can I get you another drink?" He pushed his chair back to stand up and even though I had just arrived with a full pint gave me the look to ask if I would like another as well.

"Go on then, if you insist," I said with a grin.

"Pint?"

I nodded.

"God where the hell do you put it?" Laura, a fabulously buxom woman with curves most men would drool over, looked at me enviously. "You're like a little pixie."

"Fast metabolism," I said with an apologetic shrug.

"Well, I think it's bloody unfair," Laura went on. "It's bad enough being friends with Eve, here, I mean look at her, middle forties and still a size eight, and now there's you. I may as well go home and dig out a bin liner to cover myself with."

"Stop it," Eve laughed at her. "You're bloody gorgeous as you are, and you know it."

I caught a flash of uncertainty in the woman's beautiful dark eyes. For all I behave like a man-eating trollop, I do have empathy for my own sex.

"I think you are the most glamourous teacher I have seen, that is, if you are a teacher? I saw you in the school yard yesterday morning."

"Sorry I haven't introduced you, have I?" Fae apologised. "Laura is the head teacher, and this is Fae, Ruth's niece."

"I've heard all about you already," she smiled warmly. "So how are you enjoying being back in Maypoleton? I've only been here about three years, but I love it."

Craig was making his way back to the table with a tray of drinks, behind him I saw the blond head of Matt making his entrance into the pub.

"I'm enjoying myself so far," I said as I caught the flash of a look on Matt's face.

"Where the hell have you been?" Craig greeted him with a friendly scowl. "I had to sit through the bloody quiz with these two lunatics. You'd have thought we were on mastermind."

"Now then," Laura slapped Craig on the arm with the easy affection of a good friend. "Honour is at stake you know that. But yes, where have you been Matt? We were expecting you earlier?"

Matt studiously avoided my eyes. "I tripped and landed in the ditch on Bleasfell road. Took me ages to get clean."

"Well, you're here now," said Laura as she wriggled up for him on the bench that curved around a corner.

"Thanks," he said sitting down.

"Have you met Fae?" Eve asked brightly.

Matt mumbled something intelligible into his pint.

"We met on the road on my way here. Matt kindly helped me change my tyre. Bloody sheep railroaded me into a grass verge."

"Yes, they do have a habit of doing that," said Laura with a laugh.

The conversation was then interrupted by the quiz master announcing the winning team. Judging by the groans, mutters and cheers this was taken very seriously. Under the cover of the general noise and chit chat I had chance to observe Matt as I sipped my second pint.

He was looking distinctly uncomfortable, and a flush rose on his cheeks if his eyes met mine, which they did rather a lot. At the same time, I noticed how he had a habit of tensing ever so slightly if Laura moved a fraction closer to him, which huddled up as they were, was a natural thing to do.

So that was the way the wind was blowing, was it? The hunky deputy head had a bit of thing for the voluptuous head teacher. Interesting. Watching how at ease Laura was I guessed she was clueless. As the clapping for the winning team died down, I caught Eve watching me, watching Laura and Matt.

There was a speculative look in her merry eyes, an odd mix of green-blue with a dash of brown thrown in. I recognised a kindred spirit in some respects. Eve was a lot sharper than she let on.

"So has Matt caught your eye then?" She asked me outright about half an hour later when we were in the ladies together.

We were both at the sinks, our reflections regarding each other steadily.

"He's not really my type," I answered in all honesty as I dried my hands. "I prefer a darker more brooding character. But he does seem very nice."

"He is. He's absolutely lovely. I just wish Laura could see it."

"I thought she was married, or that's the gist I got from her conversation."

Eve fluffed up her hair with her fingers and wiped away a trace of smudged eyeliner. "She is. To muppet Mark."

"Muppet Mark?" I liked this woman with her direct speech and assessing eyes.

"Absolute tosser but Laura is devoted to him. Works away a lot and I'm pretty sure he plays away a lot as well if you know what I mean?"

I did. I am exactly the sort of woman, that men play away with. I nodded with a wry smile.

"The thing is though; she has four children. She is absolutely devoted to them, and I think she just doesn't want to split the family up."

"Four kids and she works as head teacher, bloody hell is she some kind of superwoman?"

"We all think so," said Eve with a tilt to her head and another one of those peculiar looks as though she was trying to read deeper into me. "She is a genuinely lovely woman, wouldn't harm a fly. And I know there are not too many of those around."

"No there aren't," I replied steadily. And I am certainly not one of them. I wondered which category Eve fell into. I also wondered if she was trying to say something else to me. Back at the table and well into another round of drinks, Craig, Matt and Laura were talking about someone called Gawain and his father.

"He's desperate to get someone permanent for the position," Laura was saying "the staff from the agency keep letting him down."

"I know it's playing on his mind," Matt said to her, his eyes flicking warily to me once more as I sat back down with Eve. "He was even talking yesterday about moving back to the town so that he won't have the same problem."

"Oh no we can't have that! Bloody hell he's the best vicar we've had," said Laura.

"What's the problem?" Eve asked as she sat down.

Craig explained. "Gawain's father is needing more care now since his illness has deteriorated. He's desperate to keep him out of a nursing home, but the care he can get out here is just unreliable. He really needs someone to live in, or at the very least local."

"I can do that," the words fell off my tongue as smoothly as silk. I am not sure who was more surprised, them or me.

"Really?" Laura looked at me as though I was a gift from heaven. "Are you qualified?"

"I've worked in nursing homes since I was twenty."

"But I thought you were only here visiting your aunt?" Matt asked looking a little worried.

My shoulders shrugged their answer.

"But what about your own work?" Laura pinned me down with her headteacher's gaze.

"Ah."

Craig looked at me with a policeman's radar gaze. "Ah?"

Another shrug, I was very good at these. "Small matter of a recent accusation."

"Such as?"

"Murder," I said nonchalantly, and smiled inwardly as Matt choked on his pint.

"Really?" Eve and Laura sat forward with a look of intrigued delight on their faces.

"'Fraid so." I looked at Craig. "You can check it out if you like. No charges to be pressed but I have left my place of employment because regardless of the facts, mud tends to stick and when you have the local papers calling you the Angel of Death, it's very sticky mud indeed."

Eve burst out laughing. "I think you are going to fit in perfectly here, Fae. Laura why don't you have a word with Gawain tomorrow and tell him his prayers have been answered."

Laura looked equally pleased. "Absolutely. It will be super if you can stay here Fae, won't it Matt?"

Matt stared deeply into his pint and didn't answer.

CHAPTER TWELVE

The following morning, I slept late again. I woke feeling distinctly groggy which someone else might have blamed on the pints of stout, but I never usually suffered from hangovers. I could only assume that the sluggish feel to my body was the after affects, of what had happened in the graveyard.

Not the sex with Matt. That had been just fine. More than fine. I was chuffed to have stumbled so easily on such a pleasing source of entertainment whilst I was in Maypoleton. I had thought attractive men might be thin on the ground in such a remote and small village, but with Craig and Matt there was plenty to satisfy the eye.

It also appealed to my nature, wicked soul that I am, that Matt was clearly under Laura's spell and that despite this he had completely lost his inhibitions and fucked me like a mad thing up against the tree in the graveyard. I laughed to myself as I showered and dressed, remembering the look of horror on his face both before and afterwards.

He was sweet and although this was breaking my rule of not getting involved with nice men, I decided that if I was staying in Maypoleton for a while, it couldn't do any harm for once. Besides, judging by the enthusiastic way he had gone about it, Matt had been desperate for sex himself.

Maybe I could ease his unrequited passion for Laura. Surely there could be nothing wrong in doing that. In fact, I would be doing something positively good for once. I would be alleviating his suffering. I chose to ignore completely that pesky nagging voice that taunted me that it would stop me from thinking about him.

Him.

My stranger of the night with no name.

The man who had invaded my mind and refused to be banished.

Happy with this side of things, I was left then with what I considered to be the side effects of my beyond the grave encounter with my mother. I went downstairs feeling really rather less then perky. Again, Aunty Ruth had left me a note. Uncle Eric was working today, but as it was Friday my aunt was down at the stables. She would be back at lunchtime.

Glancing at the clock I saw it was eleven thirty already. Crikey I had slept late. I opted for a bit of peace and quiet and chance to mull over my thoughts before my aunt returned. I wanted to think about what my mother had shown me.

I also needed to ponder how much I told Aunty Ruth.

There was a freshly baked granary loaf in the bread bin which looked tempting. I cut two thick slices which I liberally loaded with butter and some locally made blackberry jam and made myself a strong coffee with cream and three sugars.

The kitchen had French windows which opened onto the small, paved patio garden. There was a round wrought iron table with two chairs, and I opened the doors to take my late breakfast outside. In typical April fashion, after the unsettled weather I had experienced on my drive up here, today was benignly sunny and warm. Time to make the most of having nothing to do and a bit of sunshine.

Time to think.

It was quite a dilemma.

I knew that Aunty Ruth must be suffering even after all this time from the thought that her sister had possibly killed herself. God knows I suffered from how responsible I was for Fliss, and my aunt blamed herself in some way for not being there for her my mother. If I were to tell her what I knew, surely that would alleviate this suffering which would be a good thing. But the only way I could do this was to come clean and confess what I had kept hidden all my life, apart from with Fliss of course.

I was psychic.

I was a witch.

Powerful too.

From being as young as I could remember, I could sense and feel things that my twin so clearly couldn't. Then when I hit puberty, it got worse. Or should I say stronger. I had no idea what the hell was going on with me. I couldn't control my emotions. My feelings ran wild and my behaviour with them. There was too much energy buzzing round in my head for me to contain and this led me to getting into trouble both at school and at home.

Ultimately it led to Fliss's death.

At which point I shut down this side of me.

Only of course you cannot completely deny that which is a part of you. It exists and like the embers of a fire it glows within you, waiting for the breath of life to bring turn it back into a flame.

It seemed that as I got older, and maybe this had something to do with me being the age now that my mother was when she died, it grew more demanding. Or maybe with the line of work I had been in, continually being confronted with death as the elderly residents would naturally pass away, it triggered a response.

I had no idea really and that was part of the problem. This was not something I could look up on the internet. Well actually I had but that only led to a whole bunch of weird people that I really did not want to associate with.

Could I talk to Aunty Ruth about this?

The trouble was, my aunt was a keen church goer, not in the bible thumping kind of way, just very Church of England, down to earth, every Sunday kind of way. How would she react to the knowledge that her niece knew when people were going to die and could also communicate with them once dead? It could completely freak her out and I had no wish to do that. I also was reluctant to talk about it because it was too much of a reminder of what I had done to cause Fliss's death.

My thoughts had grown no clearer when I heard the pleasant tones of Aunty Ruth's voice calling through from the kitchen.

"Hello love, you had another good night's sleep?"

Dressed in jeans and a bright pink sweater, she came to join me on the patio bringing with her a warm smile and comforting smell of horses and hay.

"I did thank you. Must be this northern air," I said getting up to hug her. I loved Aunty Ruth's hugs. They were like being wrapped in a soft comforting duvet. "How are Treacle and Toffee?"

"Just grand," she said wandering back into the kitchen to begin opening cupboards and getting a tub out of the fridge. "Do you want some soup for your lunch? It's homemade tomato and red pepper?"

Aunty Ruth could not bake to save her life, but her soups were legendary. Ignoring the fact that it was only an hour since I had eaten two doorstops of bread and jam, I nodded.

Do I say something or not?

Shall I, shan't I?

Coward that I am, I was glad when she began to talk, saving me the decision process for another time.

"Eve was telling me you had had some trouble at your work?"

Okay maybe that was not the best of topics, but I suppose it had to come up, especially after the way I had blurted it out in the pub last night. This was a small village after all, and Eve had her horse in the same stable block. They were bound to gossip.

"I know. I am sorry I didn't tell you myself. It wasn't something I really wanted to talk about, but it came up last night in the pub."

"Eve said. Happen it's a good thing," Aunty Ruth nodded at me as she heated up the soup and cut some more of the bread. "Gawain's really struggling at the moment and his father's a lovely soul. It would be a damn shame if he had to go into a nursing home or come to that matter if Gawain had to leave the village."

"Sounds like someone out of King Arthur," I said with a smile as I took the bowl of hot soup that she passed to me.

"Well exactly. His mother called him that after the knight in the legends. Most men would appear daft with a name like that," she said sitting down opposite me, "but it suits him. He's a real gentleman and so much more of a Christian that Reverend Michael who was here before. I used to sometimes wonder what on earth he was doing in a church with some of his small-minded ideas. But Gawain Temple has made a real change here. We'd all be very sad to lose him."

"Sounds a great guy," I sipped my soup thinking he sounded far too good to be true and a tad boring, but hey who was I to judge.

"He is. And he is happy to overlook your problem with the police and the fact that you left work under a cloud."

I nearly spat out my soup. "You've spoken to him about me?" She smiled and there was the tiniest glimmer of mischief in her eyes that was familiar to me. I saw it often in my own reflection.

"Didn't think it would do any harm to put a good word in. And it seems like fate has brought you here just at the right time. Besides, it would be lovely, Fae to have the chance to get to know you again, properly."

That wriggling worm of guilt, how it made me squirm inside.

She paused and swallowed a couple of mouthfuls of her soup before adding, "So I said you would come to church with me this Sunday and he can speak to you afterwards, take you to meet his father."

How could I refuse? "That would be great, Aunty Ruth. Thanks."

I meant it as well. If staying here and taking on a job as carer for the vicar's father made amends in some way for my absence over the years since Fliss's death, then it was well worth doing. I could certainly think of worse places to spend the summer.

My aunt then went on to chat in general about this and that, and I was happy to let the conversation flow. Most definitely this was not the moment to discuss my mother. That could come later. For now, it was enough to settle into what to all intents and purposes was a new relationship. I had been a teenager when I had last been here. Aunty Ruth was right, we really did need to get to know each other again.

Saturday brought with it more never-ending rain and a frequent blast of hail stones but that didn't stop my aunt and uncle spending most of the day at the yard. I joined them for the morning and then spent a very lazy afternoon in front of the fire with a good book. There was no doubt I had turned into something of a sloth since taking my enforced break from work, but I told myself that if I was going to start a new job than I may as well enjoy the time now.

The following morning was my chance to meet the saintly Reverend Gawain and his father. I had not thought to bring any smart clothes with me, but I opted for a pair of jeans that did not have holes in them and one of my more sober sweaters, a black polo neck, under my good old leather jacket. As for the pink Doc Martens, well I would probably end up being buried in them.

Fortunately, Aunty Ruth was not a dress up for church kind of woman in the same way Mum was. It crossed my mind to wonder as we walked over to the church, if my mother Rowan had been religious. We were just halfway across the green when I voiced this out loud and Aunty Ruth stopped.

"Your mother…..Rowan, well she was a little different." She seemed unable to move as though captured in a moment of time. "Fey, she was. Other worldly at times. I used to wonder if that was why she struggled like she did. If her mind was just not quite right?"

Or I wondered, was she disturbed by what she could sense and feel, on top of being exhausted with looking after twins, one of whom was a restless child.

Fey like her mother.

Was that why she named me so?

Had she known from the moment of my birth that I was different to Fliss?

"I'm sorry. I didn't mean to upset you."

"No, love, you ask away. It's right that you want to talk about her. It just feels strange that's all. I've been so used to not speaking of her. Your mum didn't want me to do that, and I understood how she felt I really did. She was only trying to do the best for you, but it was hard at times. So hard. It was as though Rowan had stopped existing and yet every time I saw you, there was this gaping bloody wound that grew bigger and bigger as you got older, and I started to see Rowan in you."

Her voice was wobbling now, and I led her to the bench I had sat on the other night. Surely it would not matter if we were a few minutes late for the service. Surely Saint Gawain, as I called him in my mind, would understand.

I let her compose herself, wiping away the tears until she was ready. Then we finished our short journey and entered the church just as everyone was standing up to sing the first hymn. The church was fairly full, and we chose a pew at the back to not cause a disturbance. Standing behind a tall gentleman and his wife, I opened the hymn book that Aunty Ruth passed to me and with her, began to join the others in singing.

Church had been a regular part of my upbringing, and I had been in the brownies with Fliss. She collected an armful of badges, I trudged along with a couple, reluctantly earned. I put my foot down when it came to progressing to the guides. That was the only time Fliss and I did things separately. She loved all that kind of thing and threw herself into it with enthusiasm.

By that time, I was already feeling pulled along another path.

But once Fliss was gone, I let myself be sucked back into the fold again, if only to salve my guilt and try and fill the gap for my parents. Which of course I could never do. Either way I had a half-hearted approach at best to being in church, but I had nothing better to do and besides I was curious to see what Saint Gawain looked like.

I pictured him as very monkish looking, mousey coloured hair, indistinct eyes, probably short sighted with glasses, and nondescript features. I imagined him being average height and a bit weedy in build. The congregation sat down and shifting my position slightly, so I was not directly behind the tall gentleman, I finally got a look at him.

Him.

My dangerous stranger.

Him.

My passionate lover.

Him.

My insane obsession.

No this could not be possible. I was hallucinating. Fantasising. Yes, definitely that. My imagination was running on overload, and I absolutely was not looking at the man who had been in my thoughts every day for the last couple of months, damn him. I absolutely was not looking at the man who had made love to me as no other man ever had.

And then paid me.

Fuck him!

Oh, but you did Fae, and it was so fucking good, wasn't it? It was too good to be just fucking. It was so much more than that.

I cursed the voice in my head and shut my eyes, keeping them squeezed together for a long moment. If I kept them shut for long enough, then surely that aberration in my vision would disappear.

"Are you alright, Fae?" Aunty Ruth whispered to me.

"Just got some dust in my eyes."

I felt her pass me a tissue. "Here, use this."

"Thanks." I made a show of wiping at the corner of my eyes and then dared to peek again. Fuck! It was a silent strangled exclamation. The aberration was still clearly visibly. The man in the pulpit was Him.

My nameless stranger was nameless no more.

Reverend Gawain Temple.

The fucking vicar for fuck's sake!

"Are you sure you're alright?"

Aunty Ruth glanced at me in concern as I let out a tortured sound, half hysterical giggle, half groan.

"Dust," I whispered again, pointing to my throat. I made a show of coughing, which was not a good idea as it made him look up from the pulpit and turn his head in my direction.

I held my breath.

A moment of stunned silence as the words that had been falling so eloquently from his lips died in an instant as his eyes connected with mine.

I held my breath still.

Then as smooth as silk he carried on, leaving everyone else no doubt thinking the pause had been deliberate. Bloody hell he had nerves of steel. Impossible to tell from his reaction that he had just spotted a woman in the congregation with whom he had had a night of wild passionate sex.

That he had paid her for!

I gasped for breath.

Bastard!

"Fae?"

I panicked for a second thinking I might have spoken out loud, but it was just my erratic breathing that was causing Aunty Ruth concern.

"You're not asthmatic, are you?"

I shook my head and did my best to compose myself, my head spinning as the next part of the service passed by in a blur.

"Are you coming up for communion?" Aunty Ruth whispered to me a little while later.

By then I was fired up with rage and humiliation at the thought of the money he had left for me, incensed at this façade. How could he stand there in front of all these people, preaching to them, addressing them as his flock? How could he do that and be the same person who had shared my bed and left me pining for more afterwards? How, for that matter could he be the same person who had brutally wiped out five men single handed?

How could he possibly be the same person?

Maybe, I thought in a blinding flash, maybe he had a twin?

I was a twin after all.

A shatteringly cruel memory of what being an identical twin had led to.

Absurdly I found that my legs were shaking as I slowly followed Aunty Ruth up the steps towards the alter rail. I was pleading with the God that I did not believe in, for this to be the answer. Saint Gawain, Reverend Gawain, had a twin.

Yet at the same time part of me was shrieking yes!

I had found him.

Wrong place to be having lustful thoughts but all I could picture was us in bed together. Do not moan out load Fae. I clamped my lips shut and dug my fingernails painfully into my palms as we inched nearer.

Not for a second did he betray the fact that he knew me as I approached so I was beginning to believe that he was in fact a twin. I could not decide at this point just how I felt about this, because in general I was beginning to feel a little peculiar.

For God's sake Fae, get a bloody grip.

He's only a man.

You've slept with dozens.

He was not just only a man though. He was a man who had filled my nights with restless dreams and my days with tormented fantasies, all blended with a large dose of anger. A potent mix and I was trembling inwardly as I stepped forward to kneel next to Aunty Ruth at the rail.

Twin or no twin?

That was the question.

His eyes met and held mine over the rim of the chalice. Sea coloured eyes, blue-grey, unfathomable in their depths. Eyes that had stared into mine as I had clung to him, lost in a turbulent storm of passion.
No twin.
His fingers lightly brushed mine as he handed me the wafer. Fingers that had touched me all over, been inside me, pleasured me, brought me to ecstasy.
No twin.
I couldn't move. I was locked in place on my knees at the altar rail as he moved past me to the next communicant. I remained like a statue as I listened to him speaking, every word sending shivers down my spine.
No twin.
"Fae, are you alright?" Aunty Ruth was already standing up and looking at me in concern.
No, I wasn't. I really wasn't alright at all. I felt as though my life was spinning on its axis, and it was making me dizzy.
"Sorry," I whispered, aware that others, including him were looking at me. "Cramp in my legs," I lied and stood up.
I caught his eyes fixed firmly upon me.
And fell forwards flat on my face in a dead faint.

CHAPTER THIRTEEN

How utterly mortifying.
I have never fainted in my life.
Yet here I was gazing up into blue-grey eyes having been gently rolled over and helped into a seated position. His face was still rather blurry in front of me which was probably a good thing. If he had been in sharp focus, I would not have been able to stop myself from looking at that mouth, well defined and sensuous, without remembering just how it had felt to have him kiss me.
Fuck.
Too late.
I had thought it and could not prevent a groan from escaping my lips.
"Here, drink this." The cool rim of a glass touched my lips. I closed my eyes to block out his stare and the rest of the congregation who were no doubt having an absolute thrill at my expense. I could hear the hushed delight of mutterings and through that Aunty Ruth's voice, loaded with concern.
"Fae, are you alright?"
I sipped at the glass. Water, not the communion wine. Pity, I could have done with a slug right now. Daring to open my eyes, I was relieved to see he had moved away slightly, and Aunty Ruth had taken his place by my side.
"I'm fine, really. I can get up, honestly."
Instantly there was a hand under my elbow, and I was lifted to my feet in a smooth easy movement. I don't normally blush, but my pale skin was now a rosy red as I felt one hand on my arm and the other behind my back.
"Would you like me to walk you back to your seat?" The caring vicar in front of his flock, of course he would offer to do that. Just as he had offered to drive me back home.

Only I could see the flinty cool look in his eyes and notice the betraying tell-tale sign of a muscle twitching near his mouth. Just as it had done when he had tried to contain his passion. Just as it had done when he was deep inside me.

Oh, hell Fae, stop right there.

"No thank you. I am fine now really, honestly." Gathering my wits about me, what little I had left, I smiled brightly, my mask firmly back in place. "I am so sorry to interrupt communion. I must have just stood up too quickly, low blood sugar level."

At last, I was seated back in the pew with Aunty Ruth and could legitimately bow my head as though in prayer. In reality, I was thinking anything but holy thoughts. How was it possible he was a vicar? And how was it possible that he was the vicar right here in Maypoleton?

The enormity of it was sending me dizzy again.

"Are you sure you don't want to leave now?" Aunty Ruth whispered to me. "No one will mind."

I eased myself back into my seat, head up, determined to shake off this ludicrous reaction.

"No. I really am fine," I repeated like a parrot. "I just haven't been sleeping well recently, all the worry over the accusations at work."

"I can imagine," Aunty Ruth said quietly, patting my hand as she did so. "It must have been a terrible time for you. I'm not surprised you have come away looking so peaky and washed out. But no matter love, you're here now and a bit of Northern fresh air and good food will soon have you full of spirit again."

I nodded and suddenly had a light bulb moment.

Spirits!

That was it. That was why I had fainted. I was still feeling the after effects of communicating with my mother the previous night. I was not used to doing something like that and especially with such personal emotions involved. No wonder I was feeling out of sorts, all wishy washy and wobbly.

Satisfied this was the case I sat up straight and prepared myself for meeting Him properly again as the service came to an end. He led the way out of the church, eyes front all the time, not looking left or right and I wondered if this was always his way.

Or did he only do this when he had a member of the congregation who he had slept with.
And paid for the privilege!
Bastard.
I had almost forgotten that, but it gave my mind something better to focus on. Anger was a good source of energy. As we were sitting at the back, we were one of the first to walk out of the church to where he was standing to greet his flock. Now the fun would really begin.

"Let's go and introduce you properly," Aunty Ruth said, "And then maybe when everyone else has gone you can have a chat with him about helping his father."

Hells bells I had forgotten that as well. Honestly my mind had lost all sense and reason. One look in those killer eyes and I was gone. How ridiculously pathetic. Focus on the anger Fae. This man treated you like a prostitute. I ignored the painfully loud voice that clanged in my head like a bell, proclaiming that I had acted like one. There were a couple of people chatting to him as we shuffled out of the porch, and I suggested to Aunty Ruth that maybe we could talk later.

I didn't trust myself to control what may come out of my mouth, like, "How dare you pay me you fucking bastard!" I loved Aunty Ruth far too much to do that.

"If that's what you want," she said with concern in her eyes. "You do still look a bit peculiar.

I bet I did.

I should have realised though that a man who could annihilate five others in the dark without even getting out of breath, was not going to let me slip by quite so easily. As stealthily as a panther he was suddenly at my side, one hand on my arm, guiding me around to face him.

"Are you feeling better now?"

I swallowed, hating the way my body was reacting just to the sound of his voice, far less clipped and short than I remembered, far more seductive with tones of warmth lacing through it. I wondered if this was his vicar's voice because the way he had spoken to me on that night had been very different.

"Yes. Thank you." I stared at him, wondering if he was going to pretend that we had never met.

As calm as anything, still with his eyes fixed on mine, he said to Aunty Ruth, "So this is your niece you were telling me about. Fae, is it?"

"That's right, Vicar."

"And you would be interested in helping look after my father, so I am told? You are an experienced nursing assistant?"

I squirmed inwardly under the expression in his eyes. He had not forgotten one little second of that night, I could see it in the way his gaze had darkened, and that luscious mouth had tightened. My hand itched to slap his face, to wipe that look right from it. Yet all I could do was to stand there like a dummy and nod pleasantly.

"Well perhaps you can come and have a little chat about that? I would be very interested to hear about your experience."

"That would be great," I managed to squeeze out, wondering if I had been invaded by somebody else. This was not how I behaved at all.

He nodded. "I will be free at three o'clock, come to the vicarage then."

"I'm usually at the yard with Treacle and Toffee at that time," said Aunty Ruth as I was struggling to respond further.

I had the shock of my life then as he smiled at her. Good grief. I thought I could pull out a killer wattage smile, I was a mere novice in comparison. I watched as Aunty Ruth melted under his gaze, regardless of what he was saying.

"It would be better if Fae came alone. That way we can get to know each other properly."

Yes, because we haven't done that. We've only spent the night shagging our brains out. How about that for a job interview! I knew he was mocking me as he turned back to look at me once more, that smile still in place but a totally different light in his eyes. Flummoxed, totally out of my depth, all I could do was to agree that I would go to the vicarage at three in the afternoon.

"Will Mrs Mannering be there?"

"My housekeeper?" A tiny element of surprise at last. "No. She has the afternoon off. My father is usually asleep at that time, so we won't be disturbed."

Straight to my core went a bolt of lust as fierce as though shot from a crossbow.

Did he feel the same?

Impossible to tell, but I spent the next couple of hours like a cat walking on hot coals. So much so that Uncle Eric who was trying to read the Sunday papers finally turned to me with an exasperated sigh.

"Fae, love, do us all a favour and go and have a run. You should have come with me this morning up the fell, instead of sitting in church with your Aunty Ruth. It's not good for folk sitting on hard wooden benches like that, not if looking at you is anything to go by."

I grinned at him. "You're probably right, I might have been better having a run instead. I think next Sunday, I will join you."

Once more Aunty Ruth checked that I was feeling alright, but I could assure her that after such a hearty lunch of roast lamb with all the trimmings and apple crumble, I had more than enough fuel to ward off any faintness. I nipped upstairs to change into my running gear and within ten minutes I was out the door, hearing a good natured, "thank God for that," from Uncle Eric as he rustled his newspapers.

There was a path that ran along the river on the other side of the stone bridge, and I headed off towards this, planning on just going so far for about twenty minutes and then turning round. I wanted to make sure I had time for a quick shower before presenting myself at the vicarage.

With every step I took, my feet light on the ground, I was whirring over and over in my mind what it meant that my mystery man was the vicar of Maypoleton. I could not have been more surprised if somebody had told me that Father Christmas was actually real. How could a man like the one who had rescued me and then spent the night with me as he had, possibly be a vicar?

In Maypoleton!

I thought of all the nights I had lain awake thinking about him, fantasizing that I would see him again. Imagining what it would be like between us. Hot and steamy sex, of course, but beyond that I had allowed myself that most stupid of fantasies, that it would evolve into something more. I had never met a man who had affected me the way he had and now here he was.

The bloody vicar!

I paused to check the time. My route had taken me over the bridge and down the wooded path along the river on the side of the village where there were more modern houses sprawling out in neat little closes and cul-de sacs. A car was coming in my direction, and it slowed down.

The driver opened the window, and Matt stuck his head out to call across the road to me. "Are you alright running, Fae? I heard about this morning in church. I was with the scouts but one of the parents told me there was a bit of excitement with the new lady passing out dead at the altar."

He was grinning broadly, and I got the feeling he was glad to have scored a little point over me. Someone who fainted in church did not have quite the same mysterious attraction as a wild woman luring him to have sex against a tree in the graveyard.

I poked my tongue out, making him laugh even more. "As you can see, Matt I am perfectly fine. Just low blood sugar that was all."

"Good. Look, about the other night," he paused, and I let him struggle with his words. "I really do have to think about my reputation."

Placing my hands on my hips, I tilted my head with a quirk of my eyebrows, mocking him slightly.

"It's a small village Fae, and I know how people can talk. I know how Eve and Laura love to gossip that's for sure." His face gave a funny little twitch as he said the head teacher's name and I knew then that Eve had been right. He did have a thing for her. My amusement increased.

"And you really don't want me confiding in my new girlfriends that I had wild, rough sex with Maypoleton's scout leader and deputy head up against a tree in the graveyard? And it was wild and rough, Matt, very exciting. I would have thought you would want me to share your prowess with the ladies of Maypoleton?"

"No! I really would not."

"You sure? Cos you definitely rate as a ten."

I could see from the cloudy look shadowing his usually sunny face that he did not like the notion at all that women could view men in this way, and certainly not him. A little devil inside me nudged me further.

"I mean, I could understand if you had only come up to about a five or a six, but you were definitely a ten, Matt."

"Does your Aunty know what you are really like?"

Ouch! A bigger ouch than he could realise. I kept my face impassive. "Alright, I'll be kind. I promise I will not breath a word of our rendezvous to another soul. But I am just wondering something Matt?"

The grip he had on the steering wheel eased a little. "What?"

"If you are that good up against a tree, what are you like in bed when you've really got room to move?"

His hands tightened once more and there was an accompanying inhalation of breath that told me he was trying to keep control. He opened his mouth and then with a shake of the head, pressed his foot onto the accelerator and sped off, driving in a manner most unsuitable for a respectable deputy head and scout leader.

"You wicked, wicked girl, Fae," I laughed to myself.

But as I began my run back to my aunt's house my amusement faded. Matt was most certainly a ten, but someone else had scored an impossible eleven. Under the blast of water from Aunty Ruth's shower, I wished I could wash away from my mind the memories of that night, as easily as I could the sweat from my run. But I couldn't. He was under my skin.

I dilly dallied for a ridiculous five minutes over what to wear and then realised this was utterly pointless. He had already seen me at my most provocative, he had witnessed me falling flat on my face in front of him. Really what was the point in trying to impress him.

And stop right here for a moment.

I was trying to impress him?

Oh no, no, no, Fae this will not do at all.

I reached for my ripped jeans and Annie's crazily bright stripey sweater, clothes I was most comfortable in, which did raise Aunty Ruth's eyebrows somewhat.

"Do you not want to wear something a little more…..?"

"Trust me, he's not going to be influenced by what I am wearing."

"Are you sure?"

"Positive." I shrugged. "He's a vicar, he will be above that sort of thing."

Her face cleared and she smiled. "Yes of course. Silly of me. And he's such a lovely man."

I returned her smile and grabbing my leather jacket set off to the vicarage. It was annoying to find that my stomach was churning as my feet scrunched up the gravelled path to the front door. Not only that but my mouth was suddenly dry, and my heart was beating faster than it had whilst I had been running.

Fae what is happening to you?

I very nearly turned around, my finger hesitating on the doorbell.

Go home, Fae, I told myself. What are you doing here?

You are home, that other voice told me and following its' command my feet rooted to the spot.

"At least you are good at time keeping."

I nearly fell forward into the space created as the doorway was opened and I found myself once more face to face with him.

"It's not all I'm good at." Defiance and a determination to claw back the ground I had lost in fainting, made me spikier than usual. Fae in full hedgehog mode, small and very prickly.

"Hhmm." A single syllable full of so much comment. "Come in then."

I stepped inside, aware only of him, the way he moved so lightly on his feet, the height and breadth of him, that after shave he wore. For God's sake Fae you'll be sniffing the air after him like a dog in a moment. It was humiliating and that recalled the other humiliation.

It burst out of me. "You paid me."

"You earned it."

Worthy of a slap and he had one coming to him. Only his hand moved so much faster than mine, grabbing my wrist easily in one swift movement. I should have remembered the men he had floored. The look in his eyes was one of amused curiosity.

"You mean that really isn't your side line to earn a little extra on the side?"

Out of nowhere came a reaction that was as unsettling as my faint that morning.

His words hurt me.

Stung cruelly.

I realised I cared and hated the way that tears sprang to my eyes. The hand holding my wrist lowered as he monitored my reaction coolly as though observing an alien species. Maybe to him I was. He was certainly alien to me in how he behaved and how I reacted to him. Whilst my mind was spinning in ever decreasing circles of confusion, my body was fighting its' own raging battle and rapidly losing. Any minute now and I would be throwing myself into his arms and begging him to take me to bed again.

His face grew stony, and I think he sensed that need within me. Did he feel it himself? Or had that night been a one-off affair. An aberration of behaviour. As I thought this, I regained a little ground. He wasn't the only one who could toss out words to be used as weapons.

"And what is the church's stance on prostitutes if that was the case?"

Unlike Matt he did not flush under my stare. "You'd better come and meet my father. I have told him you are coming." He turned his back on me and started to walk across the wide hallway.

"You mean you are actually considering employing me?" I was completely perplexed. I thought that he only wanted to see me to make it very clear, in a similar way to Matt, that his reputation was not to be smeared. Either that or to continue what we had started. I quashed the damnable little thought that taunted me; this was what I had hoped for.

"My father's needs are all that matter." His voice was clipped as he spoke over his shoulder to me. Across the hallway he paused in front of a door. "It's of no concern to me how you conduct your private life as long you do your job properly and by all accounts you do that, regardless of your delightful title Angel of Death."

No one had ever rendered me so utterly speechless before. I didn't know which part of the sentence to object at the most.

After a long moment I managed to splutter out. "How do you know? I mean, I know you will have heard about the accusations, because I told Matt and the others, but how do you know that I am good at my job? Which I am by the way. Bloody good in fact."

"I checked you out."

I stared at him. "You're a vicar. How did you do that.'"?

He ignored my comment. "This is my father's room. It used to be the library, but I had it converted when he moved in with me."

The door was opened for me to enter, and I stepped into a large airy room with double aspect windows letting in plenty of light. There was a single bed the type of which I was used to seeing in the nursing homes, with protective rails and the facilities to raise or lower it if needed, but the room's occupant was sitting in a wheelchair looking out of one of the windows.

He turned his head as Gawain spoke, "Dad, this is the young lady I told you about."

Listening to his address his father, I was convinced I was now dealing with someone with multiple personality disorder. This was not the same man who had rescued me, or who had spent a thrilling night with me, or indeed even the coolly inscrutable vicar I had had fainted in front of.

This was a son speaking lovingly to a father.

Very discomforting.

His father turned his head from the window, and I could see that although the illness had stripped the muscle from his frame, I was looking at an older version of his son. With white hair cropped close to his skull the bone structure in his face was clearly defined, only his cheeks were far more hollowed, the eyes, a similar blue more deep set under brows that were furrowed no doubt by the pain he suffered. There was no denying the intelligence and interest that came my way from those eyes.

Even without speaking I liked him.

I liked his spirit and his energy.

"Hello, I'm Fae. It's lovely to meet you." I stepped forward with a smile on my face and my hand held out. From the corner of my eye, I felt Gawain watching my every move, assessing every nuance of my voice. Go ahead. There was no play acting here.

"Well, you're a sight for sore eyes I must say. I keep telling my son, I may be in a wheelchair but that doesn't mean I have forgotten what it is like to feel like a man. I'm not dead yet you know." This was addressed to Gawain with a grunt and a smile that belied the complaining tone of his words.

Turning back to me he carried on. "So, Fae, what on earth is an attractive woman like you doing in a backwater like this? And yes, that may well be a chat up line. Well then?" There was a light in his eyes that I responded to, and I grinned back at him.

"Oh well, this and that. Escaping from a scandal if you must know."

"Indeed, I must. Scandal and gossip hey, and I bet yours is a damn sight more interesting than all the twaddle I hear from Mrs Mannering. Well then young lady, come and sit down and don't spare any of the juicy bits now. Young Gawain here is convinced I might conk out if I get too excited. I'm far more likely to die of bloody boredom. You don't mind if I swear? No, I didn't think you would. Well then Gawain, how about some tea and a slice of that cake. As boring and dour an old dragon as Mrs Mannering is, she can bake a good cake? Do you bake? No, I didn't have you down as a baker? Poker perhaps?"

"Only if the stakes are high enough."

He barked with laughter, and I thought I saw a flash of amusement briefly on Gawain's face before the mask was back in place.

"I'll bring some tea. Unless you would prefer coffee?"

Was this really the man who had made love to me so wildly and deeply?

"Tea will be lovely thank you," I smiled sweetly at him.

"Now then my dear," said his father, "Come and sit here and tell me about this scandal. Any sex involved or was it more of the cloak and dagger murder variety?"

I saw Gawain tense as he turned to leave the room.

The imp rose within me, and I said teasingly to his father. "Well, as a matter of fact I did have a very unusual encounter of that nature, but the man in question turned out to be a total prat, thought I was a prostitute, can you imagine that?"

"What an idiot!"

"Exactly, my thoughts entirely, what an idiot."

CHAPTER FOURTEEN

I may have wanted to categorise Gawain as an idiot in my mind, but I knew I was lying to myself. My rescuer, turned lover, turned vicar was anything but an idiot. After a very pleasant hour chatting to Arthur and playing a quick hand of poker, Gawain returned to the room to clear away the tray he had brought in earlier.

"Are you able to start tomorrow?" He asked after giving his father a quick glance and receiving a subtle nod from him.

So that was it? I had passed the job interview?

"Don't you want references at least?"

"I told you. I've already checked you out." Cold, dispassionate, efficient.

I struggled to hold his stare which was a new phenomenon for me. Instead, I looked at his father.

"He's checked me out?"

Arthur tapped his nose with a bony finger. "Best not to ask my dear. Are you any good at chess?"

Rising from seat I shook my head. "Not something I have ever tried I'm afraid."

"Not to worry. I can teach you."

"I'll look forward to it," I said, thinking this was the oddest job interview ever. "So, what hours do you want me here?"

"I'll discuss that with you. Dad needs a rest now I think."

"I'm fine," said Arthur waving a hand but I could see what Gawain had picked up on. Beneath the animation on his face the tell-tale signs of pain were creeping in.

"Do you want helping into bed?"

It was the most natural thing for me to ask this and was not for Gawain's benefit at all. I think Arthur was about to argue that he didn't need to be in bed, but I gave him one of my looks, with a knowing smile on my face and he gave in.

"Actually, my dear that would be very kind."

Years of training and experience were a good antidote to the disturbing presence of Gawain who was silently watching. I managed to block him out completely as I concentrated on the task in hand, making sure that Arthur was moved into his bed with as little discomfort as possible.

"I will see you tomorrow then," I said to him and then turned to my new employer. "Perhaps you had better show me the kitchen, so I know where everything is?"

"Follow me."

It was a gorgeously large room with slate floors, solid oak cupboards, a beast of an aga and a view over the garden. I was drawn to look out of the window and had an inexplicable urge to go down to the bottom of the long garden, past the pretty flower beds and vegetable plots, all neatly in order, to the very bottom where a magnificent old tree stood proudly.

"Are you listening to me?"

"What?"

"Clearly not."

I turned away from the window and nearly jumped when I realised how close he was standing to me. His grey blue eyes, with the lines at the corner were scanning my face as though trying to fathom out what was going on in my head. Good luck to him because I was certainly clueless as to that.

In fact, my brain seemed to grind to a most unhelpful halt whenever he was near me. I felt myself instinctively leaning in towards him and saw in that instant a flash of reaction before he stepped back.

"I was saying that the kitchen is usually the domain of my housekeeper, Mrs Mannering."

"Oh yes, the rottweiler," I interrupted him. "We've met."

Not by a millimetre did his mouth move to display any sense of humour at my comment.

"She prepares my father's meals but obviously he may well wish you to get him the odd snack and drink throughout the day."

"Obviously." I was not used to being ignored, certainly not by a man, most definitely not by a man I had slept with.

He carried on as though I had not spoken, detailing the hours his father required help and what exactly that would entail. In general, there were days when I would be needed to be at the vicarage early in the morning to help Arthur shower and dress and do the reverse at bedtime. This would fit in with days when Gawain himself was unable to do so due to parish commitments. Then of course there was the daily medications to see to, but the main duties it seemed were to provide company and stimulation for his father.

"He enjoys being in the garden and outside as much as possible, being taken for drives in the country, that sort of thing. I take it you would be happy to do all of this?"

"Absolutely."

What was there to not agree to? By all accounts this was going to be a very cosy kind of job, never mind the fact that I would be seeing him daily, which of course was not influencing me one iota.

Lying again Fae.

He told me how much he would be paying me, and I had to stop myself from reacting too enthusiastically in case he thought he was offering too much and decided to lower the rate. Then just to throw a bucket of cold water over my head he brought up the elephant in the room.

"That night in January….."

The night that changed my life.

"You mean the night you thought I was a prostitute?"

I have been told I have stunningly beautiful eyes, aquamarine blue and just as clear as those gem stones. I forced myself to hold his gaze with a defiant tilt to my chin which belied the churning in my stomach and the heat that rushed to my core.

Finally, a reaction.

A moment of answering heat and then the dousing of icy cold clarification.

"It won't happen again. You do realise that don't you."

"I'm sorry?"

He stifled a sigh, barely. "To be clear, me employing you to care for my father, is not an invitation for anything else. I slept with you that night because you were quite frankly desperate for me to stay with you. I understood you were suffering from the shock of the attack and of course your distress over your sister."

My jaw dropped open. "You slept with me out of pity?"

"What other reason could it have been? You don't think it's something I make a habit of doing?"

I felt something else in my stomach now.

Not desire.

A pain I could not put a name to.

For a moment I was back at that night, remembering with a cruel clarity the way I had thrown myself at him, begged, pleaded, known that he had been fighting a battle to walk away. He was not lying. He did not make a habit of sleeping with women like that. I didn't know whether that eased the blow to my gut or not. All I knew was that I had never been more uncertain of where I stood with anyone in my life.

And never had it mattered more.

"Right then, I'll be off." I mustered what dignity I could, aware that I was perilously close to tears. "No need to show me to the door. I can find the way."

Nevertheless, he escorted me through from the kitchen to the hallway and the front door.

"One more thing," he said as though he had not just fired a brutal shot at my ego, "there is no need for you to wear a uniform at all. My father doesn't like to be reminded that he needs the care, so it will help him if he can view you more like a friend."

I had my back to him, and I didn't dare turn around to face him. "I understand."

It was about the only thing I did understand. My mind was in too much of a muddle to go straight back to my aunts'. She would no doubt want an in-depth discussion over what had taken place this last hour or so and I was too shaken to be able to hide from her that I was deeply disturbed.

Disturbed?

I felt like howling my eyes out.

Get a grip, Fae!

I walked across the road from the vicarage to the village green. It was going on for teatime. I knew that my aunt and uncle would be back from the stables soon, but I needed to be alone. I needed some air. My feet propelled me to the green and the bench I had sat on the other day. As before I had the sense that this was where my mother, Rowan had sat on many an occasion and I had a longing to talk to her.

There was a young family feeding the ducks at the pond and they said hello with friendly smiles, and at the far end of the green there was a group of boys playing football. All very calm and serene. Maybe if I sat and observed, I would absorb some of that serenity.

I felt something but I am not sure if I could call it serenity. I was reeling from the effect that Gawain had on me and part of me was considering just going back home and getting work with an agency. But as soon as I thought this, there was a pulling sensation within me as though something was literally rooting me in place.

A touch on my hand?

Rowan?

"Am I meant to be here?" I sent my whisper into the soft evening breeze but the only answer I got was the ripple of children's laughter and a taunting echo from the ducks.

Still that knot that was tangling my mind and emotions and threatening to have me crying my eyes out. Was I picking up psychic energy from Rowan, or was it something else entirely? Whatever it was I was glad to have the bright voice of Eve break into my thoughts.

"Hello there, do you want a bit of company? You seem miles away?" Aunty Ruth's neighbour didn't wait for my answer and sat down beside me.

"I heard you fainted in church this morning, that must have given them all something to talk about." She was grinning as she spoke but there was something so warm and natural in her manner, I couldn't take offence.

"I suppose it did."

"Let me guess. You were so bedazzled by our gorgeous vicar that you decided to throw yourself at him?"

Astonishingly, unnervingly, a tear rolled down my cheek.

"Oh shit, I'm sorry. I've said the totally wrong thing, haven't I? Craig always says I am such a blabber mouth. Do you want to talk about it? Come on, I've seen Ruth and Eric at the stables, and they won't be back for a while yet and Craig's working. Come and have a brew at mine."

Eve had such a way with her that meant that ten minutes later I was sitting in her cosy kitchen having yet another mug of tea.

She chatted about her daughter and son, both grown up now and living out of the village and her pride in them was evident, as was the love she felt for her husband whenever his name came up.

"So, rubbish relationship then?" She asked bluntly as she sat down opposite me at the kitchen table. "Don't worry. We've all been there."

I shook my head. "No. No nothing like that." I mean how could it be. You could hardly call a one night stand a relationship. "I think it must be coming back here after all this time. It feels….I don't know. I can't put it into words. I guess it's connecting to my real mother."

"It's a powerful thing when you connect to someone who is dead," said Eve softly. There was a completely different tone to her voice now. Almost a longing, a sadness that was at odds with her bright personality.

I shot her a look across the table.

"It's a long story and one I will tell you sometime. But I think you should know, in case you don't already, Maypoleton has a particular energy that some people pick up on." Unusual eyes, a swirly mix of green, blue and brown surveyed me over the rim of her mug. "You know don't you. You would do, being Rowan's daughter, at least from what Mabel has told me."

I tried to look as blank as possible and received a cheeky grin for my efforts.

"Mabel by the way is the head of our local coven, and you are most welcome to join us."

"I'm not quite sure I follow you."

A friendly smile. "I think you do. And maybe that's why you fainted in church. You are one of us, not them." She then burst out with laughter. "Oh, and that's so funny. You are going to be working at the vicarage. Does he know he has just employed a witch to look after his father?"

I nearly choked on my tea. "I'm not a witch!"

"Course not."

Memories flooded my mind.

Spells and incantations.

The devastation that I conjured up.

"I am not a witch," I said slowly and put down my cup. "I have to go. Thanks for the tea."

"Shit, I've done it again haven't I. I'm sorry. I forget at times how hard it was for me at the beginning." She got to her feet and followed me to the door. Placing a gentle hand on my arm she spoke further. "I want to help if I can. Just let me know when you are ready to talk."

It was an effort to not shake her hand off my arm. "Honestly, I'm fine. And I really am not a witch whatever you may think. I have just not been sleeping too well these last few weeks because of the murder accusation. And thanks for the tea. Look, there's Aunty Ruth. Bye now."

My down to earth aunt and equally grounded uncle were just the company I needed for the rest of the evening. Once the front door was closed behind number 1 Cobblers Row, I could shut out the clamouring voices in my head, those ghosts from the past that Eve had unwittingly stirred up.

I could just about slam the door in my mind on the devastating attraction I felt for Gawain Temple, as I talked to Aunty Ruth and Uncle Eric about my meeting with Arthur. I could chatter away quite happily about what a nice change it would be to work for a private client instead of in such a busy nursing home where I was one of many staff. I could enthuse about how glad I was to have made the decision to come and visit and how fortunate it was that the vacancy had occurred at such an opportune moment.

Easy to do all of this and pretend that everything was fine, until it came time for my aunt and uncle to go to bed. They kept earlier hours than I did but surprisingly I was yawning when they said their goodnights and decided I may as well go upstairs too. Only then it was not quite so easy to stem the flow of turbulence in my mind.

What the hell was I doing staying here?

The phrase out of the frying pan and into the fire kept nagging at me.

I had left behind an accusation of murder, and run full pelt into what exactly?

Having spent the months since January having every other thought in my head occupied by the nameless stranger, only to discover he was the vicar in Maypoleton, was big enough. I was not a great fan of co-incidences. I was even less a fan of being treated with the utter disinterest that he had shown me. I had not experienced rejection from a male in my life since….

And this was where my thoughts became demons that raced behind me, pushing me towards a cliff edge that I did not want to topple off. But as I teetered precariously, memories screaming painfully in my head, I had Eve's comments to add to the mix.

How did she know?

Had Mabel said something?

Maypoleton was a place of peculiar energy?

I knew that from the moment I had stepped into the graveyard. My ability to connect with the dead had shot into overdrive. But what I didn't know and was terrified of, was the potential consequences of me staying here? So why was I not packing a bag and leaving this hotspot of energy that would tempt and tease me into being what I shouldn't.

Gawain bloody Temple.

That was why not.

The bastard man had got completely under my skin.

Hours later I was still tossing and turning, unable to sleep. The bright light of the moon was pouring into my room despite the thickness of the curtains. My head was pounding, thoughts of Gawain blending into Joel.

Joel Sparrowhawk, my first love.

Joel Sparrowhawk, grey blue eyes, dark haired, cocky and dangerous.

Joel Sparrowhawk who was four years older than me, who already had a girlfriend and who never looked twice at me.

Until I worked my magic and changed all that.

Until I broke the unbreakable law and used magic to bend another person's will to mine and in doing so brought about the death of my sister.

Joel bloody Sparrowhawk damn him with his grey blue eyes, cocky arrogance and air of danger, who I realised with a thumping heart had morphed now into Gawain Temple in my thoughts.

Grey-blue eyes, coolly arrogant and most definitely dangerous.

There was no way now I was going to get a wink of sleep. Three in the morning, the darkest hour of the night. I tossed aside my duvet and reached for my clothes. A walk would clear my thoughts. Only as I sneaked quietly downstairs, careful not to wake my aunt and uncle, the windows began to rattle with the pounding of heavy April rain, that sounded more like hailstones.

I snatched my car keys up and the umbrella that always stood in the porch. It took me a couple of minutes to walk quickly to the village car park and I would have been soaked without the umbrella. I didn't know where I was going to go, I just knew I needed to go somewhere.

As I pulled out of the car park and onto the main street of Maypoleton I could see that a light was on upstairs in the vicarage. A desperate longing overwhelmed me. All I wanted to do was to go and bang on the door and demand that he let me in. Beg him to take me into the shelter of his arms as he had done that night.

Christ Fae where has your self- respect gone?

Disappeared as though it had never been there.

I wanted him that badly and in turn he had make it clear he wanted nothing more to do with me. He had slept with me out of pity. The steering wheel got the impact of my forehead as I thumped against it and howled with gritted teeth. How, after sleeping with so many men, discarding them like playthings, could I now be so monumentally fixated on the one man who didn't want me?

I floored the accelerator and recklessly drove my car down the deserted main street until I came to the bridge. An impulse had me wrenching the steering wheel right, and I drove in the direction I had run previously. The road took me past the entrance to the newer housing estate and then further down the country lane where suddenly there were no streetlamps just the light of the moon.

Somebody else was awake it would seem.

About a quarter of a mile down the lane, there was a pair of semi-detached houses, set apart from any others just fields either side of them. One of them had a light on both upstairs and down. Out of curiosity, wondering who else in the village was having a sleepless night, I turned my head and in doing so spotted a car that I recognised.

My foot slammed on the brake pedal. Grinding the gears, I threw the car into reverse until I was alongside the driveway. Fuelled up on rejection, painful memories and the magic of the moon, I got out of the car and not wasting time to think about my actions, I banged on the front door.

CHAPTER FIFTEEN

"Christ Fae what's wrong? Is someone ill? Has there been an accident?"

All understandable questions considering it was past three in the morning; the weather was wild, and I had battered on his door like a thing demented.

I was demented. "Hi Matt," I wriggled past him in the narrow hallway, out of the rain and hailstones.

He shut the door, mainly I think because of the weather and not because he felt like inviting me in, an unwelcome guest, a demon crossing the threshold.

"Hi Matt?" He folded his arms across his chest, muscles nicely displayed under the black top he was wearing with checked pyjama pants. "Three in the morning, you bang on my door and just say hi Matt?"

"I saw your light on, so I knew I wasn't waking you." I unzipped my leather jacket and hung it on a peg by the front door.

"What are you doing here?"

"I told you. I saw your light on. Thought you might like a bit of company." I smiled at him with a look in my eyes that told him exactly what kind of company I was after.

He swallowed and made a manly effort to keep the conversation on track. "Fae, I know you are new to the village, but this really is not the sort of thing that we do around here?"

I arched my eyebrows oh so innocently. "Really? You mean like not having sex in a graveyard, that sort of thing."

"I mean exactly that sort of thing. Look Fae, you are a lovely woman, and very attractive."

I kissed him before the 'but' could pass his lips. But he didn't love me, and he wasn't in the habit of having sex with women he didn't love. But he was in love with someone else. But he had a reputation to uphold. But he was respected in the community. All those buts as to why he should not, must not take me upstairs to his bedroom and fuck me senseless.

I was very good at overcoming buts, not that I had to resort to these tactics often it must be said. Men being men, they respond so easily to the touch of a woman pressed against them. The soft opening of a mouth beneath theirs. The offer of pleasures to be had in the curves that melted against hard lines of muscle. The promise of wild abandonment in the throaty sounds that purred against their ears.

We fumbled, kissed and stumbled our way up the stairs, my sweater discarded halfway, my bra tossed over the bannister at the top, his top following it down to the floor. Bare chested the pair of us now, mouths locked in a kiss as he propelled me blindly backwards, each step now pressing his erection hard against me.

Back until the edge of the bed came up behind me and I naturally fell upon it, pulling him with me. He was strong and agile and soon had me lifted further up so my head was on the pillows, and he could lay full length on top of me. I arched up against him, ready to feel him inside me, ready to lose myself in that place of oblivion. I lowered a hand to reached beneath his pants, pushing them down, and clasping him firmly in my grasp.

"Oh God." He groaned and stopped kissing me for a few moments as I held and caressed him in my hands, feeling the length of him grow and harden further. After the bruising blow to my ego from he who I was trying not to think about, Matt's response was adding to my own sense of urgency.

With my other hand I guided his to my jeans. He rushed to unzip them and wriggle them past my hips, taking my pants off with them. I sensed a moment's hesitation as he moved above me, bedside light illuminating a slight frown on his face. I was not the woman he wanted to have in his bed. He didn't know that I knew this, and it didn't matter to me, but I could see in that instant that it mattered to him.

He was in love with Laura.

But she was married, and I was here, naked in his bed, with his throbbing erection in my hands. I guided him to me, lifted my hips and banished the moment of doubt and guilt. Time for that later. Right now, he was mine. He may well be on top of me, but

I was the one who was driving this. I wrapped my legs around his waist and bucked up with my hips.

"Christ."

He groaned again, and I smiled against his head as he opened his mouth to take one nipple and bite down on it. No more buts. I urged him on with my hips and arched my back up from the bed pressing my breasts further against his mouth, his hands.

I came quickly, releasing the pent-up tension and emotions that had been rampaging through me since I had set eyes on Gawain in church. My breath exploded in a breathy gasp of tortured pleasure; my eyes tightly shut. I wanted these feelings. I wanted to feel the hard masculine power driving within me. I wanted to feel that bruising of flesh against flesh. I wanted to feel the stinging sensations of teeth against tender skin.

But I wanted blue-grey eyes to look into mine.

I wanted a different voice to be moaning his cries of passion.

I wanted Gawain.

Shamefully this didn't stop me. I rode the waves of my orgasm, and greedy for more tangled my fingers in Matt's thick blond hair, ignoring that it was not the short sharp crop of someone else, and brought his mouth back up to mine. Kissing me deeply now, Matt flipped me over and I was astride him in one easy movement.

"Ride me, hard, fast," he said hoarsely, his own eyes closed now.

Was he thinking of Laura?

I didn't care. If he was, I could relate to that. She didn't want him. Gawain didn't want me. It hurt. It hurt more than I dared to even think about. So, I rode out the pain. I closed my eyes once more and used the body beneath me to ride away the pain and rejection. To conjure up in my mind the hard body of Gawain beneath me, to imagine those cold hard eyes lighting up with fire and passion, to pretend that for once in my life I had someone who loved me.

Our cries grew louder, carrying with them those locked in feelings and emotions. My body grew slick with sweat as I bucked against Matt as hard and fast as I could. His hands were on my hips, urging me on, fingers digging into my flesh.

"Don't stop, oh don't stop, oh Jesus Christ don't stop Laura." He blurted it out with a pained gasp as his body began to jerk and tighten with spasms. Our eyes opened and connected. His with shock and shame, mine with knowing understanding. At the same time the ripples of pleasure were overriding any other thought or reaction. Nothing either of us could do now, just go with it, bow to it, surrender to the rush of sensations that had us gasping, sighing, shaking with the release.

Limp and exhausted I peeled myself off him. I had some standards to maintain even if they were an illusion. I could hardly allow myself to cuddle up to him after he had just blurted out another woman's name at the point of orgasm. As hypercritical as it was, after all I had been fantasizing about Gawain, he did not know that. I broke the weighty silence once my breathing had returned to normal.

"Laura?"

"Shit. I'm sorry Fae. That was….." He sounded mortified and who could blame him? We both sat up to face each other at the same time. His hair was darkened with sweat and his cheeks flushed, a look of boyish contrition in his eyes. He was genuinely appalled with himself.

"It's alright." I took pity on him. I liked him and this was small village after all. Plus, as it looked like Gawain had closed and bolted the door on me, where else was I going to look for the sex that I needed.

"It's not alright Fae," he protested, reaching for his pyjama bottoms.

"No, it is," I assured him blithely. "I am not going to tell her."

I don't mean that," he said as he turned away from me and got out of the bed.

He had a nice body, and it was a shame to see him cover his bottom half once more, but I knew better than to push my luck. I was not going to get a second round from Matt tonight.

"What did you mean then?" I asked, reaching for my pants and jeans. I pulled them on and stood before him, my upper body still naked and rosy from the aftermath of his kisses and the flush of orgasm.

He blushed as he looked at me, his fair skin a give away from his emotions. "I'll get your other clothes," he said as he left the bedroom and went downstairs to where our tops had been carelessly discarded.

Not bothered in the slightest by my semi nudity I tripped lightly down the stairs after him.

"It's not a problem you know," I said with a smile as I took my bra and sweater from him. "I don't need you to love me or anything like that."

"Really Fae?" he said quietly with a tone I didn't understand at first in his voice. "You don't need a man to love you to just have random sex with them? In a graveyard? At three in the morning? Whether they are pretending you are another woman or not?"

I pulled my sweater over my head and realised with a shock what I was hearing.

Pity.

That was the tone in his voice I had not registered at first.

He was pitying me for needing to sleep with him so badly that I didn't care if it was in the company of the dead, or as a substitute for someone else. Something deep inside me began to wobble precariously. The only way I could prevent it from escaping was to give a nonchalant toss of my head, flicking my long blond hair over my shoulders as though I really didn't care.

"I'm not that old fashioned," I said breezily. "Sex is sex. It's fun. I enjoy it. It's good for you."

Fae, are you justifying your actions?

Really?

The look in his eyes told me he knew what I was doing and that wobble threatened further.

"I'll see you around Matt. I've taken the job at the vicarage so I will be staying a while. I'm not bothered either way. But don't worry, I keep my promises. I won't tell anyone least of all Laura that we've slept together."

"Good. And look you had better go now. The milk man comes round soon. I don't want him seeing your car here, cos then it wouldn't matter if you said anything or not, the whole village would know."

"And we can't have that can we Matt," I forced a smile on my face. "Have a good day, and thanks Matt. It was great sex."

He gave an odd, strangled grunt. "Christ Fae, it's like you're talking about ordering a pizza or something." He shook his head and opened the front door.

Shrugging my shoulders into the comforting heavy warmth of my leather jacket, I answered him with a smile but as I walked back to my car, hearing the door shut behind me, the mask slipped. Once more tears threatened to blur my vision. It was further disturbing to find that the hand turning the keys in the ignition was shaking.

I turned my car around and then accelerated back down the lane. After the stormy hailstones, the dawn light was annoyingly cheerful in contrast to my mood. My body felt better for the activity, but my mind was in a worse place than before. I passed a vehicle just as I was approaching the bridge and realising it was the milk man Matt had mentioned, felt another blow to my stomach.

How had I managed to get myself into this pickle?

Fae Winters, the woman who could get any man she wanted, now had two men who in the space of one day had made it very clear that they really did not want her. Oh sure, Matt had performed enthusiastically enough and how could I fault him for substituting me for Laura when I had been doing the same with him for Gawain. But those parting comments, that look in his eye.

Pity.

Gawain had slept with me out of pity.

Matt had slept with me out of frustration for not having Laura and pitied me for needing someone so badly that I had knocked on his door at three in the morning. I had never experienced this feeling, and I didn't like it one little bit. I also hated the fact that every bloody thing seemed to have me close to tears these days.

I wiped the wetness from my cheeks as I parked back in the village car park and walked briskly back to Cobblers Row. It was nearly five o'clock now and as I neared my aunt's house the door to number three opened. Craig Hawthorne, ruggedly attractive in his police uniform was coming out. Behind him I could see Eve in her dressing gown. She gave him a lingering kiss which he returned, and I felt that stab of envy once more, a further jab to add to the blows that Gawain and Matt had dealt me.

"Morning," I said quietly as though it was perfectly normal to be taking a stroll so early.

Craig nodded at me with a raised eyebrow and a question in his eyes that I chose not to answer. He got into his car, and I rooted in my pocket for my key.

"You okay?" Eve called as her husband drove away.

"Fine. Just couldn't sleep."

"Hmm."

I felt uncomfortable under her stare. It was far too knowing for my liking.

"I meant what I said Fae. You can talk to me anytime. About anything." A very pointed look.

I nodded and let myself into Aunty Ruth's just as she was coming downstairs to make a cup of tea, up early to go to the stables before work. There was no point me going back to bed now. Besides I had work, my new job to start today. Reassuring her that I was fine, just excited about all these changes, I sat with her in the cosy kitchen drinking tea and eating toast and then went upstairs to shower.

It was certainly going to make a pleasant change to not have to wear a hideous uniform to work. Clean jeans, skinny cut and a bright berry coloured sweater were the order of the day. After the double blows to my ego, I needed to bolster myself up a little. I braided my hair into two sleek French plaits either side of my head which emphasised the delicate bones of my face and made my eyes look bigger. A smudge of purple eye shadow made them look nearly turquoise in colour and a touch of lip gloss was called for today. That done I surveyed my reflection and frowned a little.

I had pale ivory skin, blemish free and the envy of many women. But I don't think it was the lack of sleep that was dulling it somehow. I didn't use blusher or bronzer normally but if I had had any, I would have done so.

Definitely looking peaky Fae.

I stuck my tongue out at the mirror and went downstairs to grab my jacket.

"I told the Reverend he is making a mistake in hiring you." Mrs Mannering greeted me in this welcoming manner a short while later as I presented myself at the vicarage, her grey manner suiting her dowdy clothes and hairstyle.

"Don't worry," I brushed past her, spiky attitude back in place, "it just adds to the mistake in hiring you. I know where I am going," I added as she proceeded to huff and puff and bluster an indignant reply in my direction.

I paused outside Arthur's door and knocked gently three times, my hand about to turn the handle when it opened.

"He's been in a lot of pain during the night."

Gawain stood immediately in front of me. He was dressed as though for work, in other words black trousers and shirt but no collar on yet. The top couple of buttons of his shirt were still undone and you could forget his occupation. You could just see him as a devastatingly charismatic man, with sea-coloured eyes, sharp bone structure, cropped greying hair and a body of rock-solid muscle underneath the clothes.

Which is how for that first fragment of a second my eyes and my body saw him, desire shooting humiliatingly right to my centre, never mind that only a few short hours ago I had been in bed with Matt. Humiliating also to find my tongue stuck in my mouth and unable to work properly.

"Are you able to give him a gentle massage after his shower, that can help?"

"Yes of course."

I unglued my tongue thinking that I would really like to give him a massage. All over. With lots and lots of oil, and then…..

"Good." He stepped aside to let me in, and I caught a hint of the after shave he wore. God almighty I would be drooling next. Giving myself a mental shake, I turned away from him and greeted Arthur.

In the company of the older gentleman, I felt grounded once more. This was what I was good at. The simple everyday tasks of caring for someone who could for whatever reason, no longer care for themselves. I had gone into this line of work trying to substitute myself for what Fliss would have done. Of course, she would have been a doctor, but this was the best alternative I could manage. And even though my reasons for this line of work had been with an ulterior motive, I really did enjoy it.

I especially enjoyed it when I got to work with people like Arthur who were razor sharp in their wits and who somehow had not lost their sense of humour along with their physical functions. It was also, I realised going to be an enjoyable working relationship as it became apparent that Arthur shared the same view on Mrs Mannering that I did when I asked him if he wanted a cup of tea.

"Let's go and rattle the old dragon's cage," he said with a wicked smile. "She hates to be disturbed in the kitchen, sees it as her domain. But I want a change of scene, and I am sure you don't wish to be cooped up in here all day with me, as charming a room as it is."

It was mid-morning, and I could see the effort it was taking for Arthur to be resilient in coping with the effects of a pain filled night's sleep. He was now showered and dressed and in his wheelchair. I completely understood the need not to be a prisoner within one room.

"Why does your son employ her?" I asked as I went to carefully push through the doorway.

"He inherited her with the position. Gawain got the vacancy here when the previous vicar retired. We had been living on the south coast then. He was chaplain to a couple of homeless shelters and drug rehabilitation centres."

I stumbled slightly with the wheelchair as we crossed the hallway. So that was what he had been doing that night. His car had been parked near to one of the shelters in town, I remembered that quite clearly. But he had not been in his vicars' clothes? Maybe he had been visiting for old times' sake?

"Must have been a change coming up here then?" I commented, thinking how odd that we had both lived in the same seaside town at one point, and now ended up here in the middle of wild Lancashire countryside. And odd, I knew from experience meant that other forces could be at work. My stomach re-tied itself into that now familiar knot.

What had really brought me back to Maypoleton?

There was no time to ponder on that now as I opened the kitchen door wide and then carefully pushed Arthur's wheelchair through. Mrs Mannering was rolling out pastry and it looked as though it was going to be a hearty chicken and leek pie for lunch.

"I'll bring you a tea tray through to the lounge in five minutes," she said with a reserved smile at Arthur and a studied attempt at ignoring me.

"No need," I replied breezily. "I know where everything is. Don't let me stop you. Actually, I fancy a hot chocolate, Arthur, what about you? Do you fancy a hot chocolate for a change?"

"Mr Temple likes fresh coffee with just a dash of milk, and I will bring it through in five minutes." The rolling pin worked faster.

"Can't remember when I last had hot chocolate," Arthur said to me with a smile and a nod. "My Bessie used to add cream to it, then swirled some cocoa on the top to finish."

"Well, if that's how your Bessie made it, then that's how I shall do it for you. I'm sure there'll be some cream in here somewhere. Ah here we go, and let's root out a whisk to make it lovely and frothy. I mean if you're going to have hot chocolate you may as well do it properly."

I rummaged around the kitchen, well aware that every action I took was irritating Mrs Mannering until she had resorted to slamming the pie dish into the oven with a distinct lack of control.

"I really cannot be having such interruptions whilst I am working," she tutted as her cold blue eyes surveyed the mess I had made, sprinkling cocoa powder and splashing hot creamy milk everywhere.

I was going to clean up after myself, but she came towards me brandishing a dish cloth with such fervour that I shrugged and left her to it.

"Where would you like to drink it?" I asked Arthur, "In here keeping Mrs Mannering company, or elsewhere?"

We exchanged a look, two co-conspirators already. "I think here will do nicely don't you. It's lovely and cosy with the aga going and I am sure Mrs Mannering won't mind us two chattering away."

The sound of the taps running disguised what could have been a huffing sigh from the housekeeper. She had her back to us now, but I knew she would be frowning. I smiled at Arthur and sat at the table opposite him, wrapping my hands round my mug with pleasure and thinking what a lovely job I had fallen in to here.

We did chat away and not merely to annoy Mrs Mannering. Arthur was keen to reassure me that although Maypoleton was a small village and reasonably remote, there was still a lot going on. I think he wanted to make sure that I would not worry about getting bored.

I thought of Gawain and Matt.

No, I would not get bored.

Confused and muddled maybe, bored definitely not.

"You said you enjoyed running," Arthur was saying as he told me about all the various clubs and activities there were on offer locally, most of them not surprisingly centred around the church and school, "Gawain likes to run. He's friends with Matt, you may have met him, he is the school deputy head and leader of the scouts. He organises the running events if you want to get involved in that sort of thing."

I sipped my hot chocolate and nodded. "Hm, I have met him. Lovely bloke. And yes, I know about the running events. Uncle Eric is a keen runner."

"Of course he is, I forgot. And your aunt has the horses doesn't she, so plenty for you to do there."

"And don't forget you did say you were going to teach me to play chess," I reminded him, "So don't worry, I am sure I will not get bored."

"Glad to hear it. I would hate to think we would drive you back to the bright lights of the South coast through lack of entertainment."

Definitely a snort then from Mrs Mannering who had obviously had enough of us occupying her territory.

"I need to mop the floor," she said opening a cupboard and brandishing the necessary equipment in the manner of a weapon.

I was about to argue that it looked perfectly clean, when Arthur cheerfully placed his mug back on the table and suggested that we go for a walk around the village.

"My last companion was allergic to fresh air and exercise," he said with a grimace, "I would very much like to perambulate along the high street and then maybe along-side the river."

"I would very much like to perambulate with you," I smiled and went to wash up the mugs, but Mrs Mannering took them from me in her rush to clear her space.

It took a little while to help Arthur use the bathroom and get him warmly wrapped up enough to brave the breezy April weather and again, I relished how lovely it was to be able to do this without my eye on the clock for other duties to perform, or residents to see to. I was really going to enjoy my time with Arthur, especially if he was as big a fan of being outside as I was.

I wrapped Annie's colourful knitted scarf around my neck and zipped myself into the warmth of my leather jacket and then we were ready to go. Just then the door to what I knew to be Gawain's study opened. Out he came, looking all clerical and devastatingly sexy at the same time, with one of his parishioners, an elderly woman who looked as though she had been crying.

There was a quick flash of grey–blue light as his eyes shot across the large hallway and connected with mine, and then his entire attention was back on the woman, a grieving widow by the sounds of it. I stood transfixed for a second, listening to the rich warmth of his voice as he gave the lady what comfort she needed as he prepared to say goodbye to her. I envied her that attention. That warmth.

A cough from Arthur nudged me.

"Right then, let's go. High street it is and then a walk along the river path." Cheerful, brisk, full of energy and not a back ward glance at his son.

But I felt his eyes on my back make no mistake about that.

Burning through the thick black leather.

Do not look round Fae, you will only see cold pity.

I pushed Arthur's wheelchair down the path of the front garden determined that I would overcome this temporary state of confusion in my life.

CHAPTER SIXTEEN

A new daily routine began, and I quickly adapted to the changes in my life. It was easy on so many levels. Working with Arthur was a dream job. Maypoleton was a friendly village. The remote and wild setting appealed to my soul. I enjoyed being with my aunt and uncle once more. I loved to be able to connect to Rowan's spirit. A sense of deep belonging blossomed inside me each day that I woke up to see the quaint village green, the winding river, the fells beyond.

I had come home.

Yet within this comfort blanket there were of course the odd areas of disquiet.

Two to be precise.

Gawain and Matt.

My employer was cold and clipped with me. Being around him was like watching the sun shine brightly on everyone else and yet having a dark cloud immediately overhead. No matter what I did, I could not direct that warmth or attention to me.

The brutality of this rejection drove me time and again to seek out Matt whenever the opportunity arose, which me being me, I made sure happened a lot. It helped that Aunty Ruth's routine always meant she was at the stables first thing in the morning and after work in the evenings and Uncle Eric left early and came back late from his job. With Matt's school hours it was simple to call in either before I turned up to see Arthur or afterwards.

He hated it as much as he loved it.

Each time he would protest that we should not be doing it.

But a man frustrated is easily seduced and seduce I did.

Quick, urgent sex, the fulfilling of a basic need. We were using each other and that didn't matter. He had no idea how I felt about Gawain, mind you neither did I. I had not dared to think too deeply into my thoughts on that matter. I told myself I was merely obsessed with the man because he was ignoring me and whilst that was the case, Matt could serve as a substitute.

He asked me one day why I needed it so badly. "Can't you cope with being celibate?"

We were in the kitchen, children's essays fallen to the floor as the table had been cleared so he could perch me on the edge, pull down my jeans and ram into me with hard, angry strokes. I had braced myself against the rapid hammering and the knowledge that each time he had sex with me was one more time closer to the end. He really did not like himself for doing this.

Rather sore and not as satisfied as I would have liked, I was stunned by his question. My hands were shaky as I zipped up my jeans. Matt went to the sink to pour himself a glass of water. When he turned back around, the angry expression softened slightly, and I wondered what my own face was revealing.

"You can get help you know," he said quietly with another of those pitying looks that dented my somewhat diminished ego further. "I know it's not as common as alcohol or drugs, but there is help these days. Maybe not here in Maypoleton, but there must be somewhere in Lancaster we could try and find for you."

My jaw dropped. "What? I'm not addicted to sex if that's what you mean!"

He shrugged and asked if I would like a tea or coffee. "It's okay Fae, it's nothing to be ashamed of if you are. People can't help if they are addicted to something. Ask Gawain, he worked for a while with addicts and the homeless before he came here. Maybe he can help you?"

"No! I am not addicted to sex," I ground out through painfully gritted teeth.

Matt made two coffees and handed me a mug. "Denial is the hardest hurdle to overcome," he said and began to pick up the schoolbooks that had been knocked to the floor.

I crouched down to help him. When the table was orderly once more, I fixed him with a stare. "I am not addicted to sex. I just happen to enjoy it that's all."

His smile was irritating as he stood there sipping his coffee. Perhaps it helped him to overcome his guilt at his own behaviour to lay the blame squarely at my door. Sod that for a lark.

Brushing back my hair, tangled from our encounter, I shook my head. "I can be quite happy celibate if you must know. I have been on many occasions."

My friend Annie would be laughing at this point I knew, but she was not here to counter my argument. And to some degree it was true. It wasn't the act of sex itself that I needed so badly, it was the momentary losing myself in oblivion that a wild orgasm could bring. I could forget. I could pretend the pain was no longer there. I could blot everything out just for that short space of time.

I could have used drugs or drink, but I chose sex. So maybe in some way he did have a point. But I argued to myself quickly as I stood there staring him out, it was the forgetting I was addicted to, not the sex. And this brought a shaft of pain so sharp to my gut that I felt as though the knife that had robbed Fliss of her life had been driven in to me.

"Are you alright?"

I must have winced out loud. I looked down to see my hand clutching my stomach, half expecting to see blood oozing between my fingers. I wished it would. I wished I would bleed out there in his kitchen and then there would be no more having to forget. But as cowardly as I was, that was not the answer. My punishment was to carry this pain and not to shy away from life itself.

But temporarily forget in the wildness of meaningless sex?

Yes. I would allow myself that balm, if indeed it could be called that.

None of which of course I could begin to explain to Matt. Instead, I just shrugged carelessly and put my shiny coat of armour back on.

"Look, I just misread the situation that's all. I got the impression you were as keen for it as I was, what with you being in love with Laura and all that."

A blow below the belt but frankly I thought he deserved it. I carried on. "So don't worry about me being addicted to sex. I can take it or leave it and if that's what you feel then that's fine by me." I picked up my leather jacket and walked out of the kitchen before he had chance to reply.

By the time I had got back to Aunty Ruth's and showered I was not sure if I had acted wisely or stupidly. I stood under the jets of water wishing it could wash away all the doubts and uncertainties in my mind. Coming to Maypoleton had been so good, but coming face to face with Gawain everyday was messing with my mind and emotions.

My heart and soul?

Really Fae?

There was definitely a very powerful energy in Maypoleton that I knew I was reacting to, and I consoled myself that this was why I was so wired. Not that I was addicted to sex.

Or that I was in love with Gawain.

Most definitely not.

To take my mind off this uncomfortable notion I changed into a clean pair of jeans and a favourite pink hoody which Annie had bought me as a present. It had a unicorn motif on the front, which was rather ridiculous given my age, but as Annie had said laughingly when she gave it to me, I was small enough to wear teenagers' clothes, I may as well have the fun of them.

I had pulled a face at the time, but my lovely friend had known that deep down I would love the hoody and would not hesitate to wear it. Thinking of Annie, I wondered how she was faring with her pregnancy and went downstairs to make a brew and call her. We chatted at length and after she had filled me in on the latest baby news the conversation turned to men.

It was not what I wanted to talk about. I hastily told her that I was far too busy with my new job to even think about looking at the local talent, which was in seriously short supply. I think she knew I was lying through my teeth and was about to press me in that sweet natured way she had when the doorbell rang. Glancing at the clock on the kitchen wall I saw that it was round about the time that Aunty Ruth would be at the stables, and I wondered who it could be.

"I'll call you later," I promised her and went to open the door. "Oh hello. Aunty Ruth's not back from the yard yet but she won't be long if you want to come in and wait?" I stepped back to invite Laura in.

"Actually, it's you I've come to see." The head teacher stepped into the cosy front room of the cottage. She was dressed in a fabulous red light woollen dress that showed off her curvy hourglass figure and spiky heeled shoes that I would reserve for a wild night out, not the day job.

"What can I do for you?" I liked Laura. She had made me welcome at the pub quizzes along with Eve, Craig and Matt, and she usually buzzed with a positive energy that I naturally responded to. Right now, though she had a more frazzled air about her.

"This is a huge imposition, but I am really stuck. I have a governors' meeting tonight at the school that I absolutely can't miss as I had to reschedule the last two. If I do so a third time, I really will be rocking the boat."

"Okay so what can I do?"

"It's the twins, both sets of them I'm afraid. Will and Dan are at a rugby match at Lancaster and need picking up, in literally half an hour, and I have no one to look after Tilly and Tammy either. Mark promised me, absolutely promised me he would be home in time, but he's let me down."

I rather thought the word, again, could be injected here but she didn't say so. Instead, she carried on explaining how she had thought of all other options.

"Matt is at the meeting with me so he can't go, Eve would offer but I know Wednesday night is the coven meeting. Equally Gawain always spends Wednesday night with Arthur, which is when I thought, ah ha, well if Gawain was looking after his father, then you would have finished work and maybe would be free. I know it's an awful lot to ask, but is there any way you could drive to Lancaster to pick up the boys and them take all four of them back to my house until I have finished?"

I was already grabbing my jacket and car keys. "No problem at all. Where are the girls now?"

"Outside in the car, I am totally blocking the road, but I was so frazzled to try and get this sorted."

"Come on then. You text me the postcode for the school and let them know that I will be picking the boys up and get going for your meeting."

"Are you sure?" Laura asked but we were already out of the house, and I was locking up. She waved to her daughters, ten-year-old Tilly and Tammy to get out of her car and hurriedly told them to come along with me.

Seeing how identical the girls were, with their dark hair in plaits and lively brown eyes so like their mothers, I was reminded with a stab of what Fliss and I had looked like together. Of course, we were faired haired with the lightest of blue eyes, but no one apart from Mum could tell us apart. Which had resulted in Fliss's death. I rammed this thought to the padlocked area of my mind and smiled cheerily at the girls.

They chattered away happily as we walked back up Cobblers Row and past the vicarage to the car park. Laura meanwhile had screechingly reversed her car back up the cobbled street, narrowly avoiding colliding with Craig Hawthorne who was trying to turn in.

"Ooops," said Tilly, the older of the twins as I had already been informed by her. "That was close. Mummy will get into trouble with Daddy again if she bumps the car. He went bollocksy last time."

"Bollocksy?" I grinned at her. Each girl had decided to take a hand of mine in theirs. It felt quite surreal to be walking along with a child either side of me. Surreal but nice.

"Not Bollocksy," Tammy piped up, "Ballistic, that's the word that Mummy used. Daddy goes ballistic when she gets things wrong."

"I can't imagine your Mummy getting things wrong," I said lightly as we crossed over the road and into the entrance of the car park.

"Daddy says she is always getting things wrong and that's why she should stop working and be a proper wife."

"Oh?" I thought at this point it was better to not comment. I unlocked my car and made sure the girls were properly strapped in. My phone had pinged with the message from Laura giving me the directions to the school. I fervently hoped that the sat nav on my phone would be up to the task. At least by the time we would be getting to Lancaster it would be past rush hour.

I also thought it wiser to drive a little more slowly than I would do usually down the winding country lanes that wove through the countryside before finally emerging onto the A6 to take us to Lancaster. Whilst I may be cavalier in my driving style, having two young passengers added caution. Laura had been able to message the boys' school to let them know I would be late.

Even so, by the time we got there, well after six, I was hoping that they would not be too grumpy.

Thankfully Will and Dan at fourteen years old had not yet fallen prey to the gloom of teenage years and still exhibited their mother's cheery outlook on life. Although it had to be said that Will did pull a face somewhat when he realised the reason why I had gone to pick them up. He mumbled something under his breath and at first, I thought he was complaining that he had had to wait so long.

"I got here as quickly as I could, but your Mum only asked me at half past five."

His face, grubby from the rugby flushed. Both boys had fairer skin than the girls, with lighter brown hair and must have looked more like their father. "I didn't mean that. Thanks for picking us up. Are you sure you don't mind us getting in your car like this, we're filthy?"

"What's a bit of mud. It will brush off. Do you want to get in the front? Dan you will have to squeeze in between the girls. I'm afraid it's not as big as your dads' car."

"Why isn't he here then?" Will turned to look at me once he had fastened his seat belt.

"Something came up at work your mum said."

"I'll bet," he muttered quietly and turned away to look out of the window.

Dan, who was the younger of the boys then began to talk about the rugby match as we made our way back out of Lancaster. He suddenly stopped mid-sentence as though something drastic had occurred to him.

"What's for tea then? I mean if Mum is at her meeting and Dad is working late again, who's cooking? Are you making tea for us, Fae? I'm starving!" In perfect timing his stomach emitted a prolonged rumbling.

In answer to this, the universe provided me with a solution as immediately ahead I spotted the bright sign of a Fish and Chip shop. "Chippy anyone?" I asked as I began to indicate and pull over. I gained further brownie points from the four of them, not that I was attempting to do this, when ten minutes later I told them that they could eat in the car with the plastic forks provided.

"Dad would go ape-shit if we asked to eat in his car," said Dan cheerfully.

"Mummy said you aren't supposed to say shit," said Tammy, pronouncing the word with relish.

"Mummy says shit all the time," her sister commented.

"Well, we're not in Dad's bloody car are we cos he's too fucking busy fucking….." Will's voice was low so that the other's didn't hear above their own voices, but I did. I kept my eyes firmly on the road ahead and pretended that I had not heard. From the way he had shut up so quickly I think he realised he had said more than he should.

A while later, with my car smelling delightfully of damp mud, sweaty boys and salt and vinegar, we arrived back at Maypoleton. Laura and her husband lived in a large five bedroomed property on the other side of the river in a prime location on the new housing estate. The garden was immaculate as were most of them nearby and I knew that there was fierce competition to keep up appearances.

Inside however, especially in the kitchen, it looked as though Laura's careful hand on the reins was slipping. Breakfast pots were still in the sink and in the utility room I spotted an overflowing basket of clothes that looked like they were waiting to be ironed.

"Daddy is not going to be happy," said Tammy quietly as she went to open the dishwasher which I could see needed emptying.

"Right then, let's crack on shall we. Bonus prize of ice cream or chocolate from the shop if we can get this sorted before your parents come home. Lads what do you say?"

I eyed the boys who were still in their grubby sports gear, determined that they were not going to get out of this because of their sex.

"We do have a lot of homework to do?" Dan said slowly but I could see he was thinking of ice cream and chocolate.

"We do actually," Will added. "We both have a maths test tomorrow and we are supposed to be revising for that."

"Fair enough. This is the deal then. You two get changed and then I can get that lot round the washer, girls you unload and fill up the dishwasher and I will do the ironing. Boys if you get on with your homework you still get the ice cream and chocolate, but you have to do it here, so I know you are not cheating me."

It seemed that this was an acceptable arrangement.

By the much later time of ten o'clock when Laura wearily put her key in the front door, not only had we tidied the kitchen and sorted the laundry, including the washed and tumble-dried sports kits, but Tammy, Tilly and I had gone round the rest of the house like magical cleaning fairies before I had quickly spot tested Will and Dan on their maths.

I had whizzed to the general shop in the village which stayed open till late, and honour was duly satisfied all around as we sat in a row on the massive leather sofa in the lounge that Will called the family room, demolishing a large tub of fudge flavoured ice-cream.

"Oh my God I've died and gone to heaven," said Laura as she stood with me in the kitchen having hugged her children and issued the edict that it was bedtime. "Thank you so much. I can't believe you got the kids to help you as well."

I shrugged. "A little bribery goes a long way."

"Mark says I shouldn't bribe them."

"Payment then." I said softly, noticing how her eyes were shining not with humour and energy but with tears. "How was the meeting?"

"Long, as you see and bloody boring." She answered with a sigh, going towards the wine rack that was built into one of the units. "Join me?"

"Why not." I sat at the glossy black granite island in the middle of the high spec kitchen and took the glass she proffered. Laura quickly got through one as she let off a little steam about the meeting and then asked if I wanted a top up.

"Sorry I should have offered you a beer, I forgot you drink that not wine," she said as she noticed I had hardly touched mine.

"No, it's fine honestly. I like wine as well. I'm just a bit off it now it seems," I said with a shrug.

She gave me a queer little look, opened her mouth as though to say something, and then cast her eyes around the spotless kitchen once more.

"You know you really have saved my bacon tonight. Mark would have gone ballistic if he had come home to find the kitchen in the tip, I left it this morning. He's always on at me to give up my job and he would see that as another good reason."

"Do you want to stop working?"

"Hell no! I love my job. I love my kids of course, but I was a teacher before I became a mum and to be honest if I was just staying at home all day, I would go literally bat shit crazy."

"So, get help then."

"Get help?"

"Well, you obviously have a gardener so why not someone to give you a hand around the house?"

Laura looked at me as though the penny was slowly dropping. I realised that for an intelligent, educated woman, she was suffering from the lack of confidence that comes from having a git of a husband who permanently put her down.

"I'll do it if you like," I said with a sudden desire to help this lovely lady and her equally lovely children. "At least I can regularly do a couple of hours on a Wednesday evening like tonight, and I can easily fit in a few more around looking after Arthur."

"Could you? Won't that be too much?"

"I'm used to working long hours, much longer than my shifts with Arthur," I assured her. "And I prefer being busy, really I do."

I could see this offered her a lifeline that she was keen to accept. Opting for a coffee now, we chatted some more until there was the sound of someone else arriving home. Going on for eleven her husband had finally turned up. I had yet to meet him and was curious, as to what kind of man would keep a woman like Laura so under the thumb.

A very clever one obviously, I could see that straight away as he took in the kitchen and me in one quick assessing glance. Good looking too and aware of it, with dark eyes and hair that I suspected should have been a lot greyer and was probably dyed. Tall and slim with aquiline features and a well-groomed air about him. Polished was the word that came to mind.

Closely followed by narcissist.

I could see the immediate change in Laura as he walked into the room and already, I hated him. I watched my new friend stutteringly explain who I was and that I was going to be helping.

It was interesting to see the dilemma flicker over his expression. On the one hand he was quietly angry that Laura was standing up for herself, I could see that, but on the other hand I could also see a look I was very familiar with.

Sexual interest.

Oh yes, he was a predator in exactly the same way that I could be. The difference though was that I would never become entangled with a man if they were married to someone I considered to be a friend. I was cool with him as I said goodbye to Laura and let myself out.

"What a creep," I muttered as I walked to my car. When I had passed him, as he would not move aside to allow much room to do this, I had caught that tell-tale whiff of perfume that even a shower had not managed to disguise. Did Laura know and was she pretending not to? I drove the short way back to Aunty Ruth's mulling over this and felt a sense of determination to be a good friend to Laura, in a sisterly way that would have Annie home applauding.

And then I had another thought.

How often had I been the other woman?

Too fucking many Fae, too fucking many.

It didn't sit easily with me. Not now having witnessed the other side of the picture. I never stopped to think about the wives, or the children that may have been involved behind the scenes. I was too interested in my own need to lose myself in meaningless sex and forget the pain of losing Fliss, and that crushing guilt, to ever stop to think about anyone else.

My footsteps were slow and heavy walking back from the village car park. It had been a long day and the evening especially eventful from my kitchen table encounter with Matt and the conversation that had followed to this inner self revelation. Without thinking I found I was walking into the graveyard and along the path to where Rowan lay. The voices of the other spirits were keen to talk and have their say, but I closed my mind to them and concentrated on the woman who had brought me into this life.

"I've made a real mess of things so far. I don't think you would be very proud of me. I wouldn't blame you either." I crouched down by her grave and traced the letters of her name with my fingers. "But I don't know how to change. I don't know how to stop. Help me Rowan, please help me."

"*You are already changed.*"

"I don't feel it."

"*You will. Soon. Daughter of Samhain.*"

I wanted to ask her more but just then a light came on in one of the upstairs windows of the vicarage distracting me. I was further distracted when I saw that outlined against the glass, as he came to draw the curtains was the naked chest of Gawain. Could he see me from where he was? There was only a small light in the graveyard right at the entrance and I doubted it's beam carried to where I was knelt.

Yet he did seem to be looking right at me, those sharp eyes scanning the dark. I stood up and the movement must have focused his gaze. He stiffened slightly, and I felt across the distance the intensity of his eyes, before with a swift movement he drew the curtains shut. My breath had been stopped in my chest and I let it out with a sigh, a moan more like of anguish and longing.

"*You are already changed. Daughter of Samhain.*"

And following these words from my mother a soft gentle sound of laughter.

CHAPTER SEVENTEEN

I woke the following morning with that unfamiliar grogginess that had been plaguing me since coming to Maypoleton. It was an effort to get out of bed in time to start work and truth be told I fairly stumbled through the day, hoping that I managed to disguise my unusual fatigue.

"Late night?" Arthur asked at one point when he caught me yawning.

"Midnight-ish," I said, which it had been after my chat with Rowan and playing at being a peeping Tom with Gawain.

Arthur tutted. "That's not good girl. Early to bed, early to rise, that's what they say, makes a person healthy and wise."

"Sounds bloody boring to me," I quipped knowing this would raise a smile from him. It did.

"Hhm. Well early bed tonight, Missie. I want my opponent to have her wits about her. No fun in thrashing someone who is half asleep!"

We were playing chess which had become a regular mid-morning pastime these last few weeks. Mother Nature seemed to have forgotten that May was supposed to be a nice month. Frequent heavy showers and unseasonably chilly temperatures regularly curtailed our morning walks around the village.

I promised him I would have an early night.

Well, earlier than midnight anyway.

Thursday was of course the pub quiz and that had quickly fitted into my new routine. There was the lively conversation with Eve and Laura, both of whom had a wicked sense of humour and of course the vicarious thrill of sitting at the same table as Matt. He would studiously try to avoid looking at me and spend most of the night talking to Craig. As tired as I was, I did not want to miss out on this fun and after tea with my aunt and uncle,

I joined Eve as she came out of her house at the same time that I did.

"No Craig tonight?" I noticed that his car was not there.

"He's working till late. There's been a sick bug flying round the station at Lancaster, so he is covering for someone. And Matt has just texted me to say he is snowed under with marking which Laura tells me is just an excuse cos he can't possibly have that much work to do, although I believe they were rather late at the governors meeting last night. She told me you helped out? I Would have done, but it was our coven meeting," she finished with a grin on her face, "which I keep telling you, you are welcome to join anytime."

I let this comment slip by me as we turned from Cobbler's Row on to the main street. "Is Laura coming then?"

"She is. It's the one time she gets out of the house each week by herself. I gather you met Muppet Mark last night. What did you think?"

Eve, as I had come to know was blunt in her approach. She regarded me with curiosity in her swirly green, blue and brown eyes that were so unusual.

"You are right, Muppet Mark. Suits him to a tee. Does she know he's playing away?" I asked as I pushed open the door to the pub.

"Evening ladies? Pint of stout and a vodka and tonic?" The landlady was already reaching for a pint glass.

"Actually, I'll have a coke tonight," I said surprising myself as well as Eve and Shirley.

"You off the drink?" Eve asked.

"Just been tired today that's all. If I have a pint, I'll be asleep before we've got through round one of the questions."

"So go on then," Eve continued as we made our way to our favourite table in one of the corners and sat down to wait for Laura. "I thought he was but how do you know for sure?"

I could hardly say that I recognised the type as I had so often been the other woman myself. "Perfume, it lingers doesn't it, sometimes even after a quick shower. Does she know?"

Eve toyed with the lemon in her drink. "I don't know and it's that age old dilemma isn't it. Do you tell your friend you suspect that her husband is having an affair? Or do you let her continue thinking that everything is alright in her world. I sometimes wish we could just….but no. Mabel would say that is a definite no go."

I felt a ripple of unease twist through my stomach.

"What do you mean?"

Another of those pert looks accompanied by a mischievous smile. "Oh, you know. A bit of spell making, playing at cupid and all that. Laura would be so much better off with Matt but apparently that is against the rules."

Do as thou will an' harm none.

That rule that I had so wilfully broken myself in the past.

I was saved from commenting as the subject of our conversation squeezed through the growing crowd of villagers who were now filling the low beamed country pub in time for the quiz.

"Phew made it, ah thanks my lovelies you've got me a large one. I need it." Laura sat down looking gorgeous in a plum-coloured v neck sweater that displayed a cleavage neither Eve nor I could ever aspire to. It was probably a good job Matt was not here tonight, I thought with a smile to myself, he would have not been able to stop himself from staring.

As if in tune with my thoughts, Eve said chirpily, "Wow stunning top, Laura, have you worn that to work today?"

"Yes. Do you like it? I wasn't sure about the colour?"

I don't think any red-blooded make would have given too hoots about the colour. "It looks gorgeous and so does that eye shadow, you put us both to shame, you always look glamourous."

"Do you think so? Mark always tells me I should stick to browns and blacks, but I just feel so dowdy in those colours."

"Don't listen to a word he says," I said told her firmly. "What man has any idea of style and colour on a woman."

"Exactly," Eve agreed, "They're all useless at that sort of thing. Apart from Matt though, I think he's got a good eye for colour and shape wouldn't you say so, Fae."

"Definitely."

"Hm. He did give me a nice compliment today which was rather sweet of him I thought. Anyway, what have you been chatting about?"

"Oh, this and that," said Eve breezily and then we had to be quiet as the quiz began.

A slightly earlier night did follow in that I was in bed before midnight, just. Eve and I had walked home together. I ended up going into her cottage for a quick coffee after the pub had closed, which turned into another gossip session regarding Mark, Laura and Matt, until Craig arrived home, looking dashing and sexy in his uniform.

I let myself in quietly next door, tiptoeing up the stairs. As I snuggled down into the twin bed in the room I had shared with Fliss all those years ago, I was uncomfortably aware of how much I envied Eve her relationship with Craig. He was not her first husband, I knew that. She had told me a few details of her marriage and what had happened during that break down, which had me both wonderfully intrigued and laughing at the same time. She was certainly a character, and I enjoyed the way my friendship was developing with her.

Yet as with Annie, I was still cautious about sharing too much of myself, although I had the feeling that Eve was going to be far more adapt at wriggling out the real version of me before too long. It wasn't just that she was older and perhaps a little wiser than Annie, she most definitely had a touch of that other side to her that I recognised myself, a gift to see slightly more than most.

Another restless night followed and yet again a sloth like feel to the morning that had Aunty Ruth asking me if I was sickening for something. For once we were in the kitchen at the same time as she had not yet dashed off to the stables to see to the horses. I cut myself a large slice of bread, smearing it liberally with butter and jam, a ravenous hunger arguing with a wobbly feeling in my stomach.

"I think it's just my sleep pattern is all to cock," I said, adding three sugars to my coffee and a splash of cream for good measure. "It's been a big change in a short space of time."

I had no wish still to share with her the growing feeling of connection I had with Rowan now that I was in Maypoleton, although I was horribly aware that this meant I had also not shared with her the knowledge that my mother had not in fact killed herself. I chewed on my doorstop wedge of bread, hearing Annie's nagging voice in my head. Not only was I a rubbish friend in keeping things to myself, but I was also a rubbish niece.

Today was Friday and Gawain had told me I had no need to work most Saturdays unless he had a wedding, so I made a promise to myself that tomorrow I would spend some time with my aunt at the stables and then tell her.

"You have a good day then," she said now, gathering up her car keys. "I'm so happy you are settling into this job and life back in Maypoleton. It's grand, Fae, really grand."

I smiled at her. "It is, Aunty Ruth. Grand indeed."

"And you're helping Laura out as well which is lovely, really becoming part of the community." She paused, toying with her keys. "Do you think you will stay permanently?"

I really hadn't given it any thought. I was not a great fan of looking forwards to the future. Live for today was more my style. The future scared me. It ran off into empty tunnels that I did not wish to explore.

"I don't really know right now to be honest. I mean I have let out my flat back home for a six-month period." A thought occurred to me. "I suppose if I do stay here permanently I ought to look for a place of my own."

"Heavens no I wasn't meaning it that way," she was quick to point out and came round the table to squeeze me into a loving hug. "I love having you here, so does Eric. No love, I was just trying to say how lovely it is to see you back where you belong. Least ways that's how it feels to me. Don't you be thinking I am wishing you out from here, far from it."

"Ah thanks Aunty Ruth."

I returned her hug but after she had left and I had the kitchen to myself as Eric had already made his way to his job in Lancaster, I had ten minutes or so to mull over what she had said. As lovely as it was with my aunt and uncle, it did sometimes feel a little like being a child again. They made no comments as to my comings and goings but there was no way I could ever think of bringing a man back here. My bread and jam breakfast settled heavily in my stomach as I then thought of Matt and our conversation.

How bloody insulting to suggest that I was addicted to sex.

That was him scratched off the agenda even though I may be cutting my nose off to spite my face as the saying went.

And then of course there was Gawain.

How bloody insulting to pay me for sex.
How utterly demoralising to be pitied and shunned by him. Strike two.

Maypoleton did not have a huge choice of men on offer. Mark would jump into bed with me, no doubt about that. I felt distinctly queasy at the thought. Even if I had found him attractive, which I didn't, you see Matt, I found myself having a conversation in my head, I can't be so bloody addicted if I can think this way. I could not possibly consider having an affair with him now that I was friends with Laura and now that I had begun to see the damage behaviour of that kind could do.

"You are already changed."
That was what Rowan had said to me from her grave.

I cleared away my plate and wiped the jammy crumbs from the counter. Maybe I was changing, I thought. Maybe I was changing into a woman who could indeed be single and happily celibate, in which case my twin bed in the room upstairs would do perfectly adequately. But even as I thought this, tried to picture it in my mind, I knew this would not be the case.

There was nothing I could do about it for now. I would have to accept that Matt as well as Gawain had effectively slammed the door on me, and for now single celibacy was on the cards. I would have to go running more often, I thought as I left the cottage to walk the short distance over to the vicarage.

Not fair, I thought, not fair at all.

The door was opened this morning by Gawain just on his way out to visit a poorly parishioner. How could I think I could remain celibate when I was seeing him every day? No wonder I wasn't sleeping well. No wonder I woke up with a churning sensation in my stomach. Facing him daily was like putting my feelings through a mangle. Lust, longing, emotions I shied away from naming, hit me like a sledgehammer every time I felt his eyes on me.

"Sorry," he said in that clipped manner of his as he stepped back to let me enter, creating as much space between us as possible.

Even so with a couple of feet between us I felt as though there were mere inches. I thought of how I had seen him standing bare chested at the window the night I had talked to Rowan and the way I had felt as though something was pulling us together. I remembered the sound of my mother's laughter in the cool midnight air. How could I think of remaining celibate when I was being tortured by his presence? Impossible. Then quick as a flash another intriguing thought.

Was he?

He had spent that wild night with me, thinking I was a prostitute. Did he use them regularly? I knew he had fought with himself to overcome his reluctance to sleep with me initially, but once he had, the heat and passion had been intense. How could he possibly contain that all the time? Memories flooded into my mind and my body responded, hot desire pooling between my legs.

"Are you ill"?

I had not realised I had groaned out loud.

He had been about to walk through the doorway and turned to stare at me, cold eyes searching and assessing. In that instant my face must have been unguarded. I saw the flare of light turn the blue-grey eyes stormy for a second and then lightning fast the calm was back in place.

"I'm fine," I stuttered and blushed at the same time. Me, stuttering and blushing. Ridiculous!

"Good. I will be back later. Dad would like to spend some time in the garden today. The weather looks like it is going to behave itself again. He used to love gardening before he was ill."

"Yes, yes of course," I answered, despising myself for how eager I was to please him. When he had gone, I mocked myself in the hallway mirror. "Yes, yes of course. For fucks sake Fae!"

"Less of that language if you please, this is a vicarage in case you have forgotten!"

"Christ Almighty you made me jump!" I turned round to see Mrs Mannering crossing the hallway, polish and duster in her hands.

"That too! I will not have blaspheming in this house!"

We glared at each other across the hallway and then I heard Arthur calling from his bedroom. "Is that you, Fae?"

I brushed past Mrs Mannering and then turned around to childishly stick my tongue out at her, not realising, or maybe I did, that she could see what I was doing in the mirror.

"How rude!" I heard before knocking on Arthur's door and going into his room.

"Are you and the dragon having words?" He greeted me with a smile.

"She doesn't like my language."

"Excellent. Anything that gets that old dragon hot and bothered will do for me. You swear away my dear. Gawain's language is utterly foul at times, but then what can you expect."

I began the daily tasks of helping Arthur to shower and dress, intrigued by what he had just said. "What do you mean? I would have thought being a vicar his language would be ultra clean?"

"Not always a vicar my dear," replied Arthur tapping the side of his nose, but as on previous occasions he refused to be drawn on aspects of Gawain's earlier life.

I didn't even know if he had ever been married. He must have had relationships. He was in his forties, devastatingly good looking with that hard rugged edge to him that set him apart from other men. I didn't press Arthur on this, not wishing to give away how obsessed I was with his son.

We played chess for a little while and then midway through the morning as had become our habit, we went into the kitchen for a hot chocolate and some Dragon Baiting as he liked to call it. Remembering what Gawain had said I suggested that we take our drinks for once into the garden. I had not yet had chance to sit out there with him, as the weather had been so foul apart from that very first day when we had walked into the village.

Five minutes later we were sitting near the bottom end of the long garden in a spot which caught most of the morning sunshine. It was lovingly tended with a mixture of both flower beds and vegetable patches, very traditional English country garden in style. My mum would love it. As soon as I thought this, my natural mother Rowan popped into my head.

Had she loved gardening?

A sharp smell filled my nostrils, both sweet and tangy at the same time.

Herbs.

Rowan had loved growing herbs. Healing flowers and remedies.

Are you alright my dear?"

"Sorry?" I blinked and came back to the moment.

"You looked like you were miles away?" Arthur eyed me gently over the rim of his mug.

"I was thinking about my mother. My real mother," I said quietly, and it seemed so easy to talk to him about her, about the fact that I had no real memories of her. I didn't tell him that since coming back to Maypoleton I was able to sense her presence and connect to her.

He shared snippets then about his beloved Bessie, Gawain's mother. A stoutly practical woman who had nevertheless had enough of a romantic soul to name her son after one of King Arthur's fabled knights. As the conversation moved to Gawain, I felt that conflict of emotions inside me. We chatted some more and then Arthur asked if he we could also go into the village before lunch.

"I would like to buy a birthday card for an old friend if you wouldn't mind?"

"Not at all. Let's go now."

His face lit up and I stood to move his wheelchair and turn it back towards the house.

"Don't leave me."

"Pardon?"

"I didn't say anything my dear."

"Don't leave me here!"

The voice was as clear in my head as though someone was standing next to me. The air had turned distinctly chilly and yet the sun was still shining. I turned behind me knowing that I would not see anyone. But my eyes went to the end of the garden, right to the wall where there was the ancient yew tree overshadowing a dark neglected part of the garden.

"Please don't leave me here."

"Fae?" Arthur's voice cut through to me.

I began wheeling him back up the path. As I did so an icy blast of wind gusted through the garden.

"My goodness where has that come from?" Arthur exclaimed as he shivered.

"I'm lonely here. So lonely."

A body blow to my soul that had me pushing the wheelchair as quickly as I could. Gawain was in the kitchen with Mrs

Mannering as I opened the door and wheeled his father back into the warmth.

"My it's taken a bitter turn out there," said Arthur blowing on his hands.

"I told you it was too cold. Silly girl," muttered Mrs Mannering none too quietly.

I ignored her and looked directly at Gawain. Right now, thoughts of lust and desire had fled from my mind. There was something more pressing to deal with.

"I need a spade."

"I beg your pardon?"

Arthur and Mrs Mannering both began to question my comment. I held Gawain's steely gaze and repeated myself as though it was a matter of life and death, which in a way it was.

"I need a spade."

Not just a vicar.

He knew there was something so much more than a crazy notion in my head. Even so he pushed me by the smallest action of raising an eyebrow and piercing me with a look.

Exasperated, I blurted out, "There's a body in the garden."

At which point Mrs Mannering dropped the pie dish she had just got out of the oven and Arthur clapped his hands excitedly. "I knew you would be more interesting than all the others."

CHAPTER EIGHTEEN

In a manner reminiscent of the night when I had met him, Gawain was all clipped efficiency and no nonsense, as though I had just said I want to dig up some vegetables for lunch, not that there was a body buried in the garden.

He calmed the rather hysterical Mrs Mannering who was flapping on two counts. I wasn't sure what she was more concerned about, dropping the pie dish or my announcement. Either way he soon had her shushed and in her place.

Realising that his father was absolutely not going to be wheeled out of the way from this excitement, he swiftly found a warm waterproof coat, tossed it to me to help Arthur put it on as well as an extra rug, at the same time as swapping his shoes for a pair of wellingtons.

Then, not bothering with a coat himself, he looked at me once more, those disturbingly analytical eyes scanning me as though I was an alien creature who had somehow landed in his kitchen.

"Show me." Cold, hard, ruthless.

I wheeled Arthur back into the garden, leaving behind a muttering Mrs Mannering, now busy clearing up the mess of the pie on the floor. I had not bothered with my leather jacket before and with this pressing sense of urgency within me, the fact that I was feeling cold myself was of no importance.

The late spring sky was still clear and sunny, but the air had grown much chillier and that had nothing to do with the weather. I settled Arthur close to where we had been sitting before and then bracing myself, I took a few steps towards the yew tree.

"I am here."

"I am waiting."

"I have been waiting so long."

Sadness. Sorrow. Heartbreak.

I stood in the overgrown patch of garden, neglected and uncared for, overwhelmed with emotions that had me shaking inside and tears pooling in my eyes. The earthy damp smell was infused with another scent, that of wild herbs, although there were no flowers of that description nearby. No herbs at all. Just weeds, nettles, brambles. A part of the garden grown wild and unloved.

"She is here," I said as my feet moved to a particular spot.

"She?" Gawain shot me one of those looks.

An unanswerable question, at least to him. As unanswerable as how the freaking hell I knew there was a body waiting to be discovered. I knew that my cover was blown. I knew that from this moment on there could be no more hiding what I was, but that could come later. I was being driven by a need far more pressing than my own personal desire to hide that dark side of myself. I stared back at him, wondering if I looked as wild eyed and crazy as I felt. Judging from his expression I must have done. He said nothing further but hefted the spade and began to dig.

"Are you psychic then?" Arthur asked me directly from where he was watching with avid curiosity.

I couldn't take my eyes from Gawain, fascinated by watching his body hard at work. The ground was solid and unyielding at first and he had to resort to a pickaxe from the garden shed. Strong easy movements from a body that contained power and energy, a body that had released that fire into me in a moment of unguarded, unchecked passion.

I shivered from cold, from psychic energy, from desire, from longing.

"Roger, the gardener won't go near that spot," Arthur's voice carried on making me realise I had not answered him, although from his tone he didn't appear to mind. "He and the dragon regularly have argie bargies over it," he went on. "She wants him to plant flowers there and he refuses point blank. It's quite funny to watch," he finished with a chuckle.

There was a period of silence apart from the noises of the ground giving way to pickaxe and spade, and Gawain's breathing which grew heavier as time went on. Unable to bear the inactivity, I went into the garden shed and rooted out a pair of gloves for myself and a second, slighter smaller spade. Uncaring of the mud and the dirt, but then Gawain was also showing no concern for the state of his clothes, I began to help by clearing away the tangle of brambles he had chopped through and making more space for him to work.

I began to dig with him.

Our eyes met for a moment and a shared second of energy scorched between us. He felt it I knew he did. But he shut it down as quickly as it had flared up and concentrated on his task. Now that the top layers of soil, clogged up and rooted as they were with weeds and deep roots, had been removed, it was easier to make progress.

It was my turning of the spade that uncovered her.

The teeth of a skull smiling at me suddenly, ivory light against the soil.

We both paused then. I cast aside my spade and dropped to my knees, scraping at the dirt with my bare hands.

"You've found me."

"Stop."

Vaguely I was aware of Gawain speaking to me, but it didn't matter. I could not really hear him. All I could hear was her voice. I could not ignore the touch of his hands on mine though or the physical presence of him crouching in the dirt next to me.

"Fae, stop now. We have to call the police."

"But she's been there so long, I can't leave her now," I turned my head which was a mistake as it brought my face to within an inch of his. My heart was hammering in my chest, my breathing was light and shallow. I was wired with emotions and sensations that were making me dizzy. Half of me driven by an urgent need to continue my task, the other half desperate to plant my mouth against his and lose myself in the passion of his kisses.

I saw his eyes change.

I saw the muscle twitch at the corner of his mouth.

Then I saw the clarity that he was so adapt at regaining and I was so skilled at losing. "This is a police matter now. We can't just dig up a skeleton. We don't know if this is a crime scene."

"It's not," I shook my head at him wildly. "She's been here centuries. Please, I can't leave her any longer." She won't let me; were the words I left unspoken.

Gently then, he kept hold of my hands and drew me to my feet. I was looking into the eyes of a vicar now, a man of the church and what I saw there had an even more disturbing effect on me.

I thought he could blow my mind when he was cold, dispassionate, angry.

Compassion in those eyes was another thing entirely.

Let me throw myself into your arms and rest in your embrace, shelter me from the storms within my soul.

Trembling I was aware that I was not far from having a total melt down.

"My father needs to have something to eat. I imagine Mrs Mannering has rescued the pie sufficiently. Take Arthur inside and have lunch."

Arthur was beginning to comment that he was not all that hungry, but at a look from his son he clamped his lips together and then spoke to me. "Yes, Fae if you would be so kind. I am rather chilly now as well. A hot lunch is just what I need."

To say I was reluctant to leave the grave was a huge understatement but Arthur's cheerful voice reminding me of my responsibility to him was just what I needed to break through the spell that I was under.

And there was no doubt that I was under a spell.

I did my best to push this thought aside as I wheeled Arthur's chair back up the garden path, my legs struggling with a horrible wobbliness that had set in. I also had not realised quite how cold I had become until the warmth of the kitchen wrapped itself around me like a cosy comfort blanket. I let out a long breath of relief. Back in this normal environment I had a better grasp of my senses.

"Oh, be quiet woman," Arthur forestalled Mrs Mannering's horrified exclamations at the mud and dirt I was bringing into the room, having thoughtlessly forgotten to take my boots off. "It will clean. Right now, we need some food. Fae has had quite a shock."

Bless the man, it was debateable who was caring now for whom. My mind was still struggling to process properly, and he calmly prompted me in my actions. His coat was put away along with the rugs. I helped him to the bathroom and then dispensed his lunchtime medications. I cleaned and tidied myself up as best I could, washing the grime and soil from my hands and wiping away the traces of tears from my eyes. There was nothing I could do about the filthy state of my jeans and sweater.

Ignoring the hostility from Mrs Mannering, we finally sat at the kitchen table, with a plateful of the slightly mangled, but nevertheless extremely tasty chicken and leek pie in front of us.

"Are you not going to eat?" Arthur pressed me when he was halfway through his and I had barely touched mine.

"Is it not good enough for you?" Mrs Mannering snapped at me, her cutlery attacking her food as though she wished she could jab the knife and fork into me.

"I'm just not hungry," I said and acknowledged to myself that I was feeling rather queasy. Not surprising. I pushed the plate away, not caring that I was offending the housekeeper.

Just then Gawain came back into the kitchen from the hallway. He had got changed whilst I was seeing to his father. Out of vicar style clothes now and in jeans and a silver-grey sweatshirt that made his grey-blue eyes look lighter and suited his cropped greying hair. He gave me a quick assessing look that I could not hold, then calmly asked Mrs Mannering if there was any more pie.

Clearing away my plate with a sharp look, she then smiled sweetly at him and placed his before him. He ate as he did everything else, calmly, with as little fuss as possible. In between mouthfuls he addressed his father, as though having decided conversing with me was far too complicated for now.

"Craig is on his way. He was just coming back from Lancaster when I rang him."

The thought of a second police enquiry within a few months, with me in the middle of it, was not something I wished to consider. I began chewing at the skin around my nails, a nervous habit from being a teenager.

Gawain noticed immediately. "You don't need to worry. Craig will take this all in his stride. And you can hardly be accused of anything nefarious in this instance." A subtle reminder that he had not forgotten at all the cloud under which I had left my previous employment.

It appeared that he was right in Craig's reaction to the phone call he had received. About fifteen minutes later, there was the sound of the doorbell. Arthur had adamantly insisted he did not need his usual after lunch nap and who could blame him. Under Gawain's instructions Mrs Mannering had provided a large pot of tea to drink whilst we waited for Craig to arrive.

My head was beginning to pound as Craig began to speak to me. "So can you tell me how you knew there was a body buried at the bottom of the vicarage garden?"

He sat down at the table opposite me, a mug of tea and a plate of biscuits placed in front of him by a smiling Mrs Mannering. Four pairs of eyes were focused on me. I must have resembled a surly teenager as I refused to engage contact with any of them and shrugged my shoulders, whilst still nibbling at my now bleeding thumb.

"Okay," said Craig slowly. "It's one of those is it."

"What do you mean?" Gawain asked.

"Let's just say it is not the first time a skeleton has been uncovered in Maypoleton with unusual circumstances surrounding it."

"I would have thought any discovery of a body would be unusual?" Arthur queried.

"Well yes, but there are various levels shall we say of unusual and Maypoleton would appear to have more than its' fair share. Right then, we'd best get on with it."

The matter-of-fact way he was viewing this finally had me raising my eyes to look at him. I was surprised to see a sympathetic expression on his face.

"I think you could do to have a chat with my wife sometime," he said and then followed Gawain towards the door. I shot up from the table to go after them, but he blocked my way.

"No. I understand a little of what you are going through, believe me I do, but this is not for you now. I will speak to you later."

If it was not for the kindness and genuine concern in his voice I would have protested.

"How about finishing that chess game?" Arthur suggested, his earlier suggestion of going into the village clearly forgotten.

Knowing there was nothing more I could do I went to wheel the chair out of the kitchen. Back in the calm surroundings of the bedroom, with the large sash windows that looked out onto the village, I could pretend for a little while there nothing extraordinary had happened.

Arthur was as astute as his son and made no comment at all on what would be happening outside as he settled himself back at the table and carefully picked up his rook. Concentrating on the game enabled a semblance of calm to return to my mind. Chess was mathematical and logical. It was as far away from psychic notions that urged you to dig up skeletons as you could possibly get.

There was background noise that filtered through from the hallway. New voices adding to those of Gawain's and Craigs, footsteps coming and going, doors opening and shutting. All in the periphery of my hearing. I longed to be out there, demanding to know what was going on but Arthur kept me engaged in my task as the ticking of the clock on the wall accompanied the passing of time.

Midway through the afternoon there was a knock on the door and then Mrs Mannering entered with a tray. As she did so I caught a glimpse of white suited figures passing by in the hallway. I watched enough crime dramas on television to know that regardless of my insistence that the body would be centuries old, a team of forensics would have to be called in and an authority more senior than that of Craig's to classify this as a recent burial or not. Sure enough, as the housekeeper left the tray on the table and turned to leave the room, her employer and mine entered along with Craig and another gentleman.

"Thank you, Mrs Mannering," said Gawain. "I wonder if you could now rustle up some refreshments for the gentlemen who have been working outside. They are all rather cold and wet now."

I had my back to the window and had not realised it had begun to rain. Catching the sniffy look on her face, I guessed that Mrs Mannering was not overly pleased at having numerous folk tramping in and out of the kitchen and no doubt leaving muddy footprints. This bothered me not a jot and neither I thought by the look on Gawain's face did it him.

Then for the second time in the year I was faced with questions from a senior police official. He had far less presence than Craig, being much smaller in stature and nearing retirement age but a sharp intelligence was there in his eyes.

"Well Miss Winters, it would appear from the initial assessment of my colleagues that the skeleton is considerably old although of course that will have to be confirmed at the lab. But it would suggest we are not dealing with any crime that needs to be investigated. However, just for my records you understand I would like to know how you knew it was there?"

They all would, I thought looking at them. Apart from perhaps Craig who was standing a little way back, arms folded and a thoughtful expression on his face. I couldn't speak at first. I looked at Arthur. I fiddled with the chess piece in my hand, the horse, no, the knight it was called.

"Miss Winters?" The police officer pressed again. He had introduced himself but for the life of me I could not think of his name, it had flown out of my head already. His voice was easy though to ignore and I continued my study of the chess pieces.

"Fae."

Upon hearing Gawain saying my name I snapped my head round. If he had been looking at me with that cold disinterest, I could have spat out some glib reply. I could have lied. Made up some ridiculous story. But he wasn't. He was looking at me with the eyes he would survey one of his flock, eyes that sought out the despair and fear in a lost soul.

"I'm psychic."

More than that. A witch. A woman who had used her gifts to manipulate others. A sister who had in doing so, led to the death of her twin. Not ready to tell anyone all this. Those two words had to be wrung out of me like blood from a reluctant stone. Gawain continued to hold my gaze, and it was an effort to turn away and face the police officer who was now speaking.

"I don't suppose you can clarify that for me?"

"Not really." I could but I was not going to.

"Like I said before," Craig spoke now, addressing the senior office, "It's not the first time it has happened in this village, and I am sure it will not be the last."

My eyes now shot to his in surprise and I was further intrigued when Gawain added to this.

"My bishop mentioned something of the sort when he asked me to take this position. He thought someone with my background would be a good antidote as he put it to the other worldly nonsense that bubbled up here. I gather my predecessor was quite vocal on the subject and that your wife was involved was she not?"

Craig allowed a small smile to flicker across his face. "She was. But that is her story to tell, not mine. For now, I think all that matters is that we let the pathologists do their work and then the poor soul who has been buried here can find some rest."

"Indeed," said Gawain who opened the door to indicate to the senior officer that it was time to go.

"I was right then," said Arthur once we were alone again. "You don't like it though do you, being psychic, I mean?"

Again, it was not something I could put into words that would make any kind of sense. I was shatteringly tired. It was all I could do to focus my eyes on the chess board.

"You need to go home," said Arthur with a gentle tutting noise.

"But I'm supposed to be here until this evening. Your son has a parish meeting tonight, he won't be able to get you into bed."

"The way you look my dear, you are going to be asleep where you are sitting if you don't move soon. Don't worry about me. Gawain is more than capable of making his parishioners wait, if necessary, he won't be bossed by them let me tell you that," he finished with a chuckle. "You can't boss Gawain into doing anything he does not want to do."

"Well, if you are sure," I said, pushing back my chair, the thought of escaping back to Aunty Ruth's cottage and hiding beneath the duvet an overwhelming one.

"Absolutely. I am curious about one thing though, oh don't worry, nothing to do with the skeleton in the garden," he said quickly as I must have looked apprehensive.

"Go on."

"You don't refer to Gawain by his name." Clever eyes regarded me with a hint of mischief.

"Don't I?" I said lightly. "I hadn't noticed."

"You refer to him as, 'My son.' I was just wondering why that was?"

My fuddled mind was too slow to compute a reply. I was saved from doing so by the door opening once more and Gawain himself appearing again. I looked at him and then back at Arthur who smiled knowingly at me and nodded, appearing pleased with himself.

"I have told Fae she needs to go home. This must have been an exhausting day for her."

"Quite. You do look rather dreadful."

If it had not been for the enormity of what had occurred, I think my ego would not have survived another blow.

"If you are sure, you don't need me later on?"

"Quite," he said again. "Will you be alright walking back to your aunt's? I don't want you passing out again like you did in church that time?"

What an embarrassing reminder. "I will be fine."

"You don't look fine, Fae," commented Arthur who sounded far sprightlier than I did to be fair. "Walk her back across the green Gawain my boy." Mischievous indeed and done with such a gentlemanly flair it was impossible for his son to refuse.

"My pleasure," said Gawain although I knew this was far from what he was thinking. "I'll fetch your jacket."

"No need. It's on the peg by the front door. Thanks for the chess." I said to Arthur.

"Now that is my pleasure. Thank you for such an entertaining day. I do hope you feel better tomorrow."

So did I.

Finding the skeleton had knocked the stuffing out of me. I followed Gawain back into the hallway. Catching sight of my reflection in the mirror I saw that I really did look dreadful. Gawain grabbed a coat for himself from the pegs and once I had my leather jacket on, he opened the front door.

Walking next to him across the village green back towards my aunt's was perhaps even more surreal than the urgent prompt to dig up a buried skeleton. I could cope with the notion of spirits speaking to me. I could cope with centuries old bones.

I just couldn't cope with him.

He had silence down to an art form, not uttering a word until we were standing outside number one Cobblers Row. "You are scheduled to work tomorrow, but if you don't feel up to it at all, let me know."

No mention of skeletons. No mention of psychic abilities. No mention of previous encounters. Just, would I be fit for work?

"I'll be fine," I assured him and then let myself into my aunt's cottage, longing to just crawl into bed and hide under the covers.

"Good."

I turned the key in the door.

"Fae."

God did he know how it crippled me to hear him saying my name? How it was torture me for to say his, knowing how he felt about me.

"What?"

"My father likes you."

"I like him too."

And I am hopelessly in love with you, yelled a voice in my head that I could no longer ignore.

CHAPTER NINETEEN

"Whatever's the matter? I wasn't expecting you back till later? Are you ill? You look dreadful, Fae." Aunty Ruth had been sitting reading a horse magazine and got to her feet as soon as she spotted Gawain standing behind me.

He placed a hand on my back, gently propelling me forwards into the lounge. I felt the touch of him through my leather jacket and longed to lean back against him. Instead, I stiffened and moved away, going to sit on the sofa. My legs were shaking, and I felt horribly close to fainting which I was determined not to do in front of Gawain once more. But I couldn't answer my aunt as I had to concentrate on clamping down the rising nausea and dizziness that was ringing in my ears.

"There has been a bit of an incident at the vicarage," said Gawain smoothly as though finding skeletons in his garden was an everyday occurrence.

"What kind of incident?" This was from Uncle Eric who had come through from the kitchen.

"Fae discovered a skeleton in the garden."

Typical of him to put it so bluntly.

"A skeleton?" Eric sounded incredulous.

"Oh Fae." Aunty Ruth had a very different note in her voice. "You're like your mother in more than just your looks, aren't you?" It was hard to tell whether this was a good or bad thing. "She could always talk to the spirits in the graveyard. Used to scare me to death how she did it. I often wondered if that was what led her to…..if that was partly to blame for how ill she was after having you and Fliss."

"I think I'll put the kettle on. Tea vicar?" Uncle Eric said in his no-nonsense way.

"Thank you, Eric that would be good. Milk no sugar."

I managed to raise my head sufficient to throw a sharp look at Gawain. What the hell was he playing at staying? I was having a hard enough battle not going into total melt down due to the psychic energy I had been exposed to, without him adding to it. Had he no idea how much his presence affected me?

Clearly not, as he made himself at home in the chair opposite me, his large frame filling it and his long legs stretching out in front of him. His manner was that of the concerned vicar, clear blue-grey eyes calmly appraising me, waiting it seemed for an explanation. A confession perhaps? Fuck that for a game of soldiers. My aunt on the other hand was not someone I could deny.

"Fae?" She said questioningly as she sat beside me.

"Cake."

"Cake?"

I nodded, sitting a little more upright. "I need cake, or biscuits, sugar." It was the only way to combat the utterly draining sensations that were flooding my body.

"Eric, be a love and bring in those brownies I bought from Mabel this morning."

My uncle did so along with a mug of tea for us all. "I've put three sugars in it love," he said as he placed mine on the coffee table in front of me.

I nodded my thanks and then attacked the plate of brownies as though my life depended on it. When I had eaten three in quick succession, not caring that there was now downright amusement on Gawain's face as he watched me scoffing the lot, I began to feel a little better. It was my own fault, I should have eaten more of the pie at lunch time, but then I had felt so nauseous it had been impossible. Delaying tactics now deployed and used up I had to answer the three sets of eyes that were questioning me as I sat there.

"Yes. I can communicate with spirits. I'm psychic." I snapped the words out as I looked across at Gawain.

The amusement had been replaced by sharp curiosity. I had the feeling he was viewing me as though a scientist would an interesting subject he had come across for the first time. Whether this was a step up from slutty part time prostitute I was not altogether sure at this stage. Then I turned to look at Aunty Ruth, clearly disturbed by my announcement.

"I am like my mother," I said more softly. As I did so something shifted deep inside of me. Something that I had not even known was there. It was as though a connection was made deep in my soul that had been missing and now suddenly was in its' rightful place. An oddly powerful feeling. Powerful enough to sit up straighter, hold my head a little higher and speak in a voice that was calm and held no note of apology.

"I am like my mother," I said to Aunty Ruth, ignoring the men for now, as frankly they were not as important in this moment. "And I know what happened to her. It was an accident, a complete accident. She never meant to take all those pills. She was just so exhausted, so utterly, utterly exhausted. It was my fault, I wouldn't stop crying, I wore her out."

I watched her face crumple, and the tears begin to fall. "Oh love."

"How about another tea?" Uncle Eric was not good with emotional outpourings and as Aunty Ruth and I shared a tearful hug he busied himself with collecting the empty mugs.

"I knew it," sniffed my aunt when the second round of tea was brought through. "I knew my sister would never have killed herself. I always knew it." There was a slightly defiant note in her voice as she looked across at Gawain who seemed to have taken root in his chair, he looked so bloody at ease and comfortable there.

"I am glad you have the peace of knowing this," he said, "although regardless of the church's teachings, I must tell you I would never have thought any less of her if it had been the case. Suicide has crossed my path enough to know that we must never, ever judge those poor souls."

I might not have been in the room then. His whole attention was on my aunt and on reassuring her. It was stunning to see the transformation in Aunty Ruth's face as he spoke, compassion oozing out of every syllable he uttered. I felt incredibly jealous, ridiculously so.

Then that spotlight was turned on me. "It must be difficult for you, Fae?"

Oh no.

Please do not look at me like that.

Do not look at me as though I am just another of your flock, a lost sheep most definitely straying from the path.

No, do not do that to me.

Do not look at me as though you care whilst shutting me out of your heart.

Do not dare do that to me.

I managed a careless shrug. "Why should it be?"

You are lying, his eyes told me with a flicker of speculative light in them. But he said nothing.

It was my aunt who spoke next. "But you don't do any of that spell stuff do you love? I used to fret about our Rowan and think it could have got her into trouble? I know Mabel and her daft bunch of women, Eve included, like to dabble with spells and incantations and the like, but it never sits comfortable with me. I wouldn't like to think you dabble. Just in case it does turn you funny, like Rowan. I'd hate anything bad to happen cos of something like that."

Like Fliss dying because of a spell, I cast. "No," I lied. "I have never dabbled as you put it. Nor will I." The latter part at least was true. I had no intention of ever again using magic of any kind.

"So, who is the skeleton then?" Uncle Eric as practical as ever asked the question that perhaps we all should have considered before.

"Fae?" Gawain looked at me.

"I don't know. I just knew she was there."

"Is there anything in the parish records, Vicar as to who might have been buried in your garden? And why was she buried there?" Aunty Ruth suddenly asked the other pertinent question.

"Reverend Michael never said anything to me about a buried body when I took over from him," said Gawain. "I shall have to do a little digging of my own, or perhaps others in the village might have an answer to the mystery. For now, I must go back to Dad. Fae if you wish to take tomorrow off that will be perfectly acceptable. I can imagine that something like this is very draining, although I have to say the cure of chocolate brownies seems to have done the trick, you do have a little more colour in your cheeks than you did earlier."

Stop being so nice, I can't bear it.

"I'm sure I will be fine."

When he had finally gone and I could relax a little, Aunty Ruth fussed around me like I was an invalid. To be truthful it was nice to be so cosseted. She ran me a deep hot bath and brought me up a cheese sandwich and a glass of milk, just like she used to do if Fliss and I were poorly when we were girls. Then, despite the early hour, I was happy to crawl into my bed and pull the duvet over my head.

Astonishingly I slept well and even more surprisingly, Aunty Ruth was still in the kitchen the following morning when I dragged myself downstairs to go and have breakfast.

"Are you not going to the stables this morning?" Usually, she was there by now. I checked the clock on the wall, it was nearly seven thirty.

"It's Saturday love. I don't have to rush there. Did you sleep alright?"

"Like a dead thing," I said with a yawn and then grimaced slightly at the choice of my words.

"You still look proper peaky though, love. Are you sure you aren't sickening for something?"

I shook my head, ignoring the fact that I felt as though I had a terrific hangover without the fun of being drunk the night before. "I'm fine. I did have a sick bug weeks ago before all that trouble at work. But this is just reaction to yesterday."

"Gawain called earlier. He was most insistent that you had today off work."

I had to admit, the thought of facing him today was more than I could bear. For the first time in my working life, I took the easy option. "Perhaps staying away from the vicarage is a good idea," I mumbled.

"Well then maybe some time down at the stables with me is just what you need today. Plenty of fresh air, a bit of exercise and something down to earth to take your mind off what happened yesterday."

It was exactly what I needed. You can't get more down to earth than mucking out stables, filling hay nets and water buckets and grooming horses. Maybe I would even have a ride. I managed to overcome the nausea that was still lingering from yesterday and ate a hearty slice of fresh cobby bread covered in butter and jam and then went with my aunt to Farthing Hall livery yard. Not surprisingly word had flown around already. But far from being besieged with a mountain of questions, the only comments raised were as to how I was feeling myself.

"Are you alright, love?" Sally, the owner of Farthing Hall asked when she saw me getting out of Aunty Ruth's car. "There's plenty of biscuits in the tin if you want something to eat whilst you are down here," she nodded her head towards the tack room where there was a kettle and a constant supply of tea and coffee.

"I'm fine thanks," I replied and looked at Aunty Ruth with a question in my eyes.

"They found a skeleton buried here a few years ago," she explained once we were in the quiet hush of her stable block. But that was as far as she wanted to go and knowing that she felt uncomfortable with the whole subject I was happy to lose myself in the tasks at hand.

"I'm going to school Treacle this morning," she said leading her beloved horse out onto the yard to tie up so she could change the bedding, "Would you like to take Toffee for a ride? She's an excellent hack and the weather has finally improved after all that rain."

I followed her example leading her other horse to tie up next to Treacle and stroked the palomino mare on the neck. She was a gentle enough horse as I had come to know since moving back to Maypoleton, but I had only ridden her once and that had been in the school under the careful eye of my aunt. I was touched that she trusted me enough to take her horse out onto the road but wasn't sure that my own capabilities were up to it. I said as much and then Eve walked past on her way back from the tack room, arms full of saddle and bridle.

"I'm hacking out with Sam, why don't you come with me. Toffee will follow him like a lamb, you'll be perfectly safe. She could see me hesitating and then said softly. "I think it would do you good. You must be feeling like shit after yesterday."

Her blunt manner and understanding, was just what I needed, as well as perhaps the exercise and calming effect of being on a horse. "Thank you. I'd like that."

Eve expertly tacked up Sam and then came to check that I had done the same with Toffee. "There's a bridle path through part of the grounds," she said once we were both mounted, "and then we can go on the road, but don't worry, it's quiet and it's only for a short bit until we can get onto the fell."

I had forgotten how soothing the rhythm of a horse could be, the gentle rocking and swaying of the animal beneath you, and the soft blowing of their breathing, together with the occasional snort and toss of the head. Unusually for Eve she was quiet, and I was grateful that I was not being bombarded with questions. We made our way slowly through the grounds of Farthing Hall, passing a tiny one and a half storey white cottage, straight out of a fairy tale.

"Oh, that's sweet. Who lives there?"

"Dad lives there now," said Eve pulling on the reins to halt the horses for a second. There was a wistful expression on her face, one of longing and sadness that was most unlike her. "It was haunted," she said softly, "but not anymore."

"Haunted?"

Eve turned in her saddle to look at me. "Maypoleton is full of ghosts, Fae, and they reach out to some of us in ways you could never imagine." She sounded so sad that the questions I wanted to ask her died on my lips. Then she gave herself a little shake and offered a friendly warning. "Be careful, Fae. If you've answered the call of a ghost you may end up with far more than you bargained for."

Then she asked if I felt like trotting for the rest of the way through the grounds until we came to the road. I didn't have chance to dwell on her words as I was concentrating on getting back into the rhythm of rising and falling in time with the horse which looked as though it came so naturally to Eve, even though I knew she had only been riding herself for a couple of years.

But with the bouncing motion came a sense of calm and then with the steady clip clop of hooves on tarmac as we joined the road and slowed into a walk, I felt more and more at ease with myself. It had been a good suggestion of my aunt's to join her at the stables. I reached down to pat Toffee on her neck, grateful for the peace that had been missing from my mind for such a long time.

This was more like it.

Fresh air, open space, miles of moorlands and fells around us, only the occasional car passing by. A perfect tonic and it remained so until a while later when we had left the road to follow a narrow path that sloped around the lower circumference of a hill.

"If we take this route," explained Eve, we can go in a circle and come back to the stables. "There's a little bit uphill but it's good for the horses. Are you okay to do it in trot, just lean forwards a little as you rise and then when we go downhill, we can go back into walk."

I was enjoying myself so much I nodded my head and kicked lightly against Toffee's sides. It was quite an adrenaline rush trotting up the hill, feeling the energy of the horse beneath me, sensing the excitement in the animal as it was keen to follow the other one.

"Hi there!" I heard Eve calling out as she was on front of me, and she slowed Sam down to a walk.

I pulled back on Toffee's reins, although there was hardly any need to do this as she naturally followed Sam's lead. Aunty Ruth was right, she was such an easy ride. Feeling pleased with what I had managed to accomplish I had a beaming smile on my face as I pulled up alongside Eve to see who she was talking to at the top of the hill. My smile froze I place as I spotted Matt in his running gear and with him Gawain.

Neither of them looked particularly out of breath which was testament to their fitness, and I knew very well how much stamina each had in bed. Seeing them side by side, I was hit by a sledgehammer blow. How could I have possibly have slept with Matt? As attractive as he was, he had nothing like the effect on me that Gawain had. I literally felt as though I had been punched in the stomach as his flinty gaze settled on me, my mind going dumb as he spoke, not in that awful sharp manner but with concern.

"Are you alright this morning?"

"I'm fine," I squeaked sounding so unlike myself that Eve turned and shot me a glance. "How is Arthur? I hope he wasn't too disturbed by yesterday?" Thinking of him grounded me a little.

"Disturbed? He's loving it," answered Gawain and then he smiled.

I nearly fell off my horse. God almighty do not smile at me like that. Then I realised he was not smiling at myself exactly, more at the thought of his father.

"Mrs Mannering's in a tizzy though," said Matt conversationally and I got the sense that he was relieved that I was not giving off any flirtatious vibes towards him.

"I'll bet," said Eve with a rather sour note in her voice. "Not a great fan of skeletons, or those responsible for finding them."

"I don't suppose you know anything about this one, Eve?" Gawain asked her. "Or any of your friends?"

"In my coven you mean?" Eve was back to the teasing that I associated with her after her quiet spell earlier. "Not as far as I know, but I am sure we can do a little divination and come up with some answers if you like."

"There is really no need for you to do that," Gawain said steadily.

I wasn't sure if Eve was joking or not, but she was definitely making mischief when she added next, "So what does your housekeeper think of you employing one of the other side to work for you?"

"I'm not on anyone's side," I interjected quickly. "I just found a skeleton that's all. It's no big deal."

"I beg to differ," Gawain said looking at me probingly. "I have never come across anyone with psychic abilities like you before. I would say you are pretty special Fae."

How I wanted him to say that to me, but not in this way. I was cross that he was happy to view me as a subject of curiosity and nothing more than that.

I shook my head and shrugged my shoulders at the same time. "I told you. It's just a skeleton. It's no big deal."

Next to me Eve said levelly, "I think you might be wrong there."

Fool that I am, I chose to ignore her. So, what if I was a little psychic, so what if this had led me to uncover a skeleton. It was hardly a life changing event.

Or so I thought at the time.

CHAPTER TWENTY

"Are you sure you're quite alright?"

"I'm fine," I answered Gawain as he held open the door to me on Monday morning.

I usually let myself in as the door was never locked but he must have seen me crossing over the green. Aware that I was a trifle late, I was flustered and on the back foot. I was also annoyed at the reason I was late. A couple of older ladies, out walking their snappy little dog had accosted me and told me in no uncertain terms that my sort should not be working anywhere near the vicinity of the vicarage, let alone be responsible for the vicar's father.

"I am sure you will find that you are not required there this morning," one of them had said in her sniffy voice. "Margaret has told us all about you. You only got the job out of the kindest of the vicar's heart. A genuine saint he is."

"Absolute saint," said the other lady who I think was her sister. "I mean who else would employ someone who was sacked from her previous job for suspicion of murder?"

Still shaken up from the discovery of the skeleton I was slow off the mark and grumpy from a bad night sleep, waking that morning to feel distinctly queasy.

"Who the fuck's Margaret?" I snapped, not caring that I shocked them.

"Really!" They whirled around from me, muttering together in whispers of horrified delight.

I trudged on to the vicarage, my truculent mood not enhanced when the door was opened by Gawain who immediately asked if I was alright.

"I'm fine," I snapped.

"You don't look fine." Gawain's voice was both questioning and caring at the same time. "You look bloody awful in fact."

Catching sight of my reflection in the hall mirror, I had to agree with him. My bad mood worsened.

"Who the fuck's Margaret?" I snapped again.

Psychic overload, lack of sleep, nausea and yes, frustrated desire when in close proximity to him were not a good combination. I was in the mood for a bloody good fight. Or a bloody good fuck and as both Matt and he had made it clear that the latter was not an option, then the gloves were off.

Not a whisper of a reaction to my mood or my language.

"I assume you are referring to Mrs Mannering. Have you eaten this morning? You look as though you are going to pass out. You haven't got some kind of eating disorder, have you?"

"No, I haven't, and no I fucking haven't!" I brushed past him, hating the way my body responded to the nearness of him as I hung my leather jacket on the peg. "I just wasn't hungry that's all."

"I believe it can have that effect." His voice carried after me as I stomped across the hallway.

"What?" I whirled around quickly which was a mistake as I felt rather dizzy in doing so. I saw the frown on his face and the look of interest deepen in his blue-grey eyes. "I'm fine! What did you mean? It can have that effect?"

"Psychic energy. I have been reading up about it. Fascinating. I would like to discuss it with you later." Cool, curious, intellectually intrigued. That was the light of interest in his eyes. An intelligent man of the cloth, eager to probe the thoughts of someone with a much different view on life. No hint of heat or passion. Not a flicker of interest in myself as a woman. How had I ever kidded myself the odd time I had thought there had been?

"Well, I don't feel like discussing it with you," I said childishly, my pride and ego too battered right now to really care what he thought. I was, however, happy to discuss it with Arthur later on that morning. Once we had gone through the daily routine of shower, medications, and a bit of physio, Gawain's father was keen to be taken out into the garden

"Of course, I would understand my dear if you would rather not," he said softly as I helped him into his wheelchair. "But in all my days I have never met anyone quite like you and to be truthful my dear, you are such a welcome breath of fresh air in this fusty old vicarage. You remind me a little of Gawain's mother. She was a lively character with a vivid imagination. I do miss her so much you know."

His eyes had strayed to the photos by his bed of a pretty woman with laughing eyes and a generous smile. I couldn't refuse his request and making sure he was well wrapped up I opened the door to push his chair through the hallway. As I did so, it was impossible to not see Gawain escorting the two ladies who had spoken to me earlier into his office. One of them turned her head to give me a satisfied smile and I let out a heavy sigh.

"Got on the wrong side of the Misses Tweed, have you?" Arthur asked astutely. "Thick as thieves with the dragon you know. Oh, good morning, Mrs Mannering and how are you today?"

Clearly not happy at being referred to quite loudly as a dragon, and even more unhappy to see me behind the wheelchair. "It's not right you being here," she said, standing in the doorway as though to block the entrance to the kitchen. "I said as much to the vicar. It isn't right that a heathen witch is employed in such a Godly house."

"She's not a witch you damn fool woman!" Arthur barked out. Then he suddenly turned his head round to me with the most devilish look in his eyes. "You're not by any chance, are you?"

"No, I am not," I said to his disappointment, and I felt a twisting stab somewhere deep inside of me, as though I was denying part of who I was, and it was wrong to do this.

"Oh well, can't have everything. Well, what are you doing still standing in our way woman? We want to go and sit in the garden. Hot chocolate first though Fae, hey?"

"Do you have to? You always make such a mess!"

Yes, we did, and I only left the mess because she was so horrible to me. I also knew that Arthur got a certain mischievous satisfaction in doing anything to irritate the housekeeper.

"Why do you dislike her so much?" I asked him a little while later.

I had taken the steaming mugs of hot chocolate and a plateful of biscuits out on a tray to sit by the small table at the bottom end of the garden. My legs had begun to tremble and my stomach to churn as soon as I saw the now empty shallow grave that was mere feet away from us. Talking about the housekeeper was a good distraction to how my body was feeling.

"She thinks I would be better cared for in the nursing home in Lancaster."

I was dunking my biscuit in my drink and nearly dropped it into the frothy liquid. "You are kidding me? That's not exactly Christian."

"She thinks I take too much of Gawain's time away from his other parishioners."

"Bloody hell. Does he know this?"

Arthur shook his head. "She has never said anything. I just know. People can treat you as though you are stupid if you are in a wheelchair. They say things around you forgetting that it is only your body that doesn't work properly, not your mind. I overheard her on the telephone one day. It was shortly after the other lass, before you had to leave. She was talking to the Tweeds and mentioned that it was maybe a good thing that my previous companion had to leave as now the vicar would feel more inclined to put himself first and the needs of his flock."

"Hells bells." I ate my soaked biscuit, the first food I had eaten all morning and contemplated this.

"Exactly. Now you know why I call her the dragon. Are you sure you are not really a witch? It would be lovely if you could cast a spell on her or something?"

"I promise you. I am not a witch."

"*You are a witch.*"

A whisper on the wind, a rustle in the leaves. My eyes shot to the disturbed patch of earth.

"Pity that. I was fascinated when Gawain told me there was a coven here in the village. Lovely ladies they are too. Much jollier lot to be honest than some of the WI that come round. But I suppose that's to be expected."

"Mm," I answered a little distracted.

"So, who do you think she was then?" Arthur had spotted the way my eyes had fixed on the now empty grave.

"I have no idea."

"Gawain has spent all weekend trying to research her. He was talking about going into Lancaster to see if there are any records there. You do know don't you that this area was a hot spot for witches back in the day. We're not far from Pendle you know."

I did know all about Pendle and the poor mistreated women who had been hauled off to prison in Lancaster and then hung. But whoever the skeleton had been in the grave, that had not happened to her.

"*They hung me. Here in the village. They hung me.*"

Sorrow. Anger. Sorrow.

The heavy emotions washed over me. It was all I could do to concentrate on listening to Arthur. He was talking about the other time when a skeleton had been found here in Maypoleton. I knew now of course, that Eve had been the one to discover it, but not all the details. As fascinating though that might have been, I was more interested in blocking out the energy that was coming my way, wave after wave of dark, saturated emotional energy.

It was knocking me sick. "Do you mind if we sit somewhere else?"

"What? Oh yes of course. How clumsy of me to suggest we sit here in the first place. I am such a buffoon." Arthur was instantly apologetic.

I was quick to reassure him "You are nothing of the sort. It just feels a little chilly here that's all."

"Does it?" He looked surprised and well he might as the sun was being especially kind right then and bathing us in her warmth.

I felt chilled to the bone though. "How about I go and fetch that book I was telling you about? We can start to read it this afternoon if you like?" I had told him about the Bulldog Drummond stories that Mr Carlisle had so enjoyed having read to him before he died. Kelsey had allowed me to take the one I had been reading as I left the care home.

"Jolly good idea. I like the sound of this Bulldog Drummond chap. Sounds a bit like my Gawain." Arthurs eyes twinkled with a speculative light as he looked at me. Aware that I now had flushed cheeks in contrast to the pallor of my complexion I tipped my head forward slightly allowing my hair to cover my face, so I didn't need to reply. As I released the brake on his chair and began to wheel it back up the path, I heard her voice again.

"*My name is Eliza.*"

I nearly stumbled. Laughter accompanied the next comment.

"*We share the same name. We share more than that. We are the same.*"

Fae Eliza Winters.

With Rowan dying when I was so young, I had never been able to ask her about my middle name. I wondered now with more of that churning feeling in my stomach, if there was some distant family connection to the skeleton I had uncovered. It would perhaps explain a little of how I had been drawn to it.

But what did she mean? We were the same.

More laughter, playful, mischievous.

"We are both witches."

I am not a witch! I affirmed this silently as I walked up the garden towards the house. Mrs Mannering was busy ironing pristine white bedding, steam rising from the fresh smelling cotton sheets. My mind went to picturing Gawain's head on the pillow. His stern features softened in sleep. What, I wondered would he look like asleep? My heart ached stupidly at the thought, and I mentally kicked myself. What the hell did I care what he looked like when he was asleep?

"You care because you love him."

Bloody hell she had followed me inside!

"Right, I won't be long," I said to Arthur, desperately needing to get out of the house for a little while.

"Where are you going?" Mrs Mannering demanded haughtily. "You have only just got here."

"She's very kindly offered to go and bring me one of her books for me to read." Arthur butted in before I could snap out a churlish reply. "Would you mind wheeling me to the front garden whilst you go?"

Once I had settled Arthur in a comfortable spot where he could be sociable with the odd villager who would walk by, I set off at a brisk pace to Aunty Ruth's. My mind was alternating between being full of Eliza, whoever she had been, and tormented thoughts of Gawain thrilling my body and capturing my heart in one crazily wild night of never to be repeated passion. I didn't realise that tears were blinding my eyes, or that my legs were shaking, until I tripped and went flying on the uneven cobbles that still lined the road where Aunty Ruth lived. Strong arms came out to halt my tumble. "Whoa, steady there Fae. Are you alright?"

I was pulled up to my feet to find Craig looking at me with concern in his clear grey eyes. Off duty today by the looks of him in jeans and a t-shirt and again I was hit by a surge of envy for Eve. Lucky bloody woman.

"I am fine," I reassured him, even though I was feeling frankly anything but.

"Maybe you could do with a couple of days off work? I am sure Gawain would understand."

"Really I am fine," I insisted that I was perfectly okay to walk the rest of the way to my aunt's house unassisted.

He gave me a look to say that he knew I was lying but he was not going to challenge me on it. I let myself into number one Cobblers Row, glad that there was no sign of my aunt and uncle. Racing upstairs I quickly rooted through my belongings to fetch the book I wanted. As I picked it up, I thought of Mr Carlisle and that last evening I had spent with him. His death and the suspicions around it had led me here. Had that been a good thing I wondered now? Part of me wanted to run as though the devil himself was after me.

Run away from the agony, sheer fucking agony, of being around Gawain.

Run away from the fear that was rippling through me at what I was unleashing.

Run away from the past, the present and whatever the future may hold for me here.

I caught sight of myself in the hallway mirror. My face. Fliss's face. "Run or stay? What should I do, Fliss?"

I saw her as clear as though she was next to me, behind me in the mirror. Her face was full of love, gentle warmth as there had always been shining in her eyes.

"*No more running Fae.*"

"What do you mean, no more running?"

"*You have been running ever since that night. Running from who you are.*"

Bitterly, silently, with a nod to her in the mirror I accept this was the truth.

"So, I stay then?" Another lingering smile and then she was gone. I blinked away more tears, traced my fingers over the mirror, willing her to come back. When I realised she was not going to, I opened the door and made my way back to the vicarage at a steadier pace this time, aware that my body was still feeling most peculiar.

Arthur was chatting to a couple of ladies from the village as I approached. One had three dogs of various sizes and breeds on leads with her and the other, a very attractive brunette was holding the hand of a toddler. I was aware that although both greeted me with smiles and friendly hellos, the woman with the child was giving me a deeply searching appraisal. Which of course had me replying with a cocking of my head, a raising of my eyebrows and a 'who the fuck are you?' stare.

"Fae, this is Cheryl," he said gesturing to the woman with the dogs. "She's our local dog walker and very good at it too as you can see."

I could. The dogs were all sitting quietly next to her, and I could understand why. She had a naturally calm energy about her. Not so the brunette who was no positively radiating animosity.

"And this is Lucinda," Arthur was now introducing her, "and this delightful little chap is Toby. Lucinda also has a daughter who has just started at the school."

I offered a smile and received one in return, but it didn't match the look in her eyes.

"Gawain sings her praises too," added Arthur looking at me with what I am sure was a glint of mischief in his eyes. Then he spoke to her. "You have really made a difference to the Sunday school attendance since you moved here."

"I have," she said, speaking for the first time and boldly challenging me with a look. "Gawain is often telling me that he doesn't know what he would do without me now."

So that was the issue, was it? I was stunned at the boulder of emotions that hit me in the stomach. I had never, ever, in my life felt such an instinctive reaction against a woman. But then I had never, ever, fallen so stupidly, madly, fucking insanely in love with someone.

Someone who despised me.

What I wondered, did the saintly, and not so saintly at times, Gawain Temple think of this attractive woman who clearly had her eyes on him? Then I consoled myself that it didn't matter anyway as she had a family so that put her out of the picture.

Sadly, my illusion over this was dashed a few minutes later. We said our goodbyes and went back inside. Once we were settled in the comfort of his room that overlooked the green, Arthur filled me in on the background of the two women.

"Lovely ladies both of them. Cheryl's family have always lived around here, she's Mabel's niece, you know Mabel, don't you? Of course you do," he said referring to the woman who ran the bakery. "Lucinda is fairly new here. She moved to the village for a fresh start after her husband died. Poor thing, left on her own with two young children. Tragic."

His tone of voice had me looking at him sharply.

"She plays the grieving widow very well." Was his answering remark to my probing stare.

"Plays?" I asked as settled myself comfortably in a chair opposite him, the book on my lap.

"I may be old my dear, and creeping with decrepitude, but I am very observant."

I flushed under his gaze.

He went on. "A woman who is genuinely devastated at the loss of the love in her life, does not immediately throw herself at the most eligible man in the area."

"Oh?" I thought I was being casual enough. Apparently not.

Arthur leant forward and patted my knee. "Don't worry my dear. Lucinda is totally unsuited to my boy."

My shoulders jumped up in a not so nonchalant shrug. "It's no concern of mine."

"Hhm," he said with a look that told me he knew I was in love with his son. "Would you like to read to me my dear, my eyesight is not as it used to be, and I get headaches very easily these days."

Thankful that he was not going to delve any deeper for now, I tucked my feet beneath me, curled up in the cosy chair and opened the book. I found reading out loud a pleasant past time and something that always managed to calm me. It was a joy to bring the story and characters to life and to hear the odd chuckle of amusement from Arthur as I did so.

"Ooh I like this fellow, Bulldog Drummond," he said at one point when I was taking a break to have a sip of water. "Just like my grandfather. And Gawain for that matter."

Instant flashback to that night.

Five men knocked to the floor.

Wild deep passion.

I needed another sip of water and nearly choked on it when I heard the voice behind me.

"Who is?"

He had entered the room so silently I had no idea he was standing there.

"Ah Gawain my boy. You would love this book. Full of no-nonsense heroics."

"You read very well." Clipped, no nonsense. A statement of fact addressed to me. And then, in an equally dispassionate voice. "A few moments of your time if you wouldn't mind. Dad will be perfectly fine by himself for a while, won't you Dad?"

"Oh yes of course. Fae off you go with my son, he clearly has matters of import to discuss with you."

Arthur waved a hand at me airily and as Gawain had turned his back already to walk through the door, he winked at me. And then laughed as I couldn't stop myself from scowling.

"Yes, I thought so", he chuckled as I handed him the book, quelling the urge to give him a light wallop with it.

I stomped after Gawain, feeling all my defensive prickles rising uncomfortably to the surface. Attack was always my chosen form of defence. Having been faced with the thought that the attractive young widow and mother was after the focus of my unrequited desire, I was in battle mode.

"What?" I demanded as I followed him into his study and inner sanctuary, closing the door behind me with something of a slam.

Raised eyebrows and a coolly probing stare met my defiant glare. "What?"

We stared at each other for a moment. A volcano and an arctic glacier in the same room. You would think that the volcano would have the upper hand and melt the ice. But it seemed in this case the arctic freeze was stronger.

I hated him at that moment.

I hated how my heart felt as though it was on fire.

I hated how my soul felt as though it was screaming in torment.

There was a tiny moment of relief and satisfaction when I caught a glimmer of something, something other than disdain in his sea-coloured eyes, and then fear overrode other emotions as he spoke.

"Are you a witch?"

CHAPTER TWENTY-ONE

"I'm a witch, I'm a bitch so what of it."

The wild words blurted out of my mouth. He was not impressed. The dark light of disapproval fuelled my rebellious spark. I am my own worst enemy. Self-sabotage and I walk hand in hand together, best of buddies. The more I sensed his deeply controlled anger, the more I fired up.

The sluttier I became.

I tilted my head to one side, allowed my silky blonde hair to fall beguilingly over one eye. My mouth curled up in a smile to beckon and bewitch. I knew my eyes, such an unusual shade of aquamarine could dazzle and blind if I so wished.

I so wished.

I so wanted.

I so desired.

The energy in the room shifted. The volcano was now suddenly so much stronger, and I watched as the conflict within him had the effect of the glacier melting fractionally. It was not much but it was enough for me to take a move forwards.

"Well, what do you think I am? Or maybe I should be asking, what would you like me to be?" As the words came out of my mouth I heard his intake of breath, accompanied by a sudden flash of anger in his eyes as though he knew in that second that he had let his guard down. Leaning against the hardness of the door, I felt for the handle and with a jolt of satisfaction realised there was a key.

I turned it.

The witch and the vicar in the study.

The fire in my heart ignited.

With yearning deep in my soul, I walked towards him, placed my hands on his chest, raised myself on my tiptoes and planted a kiss on his lips. Firm, cool, unyielding. But the beat of his heart beneath my hands told another story. I leant in so my body, touched more of his. Another kiss, again on denying lips.

"Don't tell me you haven't thought about it?" I could not believe for a moment that he had not been plagued by the same manner of repeated dreams reliving that night. Those daytime feelings of longing, of separation as though some part of him was missing. I could not believe that he had not been suffering the torment deep down in his heart and soul that I had these last few months.

It simply was not possible.

Because if that was the case then I was completely doomed. Lost.

He had to feel something!

He did.

He was a man after all.

A man with a clerical collar on, but a man, nevertheless. I leant in even closer, feeling that maleness of him against me as once more I reached up and pressed my lips against his. This time a response. An angry, bruising kiss, his hands clamping around my head holding me firmly in place.

The kiss deepened, his mouth now taking the lead over mine, opening, searching, probing. I was more than happy to sink into the heat of his embrace, to soften and melt into him. Different to Matt. Different to the other men. Different in that my heart and soul were on the line here and I was utterly helpless to prevent that.

Surely, he felt the same?

Surely, despite my wayward approach he knew deep down what I was feeling.

Surely, the way his hands were now roughly caressing my body told me I was right.

Limpet like I clung to him, unable to stop the moans of desire slipping from my throat, weakening into whimpers of need and want. His hands cupped my bottom over the denim of my jeans, pulling me up tight against the swelling hardness of him. Slick with heat, I felt the torture of being so close, yet so far away.

Not enough to be against him.

Not enough to feel muscle under clothes.

Not enough to have him still so rigidly in control.

I wanted skin on skin.
I wanted him within me.
I wanted a shared communion of something far more than just sex.

Lost as I was in the depth of his kisses, demented as I was for the touch of his hands on my bare body, I gave myself up completely to the rage of fire that was burning from the inner most depths of me. I was blissfully happy to feel him reaching for the zipper of my jeans, delirious with delight to feel hands now on my skin, mindless with lust as fingers, hands roughly explored my achingly wet core.

"Christ, Fae."

I opened my eyes then as his mouth left mine to utter those words. A sea of dark unreadable emotions met my gaze. His face harsh, cruel almost. One hand was pleasuring me, fingers plunging deep inside, forcing me to buck and writhe against the motion. The other hand cupping the back of my neck, thumb pressing ever so slightly against my jawline.

He watched the expressions so clearly revealed, fly over my face as easily as clouds across the sky on a breezy day. All the while his face was stormy, unyielding. Ungiving. Even the giving of his touch was somehow measured as though he enjoyed seeing me so abandoned and in need, knowing that he was the source of such desperation.

And desperate was the word here.
Desperate to fall into oblivion.
Desperate to scream with release.

He sensed the moment, as my body began to arch like a bow, knees giving way, my head tilting back, throat exposed, primal noises ripping out from my soul. The hand on the back of my head moved to my mouth. My eyes went wide as he covered my lips with his hand and warning look in his gaze.

I felt anger and rage then at the same time I felt the waves of orgasm begin to crash through me. Unrelenting, he drove in deeper with his fingers, his hand, pushing me further and further, all the while forcing me to remain silent. I bit against his hand, saw his eyes narrow, felt his other hand deeper, rougher still punishing me with a last brutal climax that had tears streaming from my eyes.

Sated in body, but denied in heart and soul, I went limp, unable it seemed to support my own weight on legs that had lost all bone and muscle. I had never felt so intensely fucked and at the same time so deprived. Utter torture. But it was not over yet. Breaking the silence his words were like bullets from a gun.
"I need to come. Suck me."
Dazed.
Drunk.
Doomed.
I could only nod my head at him weakly and slide down in a wobbly heap to my knees. He was quick to unfasten his trousers, quick to release himself, quick to get hold of my head and guide me into place.
Someone else had invaded my body.
This could not be me, on my knees giving someone a blow job whilst their hands tangled in my hair forcing me to take in as much as I could, more, than was comfortable.
This absolutely was not Fae Winters submitting to the urge to please and to give, all the while feeling, knowing, that I was being used.
It had always been the other way round.
With each suck, each lick of his shaft, each stroke of my tongue, I felt my heart begin to splinter as the awareness grew inside me that I would do anything, anything at all to please this man. I hated myself as much, I realised, as I had fallen so stupidly, wildly, uncontrollably in love with him.
But I couldn't stop.
I couldn't pull away, even if I had been able to.
I could no more deny him this pleasure than I could deny myself the air that I breathed.
I gave him all I had and then some more until with a juddering jolt he came, filling my mouth, demanding I swallow as his hands kept their hold. I coughed, I half choked. His hands held my head until every last drop had been shot from him and taken down my throat.
Hot, salty, the very essence of the man and greedily I took it. If that was all I could have of him, then I would take it and savour it. At the same moment I swallowed, my mind was once more screaming at me as though I was another person entirely.

Get the fuck up off your knees Fae Winters!

Tears streamed down my face.

My whole body was shaking, and I struggled to get to my feet. The hands that had been clasped around my head, holding me roughly in place reached for my arms to pull me up. He had tucked himself back into his trousers, zipped up and no signs on his face at all that he had just let himself go with a woman he had accused of being a witch. A woman he had once more treated like a whore.

Unloving.

Ungiving.

Cool sea-coloured eyes, more grey than blue right now looked hard into mine. I had the sense he was about to say something equally as condemning as the look on his face, but there was a sudden flare of light that softened his expression. Was it, I wondered, because my lips were trembling? Was it because of the tears rolling silently down my cheeks? Was it because I was shaking as though I was in shock?

Whatever it was, it undid me even more.

To be handed a tissue, to gently be guided to a chair, to feel a comforting hand on my shoulder was more than I could bear. A damn broke and there I was, howling my eyes out, keening like a woman in mourning. I was, I realised.

A woman mourning for the sister she had killed.

A woman mourning the mother she had grown up without.

A woman mourning the loss of herself in guilt.

A woman mourning the love that she had just realised was way beyond her reach, no matter what her soul told her.

A dozen tissues and what seemed like an age later, I finally raised my head, careless now that I must look an utter mess. He seated himself in a chair opposite me and had the calm air of someone with nothing else in the world to do right at that moment, other than to be fully present and focused on the snuffling, tear sodden wreck in front of him. I felt about six inches small, and yet when he spoke, he made me feel suddenly taller in my chair.

"You have never grieved for her, have you?"

I remembered that night, how he had spotted Fliss's photo. How that had been the moment when he had lost the battle within himself and stayed. That moment of gentle heart compassion that had turned into wild physical passion.

I shook my head, shredding the last remaining tissue I had in my hands.

"Why can you not forgive yourself?"

I stiffened and my eyes must have shown alarm.

Calmly, he went on. "I read all the reports in the newspapers, checked you out before offering you the job here. You were not to blame for her death were you."

He was good.

He was bloody good.

He had no need of psychic ability to get through a persons' defences.

The subtle change of intonation at the end of the sentence. The invisible question mark. You were not to blame for her death, were you?

My heart pounded and not with unrequited love.

It thumped painfully in my chest with fear.

Banged resolutely against the walls of my ribcage, demanding that I release the burden held within. Somehow, I won that battle. I found a tiny remaining sliver of backbone, sat up straighter, sniffed back my tears and reminded my head that, it could cock to one side and yes, my chin could tilt up, and look, my eyes could hold that stare.

Well done, Fae.

Not sure it made up for how I had completely demeaned myself in front of him, but hey some self-respect at last was better than none at all.

"Of course not," I lied as I always had.

He chose not to press it at that point. Instead, just when I thought I was regaining lost ground, he brought the conversation back to that minefield of a topic. "Are you a witch?"

"Of course not," I lied once more.

We both jumped then as the door, which I had locked and should still have been locked, suddenly opened and slammed shut, an icy draught entering the room.

"You are a witch. We are both witches."

"Fae?"

How I managed to do it, I do not know, but I gave the most careless of shoulder shrugs. He let out an exasperated sigh as though he knew I was lying. Seemingly unconcerned that the door had developed a mind of its' own, he stood up and went to relock it, and then once more in his seat, he carried on talking as though nothing strange had happened at all.

"You are clearly psychic at the very least. I am well aware that Maypoleton has a draw for energies of this kind. Craig will have told you that the skeleton you discovered was not the first to be found locally, and in that instance, there was a case of supernatural energies being disturbed. His wife was nearly killed because of it."

I had to show my astonishment. Eve? Really? That chirpy, flirty woman with the laughing eyes and happy smile always on her face? What on earth had she got involved with? Before I could ask, and to be honest I think he would not have told me anyway, he continued with a clear warning in his voice.

"I accept there are many things in this life that we cannot explain. I am not afraid in any way. And if you do consider yourself to be a witch," he held up a hand to halt my protest, "Fae, please don't lie to me again, you do yourself a disservice in doing so. There is a fully functioning coven right here in Maypoleton, so I do know that witchcraft is alive and kicking right here in this present day. All I am going to say, is this. I absolutely will not tolerate any behaviour, or actions that may bring harm to anyone within this parish. Do I make myself clear?"

I shrugged again, clearly irritating him.

"Fae?" he looked at me warningly and I remembered the five men he had floored.

"You have made yourself clear," I said with a somewhat throaty voice. "I promise I am not a witch, and I would never do anything to harm anyone in this village."

His eyes narrowed but at that point there was nothing else he could really say, other than to drive a white-hot dagger into my heart by adding, "What happened before, I am a healthy male, you are a healthy woman. We have needs. We are human. It should not have happened. It did. It will not happen again."

The coldness of it lit a new fire within my soul.

A fire of anger, pain and rejection.
A fire that was going to run amok and cause havoc.
"Of course," I said nonchalantly as though my heart was not being shredded into pieces and then cruelly discarded. "May I go?"
He nodded and I stood up. Then, just to mess with my mind and emotions even more, he said in that wickedly gentle tone of voice that was so utterly devastating. "Fae, anytime you do wish to talk about your sister, I will always be here to listen. Forgiveness of yourself is the key to peace in your heart."
Fortunately, I had my back to him because I am not sure what my face must have looked like. I just nodded and opened the door. As I did so the voice was as clear as though someone was standing right next to me, echoing my words of earlier, with a distinctive note of mischief in them.
"I'm a witch, I'm a bitch."
Eliza.
The woman whose body had lain hidden in the grounds of the vicarage for centuries. Present with me now, in all but physical form. Her energy had joined us in the library. A confusing, swirling, cyclone of energy that was wrapping around me and sending me dizzy. Not what I needed on top of the shattering encounter I had just had with Gawain. I needed even less to then be confronted with the dragon as I made my way across the hallway to go back to Arthur's room.
"I see that the Reverend has made it quite clear then?"
Mrs Mannering stood before me, brandishing a long handled sweeping brush as though it were a weapon. She eyed the evidence of my crying with satisfaction. "We don't stand for any of that heathen wickedness here. He's far too tolerant of that dreadful bunch of women in the village, they should be banned from cavorting in the manner they do. But rest assured my girl, there will be no cavorting of that kind under this roof. I hope that's now clear to you." She began to sweep the parquet floor tiles with anger in her movements.
I thought of what had just occurred only a few feet away. The stinging pain of rejection brought the spark of rebellion to the fire in my soul. "I will cavort in any way I wish to, with whomever I wish to, wherever I wish to." Ignoring the fact that I

knew my eyes were red and swollen, I held her stare. "I hope that is clear to you." My voice was as icy as the temperature suddenly became.

I saw her shiver. I saw the broom being torn from her hands and tossed wildly across the hallway, just as Gawain walked through the door. It hit him in the chest. Mrs Mannering's face was a picture of shock and fear. I hoped my own expression was neutral as I endeavoured to hide my surprise. That had not been of my doing.

"Mrs Mannering? Are you quite alright?" Gawain calmly picked up the broom and looked at his housekeeper with concern in his eyes.

"I......I…..she….," the dragon stuttered as her eyes went from me to Gawain and her finger pointed at me. "She did it, she's a witch!"

Gawain looked at me sharply, the warning he had only just given me very clear in his eyes.

I am good at shrugging. In fact, I would say I excel at this gesture. I gave perhaps one of my best with a roll of my eyes for good measure.

"I have no idea what she is on about. Now if you don't mind, Arthur's morning has been disrupted enough, he will be waiting for me to continue reading to him."

"Fae." My back was already turned as he called my name. "Remember what I said."

I did not bother to reply as I opened the door to Arthur's room.

Eliza did. Hissing out the words in fury. *"I remember everything. Everything!"*

Only I could hear her, and I wondered what she meant. For now, though I needed to focus on getting a grip on my emotions. There was too much going on in my life that was a mess without having the time or energy to worry about the feelings of a centuries old ghost. And perhaps it highlighted the depth of my feelings for Gawain and the turmoil this created within me, that I paid no heed.

Which of course was a mistake.

The warning signs were there.

I stupidly ignored them.

CHAPTER TWENTY-TWO

"You know I am close friends with Eve, so you will know that I have no problem whatsoever with her witchy goings on."

Laura was sitting at the kitchen table in Aunty Ruth's house. She had brought round the most sumptuous chocolate cake that she had baked herself. How she found the time to bake on top of juggling her role as head teacher and mother of two sets of twins was beyond me. I had every admiration and a genuine fondness for her, which is why I felt so relaxed as she began the conversation.

"I think I know what you are going to say." I smiled to put her at her ease. "Do you take sugar in your tea?"

"Just one please. I know I shouldn't. Mark is always going on at me to lose weight, but sometimes you just need that little bit of something don't you?"

I hid my distaste at the thought of her husband. What a muppet! "Absolutely and a chocolate cake like this definitely classes as a lovely bit of something. Right, one cup of tea and one slice of cake. Aunty Ruth is at the stables with Treacle so we can have a nice cosy chat and let me put your mind to rest. I am not a witch."

Again, the lie.

I paused for a second and wondered if I was going to receive a rebuke from Eliza as I had in the library with Gawain. All was quiet so I went on.

"Really I am not," I said in response to Laura's raise of the eyebrows. "I am psychic yes. I can hardly deny that. I knew that there was a skeleton buried in the vicar's garden, but that's all there is. And I promise that when I look after the twins on a Wednesday night, there will be no witchy goings on, cos of course I am not a witch. I guess that is what you are worried about?"

Laura finished her mouthful of cake, nodding as she did so. "You understand don't you. I love Eve to bits and find her fascinating, if a little scary at times. But being the head teacher of the primary school and a church school at that, I have to walk a certain line."

I smiled warmly at her. "We all have to walk a certain line." Mine was covering up who and what I was.

A witch responsible for the death of her twin sister. A witch capable of not only discovering an ancient skeleton, but also of bringing her spirit back into existence. A witch who was stupidly, disastrously, in love with a vicar. A witch who was feeling the sting of bitter rejection and therefore not as grounded as she should have been. In other words, I was a witch not in control of my emotions and therefore my power; a dangerous state of play but not one that I was ready to admit, either to myself or to Laura.

We chatted in general, and it became abundantly clear that Laura was a woman who had no idea of her own worth. Little comments she let slip drew a picture of a narcissistic husband who was not going to be satisfied until he had worn away her self-belief. But there was a hint of steel in Laura that was helping her to stand her ground and not give way to his demands to relinquish her role as head teacher.

"I adore my children, I really do," she said as I poured us both a second cup of tea and cut another slice of cake. "But I would go round the bend if I didn't have my work. I need to be active; I need to do something for myself!"

"Of course you do," I said encouragingly. "And I am more than happy to help on Wednesday evenings and any other time for that matter when I am not with Arthur. I like to be busy too."

Laura gave me a sly smile. "Yes, but Fae, surely you don't want to tie up all your free time. I mean you must want to have a personal life of your own." Her soft brown eyes lit up with interest. "Come on, your turn to share. Is there a man in your life back home? I kind of hope not to be honest. I am hoping you will stay here with us in Maypoleton." She looked at me over the rim of her mug and waited for my answer.

I found it difficult to speak. Absurdly tears filled my eyes. Pain stabbed me in the heart.

"Oh love, I am sorry. Did you come here to get over a relationship?" She put down her mug and her hand reached across the table for mine, a gesture of sisterhood. The knowing how it felt to have a broken heart.

Did I have a broken heart?

Was this why I was such an emotional wreck these days?

Bad enough to have a brutally bruised ego, thanks to both Gawain and Matt's attitude towards me. But to have the crashing realisation that I had stupidly given my heart to Gawain and yes it was torn, ripped into pieces, was way out of my sphere of understanding. I crumpled some more and with tears rolling down my face, I nodded. Better to let her think I had left behind someone who had hurt me, then have her know the humiliating truth.

"Bloody men hey?" Laura gave my hand a little squeeze. "And what an idiot he must be to let you go!"

I gave a snort at this and gently withdrawing my hand from hers, wiped away my tears.

She continued. "You are one of the most stunningly beautiful women I have met, any man who turns you down needs his head seeing to. But these things happen love, and I know this is perhaps not what you want to hear right now, but I do believe everything happens for a reason." Her face took on a bright expression. "And maybe that reason was because you were meant to come to Maypoleton, and maybe you are going to find true love right here in the village!"

How that shard of glass twisted in my heart, shredding some more, bleeding out some more. "Not really looking for a man right now." Fae really, do you ever stop lying?

"I know you probably feel that way, but the best way to get over a broken heart is to look for love with someone else. That's how it was with me and Mark," she said. "I had just been dumped by someone I thought was the love of my life, a right bastard he was too. And then I met Mark. And look how happy I am now!" She nodded her head at me enthusiastically and there was a smile on her face but somehow the light in her eyes was not quite as bright as it should have been. "I tell you what, let's get together with Eve and have a night out. We could even go into Lancaster; I used to go there all the time before the twins were born."

In the past the thought of a night out with a couple of lively female friends in search of prey, would have been at the top of my agenda. Now when I considered this, all that was in my head, was the memory of that night back in January. The night I had met Gawain.

"If you don't mind, I really don't feel up to that." Fae what the hell has he done to you? How has he turned you into such a pile of mush?

"Alright, don't worry, I won't push you on that. But maybe………"

"What?"

"Well maybe there is someone right here for you?"

Another twist of that glass in my heart. "I don't think so."

Laura looked thoughtful. "What about Matt? He's single. And such a lovely bloke."

I choked on my tea. "Sorry, went down the wrong way," I said when I finished coughing. "No. I mean yes, I agree, he is a lovely bloke." And a bloody good shag, I thought to myself, remembering the frequent times we had been together. But I also could remember blisteringly clearly, how he had called out Laura's name whilst making love to me. No correction, whilst having sex with me. Matt had never made love to me.

A shudder ran through my entire body as another thunderbolt hit me.

No man had ever made love to me.

Apart from that night with Gawain.

Despite his reactions since, there was an element of my soul that screamed loudly at me that there had been more between us than just sex. A connection of some kind that went far deeper than the physical. Something had touched us both that night.

I knew it.

Felt it.

Believed it.

So how could I have got it all so fucking wrong? My head was beginning to hurt.

"So how about it then? You and Matt I mean?" Laura was looking at me encouragingly. "Maybe you could ask him for a coffee or something?" She looked so excited at the idea I felt a real glump for letting her down.

"I'm sorry. I really don't feel up to that right now. And honestly, I don't think Matt sees me in that way at all." Cos he is madly in love with you!

"Oh, that's a shame. Never mind. Hhm, who else is there, let me think." She pursed her lips and blew out a breath. "I mean there is Gawain of course. He is single. But then there is Lucinda."

Lucinda, the woman I had met the other day with Arthur. The attractive young mother and widow who just happened to help at the Sunday school. A proper picture of virtue. A perfect match for a vicar.

"Lucinda?" I said casually.

"Yes. Lovely woman. I mean they are not dating as such, or so I believe. But it's pretty obvious that she likes him and to be fair, who wouldn't! Such a gorgeous man, ridiculously sexy for a vicar! Anyway, there is a lot of speculation that they will get together and most people in the village agree they would be a really good match. But we think that Gawain is waiting until she has had more time to grieve for her husband." She grinned at me. "Which maybe gives you time to make a move?"

I thought of all the moves I had made so far.

I thought of his cold reactions.

I thought of his brutal rejections.

That cruel shard of glass that seemed embedded in my heart gave another violent twist. The pain of it shot down to my stomach, twisting and turning in my gut until the tea and cake churned up into a nauseating concoction.

"Are you alright?"

I nodded.

"You don't look alright. You look as though you are about to be….."

I was.

I shot past Laura and thankfully made it to the tiny downstairs loo just in time. Head into the bowl of the toilet, I was suddenly and wretchedly sick. Tremors ran through my body as the spams worked on emptying my stomach.

"Oh, you poor love. Here, let me rinse this cloth out then you can wipe your face. There you go. It's alright, take your time."

Laura's warmth and caring was too much. For the second time in a couple of days I was reduced to a blubbering mess of emotions. We went back into the kitchen. Laura poured me a glass of water and placed it on the table before me and then got on with clearing away the tea and cake. "Do you want to talk?"

I sniffled and snuffled and shook my head. "I'm fine honestly. Sorry about that. Don't know what came over me."

"The bastard really did a job on you didn't he?" For the first time since meeting her, a flinty expression came into Laura's eyes.

"Sorry?"

"The bloke who broke your heart, the fellow back home. He really messed you up. Bastard," she said again with feeling.

I let my head fall onto the table, hair spilling out messily and groaned. Fae Winters get a bloody grip woman! How the freaking hell had I got myself into this state? I no longer recognised who I was. Fleetingly I thought of all the men I had so cruelly discarded and had the awful realisation that perhaps this was no more than I deserved.

The Law of Threefold.

I snorted and groaned.

Stupid, stupid, stupid Fae.

I had brought this all on myself. Do as thou will and harm to none. The Wiccan law. I had certainly done as I wanted, but I had never once considered the harm I was doing to others, either the men I was using, or the wives and girlfriends that I was perhaps inflicting pain on.

The law of threefold.

That which you create, comes back to you threefold.

Or more.

This was definitely a case of more! I groaned and raised my head. Thank goodness my aunt and uncle were at the stables. It was bad enough to feel so exposed in front of Laura. I felt distinctly uncomfortable as I looked at her. I was not used to letting myself go. I had never allowed myself to get close to any female friends. I remembered how I had not even told Annie about Fliss.

Thinking about Annie, I wondered how she was faring with her pregnancy. Some bloody friend I was! I had been here two months now and my contact with her had been minimal. She would be about six months pregnant, a lovely bump visible, her bonny face blooming with the joy of the new live she was carrying.

I had a flash of seeing her in my mind's eye, cosying up on her sofa with Shane, laughing as they turned the pages of a baby name book. They were playfully arguing over what names to choose. Shane wanted Rory for a boy and Molly for a girl. Annie agreed with Rory but not Molly. Her choice for a girl's name was Jennifer Fae. A waterfall of emotions drenched me as I saw this scene with my third eye as clear as though I was sitting in the room with them.

I hated, absolutely hated that the primary emotion was jealousy.

That evil serpent had well and truly wrapped itself around my heart and was squeezing tight. Rampaging through me was the overwhelming knowledge that all I had ever truly wanted, was to have what Annie had. A loving husband and a child with him. Was that really too much to ask for?

Thoughts flew back to Fliss and what I had deprived her of. A chance of any kind of life.

Yes Fae, it was, it is, too much to ask for. You don't deserve any kind of happiness in your life. You stole that of your sisters. The gods are never going to allow you to experience the simple bliss of family life. I knew it and understood it.

Accepted it?

At the moment, it was hurting too fucking much to accept but I was resigned to the knowledge that I had no choice. I thought of Gawain and the attractive Sunday school teacher with the ready-made family. I pictured them together, knowing that this was more than likely what the gods and the Universe had in mind.

Yet another choking stranglehold of jealousy.

Accepted it?

No fucking way.

"I'm a witch I'm a bitch."

I heard again in my head the replay of Eliza's words, echoing mine. I felt the emotions that had been behind those words and knew that it was the mirror of my own. Hurt, pain, rejection, anger, hate even. Heavy dark emotions that could pull a person into a very dangerous place indeed.

Especially if you are a witch.

All of this whizzed through my mind in a matter of moments, a cauldron of chaos brewing deep within me. I gave myself a little shake as I realised that Laura was looking at me oddly.

"Are you sure you are alright Fae? You really don't look good at all."

No wonder, I thought. I was poisoned by my own thoughts and actions.

"I'm fine."

Her face was a picture.

I had to smile. "Alright, I am not fine. But I am if you know what I mean." I heaved a big sigh. "Okay I admit it. The bastard did a really good job on me. He totally fucking broke my heart. Tore right into it, shredded it, and then tossed the pieces onto the fucking scrap heap."

"Bastard!" We said this together and at least I could laugh. A little.

"Oh, honey we have all been there," Laura said, once more reaching for my hand in that gesture of sisterhood. "Some of us more than once," she added ruefully. "But the pain will ease, trust me on that. It will take time don't get me wrong, but it will ease."

"I hope you are right on that cos I fucking hate feeling this way. My emotions are all over the fucking place, I can't stop crying, I feel physically shattered. I have never been so tired in my life, which is so not like me. I keep feeling sick at random times, mind you that can be the after effects of the psychic stuff. But yeah, I admit, I feel totally utterly fucking crap!"

It was a relief to say it.

Laura's face took on another interesting expression.

"What?"

She opened her mouth to speak. Shut it again and looked at me consideringly.

"Go on, spit it out."

"Well, I was just wondering if there was any possibility….."

She didn't get to finish her sentence as the doorbell rang.

I got up to answer the door and found Eve standing there. "Oh hi, Aunty Ruth's at the stables with Uncle Eric."

Eve smiled at me. A very knowing smile. "It's you I have come to see. May I?"

"Of course," I stood back to let her in. "Come through. Laura's here. We were just having a brew and some cake. Would you like some?"

"I never say no to a brew and cake, especially if Laura has made it." Eve followed me through to the kitchen and hugged her friend before sitting down at the table. I brewed up once more and cut Eve some cake and then sat down wondering what she wanted to talk to me about.

"So?" I asked with a raise of my eyebrows. "What was it you wanted to see me about?"

She gave a little mischievous smile. "I may be wrong, but I was picking up on a lot of energy and I felt I had to come and see you."

Eve, like me was psychic. Eve, like me had uncovered a skeleton right here in Maypoleton. I felt slightly uneasy at what else Eve may be able to discern.

"Go on."

She tilted her head back and there was a little pause before she spoke. Her words when they came hit me like a thunderbolt from the gods.

"I think you may be pregnant."

CHAPTER TWENTY-THREE

"That's just what I was about to say!" Laura exclaimed, looking delighted at the bomb her friend had just dropped.
They looked at me with eager expressions.
I sat there locked in place, not able to move and absolutely, not able to think. Every cell in my body and brain seemed to have momentarily frozen in place. The kitchen clock punctuated my silence, ticking away for what seemed like ages but was perhaps only thirty seconds or so, a minute at the most.
"I'm sorry," said Eve, looking quite the opposite. Her smile resembled that of a cat having its bellyful of cream. "I perhaps should not have blurted it out quite like that. Craig is always telling me my mouth gets me into trouble at times."
"Which it does," Laura commented affectionately.
"Which it does," agreed Eve.
"So?" They both leant forwards a little towards me.
I unglued my tongue from the roof of my mouth. "So?"
"Are you pregnant?" Eve's swirly green, blue, brownish eyes were dancing with merriment and anticipation. "Mabel has been working with me and the girls at the coven to heighten our intuitive knowledge. I was in the kitchen making Craig's tea and I could feel all this energy coming from here. I knew there was something going on. So, I went through everything that Mabel had taught us and bang, there it was like an explosion in my mind, the thought, no not thought, the *knowing* that you are pregnant."
Bloody Mabel and her bloody coven!
Bloody Eve wanting to experiment with her talents.
Bloody bloody hell was there any truth in it?
"You are already changed."

I remembered with a sudden jolt, yes with that deep sense of *knowing* that Eve talked about, what Rowan had said to me in the graveyard.

Rowan, my birth mother. *"You are already changed."*

I did that classic thing. I dropped my hands to my belly. Clasped them around the new life that was growing there.

In wonder.

In awe.

In total fucking fear!

"No." I shook my head and stood up abruptly, the noise of my chair scraping against the tiled kitchen floor, as harsh as my denial. Turning my back to the pair of them I went to the sink and poured another glass of water. I closed my eyes as I drank it and tried to think straight. "You are wrong. I am not pregnant."

Another silence in the room and I imagined Laura and Eve exchanging a meaningful look whilst I tried to ignore the impossible truth.

Eventually Laura spoke, her words delivered more gently than Eve's excited outburst. "Are you sure there is no chance. You said yourself just minutes ago how dreadful you have been feeling of late. How tired and emotional. Sick at odd times. All those are common signs of pregnancy."

I wasn't having it. Contrary to my earlier thoughts about Annie, my jealousy over her cosy situation, the notion that I may be pregnant was just not something to consider. For one thing, who the fuck was the father?

Shit!

I rapidly tried to think whilst all the time my mind was screaming in denial. Sweat began to form on my body and a buzzing began to fill my ears.

"Fae, are you alright?" Laura was behind me. Her hands gentle on my shoulders as she guided me back to my chair. A couple of minutes must have passed as I sat there, face in my hands, not looking at them.

Finally, I could speak. "I can't be pregnant." I let out a huge sigh of relief. At last, my brain cells had co-operated. Raising my head, I looked them both square in the face and shrugged my shoulders. "I am on the pill."

"So was I," said Laura carefully. "With Tammy and Tilly. I had a sick bug and threw up my pill for a couple of days. Mind you I sort of wanted to get pregnant again, so I as soon as I could I took a test and hey ho, my second set of twins."

"Besides," Eve butted in, "regardless of sick bugs, the pill is only 99 percent reliable." She flashed me a grin. "There is always that one percent. Could be you."

Damn her, I thought, returning her grin with a scowl. She was bloody wishing this disaster on me.

Disaster?

Fae, a while ago you were desperately wishing you could experience what Annie had. Exactly! My mind argued. Annie had a loving husband. If I was pregnant, then it could be with either of two men, both of which pretty much despised me. If that wasn't a disaster, I didn't know what was!

"Are there any other possible symptoms?" Laura went on with her careful probing.

Eve was less careful. "Yeah, sore boobs, tight jeans?"

Holy fuck.

Eve's eyes shone with glee. "Yes! You see, you are."

I shook my head again, at the same time, reluctantly acknowledging these two facts. I had put the slight increase in my waist and fuller breasts, down to Aunty Ruth's good home cooking.

"You are already changed." Rowan, my mother, knew from beyond the grave. She had told me herself.

In a soft tone of voice, Laura asked, "Is it the man you were involved in back home? The one who broke your heart?"

Eve flashed a look at her and then at me. "Oh hon, sorry. Have you been shafted? Dumped?"

Had I? Not really. Used like a prostitute. Paid like a prostitute. Despised as though I was a prostitute. Did that fall into the same category? I was totally out of my depth here. Drowning in a sea of utter confusion and overwhelm! I was pregnant and two men could be the father.

"You are already changed."

I thought back to arriving at Maypoleton. I remembered with stunning clarity that first and only time I had been to church with

Aunty Ruth. Setting eyes on Gawain in the pulpit. Fainting spectacularly at the altar as I went for communion. Gawain was the father of my child.

My soul lit up with a rush of emotion that was new to me. I could only imagine it was joy. I had never felt like this before. As though my heart had suddenly become alive, was beating properly for the first time ever. A heart breaking out of its frozen prison where it had been locked up and lonely since that cold dark night so long ago.

The thirty first of January, the year that Fliss and I were both fifteen. That momentous day when I asked Fliss to take my place. I was grounded, not allowed out. I didn't just ask Fliss. I begged her. Pushed her to pretend to be me and meet bad boy Joel Sparrowhawk. Just so I could work my love spell. Just so I could take what I wanted. Something that didn't belong to me as he already had a girlfriend. She hadn't wanted to go. But she did. Because she loved me.

And she ended up with a knife in her belly.

I felt that visceral pain again and gasped in shame, guilt, and grief.

Clasped my hands to my belly, remembering the thirty first of January this year. How I had prowled the promenade late at night, looking for trouble, looking for a pain that would assuage that shame, guilt and grief. I nearly got it, so close to being gang raped. Instead, I had ended up with Gawain Temple in my bed. And now not only was he lodged firmly in my heart; his child was growing inside me.

"I am pregnant." I let the words fall softly into the awaiting silence. They sounded strange to my ears. Thankfully neither Eve nor Laura said a word. I experimented with the words again. "I am pregnant. This time with more conviction. I am a witch. I believe in the power of three. "I am pregnant."

"And so it is!" Rowan's voice was crystal clear. My mother's presence was there with me. Her joy filtered through to me. A blessing from a mother to a daughter, the best of blessings for what is more precious perhaps than for a mother to see her own daughter becoming a mother, fulfilling the deepest most primeval role it is possible for a woman to fulfil. A stupid grin must have appeared upon my face for suddenly Laura and Eve

were laughing with me, high fiving and clustering around to envelop me in a congratulatory hug.

"Oh my God, Fae, you're going to have a baby!" Laura was in tears herself now.

"I knew it!" Eve raised her fist in the air, perhaps more of an acknowledgment of her intuition being on target than anything else. "Wait 'til I tell Mabel."

"No!" My exclamation was sudden and loud. "Bloody hell no."

"What?" The two women sat back down. Eve was regarding me closely.

"No, no, no, no no." I shook my head as though my verbal denial was not enough. "Noooooo."

"No what?" Eve pressed.

I stood up then and began to pace around the kitchen. "How the fuck can I have a baby?" Christ Fae you make a mess of looking after yourself, what the hell chance did a child have with you? "I can't. I mean it's ridiculous. A baby should have a proper home, a proper family. I'm just a………."

"You're just a what, Fae?" Laura this time, with a cautioning hand on her friend to tread more softly perhaps.

I shrugged my shoulders at them. My own words and those of Eliza's came back to taunt me. I'm a witch, I 'm a bitch. Hardly something I could share with them. Instead. "I'm just a fuck up."

Eve snorted. "Trust me Fae, you are so not a fuck up. If you want to know what a fuck up is, let me tell you….."

"Perhaps another time." Again, Laura stepped in, pressing the pause button on whatever Eve was going to share. In a very practical tone of voice, she did her best to reassure me. "Fae, women have children by themselves every day. This is not the Middle Ages. You are not going to be ostracised for being pregnant out of wedlock!"

"I'm not bothered about that!"

"Then what? If it's the finances then the father must help, even if you are not in a relationship with him," said Eve and then added, perhaps not so helpfully, "even if he is the cockwombling twat that dumped you."

Laura frowned at her. I had to laugh. I was beginning to like Eve more and more. Her outspoken bluntness was something I could relate to.

"I think what Eve is trying to say," said Laura, "Is that there is help and support for you. You don't have to do this alone. And yes, practically, the first thing to consider, assuming of course that you are going to keep the baby…"

"Of course she is!" Eve interrupted her, looking astonished at the suggestion that I might not. "You are, aren't you?"

As terrified as I was at the thought of being pregnant, the knowledge that there was a life growing inside me, there was no bloody way I could get rid of it. I had been responsible for one death. The weight of that guilt had driven me to the edge of despair and back so many times. A sudden overwhelming thought that this was forgiveness and maybe, just maybe, a release from that guilt, washed over me. My legs began to shake, and I sat back down.

"More tea?" Laura asked in a motherly, practical voice.

I nodded and there was a peaceful pause as she bustled about Aunty Ruth's kitchen and cut yet another slice of cake to accompany the brew.

"Eating for two now honey," said Eve with a mischievous grin as I tucked in to the chocolate concoction.

"I don't have that excuse," said Laura ruefully, "and I need to lose weight, but sod it."

"You don't need to lose weight!"

Eve and I laughed as we both blurted this out together. Then of course it was back to me and the baby.

"I can support myself," I said slowly, with a touch of clarity thankfully returning to my thoughts. "I have been left some money." I explained about Mr Carlisle's will.

"Wow!" Eve nodded her head in appreciation of this and then in her quick-witted way remarked, "Not surprised you were accused of murder. I bet the relatives were totally pissed off at you!"

"Eve!" Laura slapped her on the wrist

I had to agree. "She's right though." I grinned. "Totally pissed off. But thanks to the lovely soul that was Mr Carlisle, when the probate has been sorted there will be enough for me to buy a little house. At least I won't have to worry about paying a mortgage or finding the money for rent."

"Ooh, I think there may be a house coming up for sale on Tanners Yard. Susie Watkins was telling me the other day that she is thinking of moving back down south to be nearer her mother. She'll be looking for a quick sale if she does. Lovely little house, very like this one."

"Perfect!" Eve nodded in agreement.

"I'm not sure staying in Maypoleton is the right idea." I said very slowly.

"Why not?" Blunt and to the point, Eve fixed me with that peculiar swirly gaze of hers.

Hoping to hell there was a veil over my eyes, I struggled to reply.

"Maybe it's better for Fae to be back down south herself, close to the baby's father. Even if you are no longer in a relationship with him, you may want him to have some involvement with the baby, and for the child's sake perhaps as he or she grows up?" Laura as ever, the voice of wisdom.

Another hammer blow to the heart.

What was Gawain going to say?

Could I even tell him? The fact that I was pregnant was not something I could hide, as good at keeping secrets as I was. But could I tell him that he was the father? Would he want to know? I suspected that knowing what I did of him, which at this point was very little and all of that very conflicting, was that he would view this as a responsibility that he would not shirk.

He would step up to the mark.

He would do his duty.

He would fulfil his obligations.

Did I want to be an obligation? Fuck no! Again, my hands went to my belly. This was my child. The gods in their wisdom had decided that I was fit to be a mother. Then be a mother I would. But that did not necessarily mean that the father had to be involved. I closed my eyes imaging the look in Gawain's should he hear the truth. I could see so clearly the initial moment of wonder followed so swiftly by the horror that he could be stuck with a woman he despised.

No.

That was not going to happen. Could I bear to stay here though and be so close to him? Just now that was not something I could answer. I was great at delaying dealing with things and that was most definitely something to be put on hold. For now, I had to get my head round the fact that I was going to have a baby.

I said as much to Laura and Eve. "One thing at a time I suppose. It's a huge thing to get my head around. For now, though, please don't say anything to anyone. I need to process this myself first."

"Absolutely," said Laura with a warning look at Eve. "And you also need to get yourself checked out with the doctor. We have a really good surgery here. Doctor Jay is lovely."

"She is," agreed Eve. "And you need to get a scan booked so you can find out the due date."

"I don't need a scan to tell me that."

I knew for a certainty when my baby would be born. The date of conception would forever be etched in my mind. It was the date that Fliss had died and the date when Gawain had spent the night with me. I did a quick count on my fingers. I felt something tingle deep inside.

"Samhain."

"I beg your pardon?" Laura looked at me.

Eve grinned and explained to her friend. "Samhain. Halloween."

"Oh, the thirty first of October. Gosh that means you are four months gone already."

A look was shared between them. I got it. More than likely, it was too late even if I had wanted a termination. A shudder ran through me at the thought. Yes, maternal instincts had kicked in. This little girl was going to be born at Samhain. How did I know it was a girl?

Rowan had told me. *"Daughter of Samhain."*

And I knew that she would be a very special child.

What I didn't know at that moment, was the disastrous chain of events that were going to play out before then, the chaos that was going to ensue and the lives that were going to be put at risk.

All because of my actions.

I knew none of that, so I sat there grinning with my hands on my belly.

I was going to give birth to a *"Daughter of Samhain,"* and nothing else mattered.

CHAPTER TWENTY-FOUR

You would think that having been accused of murder, losing my job, temporarily relocating to another part of the country, gaining employment with a man I had stupidly, irrevocably lost my heart to, and discovering I was pregnant by the same man, would be enough for the Universe to deal out to anyone in one go.

Apparently not.

There was the minor, or maybe not so minor matter of the skeleton that I had uncovered. The spirit of Eliza, whoever she had been, had also made an appearance in my life and whilst I fully understood that everything was supposed to happen for a reason, I was still hugely unprepared for how events rapidly began to unfold.

Had I known what wild cyclone of energy I was creating, I would have packed my bags that very next morning, got in my car and driven back down to the place I normally called home. Truth to tell, when I woke the day after my long tea, cake and confessional with Laura and Eve, I did consider this.

It was Sunday and I was not working. The beginning of June and the sun had crept through the gap in the curtains early. I slept with the window open, even in the middle of winter, and I could hear the dawn chorus, so much more vibrant here than back in my flat. Vibrant yet softer. No rowdy seagulls, more the melodic sing song of garden birds occasionally interspersed with the knowing caw of a raven.

I lay there in my bed, letting the sounds drift over me as I thought about my options. For a start I had to tell Aunty Ruth and Uncle Eric. Despite Laura and Eve's reaction and despite knowing how much my aunt and uncle loved me; I was anxious about how they would take my news.

I had lived so long with the heavy weight of guilt over Fliss's death and the knowledge that my parents, well Mum certainly, wished that I had been the one with the knife in my belly and not my sweet, gentle sister. Coming here to stay with Aunty Ruth had been a balm to that deeply wounded part of my soul. I was reluctant to spoil what I had found in this cocoon of cosiness. What if they were both disappointed in me? Especially as I could not tell them who the father was. I shuddered at the thought.

Hellfire, I thought with a reluctant giggle, and then giggled to myself some more. Hellfire and Damnation is what a lot of the villagers would wish upon me. How dare I lead their saintly vicar astray! The wicked side of my nature got the better for me for a short while. I imagined myself going into church and boldly standing up as he was about to preach his sermon and making my announcement.

No, no, no, Fae.

You are in enough trouble already.

Do not cause more.

Which of course I did, but I had no inkling at that moment how I was going to do so. I was more concerned about this initial hurdle that I had to somehow circumnavigate. And time of course was an issue. I ran my hands over my belly, still relatively flat, but definitely with more of a rounded shape to it than the concave smoothness I was used to and my breasts, as small as they might be, were overflowing the cups of my bras.

No avoiding it Fae.

Should I stay, or should I go?

That was the big question, and it was going round and round in my head. I sighed deeply, wishing I had someone to tell me what to do. Then I realised I did. Rowan would know. My mother would know. She knew I was pregnant. I heard the caw of a raven, very loud outside my window. Yes, she was telling me. Get the heck out of your bed and go and speak to your mother.

Flinging back the covers, I got up, quickly dressed in jeans and a hoodie with the slogan, "Don't mess with my chakras" went to the loo and cleaned my teeth. Staring at my reflection in the mirror I wondered I looked any different. I did. Peaky and off colour. I stuck my tongue out at the mirror. Not exactly blooming so far Fae!

Downstairs Aunty Ruth was already busy in the kitchen. She would be going to church later, and Uncle Eric would be off for his long Sunday morning run, but first there were the horses to attend to.

"Morning love, do you want come down to the yard with me?"

She automatically went about making me a cup of tea and popped a couple of slices of bread in the toaster. Eve would no doubt be at the stables with Sam. I wasn't sure I could cope with being in her presence not having told Aunty Ruth my news. I heard the raven again. A more pressing appointment was calling me.

I shook my head. "Not today if you don't mind. I want to go for a quiet little walk. Thanks," I said as she placed my tea and toast on the table, "and I want to have a chat my mother."

She frowned a little at this, discomfited perhaps that I could talk to spirits, that I was like Rowan in that way. "You know you can always talk to me Fae." She sat opposite me with her cup of tea and two slices of toast. "About anything. Me and your Uncle Eric will always support you in anything, you do know that don't you."

"Course we will poppet." Uncle Eric came into the room just then, dressed for now in his stable clothes but later he would be in running gear. "Whatever you need help with Fae, just ask."

Those wretched tears, threatened to make an appearance once more. Bloody hormones I thought with a grunt that made them both look at me oddly. "I'll tell you later," I said, realising that by now they both knew something was up. "I do want to go and spend some quiet time with my mother first though."

They shared a look but accepted this without comment.

"Fair enough love." Uncle Eric dropped a kiss on the top of my head. "I suppose it must be strange you being back here after all this time." He gave my shoulder a little squeeze. "But then you tell me and your Aunty what's meithering you, lass cos summat is." His Lancashire accent was always more pronounced when he cared about something, and I patted the hand that was on my shoulder.

"Thanks Uncle Eric. Thank you both of you. I will speak to you later, I promise."

The conversation then flowed a little easier as they moved onto my aunt's favourite topic which of course was Treacle and

Toffee. I then realised that it was not so much my aunt and uncle I was concerned about. It was more the reactions of some of the villagers. Especially those in the tight circles of the church. I didn't want my aunt to be subjected to vicious gossip once my condition become known.

Then I snorted to myself at the choice of word I had used. Condition! Bloody hell Fae you sound like a Victorian chamber maid who has got herself into trouble! With that thought in my head, I cleared away my pots, gave them both a hug and kiss and told them I would have a good chat later that day.

"Roast lamb for dinner," said Aunty Ruth as I headed to the door.

"My favourite." I flashed her a smile and felt a huge surge of love for her. I went back to give her another hug.

"It's not that special," she said returning my hug.

"No but you are."

"Go on with you, you daft thing."

Northern love. Northern warmth. Northern soul.

I was not a Lancashire lass born and bred as they said up here. I had been brought up on the South coast, but I had been born here. Was that what the raven was trying to tell me as she followed me to the churchyard. I was a northern soul, born here, and here I should stay, connected to my roots, to where I belonged.

Did I belong here?

Was this quirky, pretty little village, hidden away in the rugged rolling landscape of these fells, forests and hills, where I belonged? I hadn't felt like I had belonged anywhere since Fliss had died. I had not even wanted to be on this earth. Lost for such a long time, adrift in an endless sea of desolation and despair. Fate, the gods, as I liked to say, had brought me here, with a daughter in my womb. Was she supposed to be born here?

"Daughter of Samhain."

The words were a gentle kiss on the wind as I knelt in front of Rowan's grave. It was beautifully peaceful on this quiet early summer morning and I let the atmosphere wrap itself around me, carefully blocking out any voices from the dead other than the one I wished to hear.

"That's your answer, isn't it?" I sat back resting on my heels, legs folded beneath me, heedless of the still damp grass. "She will be born at Samhain and here is where she will be born."

A silent reply came to me then. A shift in the energy around me. Hard to explain other than I felt suddenly as though the air was lighter, the light was brighter, the pulsing of my heart gentled. A sense of *knowing* that this was the case and as such there was no more question or doubt in my mind that Maypoleton was where I was going to make my home.

My home with my child.

My home with my daughter.

My home with Gawain's daughter.

As though I had conjured him up with my thoughts, which no doubt I had, and maybe Rowan had a hand in this too, there he was. I felt his presence before I saw him. I knew he was approaching, even though his footsteps were silent on the dewy grass. The witch in me, that side of me that I denied, wanted him to know that I knew he was there.

I spoke before he could. "I have no memories of her." Psychic connection yes. Memories no.

"That must be difficult for you." His voice caring, compassionate. The voice of a vicar, not a lover.

I closed my eyes against the sting of tears. "Not really," I replied, still with my back to him. "You can't miss what you don't know." Another lie. Would I ever stop lying?

The raven flew close by, landed on a headstone, looked at me and cawed. I felt a lump in my throat, as though a stone was lodged there, waiting to choke me unless I expelled it "Not like Fliss. I miss her every single day. Every……..single……..day. I have felt so…… lost. Displaced. As though without her, I had no right to be alive. To be on this earth. To belong anywhere."

A long slow exhale drawn out with relief. It was almost dizzying to have let go of that burden. To have confided in him as I had the other day in the library. Behind me I felt his stillness.

I felt more than stillness.

I felt a pull of energy so strong it had me whipping my head round, despite me not wishing to look at him.

The raven cawed knowingly.

In that moment I saw.

Deep, dark, dangerous pain.

The mirror of mine reflected in his eyes.

The raven cawed knowingly.

Was he as stunned as I was by the revelation? And what exactly was being revealed?

The raven cawed knowingly and flew away.

Shaken, even more than before, I broke the contact and returned my gaze to Rowan's grave. I took my time as the thoughts softly evolved into words. "It feels right to be here now. This is where I was born. This is where I belong."

This is where my daughter will be born. Your daughter.

These words begged to be released but they would not fall gently from my tongue as the others had. They would shoot out like bullets from a gun. And I feared the ricochet effect. I hated to be scared about anything, but he created that fear within me.

"Ruth and Eric will be delighted," he spoke warmly sounding genuinely pleased although whether it was for my aunt and uncle, or for himself, it was hard to tell. "Your aunt has told me how much it would mean to her for you to stay. And it is always good to have a new member in my flock. I know you don't attend church with Ruth, but you are always welcome, you do know that don't you."

Kill me with kindness why don't you?

The caring, loving warmth in his voice.

For a member of his flock.

I stood up, wincing a little as pins and needles shot through my numb legs. "I don't think I am a flock kind of person." I turned to face him, bracing myself for the impact his presence had on me, that immediate kick of desire to the belly, that would be as clear as day on my face. Making sure I had a bland expression firmly in place, "I am more of a lone wolf kind of soul," I said lightly.

"Even a lone wolf needs a pack from time to time."

"Not this one."

Deep grey blue eyes probed into my soul. The connection between us was reflected in a darkening of his pupils. A tiny pulse of the muscle at the corner of his mouth drew my gaze to his lips. Big mistake as the longing to have his mouth on mine was sudden, intense.

"If not a pack, then a mate at least."

I was not mistaken. He felt it. I had not imagined it. There was a connection. There was a bond. My heart leapt joyously, and a curving smile replaced the empty mask on my face. From the depths of my belly, where my, our daughter nestled in place, I felt the words beginning to rise within me.

I am pregnant, with your daughter.

I could say them, let them fly from my heart.

I would see his eyes light up with wonder and love.

"There is always a chance for a new start Fae." He cleared his throat and gave his head a little shake as though to also clear his mind and reset his thoughts, apparent with his next words. "You do not have to carry on as you have been doing. You are worth more than that. And God willing you may find that love and peace here. You deserve to have a loving relationship in your life, Fae. We all do."

Confused slightly at the tone of his voice, back to that of a vicar I must have revealed too much in my face. Far too much. "Oh Fae." His turn now to let out a sigh and it was difficult to read the emotions behind it. "I am not the man for you."

"What?" Not exactly erudite I know but it was all I could blurt out.

A killing compassion. "I am not the man for you."

God knows what the expression in my eyes was now telling him, because I had no idea at that moment quite where my emotions were heading.

"I am not the man for you, Fae." He reached out a hand, to place it gently on my shoulder. A touch of consolation. "I know we have been intimate, and on both times that should not have happened. That is my weakness, not yours. But I do not see you as my partner."

Where the fuck had my pride gone?

I was crumpling again before him, my desperate need to have him wrap his arms around me, hold me safe, shelter me from life, from myself, was overwhelming. My lips began to wobble, and the treacherous tears threatened.

"Why not?" Hoarse words ripped from my throat.

He looked away.

Damn him he looked away!

He looked away to hide the lie in his eyes from me.

Angrily now I pressed the point. "Am I not good enough for you? Is that it? Because you are a vicar and I am a ….." I nearly, so nearly said, witch, then.

He misread my hesitation. "A fallen woman? Is that what you think you are Fae? A woman who throws herself at any man and so belittles her body and soul in doing so?"

"No!"

I glared at him, hurt and pain fuelling my anger. Because he was right. Partly. I had thrown myself at any man in the past, yes, and heaven help me I was being punished for it now because standing right before me was the only man I had ever given my heart to, and he was tossing it right back in my face.

He read the anger correctly and tried to console me which only made it worse. "Fae, you are a beautiful, courageous, caring woman. You are passionate, funny, strong, and yes dammit, Fae if it makes you feel better to hear it, you are as sexy as hell, and I cannot deny that I have been attracted to you."

"So why then? You must know how I feel about you?"

I pushed, I pressed, I demanded to hear another answer. He looked away again and when his gaze returned to mine, I could see he was having a battle with himself. Good, I thought, with a flame of hope burning in my heart.

He extinguished the flame. "I have met someone."

"What?"

"There is someone."

I shook my head. "No. You are single."

Damn him to hell for that boyish smile that flickered across his face. "At the moment, yes. But there is someone I am interested in."

"Interested? What the fuck does that mean?" I couldn't hold it in.

He frowned now as though I should not be questioning him. Rattled further, my defensive spikes coming to the fore, I pushed harder. "Well, are you with someone or not?"

"This is not really your business Fae."

My spikes were well and truly exposed now, sharp and nasty, in all their poisonous glory. "And would it be your flock's business to know that you had fucked your father's carer in the library?" Poisonous arrows indeed Fae, you stupid woman. Stupid because I knew as soon as I let the words fly from my mouth that I was only going to be hurting myself in the process. Self-sabotage at the highest level.

"Do not attempt to blackmail me, Fae."

In truth that thought never crossed my mind. I only wanted to vent my rage, my hurt and my pain and I had no idea how else I was supposed to do it. The look in his eyes now was that of the man I had met on the promenade, the man who had floored five men in one quick, easy, brutal assault.

A very dangerous man.

The worst thing was, it was not the danger emanating from him that demolished my defences, that withered those spikes of mine. It was the icy cold dispassionate look in his eyes. If I had held out any hope of nurturing his feelings for me, I had well and truly wrecked them. Miserable now, I dropped my guard, metaphorically tossed down my weapons on the floor and did something I never resorted to. I apologised.

"I am sorry. I didn't mean that."

His killer stare probed.

"Okay I did. I was angry. Lashing out. I really like Arthur. And he likes me. And I am bloody good at my job." Thank fuck I could claw back some pride with this. I tilted my chin up as I carried on speaking. "Please don't deprive him or me the chance for us to work together. I am not going to say anything."

"I am not that petty Fae. Provided you carry on as you have been doing," I must have rolled my eyes at that point with a mocking glint in them because he went on to say, "and I do not mean any repeat of that incident in the library, and provided nothing more is said on the matter, than you have no fears over your job. I am quite happy for you to care for Dad for as long as necessary."

Something of a relief, but of course me being me, I had to spoil it. "I do have some pride you know." Not much it has to be said, but some. "Do you think I want your precious congregation knowing that you think I am ok to shag but not to share your life with?"

His compassion was far worse than his icy coldness. "Oh Fae, you have so much you need help with."

That stung. But not as much as what happened next. His phone rang and naturally he answered it. "Excuse me," he said politely before speaking to the person on the other end. "Good morning, Lucinda, are you alright? No, no, please don't worry. Of course, you must stay at home and rest. Would you like me to call round later? I can give you communion at home if you are too ill to attend church. No, I am not frightened of catching anything from you. I am a hardy soul," he laughed softly and in that moment I knew. "I will see you later."

The other woman.

Lucinda.

The woman he saw as his partner.

I was the other woman in this case, as I had been on so many times before. But never had it hurt like this. I pictured them together. The quiet, respectable Sunday school teacher. The attractive young widow with two small children. The ready-made family unit. The perfect fit.

And what the fuck was I?

The slut who had begged him to sleep with her that night. The witch who carried his child in her womb because of that night. I wrapped my arms tightly around my tummy.

"That was Lucinda….."

"Gathered that," I interrupted spikily.

Looking at me oddly, he went on, "She runs one of the Sunday school classes, but she has picked up a sick bug from one of her children."

"Tricky things sick bugs," I said harshly, thinking that it was a sick bug that had caused the pill to fail. "You never know what they are going to lead to."

Another look from him as if to question, what route was I travelling now? I responded with a "What the fuck do I care about Lucinda?" stare, which of course was a total lie as I cared. I really fucking cared! But not in the way he would have liked.

"I will say it again, Fae. I think you need help. It would not be appropriate for me to guide you in this instance, but I can put you in touch with someone. I know a very good counsellor."

"I do not need fucking counselling." And I do not need any fucking help from you! I screamed silently at him.

"Very well. If you change your mind, Fae, you must let me know. I do want to help you, you know."

I don't want your help!

I want your arms around me.

I want you in my bed.

I want your love.

"Look, I had better go. It will soon be time for early communion. Are you sure you are alright? I am worried about you."

I waved him away with a hand. "Nothing to worry about with me. Totally fine. Away you go and tend to your little sheep."

I saw the glint of impatience sharpen the look in his eyes for a second before his vicarly vibes came through once more.

"I will pray for you, Fae."

Fuck off.

"I don't need your prayers either."

A sad, deeply patronising look and a shake of his head.

Seriously, fuck off!

He turned and walked away leaving me alone in the graveyard. Or was I alone? As he went out of sight, leaving me with my jumbled emotions, I felt another presence. "Rowan?"

"Eliza."

The spirit of the skeleton I had uncovered. It felt natural to talk to her, even though I could not see her.

"What a mess hey Eliza? What a fucking mess."

"I share your pain."

"Really?"

"We are soul sisters. I share your pain."

I felt the tears I had been holding back, begin to fall. "I feel so alone."

"You are not alone. We are soul sisters. I share your pain."

That was alright then. I had a centuries old spirit on my side. What could possibly go wrong?

CHAPTER TWENTY-FIVE

It seemed the right time to tell my aunt and uncle that afternoon. I waited until I had helped Uncle Eric wash up the pots after lunch, something we had got into the habit of doing together after my aunt had done all the cooking. Then, as we sat in the pleasant courtyard garden, fragrant with the scent of the herbs and flowers, I told them my news.

I should have known better than to fret over their reactions. A baby it seemed, whatever the circumstances was cause for celebration. And when I told them that I had every intention now of putting down my roots in Maypoleton, that was even better. As Laura had done, Ruth quickly pointed out that there was a house coming on the market in Tanners Yard, another cobbled side street with cosy two up two down cottages like theirs.

They were both discreet in the gentle probing as to whether the father was going to be a part of our lives and a little disappointed when I said no. But that quickly turned into a practical conversation as to how I would support myself and the baby when she came. Again, it was good to reassure them about the inheritance from Mr Carlisle.

I did not at that time envisage myself as a stay-at-home mum, but Aunty Ruth gave me a wise smile, patted my hand and told me that I could make my mind up about things later. Equally, she was quick to let me know that if I did wish to carry on working, then she would be delighted to help with childminding and that there were others in the village who did this for a living.

When it came to me booking an appointment with the doctor to get a scan organised and telling Gawain, as he was my employer, I was adamant that nothing needed to be done just yet. I knew without a shadow of a doubt when my daughter would be born, and I also knew that no hospital appointments would be needed at any stage. This child was meant to be.

As for telling Gawain, I wanted a little bit of time holding the news to myself before I let him know I was pregnant. My defences were in need of restoration before I undertook that battle. I was not so much of a fool that I didn't realise how vulnerable I would be emotionally as soon as he found out, especially if bloody Lucinda was making an appearance in his life. For the time being it was going to be business as normal.

Which in my case rarely appeared to be the normal kind of norm.

Who else do you know who has a friendship with a centuries old witch called Eliza?

She began to make herself known in the following weeks as I carried out my daily tasks with Arthur. And it was clear right from the start that if any battle lines were to be drawn, she was totally on my side.

If Mrs Mannering ventured a comment that was not in my favour, then a door would slam suddenly in her face, or a cup would fall from the counter onto the floor, a pan would mysteriously boil over when the gas had been switched off. Arthur thought it was wonderful and was convinced, as was Mrs Mannering that it was all my doing. When things came to a head, it was Arthur who inadvertently was the trigger.

We had been out for a walk in the village. A lovely June morning the perfect excuse for a cluster of young parents and grandparents to gather round the village pond with their babies and toddlers, throwing bread for the ducks and gossiping. They all loved Arthur, and he was happy to be invited to sit with them whilst I nipped into the shops and ran a couple of errands for myself. And I certainly did not wish to linger anywhere Lucinda happened to be, as she was on that morning with her youngest child in tow.

When we got back to the vicarage, Arthur decided he would like one of my special hot chocolates. I could tell he was in a mischievous mood as he asked this, knowing that the dragon would be in her domain, busy preparing food. He also knew that she hated the mess I made and the fact that I was encouraging Gawain's father to indulge in what she saw as rubbish.

"Tot of whisky in that Arthur, seeing as it's Friday?" I asked him before delicately placing marshmallows on top of the frothing chocolate.

"Seeing as it's Friday," he said with a wink at me, and a grin as we both heard Mrs Mannering huffing with her back turned to us.

She pounded away at a mound of dough, and I got the impression she wished I was the pastry about to be flattened with the rolling pin.

"You not joining, me? You usually do."

I shook my head at Arthur's comment. "Not today."

Alcohol was off limits now. It was too late to worry about what I may have done before realising I was pregnant, but at least from now on I could do the right thing. He raised an eyebrow, and I knew that soon I would have to reveal my secret. I didn't realise that it was going to come out so quickly though. His next words took the conversation on a route from which there was no going back.

Divine timing?

The Universe at play?

Or Eliza?

"So, there's going to be another member of Gawain's flock in a few months," he began ever so casually, leading me to think that someone new was moving into the village.

I said as much.

"Not moving in, being born. There's going to be a new baby in the parish, isn't that lovely news." He was looking at me over the rim of his mug and I choked on my chocolate. "Are you alright, Fae?"

I coughed, spluttered, wiped my mouth and nodded.

Mrs Mannering ceased her pounding to turn around and enquire. "Who is the family?"

"Not a family as such," said Arthur, appearing to enjoy stringing this out. He took his time chewing on one of the soggy marshmallows. "It's young Shelly Marshall."

"Shelly Marshall? I might have known!" Mrs Mannering's expression was one of disgust. "Little slut. I told her mother that she would get herself into trouble one of these days, hanging around with those lads as she does, and those short skirts she wears and tops that show off, well, everything! Little tart!"

"I take it you don't approve of single mother's then?" Arthur stoked the dragon's fire further.

I sat back and watched this playing out, relieved that he had not been referring to me. I thought perhaps he had guessed, especially with not having the whisky in my chocolate. Mrs Mannering went off on what was clearly one of her favourite subjects, the loose morals and low standards of todays' young people.

"In my day, people did things properly. There was none of this sinful behaviour going on."

"On I think there was," Arthur butted in dryly. "As old as time itself is the act of fornication."

"I will thank you to not use such words in my kitchen!" She fairly glared at him, forgetting perhaps that it was not in actual fact her kitchen.

"I thought you would prefer it to fucking?" Arthur then showed his truly mischievous side, and he winked at me.

Mrs Mannering could not speak. She stood there, with the rolling pin in her hand looking as though she would dearly love to swipe him with it! I think if he had been anyone else, she would have done. I could feel the anger boiling up inside her, heat beginning to emanate off her as her face reddened and the fury demanded an outlet.

"I have had enough!" She banged the rolling pin on the table.

Fair play to Arthur he didn't jump at all, merely took another sip of his chocolate and glanced across at me to see if I was finding this as amusing as he was. I was. We sat there in silent merriment as Mrs Mannering lost the plot.

"It's all her isn't it!" Now the rolling pin was aimed in my direction. "Everything has been different since she came! Bad language, messing up my kitchen, digging up dead bodies, and now encouraging you to stick up for a cheap, dirty little slut who is no better than an alley cat! I won't have it; do you hear me? I have kept house in this vicarage for nigh on twenty years now and never in all that time have I been subjected to such rudeness in….. my….. kitchen!" She punctuated each word by banging the table with the rolling pin.

"It's not your kitchen," I stated boldly.

"You shut up! You shouldn't even be here. You've only set foot in the church once since you arrived, you dabble in witchcraft, I know you do, you evil little madam, do not attempt to deny it, all these weird goings on."

I rolled my eyes at her. "I am not doing anything."

Unfortunately, as soon as I opened my mouth to say this, there was a terrific crash. We all jumped, and Mrs Mannering let out a horrified exclamation as the top shelf of the dresser suddenly came loose and piles of crockery tumbled to the floor, smashing on the hard tiles.

"What on earth is going on?" The door burst open, and Gawain stood there. I could see that Lucinda was standing behind him in the hallway. I looked to see if she had her youngest child with her, but it seemed to be just her now. Looking at the wreckage in the kitchen, Mrs Mannering abandoned the rolling pin and slumped into one of the chairs. She put her face in her hands and began to sob noisily and to my ears somewhat falsely.

"I can't take anymore. Really, I cannot."

"Margaret, whatever is the matter?"

I did not like the way that Lucinda sidled past Gawain who had stepped further into the room, to pull up a chair alongside the housekeeper. "You tell me all about it."

Out then came a muffled, but still audible rant about my shocking influence on Arthur and my wicked ways of witchcraft. I was not surprised that Gawain merely stood there in complete silence waiting for the outburst to subside. Finally, Mrs Mannering raised, her head, gave a huffy little sniff and pointed a finger at me.

"She has to go."

In the calmest, quietest voice possible, Gawain spoke very slowly, addressing neither myself nor Mrs Mannering, but his father. "Would you care to explain?"

Arthur did look a little sheepish. "I have perhaps been a little provocative."

The piercing look from Gawain prompted a further confession. "I happened to mention Shelly's pregnancy but perhaps I could have worded things a little better."

"And this?" Gawain just turned his head ever so slightly to indicate the now wonky shelf and piles of broken crockery.

Arthur slid his eyes to me, and I shook my head.

"Nope, not my doing."

"Fae?"

Eye to eye contact. A blistering heat beneath the icy surface. A distinct warning.

"I didn't do anything."

There was a momentary silence as the energy fairly crackled between us. In the corner of my eye, I saw Lucinda move.

"Well regardless of what has happened, there is a mess to clear up. Let me do this for you Margaret, and then how about I make you a nice cup of tea."

"Oh, would you my dear, that would be so lovely of you. So kind. Isn't Lucinda kind, Reverend?"

His eyes were still locked onto mine, but at that he tore them away. "Pardon, oh yes, Lucinda thank you, very kind indeed."

"Such a blessing to have Lucinda in the parish now, isn't it, Reverend?" Mrs Mannering was clearly on a roll. "You're a saint, you really are," she continued to gush as my rival sought out a dustpan and brush and got to her knees.

Saintly indeed, I thought with an ill-disguised snort.

Gawain flashed me another look and opened his mouth to speak. Judging from the expression on his face what he was going to say would not be in my favour.

I think Arthur spotted this because he piped up, "Well let's all be saintly shall we then Mrs Mannering? Perhaps this is the perfect time to rethink your own views on unmarried mothers in the parish and celebrate young Shelly's news, rather than wishing she was locked up in the stocks?"

Mrs Mannering's angry red flush had been fading, but a flood of pink embarrassment washed over her face as Gawain intercepted the look between her and his father.

Thank you, Arthur. I smiled at him a silent acknowledgement that he had deflected the heat from me.

Momentarily.

It was about to come my way in another direction.

Gawain nodded at his father. "Agreed. And that perhaps should be our focus. Rather than creating friction between each other which is clearly what is happening here."

He then looked at Arthur, Mrs Mannering and me as though we were a bunch of kids who had been pettily squabbling before glancing once more at the shelf that was half off its bracket. I think he decided at that point that discretion was the better part of valour and now was not the time to probe any further with that one.

He went on. "Maypoleton is an ancient village, but that does not mean that we must behave in the way our ancestors did. I will make it very clear in my sermon this coming Sunday that all are welcome in my parish, and most certainly any new souls that will be born here."

I saw her then.

Standing right behind him.

A little wavery at first, just a blurry shadow, black, white and grey. Then the faintest hint of colour to suggest that she was fair, long pale hair around a delicate face. A young face, a slight, slender body. With a noticeable curve in the belly, she had her hands clasped around.

Eliza.

Pregnant.

A gasp escaped me.

"Fae?" Gawain said my name sharply, but I was not looking at him. I was looking at her. She smiled at me. A bright, lively, mischievous smile.

She put the words in my mouth and out they came. "I am pregnant."

The room had been quiet, apart from the noise that Lucinda was making, emptying the broken pieces of crockery into the bin. Now it was silent, and all eyes turned to me. I dared to turn my head at last to meet that laser gaze which locked onto mine. I could feel everyone almost bursting with the effort to contain their exclamations, but it seemed that no one dared utter a sound before Gawain did.

"You are pregnant?"

Only I knew what he was thinking.

He gave absolutely nothing away from the tone of his voice which was deceptively mild and light. I looked behind him, but she had disappeared. Little minx had scuttled off now she had made me blurt out the secret I had wanted to keep just a while longer.

"Fae?" Arthur's voice was gentle in my ears and so was the touch of his hand on mine as he reached across the table.

"Guilty as charged."

"I thought we had just established that being a single mum is not a crime." Arthur squeezed my hand. "Nothing to be frightened of, is there Gawain? Gawain?"

He had to repeat his son's name to break the hold his gaze had on mine. "No, not at all." He cleared his throat. "But this is something we need to talk about, Fae." He addressed me as though he were a head teacher and I an unruly pupil. I was tempted to stick my tongue out at him. "Shall we go through to my study?"

"If we must," I let out a sigh and watched as his eyes narrowed.

Lucinda then butted in as I got up from the table and went to follow Gawain. "Shall I expect you then at six as we agreed?"

"Pardon?" Gawain looked momentarily confused and understandably so, I had just planted a potential land mine into his path. "Yes of course. I will look forward to it." He then said to Mrs Mannering, "Lucinda has very kindly invited me round to have dinner with her this evening to begin planning the children's activities for the summer fair."

A conspiratorial look flicked between the housekeeper and the lovely young widow. Lucinda was smiling at him and the look was reciprocated with warmth. Twisting in my gut was a sharp dart of jealousy. That was the look I wanted to see on his face when he looked at me. All I got when he turned back to face me was that cold impenetrable mask. Silently I followed him out of the kitchen and across the hallway to his study.

"Wait here. I won't be long." He shut the door and then I heard voices in the hallway as he said goodbye to Lucinda, was clearly giving Mrs Mannering instructions to go home early, the squeaky wheel of Arthur's chair and the sound of another door closing. He obviously wanted everyone out of the way so we could have our discussion in peace and not be overheard. Alone at last, I thought somewhat giddily as he entered the room, quietly closing the door behind him.

I was finding it difficult to breathe.

All I wanted to do was throw myself into his arms and have him hold me.

I wanted the happy ever after.

"Is it mine?" That brutally clipped voice shattered the illusion into a thousand pieces. He had already broken my heart, but apparently hearts can splinter again and again. The thought that I might be carrying his child was abhorrent to him.

"No." Fuck him!

If he didn't want me, he would not have his child.

I was not now looking at the benign smiling vicar that everyone else saw. I was looking at the lethal killing machine that had single handedly taken out five men. Whatever, whoever he had been before becoming a vicar, was not someone to play games with.

"I have told you before, Fae. Do not lie to me."

I remained mute, fighting an inner battle. I wondered if Eliza would reappear to nudge a further confession from my lips. She didn't and in the end, it was not necessary. He did that himself.

"When are you due?"

"Samhain." I said defiantly.

His eyes darkened from blue-grey to almost charcoal. My answer had both confirmed his suspicions and jarred at him in another way. "So, it is mine and it will be born at the end of October." Cold, flat, unwelcoming, contrary to how he had spoken in the kitchen about Shelly Marshall. It must have been an indication of how deeply he was disturbed himself as he gave way to a little emotion. His next words cut me even deeper.

"Christ Fae, what a mess. I am the vicar here, you are......"

I burned with anger and out it came. "I am witch. Yes. I am. Deal with it."

Way to go Fae, two stormy confessions in one day. He did deal with it. With another blow of the axe to my heart.

"I knew it. Fucking hell. It's not a mess, it's a disaster." Quietly spoken and more to himself than to me.

Anger tipped over into rage. "My daughter is not a disaster." I hissed the words at him then with a venom that took me and him by surprise. The air went very cold, as though the heat of frustrated passion had just been buried by an avalanche of icy snow.

"Your daughter? How do you know it's a girl?"

"I know. My child is a girl, and she will be born here, bred here, raised here. Whether you like it or not!" Unable to hold myself together any longer, I stood up and went to the door, slamming it behind me as I made my escape.

CHAPTER TWENTY-SIX

As much as I would have liked to have stormed out of the vicarage entirely and taken myself off for a long lung busting hike, my footsteps carried me across the hallway to Arthur's door. I had my hand on it, when I heard Gawain behind me.

Close behind me.

"Fae."

There was so much to decipher in the way he said my name. But right now, I could not cope with anything other than functioning at the most basic of levels. My whole body was trembling with a wild cocktail of pain and rage. If he had held me in his arms, then I would have turned to mush but there was no way that was going to happen. The alternative then was to lock into that suit of armour and get the hell on with the day.

"Your dad will be waiting."

"Fae."

"What?" I whirled around to face him which was a really stupid thing to do. I would have been so much better just walking through the door. That way I would not have seen the look in his eyes which told me he saw right through my spikes, my coat of barbed wire, the titanium breast plate I had strapped over my chest, too late to protect my heart, but there, nevertheless.

In the fraction of the time it had taken us both to get from the study to here, he had somehow managed to get his act together. The role of the concerned, compassionate vicar. Not only vicar, but employer.

"This is a lot to process Fae."

"No shit Sherlock."

He ignored my sarcasm. "We will need to think about a replacement for you when you go on maternity leave." A slight frown did cross his face then. "I have to say that will be tricky. Arthur has taken a real liking to you."

Shame his son hasn't.

"And we will talk further, Fae about the other aspects of the situation."

Situation? Was that how he saw it?

"Other aspects?" I glared at him.

"Financial support at the very least."

If you won't give me your heart, I don't want your money.

"Fuck off." I couldn't help it.

He was so in control and detached and I was so lost and unravelling fast. Not to mention that I was now feeling the dizzying effects of the encounter with Eliza. I knew that when I connected to spirits it left me feeling out of kilter and peculiar. So far, I had only had them come through to speak. Never to be visibly present. She was there behind him in the hallway, as I had seen her in the kitchen.

Fair, fragile, pregnant. *"He didn't want my baby."*

"Fae?" Gawain's voice penetrated the confusion in my mind, distracted as I was by Eliza's presence and what she was saying.

"He didn't want my baby."

I did my best to pull myself back. To the fact that I was battling to get a grip on my emotions and that I actually had a job to do. Pride in my work was about the only thing I could cling to right now. "I have to see to Arthur," I said with a shake of my head.

"He didn't want my baby!"

Such painful emotion it was a blow that reached across the hallway, a connection that crossed the boundary of time itself. I staggered against the door frame, my hands instinctively going to my belly.

"Fae?" Genuine concern in his voice now and why wouldn't there be, I must have looked dreadful.

I collapsed into his arms as the roaring in my ears became too much to block out. Dimly I was aware of his voice trying to get through the fog. Part of me wanted to respond and the other part of me just wanted to sleep. There was a muffled conversation, and I think I heard Arthur's voice, gentle and reassuring.

Movement then and a sense that I was being carried.

A door opening and then the soft comfort of a bed beneath me.

Arms letting me go.

"Don't leave me."

Ever so faintly I heard the response, "Fae, I am going to call Dr. Jay and get her to have a look at you."

"Don't need a doctor, just need to sleep."

"I am worried about you."

"Don't need you to worry about me, just need you to love me."

A strangled sigh. "I am going to call the doctor."

I think I grunted then and rolled over onto my side, childlike and vulnerable, curling up as small as I could. The covers were arranged around me, and I drifted off, giving in to the overwhelming need to sleep. A deep sleep which at some point was disturbed. A kind female voice was gently breaking through to me.

"Fae, I am Doctor Jay. Gawain here is very concerned about you. Fae, can you wake up?"

I groaned. "If I must."

A touch of amusement was present in her voice. "I am afraid so, Fae. Just for a little while and then I can let you rest."

Reluctantly I shook off the sleep, feeling as though I had taken a bucket full of alcohol and drugs. Opening my eyes and focusing was a real effort. I saw a very attractive woman, wearing a bright red short sleeved dress, sitting on the edge of the bed, a large leather bag open at her side. Behind her, with his arms folded across his chest stood Gawain. I didn't dare lift my eyes to meet his for fear of what I would give away to the doctor. I did however quickly glance around the rest of the room to check if Eliza was also present. She wasn't and I let out a sigh of relief which the doctor understandably mistook.

"Gawain tells me you are pregnant, Fae?"

Has he also told you he is the father? No of course not. I nodded my head in answer.

"Do you know how far along you are?"

"She will be born at Samhain," I said, no longer caring how this would sound.

Doctor Jay merely smiled at me. "I take it you are friends with Eve and Mabel then." Over her shoulder she addressed Gawain with a touch of amusement clearly in her voice. "It appears you have a witch under your roof Reverend. How does Mrs Mannering cope I wonder?"

"The matter in hand?" Quietly spoken and in keeping with the tone of a vicar, but yes there was a touch of steel there.

"Of course." Doctor Jay sat up a little straighter and began rooting in her bag. "Blood pressure first, Fae, and then we will have a little look at your tummy if that's ok?"

I nodded and held out my arm, still not looking at Gawain.

"Okay," said Doctor Jay slowly when she had taken the reading. "That's very low Fae. Do you usually suffer from such low blood pressure."

I shook my head. "Nope. Fit as a fiddle normally."

"Being pregnant is not normal."

Doctor Jay and I both looked at him then.

"Well obviously it is normal," he said sounding slightly exasperated, "But it is not normal for Fae."

"Quite," replied Dr. Jay "and it's something we need to keep an eye on."

"I am fine, honestly," I said, although in truth I was feeling way less than fine. I really just wanted to go back to sleep. My body was feeling most peculiar. I had the sense that Eliza was trying to come through again, and the energy was hitting me hard.

"You don't look it, Fae. Let's check that tummy out now. Gawain, do you mind?"

He left the room whilst she gave me a gentle but thorough examination and talked to me about getting booked in for a scan at the ante natal clinic. I argued my point that there was no need for either. When she started talking about admitting me to hospital right there and then as I was beginning to sound slurry and my body had started to tremble, I had to blurt it out.

"No hospital! I am fine. This baby will be born at Samhain with no intervention from the outside. And I do not need to go into hospital now. I just need to sleep. It's a psychic overload that's all!"

She closed up her bag and looked at me thoughtfully. "In any other circumstance I would over-ride you Fae. However, this is Maypoleton. Strange things happen in Maypoleton. I am not a member of Mabel's coven, but I know her well and Eve of course who experienced something similar to you a few years back when another skeleton was discovered here. So, I will respect your decision. For now. All will say is that please be careful."

"What do you mean?"

"From all accounts Eve got more than she bargained for. I would hate to see you come to any harm, or anyone else for that matter."

"No harm will come to anyone," I blithely assured her.

"Hm. Well for now I am going to suggest to Gawain that you stay here if you can and sleep off whatever it is that you need to sleep off. And if you do change your mind about getting checked out, then let me know straight away. Other than that Fae, you are a healthy young woman, your aunt and uncle will be taking good care of you, and I am sure you will find that the rest of the village will also help in any way that is needed. You are in a good place here, Fae."

I smiled at her for the first time. "I know," I said, "I have come home." And with that I snuggled down once more to sleep, a small part of me aware that I was in Gawain's bed, and this would be royally pissing him off. I had a smile on my face at that thought.

I was not smiling later.

I was screaming.

I was fighting for my life.

Hands were clawing at me, voices yelling, jeering in my ears. Fists cruelly pummelling my stomach. Feet brutally kicking me. Hair ripped painfully from my scalp. My body dragged hard across wet cold ground. Mud, stone, rotten food thrown at me.

I fought.

I kicked back.

I screamed.

"Fae."

Very dark now, and a howling wind freezing through to my bones. That didn't matter. The cold did not matter. My stomach was on fire. I howled out in agony. In rage and hate. My body shook in desperate agony.

"Fae!"

Burning hot wetness now. Blood pouring out of me. My child's essence bleeding into the muddy ground. A grief that

would last centuries. A scream of defiance, a promise of revenge. The weight of a rope, heavy, so very heavy, but not as heavy as the pain in my heart.
Choking.
Gasping.
Dying.
"Fae, for the love of Christ wake up!"
It must have been his strength of faith and those words he used. I came back from wherever I had been, my hands tearing at my throat as though to loosen the rope I had felt around me, my breath coming in short, sharp, painful gasps. He was there beside me on the bed, the covers tangled as I thrashed about, my body shuddering violently as though I was in the grip of paranormal convulsion.
I was.
Eliza's last moments.
Her death throes.
"Fae, Fae, please, be calm, you're safe." Gawain's voice was soft but urgent. His hands had reached for me. I felt the strength of him, as he grasped my shoulders and tried to hold me still, tried to subdue the tremors with his touch.
I heard him, yet I didn't. Part of me was still there. I felt him, yet I didn't. Part of me was still there. I saw him, yet I didn't. Part of me was still there.
There on the village green. Dragged cruelly by my hair. Locked in the stocks. Bombarded with missiles. Released from this only to be kicked and battered. My baby killed before I was killed myself.
"My baby," I moaned this out loud.
"My daughter," a broken sob.
"They killed my daughter!" A promise of vengeance growled out from low in my throat, deep in my soul.
Too much emotion, an outpouring of feelings from centuries past, blended potently with my feelings of the here and now. A deeply intoxicating brew. Magic. Poison. A magical poison. A poisonous magic. All of these. A powerful creation of energy that pulsed suddenly in the room, that came to life in that fullness of the moon. More magic at play.
That energy, that magic, drew him to me.

"Fae, for the love of God, be calm, be still."

His arms wrapped around me, and I began to feel him in the flesh. The horrors of the past receded as I took in the now of where I was. In his bedroom at the vicarage. Wearing just a t-shirt and my underwear. Had he removed my jeans earlier without me knowing, so I would be more comfortable in sleep? As I turned into him, seeking comfort, warmth, love, I was aware that he was also just in a t-shirt and his boxers. My eyes caught sight of a woollen throw tossed onto the floor next to the armchair that sat under the window. He must have been attempting to sleep there, whilst keeping an eye on me, as I slept.

That meant something.

I took it to mean something.

I made it mean something.

My limbs snaked around his, smoothly, surely, as though we were meant to be one. Bare legs and arms entwining, the touch of skin upon skin a spark to that flame.

"Fae," a gasp and a wall of resistance. "Fae, you had a nightmare."

"Not a nightmare," I whispered into his neck, my mouth beginning to press tiny biting kisses against the vein that throbbed there. "It was real, it happened."

"Jesus, Fae, no." Even as the denial came from his mouth, one hand was trailing along my bare thigh. "Fae, you need to sleep, you need to rest."

"I need to be loved." My hands felt the strength in his arms, explored the muscles in his chest.

"You are loved. God loves you."

"I don't need God's love. I need yours."

No pride, no self- respect, no barriers. Where the fuck had my armour gone? Right out of the window into the moonlight, alchemised by the haunting trauma of the past and this soul deep connection of the now, into a painful longing that would not, could not be denied. I didn't know if I was standing at the gates of heaven or the entrance to hell. It could have been either.

I shifted fluidly in his arms, the arms that held whilst at the same time, tried to pull back. I felt the hardness of him as his body responded even whilst his mind was denying the attraction. My hands slid beneath his t-shirt, pushed up the material. At the same time, I moved some more, one of my legs straddling across his, my bare thighs holding his in place.

"Fae stop." His hands were light on my back, trailing down over my t-shirt then fingers exploring beneath the hem, reaching up to the clasp of my bra. He was in as much turmoil as I.

I knew this.

I used this.

"I can't stop."

I shoved up his t-shirt, kisses pressed wildly around his navel, my fingers making little circles that teased lower and lower. I moved some more, fully across him now, feeling the hardness of him beneath me. Desire was flooding through me so much he must have felt my wetness through my underwear and his. He groaned and unclasped my bra beneath my t-shirt. Hands urgently on my breasts, fuller and more sensitive than they were. I shrugged off my top, tossed aside my bra. Knelt astride him for a moment, poised above him, ready to take him.

"God, Fae, you are beautiful." A tortured confession ripped from him.

I bent my head to kiss him. As I lowered myself, his hands pulled me close, fingers feverously tracing my back, my belly, my breasts.

"I love you," I whispered, beyond helping myself from denying these words.

"I can't love you."

"You can."

"I love someone else."

An arrow of jealousy straight to the heart.

"She is not here. I am." I called in the power of that moon then. I called in the power of Eliza through the centuries. I called in my own power.

"Oh Christ Fae," he groaned in defeat and then swiftly flipped me onto my back.

CHAPTER TWENTY-SEVEN

In a matter of moments, we were entangled together, limbs coiled snakelike. Hands searching and seeking, mouths touching and tasting. Whatever he thought, however conditioned he was that he could not, should not love me, his kisses told another story. As his mouth came together with mine, I knew the truth of it. I clawed my fingers around the back of his head, savouring the bristly feel of his short-cropped hair as I demanded more contact.

His lips opened against mine and our tongues began a duelling dance of passion, and desire. No doubt he would call it lust. I called it love. Love on fire with lust yes, but love from the deepest place in my heart, burning with heat. It blazed its way through every cell in my body, beyond that to each particle of my soul, the very essence of me.

He groaned against my neck as he briefly tore his mouth away. Gasping for breath I felt his heart hammering against mine, beneath the cotton of the t-shirt he still wore. Not good enough. Total skin on skin was what I wanted, desired, needed. His hands went to help me shrug it up his body and then cast it aside. Swiftly too his boxers and my briefs.

Bliss.

A shiver of desire in anticipation of what was to come. That very first full body contact, head to toe, naked and knowing. And there was a sense of knowing. That this was so very right. That I belonged here with him. His body on top of mine. His hands on my breasts, my belly, my thighs. So many hands had been where his now were, but no one else had ever made me react like this.

I arched up against him, my body asking, demanding, begging for more. Unable to stop myself, I groaned out loud as in response he bent his head to bite on one nipple and at the same time stroked a hand up the soft flesh of my inner thigh and gave me that touch that made me whimper.

"Christ Fae, you're so wet." He made it sound like a curse, as though he was angry at how aroused I was. And as if to appease this anger he shoved two fingers in hard, deep.

I spasmed off the bed, pushing hard against his hand to feel more. His mouth claimed my other breast, teasing the hardened nipple with tiny bites of his teeth, sucking and pulling at the same time his fingers were going deeper and deeper. My hips had a mind of their own, lifting up, writhing serpent like against him.

Tremors began to build.

The urgency increased.

Sensing it, he lifted his mouth away from my breasts and looked momentarily into my eyes. Dark with passion, impossible to read any expression, just that sense of detachment as though he was watching me from a distance, and this was not really him bringing me to a furious climax.

Yet it was him, his body that had set mine on fire, his mouth that had fuelled the flames and his touch that created the explosion of energy that could no longer be contained. He let it roll out, watching as my eyes widened in shock, my mouth dropped open, and I cried out in relief. He didn't let it stop. There was more to come. It was as though he was taking satisfaction in drawing out my pleasure as long as he could, whilst all the while, denying himself the same.

I could feel how hard he was against me, pulsing with vitality, throbbing with life, the life that was growing inside of me now. His child, to be born out of his seed. I reached out to touch, to hold, to claim. Male power at its most primal and I wanted it inside me.

"Please," a word I could not stop passing my lips. "Please. I need you."

He needed me.

He may deny he loved me.

But he needed me.

At last, his legs were across mine, one knee nudging me wider, hands under my bottom. We both cried out at the same time. Wonder in my voice. Shock in his. How could it feel so good? Maybe we had the same thought, born out of different feelings. I loved him. He despised me. Shock and wonder.

Wonder and shock. A connection that raged through and obliterated every other thought.

We were meant to be one.

Nothing else mattered.

And so, it began.

That first moment when we were one, when the full hard length of him penetrated deep within my core. A moment I wished so desperately to freeze in time. To just be there with him for all eternity. To feel that connection to another soul that was meant to be. I closed my eyes against the tears that threatened. I knew I had come home.

Even if he didn't.

My hands roamed his back, smooth sleek muscles, rippling under my touch. He returned the favour, moulding my body to his, following every line of my curves. Gently over the more tender, swollen breasts, slowly over the belly that carried his child, firmer underneath my bottom to bring my hips even closer to his.

We fought a little at first, two bodies over eager to feel, to give, to receive, the rhythm not quite there. He was pushing, I was demanding. Then it began to flow. Fluid movements, a perfect synchronicity. A rise and fall, his body dipping into mine, taking me with him. Then my hips drawing him in further, my hands now on his bottom, firm, tight muscles, that clenched beneath my touch. I dug my nails in. Bit him on the shoulder. Teeth drawing a gasp from him.

More.

I needed more.

So much more.

An unspoken demand. Words not necessary. That feel and touch in the light of the moonlight, the pulsing beat of the heart that grew more rapid, urged on a quicker, more primal beat. Breath coming ragged from both of us, a sheen of sweat making the contact between us slippery and smooth.

The duvet was tossed aside, far too hot under its covers. We were burning up with the heat of our desire. I wrapped my legs around him, trapping him in place and opening myself up even more. Deeper, deeper.

My body called to him.

My mind called to him.

My heart and soul called to him.

He heard my body at least, and drove in harder, deeper, matching the pace that now I was setting. Another orgasm was coming, and I was lost to all but that sensation. Wild beneath him, I raced on, soft cries escaping my throat, urgent pleas, the echo of my need. He listened, he answered. Pulled my hips even closer to his, pounded away.

"Oh God don't stop!"

No need really to call this out loud. He could no more have stopped than I at that moment and I knew it. I sank into the bliss that bordered on pain as the sensations he created spiralled from my deepest core to every cell in my body. Lifted to another level with passion, my body arched up off the bed, slamming into his as I lost myself completely.

My cries now a primal release.

A savage moment of joy.

Tremors raging through me in an unstoppable wave.

An easing of it, almost a relief to escape the intensity. Then just as I was floating back down, softening, ready to sink into satiated oblivion, he stoked another furnace. He uncoiled my legs from around his waist, pushed my hips wider apart, raised up on his elbows and for a moment just held himself there.

Our eyes met.

I longed to put my hands up to his face, to tenderly touch his cheek, press a finger against his lips, to smile lovingly at him.

Don't.

A silent answer from his eyes.

Don't touch me like that. Don't make those gestures of love. This is not love.

For him no. For me yes.

This was love. This was more than love.

My life and soul were on the line. How could he be so blind in the full light of this moon? How could he not see? But he couldn't. All he could see, feel, was the body beneath his, the body that he had taken to the edge of pleasure, the body that was still there for him to seek and find his own pleasure. If he would not give me his love, then I would take whatever I could from him.

"Go on." I urged him softly, sensing that he was still on the verge of holding back. That stranglehold of control that had him quivering with yet to be released passion, so firmly in place. A war within his mind, his body, his soul. To let himself go fully, completely. A violence buried deep in his heart that he was so desperately trying to hide in this version of his life.

The calm respectable vicar.
The brutal deadly fighter.
The man in love with another woman.
The man who wanted to fuck me so badly.

I saw that clearly at least in his eyes and siren like I smiled then, lazily, temptingly, enticingly. "Go on," I whispered softly again. "I will take it. I will take all you have to give me." I will take your body, your heart, your soul. Words unspoken a vow from somewhere deep inside me. I will make you love me.

"I will make you love me."

I shivered and my eyes must have widened in shock. Eliza's words, feelings. Emotions from centuries past breaking through the barriers of time, to this place, this moment. To the energy that was surging between us. I felt a rush of heat through my body top to toe and bucked my hips up against his. If my words had not had the desired effect, that heat, that energy did.

He knelt up, roughly pulling my body to fit perfectly in place where he wanted me. Then the control went. Something inside him gave way at last. The barriers crashed. The walls tumbled away.

He wanted me.
He needed me.
He took me.

I could do nothing other than be taken and that was all I wanted in that moment. To feel the hard masculine strength of him, bruising into me. To hear the slap of flesh meeting flesh, the harshness of that sound accompanying the rasping of our breathing as this turned into deep animal pleasure.

I was tender, sore. I wanted more. My body responded with the rising of another climax that promised to be on the verge of pain as the tremors began to surge through me. I couldn't stop coming. One dizzying wave after another that had me crying out shamelessly, begging pleading for him to stop, to not stop, to tell him I couldn't take any more, to demand more. No matter my words he did not stop, could not have stopped. I knew that as his body worked even harder to bring him to his own release.

Fast, hard, yes with that edge of pain.

Faster still, harder still.

Then a slow, deep, driving, penetrating thrust, pinning me in place. Another meeting of our eyes as he poured himself into me, my body welcoming his essence with more wild spasms of my own. A long intense moment. A moment of truth. In that moment he was mine.

Then he closed his eyes and pulled out of me.

Bereft, I watched him walk through to the ensuite shower room, admiring the way his body moved in its naked glory, catching sight of the scars that the moonlight exposed. What had happened to him? What was his story? I longed to know. I longed for him to share it with me. Lost in this reverie of thought, it was something of a shock when he came back with a wad of tissues.

"Here," he said quietly. "You may want to clean yourself up."

Clinical, detached. He was right though. I was soaking from my desire and his release. Somewhat subdued I wiped myself with the tissues and watched as he bent to find his t-shirt and boxers.

"I'll go and sleep in the spare room."

What the fuck?

I actually said it. "What the fuck?"

A touch of impatience in his voice. "Fae, this should not have happened. I know that. You know that. We are not right for each other."

"We are!" I protested. "Can't you feel it?"

More impatience, a heavy sigh. "I feel…….attraction. I said that before Fae. You are a very attractive woman. But I do not see you as my partner. You know how I feel about Lucinda."

"She is not carrying your child." A low blow but one that I had to hit with.

He hissed between his teeth. "I wondered if that was going to be used. I thought you said you wanted nothing from me in that respect?"

Can't you recognise a lie when you see one?

Can't you tell when you have utterly shattered someone's heart?

Can't you feel when your soul is meant to be joined with another's?

I struggled to speak. My throat was constricted, not just by a building mass of emotion that begged to be release in a wild crying fit, but with the feeling of that rope around my neck. The rope, that I knew now had choked Eliza to death. I put my hands to my throat, my breath coming in ragged gasps as I let the tears fall.

"Don't leave me. Please don't leave, not tonight. Stay with me tonight at least, give me that." My desperation was overwhelming, and I knew that it was not merely my emotions that were driving this need. The past was colliding with me right there in that room. Eliza's passion, Eliza's love for the man who had rejected her, the man who had fathered her child, here in this very room. It was all too much and I began to sob and shake in earnest.

I didn't want this.

I hated this.

I was lost in this.

It came back to pity again. That humiliating reason for someone to do something. Out of pity. His attitude towards me changed from that of anger to that of pity. Part of me preferred the anger, the Fae that I knew as me. This other Fae, this feverishly fucked up version of me that I saw as an imposter, welcomed the pity.

Because that meant he would stay.

He did, and not only did he stay but he held me close that night.

He whispered words of comfort and reassurance as I lost myself in the terrors of the past.

Worn out by his lovemaking and my emotions I fell asleep almost as soon as he was beside me. But it was not a normal sleep. Eliza's spirit had called me back to her time so that I could see clearly what had happened to her, to know and to feel what she went through.

A young kitchen maid with a bold saucy attitude, bright eyed, full of laughter and mischief. The dashing young vicar, who had not wanted to become a man of the church, but as the second son in a large respectable family it was considered the right thing to do. It was also considered the right thing to do as the vicar of the parish to marry a suitable young woman of a family from a similar standing in life.

Not to shag the kitchen maid and then get her pregnant.

How many times has this story played out in history?

And how often would a happy ending occur?

It certainly did not happen for Eliza. I saw her weeping in fear as she discovered her condition. I witnessed the emotional scenes that took place in this house, this room as she begged and pleaded with him not to abandon her, or their child. I heard the weakness in his voice, the vicar of that time as he protested that he could not possibly marry her, she was beneath him. Not only that but he had already chosen a suitable wife.

I felt her anger, her rage.

It had me jolting off the bed, wild energy coursing through me.

I heard Gawain's voice trying to break through, felt his hands trying to shake me out of this state, but it was no good. Eliza was determined to make me see everything, like before only not fragmented this time.

I saw how she then changed from the laughing, loving young girl, to the spiteful, vengeful witch. She always had been a witch, but a healing, caring, witch of the light. In his rejection, she lost that light. The dark claimed her soul and her craft turned to a thing of wickedness. The vicar's fiancée suffered a horrific death, a violent bout of poisoning, of herbal lore, witchcraft at its most foul.

Then retribution.

The anger and vengefulness of the villagers and the vicar himself.

The violent end of Eliza's own life and that of her child.

A night of horror for me as I lived and shared these moments with her, all the while being held in the arms of the man I had fallen in love with, the vicar of this parish now, the father of my child, the man who had rejected my love for that of another.

I woke feeling utterly exhausted.

Gawain was standing at the window opening the curtains to let the bright June sunshine pour into the room. It was disorienting to have the light upon me from where I had been in my half sleep, so dark and terrifying. I felt bewildered and lost and the words he greeted me with didn't help.

"Fae I am deeply worried about you." He came to sit on the end of the bed. He was dressed in jeans and a t-shirt and clearly had had a shower, he smelt gorgeously fresh and clean.

I felt as though I had been dragged through the mud as Eliza had. I struggled to listen to him.

"I think you are suffering from PTSD. I have seen a lot of this in my work. You told me about your sister, and I think you still need help with this. Please let me find you a counsellor."

I stared at him blankly. A shred of self-preservation crept in, thank God! I kept my mouth shut and let him think this. If I told him really what was going on he would more than likely stop me from looking after Arthur and as perverse as it was, the thought of not having the chance to come here every day and be near him, torture though it was, was unbearable.

As I remained mute, and no doubt looking wild eyed and more than a little crazy, he took hold of my hand. Nothing lover like in the gesture, oh no. He had regained control and was back in full vicar mode.

"I want to help you, Fae. In whatever way I can. I am not the man for you. I stand by that, but I will also stand by you, Fae, in all other respects."

Ouch, ouch, triple ouch.

"Will you let me arrange a counsellor for you?"

I heaved a sigh. "If it makes you happy."

"It would."

I shrugged. What the fuck. I could play along with it. "Okay."

He smiled and I wanted to hit him. "Good girl."

Patronising cockwomble!

I smiled back.

"I'll go and make you a cup of tea and then you can shower." He stood up and walked to the door. He then turned around to face me and added, "It will all turn out alright Fae, you will see. It's all positive. All part of God's plan."

How the fuck was this all positive?

As for God's plan, well frankly I was mightily pissed off with my gods right now.

And turn out alright?

Neither of us knew on that bright sunny morning just how wrong it was all going to turn.

CHAPTER TWENTY-EIGHT

When I finally staggered downstairs into the vicarage kitchen, having spent an age in the shower trying to wake myself up, Gawain told me in no uncertain terms that I was to take the day off. It was a Saturday and usually one of my workdays, but he was adamant. I was to go home and sleep. And on Monday morning I was to take a trip into Lancaster for an appointment with a counsellor. He pushed a piece of paper towards me with a name and address written on it.

"He's very good. I have arranged for you to have weekly sessions, all paid for in advance."

I pulled a face at him but before I could speak, he continued making it very clear this was non-negotiable. "I cannot have you breaking down whilst you are looking after Arthur and of course….." a pause, "there is the baby to think of."

The baby.
Your baby.
Our baby.

I was about to argue with him, just for the hell of it, when I saw a shadow pass over his eyes. There was something very dark and haunted within that grey-blue gaze, a pain that I recognised as grief and loss. What was his story? I had not yet managed to wheedle anything out of Arthur, he remained close lipped on the subject of his son's former life.

Instead, I raised the question. "How have you managed to get an appointment so quickly?"

"He's a friend of mine. You aren't the usual sort of client he sees, but he is happy to make an exception in your case."

I took the piece of paper, folded it up and put it in my pocket, reluctantly aware that he was right. I was in one hell of a fucking mess. Whilst I did not give two hoots about my own welfare, I had been courting a death wish for the last fifteen years, there was my daughter to think of now. I did not want to bring her into the world with me in such an emotionally off the wall state. A flash of insight, a glimpse into the past, the link with Rowan as she had connected with me from her grave.

I gasped as the blow of it was physical, a hit to the solar plexus.

"Are you alright?"

I wasn't. On the back of what had happened last night, this was all getting far too much.

"Rowan."

"Who?"

"My mother, my birth mother. She is buried here."

"Yes of course, I know the grave, I have seen you there." He nodded encouragingly; vicar mode fully switched on.

"She took an overdose, accidentally. She didn't mean to kill herself. She was just so exhausted, with me, I wore her out. She couldn't cope. I killed her, just the same as....." Hysteria was creeping in, the fear that maybe history was going to repeat itself, that I would not be able to cope as a mother. That Rowan's feyness, her sensitivities which I had inherited in spades, was going to be my undoing as a mother. That I would leave my own child to grow up without know who she truly was.

"Fae, you have not killed anyone." He pulled the chair he was sitting on around the table so he could take hold of my hands in his. "Look at me Fae, look at me." He repeated this when I didn't want to raise my eyes to meet him. Far better to let the curtain of my hair fall over my face. Tenderly, heartbreakingly so, he lifted a hand to move it back over my shoulders touched my chin ever so lightly to turn my face to his.

"You have not killed anyone," he said again, a world of wisdom, of pain and compassion in his eyes and his voice. "You feel the guilt that you have, but you have not. Trust me, Fae, I know the difference."

The clock ticked on the wall, an everyday sound punctuated a moment of silence that held so much emotion and such a deep connection between two lost souls. Because despite what he said, regardless of however he behaved, I knew he was as bloody well lost as I was. I also knew that he was never going to admit this. He pulled back from the moment first, of course he would

"Never mind what I said about taking the rest of the day off, Fae," more matter of fact now he stood up, as though he needed to distance himself from me physically as well as emotionally and spiritually. "You are going to take the coming week off as well. No arguing." He held up a hand to stay my protests.

"I never take time off work."

"Well maybe you should have done before now. Maybe this is why you are reacting as you are?" He looked relieved at my comment as though this explained my oddities a little better. "Exhaustion can send anyone off track and when that happens the trauma we have buried within us, comes barging out of the box to haunt us."

He knew all about this, that much was obvious.

Still, I argued, as much as anything because I was stubborn and argumentative at the best of times. "Who will look after Arthur?"

"Don't you worry about that. Lucinda has offered previously to help with Dad whenever needed."

Fuck no, that's a really bad idea! "How can she? She has her little one to look after, the one that's not at school yet?"

"Toby?" He smiled, a look of genuine warmth that stirred more jealousy within me. "He is a lovely quiet little boy, and Arthur is fond of him too. It wouldn't be a problem for him to accompany Lucinda and her mother is always happy to look after him as well. So, you see, Fae, there really is nothing for you to worry about."

The hell there was.

My rival in my place.

Not good. Not good at all.

Nothing I could do about it though. Gawain, as I had come to know was unstoppable, unchangeable in his thoughts. I may as well try and stop the sun setting at night.

"What the hell am I going to do with a week off?" I said grumpily as I stood up.

He did smile then, an acknowledgement perhaps of my work ethic, which at least was something no one could find fault with.

"Well aside from seeing Mick on Monday," he referred to his friend the counsellor, and getting some much-needed rest, why don't you go back home for a quick visit. Surely you must want to see your parents?" His eyes flicked towards my stomach. "You have news for them after all and face to face is a nicer way to share it."

Oh fuck. "You reckon?" I said, wondering what Mum would say on the subject. I knew it would be a mixed response.

"Oh Fae, stop being so hard on yourself."

I shrugged. "Don't know how to."

"I know." He said this softly, and again there was an invisible cord that wrapped itself around us, tugging at my heart strings and possibly his. "Mick will help." He ushered me out of the kitchen and across the hallway.

"What about saying goodbye to Arthur?"

"He's asleep." Sure, enough the rumbling resonance of deep snoring was audible through the door. "Don't worry, Arthur will understand. Go home to your aunt's, rest this weekend, keep that appointment on Monday, and then go and see your parents." Instructions issued in an authoritative manner that brooked no arguments. To press the point, he added. "And don't worry about pay, I will pay your wages as normal."

I gave up.

Wordlessly, because really what more could I say at this point, I grabbed my jacket off the peg, shrugged myself into it, and walked out of the door. Gawain had phoned my aunt and uncle the day before when I had collapsed. Naturally they were concerned and relieved when I told them what Gawain had suggested or rather decreed as to what was going to happen.

"I don't reckon much to the counselling idea," said Uncle Eric in his no-nonsense way. He was a typical northern bloke, a little gruff on the outside but warm hearted within. "Reckon you are fine as you are with me and your Aunty to look after you. And the little one." He added with a gentle touch on my shoulder.

We were sitting in the courtyard garden of their cottage. It was late morning, and they had just returned from the stables to find me making a pot of tea for them. I had nipped into Mabel's bakery on the way home, the need for a big sugar rush too great to ignore. The shop had been crowded as it always was on a Saturday morning with Mabel and one other assistant busy serving the queue of customers.

As she had done that first morning upon my arrival in Maypoleton, Mabel greeted me with a particular smile and look on her face. When the other lady had been about to serve me, she waved her aside.

"Let me see to Fae," she said and began picking out the assortment of pastries I had been going to ask for, without me even saying anything. Then the head of the village coven gave me an even bigger smile and whispered ever so quietly so no one else could hear. "I am so happy for you my dear. And don't worry. As bleak as things look now, all will be well."

My face must have shown some shock because she came from around the counter. On the surface it looked as though she was merely passing me the box of assorted pastries. In reality it was more to pass on a blessing.

"What is meant to be, will come to thee. A love that is pure, will always endure. Stay in the light, and all will be right."

"Thank you," I said a little uncertainly.

I knew that she knew about the baby, not because Eve or Laura had told her. I trusted them not to do that. Mabel knew because she *knew*. And I expected that living within a very tight knit village everyone would soon know. This did not bother me in the slightest. Becoming a single mother was hardly going to be the shocker that being accused of murdering folk in a care home had been! I had survived the glare of that ugly spotlight. This would be a breeze in comparison.

However, as I turned to leave the shop, Mabel did raise her voice slightly and repeat those last few words, a slight frown on her face as though something had just occurred to her or rather *come through to her*.

"Fae, remember, stay in the light and all will be right."

Our eyes met. From one witch to another there was an understanding that a warning was woven within the words, even if neither of us really knew what it was about.

I respected her wisdom, her craft, her *knowing*. "Thank you, Mabel, I will."

Which of course I totally did not, but at that moment I meant what I said.

In the breezy warmth of my aunt's garden as I poured the tea and shared out the cakes, I talked more about my plans for the coming week. Aunty Ruth shushed her husband's comments about the counselling and gave me her nod of approval.

"I think that is a really good idea, love and I for one am very grateful for Gawain for arranging it for you. Who knows, if your mother had had help like that….."

A moment of sad silence, broken by Uncle Eric's gruff warmth. "What's done is done, can't be changed. What matters now is that Fae is going to have a baby, and it will be grand, absolutely grand to have a nipper dashing around the place. Keep us all on her toes hey, lass?"

How I loved this kind, down to earth man. "Absolutely. And I must go and tell my parents, as Gawain has suggested, it's as good a time as any to do this and have a bit of a break as well."

First though I had to face the counselling appointment that Gawain had organised. Mick Hardcastle was a nice enough man, sharp eyed and intelligent, but then anyone connected with Gawain would be. I got the sense that like Gawain this was a second life for him, and that formerly he had been something very different. He was very good. So good that he had me squirming inwardly at the accuracy of the questions he carefully delivered my way.

Reluctantly, I had to consider that Gawain could possibly be right. Matt too for that matter as he had also suggested I needed counselling, for my sex addiction as he had put it. Maybe there was something to be said for the space in which to talk. Not that I had talked. In fact, I had remained pretty much silent, only nodding, shaking my head, or giving the odd little grunt.

I cried a lot. Silent tears, desperate to have a voice attached to them. Screaming in my head to let them loose, to be heard, to be held, to be forgiven. But I was not ready to let these flow just yet.

I did however, shake his hand at the end of the session and thank him with a genuine promise that I would be back the following Monday. He gave me a warm smile then, with a look in his eye as if to say that if Gawain had anything to do with this, there was no choice in the matter for me.

After that it was the long drive back down South to stay with Mum and Dad for a few days. I had phoned them in advance to warn them of my arrival. Needless to say, this put Mum in a fluster as she had filled my old bedroom apparently with a mountain of paraphernalia needed for the forthcoming village show and why could I not stay at my flat? When I reminded her that I had rented this out, she huffed and puffed and agreed that she could move everything into the garden shed.

Not surprisingly Mum was not over enthusiastic about my news. I knew this was on multiple levels, but the primary one of course that this was not Fliss's baby. That Fliss was not here to have a baby of her own. That once more, I had stolen something from my sister. The right to be a mother. Nothing said of course, but it was there within the subtext, the nuances, the heartfelt sighs and wistful looks. All sharp shards of glass twisting in my soul.

Dad on the other hand was delighted and without Mum knowing he passed me an envelope with a large bundle of notes inside. And more than that, a quiet conversation just the two of us, that he would be opening an account for my daughter and a monthly sum would be put in there. When I argued that I could take care of myself, especially with my good fortune in the shape of Mr Carlisle's will, he hushed me, quietly and determinedly.

"Fae, I have more money than I know what to do with. My books are selling well, I want you to have the chance to enjoy being a mother. I want you to have the choice to work or not. If working is right for you once the baby is born, then fine, I respect you are such a hard worker Fae. But and this is important, if you feel in your heart that you wish to spend the time with your daughter, at least until she is of school age, then I want you to have the freedom of choice. Especially as the father will not be involved. I remember….." He paused then and I wondered if he was thinking about Rowan. Of course he was.

Wrapping my arms around him I hugged him as tightly as I could. A blinding moment of insight clear in my mind. He understood my guilt over Fliss. He felt the same over my mother. How had I not seen that before? I loved him possibly more at that moment than I had ever done in my life. Two days though under the same roof as my parents was enough and I parted from them to go and visit my friend Annie who of course was blooming with her own pregnancy and utterly delighted with the news of mine.

Understandably there were the questions and gentle probing as to the father, but I was skilled in only letting on that which I wanted to share. I simply told her it had been a one-night stand, and I was not going to ask, or expect the father to be involved. She then naturally asked if I had met anyone of interest in Maypoleton, her romantic heart simply begging for mine to be as happy as hers. Sadly, I could not give her any hope on this matter.

Trying desperately to quell the pain and bitterness that was becoming an ever-growing seed in my soul, I lied to her yet again. "Honestly, I am fine just as I am. You know me, Annie, I am not cut out to be someone's wife."

She gave me a somewhat arch look as though to say, she did not really believe this. Surely every woman wanted that fairy tale?

I pressed on. "But I am going to be the best bloody mother I can be, and that is all that matters now."

Did she hear the doubt in my voice? How could I possibly be a good mother?

"You will be Fae. Your daughter, or son, it may be a boy," she said in the face of my shaking my head, "is going to be so lucky to have you as her or his mother. And are you definitely set on living in Maypoleton?"

Bring my daughter up in the village where her father lived? Watch her grow up, go to school, in the village where her father would be married to the lovely Lucinda? Bring my daughter up in the village where her father may have children of his own, half siblings to her?

Was I really going to do this?

Was I really going to inflict this wound upon myself.

Was I really this stupid?

It appeared so. "Yes," I said with conviction in my heart. "It's a wonderful place to bring up a child and I love being so close to Aunty Ruth and Uncle Eric. Plus, the property prices are so much more affordable there. I can easily buy a lovely little cottage outright with Mr Carlisle's legacy." I ticked off the points on my fingers. And then it came down to this. "Besides, it feels right. It's where I belong."

And this was the truth of the matter.

I knew it beyond all doubt as I made my return journey back up the motorway. With every service station that I passed I knew I was heading in the right direction. As I took the turning onto the A6 and then onto the smaller, winding country roads, I felt a lifting in my soul. Parking my little car in the village car park next to the church I found it natural to walk from there to the graveyard.

Kneeling beside Rowan's headstone, feeling that connection with my mother, I experienced an odd sensation. An emotion I could not recall feeling before. Something alien and foreign to me.

"It is joy, beloved daughter of mine. It is joy."

Laughter on the wind, sunshine in my heart, love from beyond death. I found myself laughing too. In that moment there was peace in my heart, and yes joy. These were the emotions that I was not accustomed to. I crouched there for some time letting myself feel. Opening myself up to the possibility that even without Gawain's love, I could be happy.

Me and my daughter.

We could be happy here.

We would be happy here.

I made a promise there and then, to Rowan and to my daughter. We would be happy here. As if in answer, I felt a fluttering then. Tiny, like the wings of a butterfly gently teasing the insides of my belly.

My daughter. "I feel you little one. I feel you." And then another rush of emotion that overwhelmed me in its power. "I love you little one."

Powerful emotions are powerful energies. I knew this. So, I was not surprised to feel a change in the atmosphere. A chill within the sunlight, an altering of the air that few people would detect. And then she was there with me. The other mother from the other time.

"I loved my little girl. She would have been born at Samhain too."

I turned to see Eliza standing close by. Clearer than that time in the kitchen. But ethereal enough to know she was a ghost, a spirit, an echo of the past.

For the first time I spoke to her. "Hello Eliza. I am so sorry for what they did to you."

"They killed my baby."

"I know."

"They killed me."

"I know."

The sorrow of that brutal event crashed through the barriers of time, immense, consuming. The sorrow I carried within my own heart strengthening the link between us. A powerful, dangerous link.

"This time all will be well."

Her words reminded me of what Mabel had said. "What is meant to be will come to thee. When love is pure, it will endure."

"This time all will be well." I promised Eliza as much as I was promising myself.

I completely forgot what else Mabel had said. "Stay in the light and all will be right."

I was about to step into the dark, but I was blind to it then.

CHAPTER TWENTY-NINE

After the rather abrasive aspects of Mum's attitudes towards me, I was heart-warmed by the comfort blanket that my aunt and uncle wrapped around me in the following days. Their love ensured that at least in some areas I was snug, safe, and secure. Reeling as I was from the recent events I was glad to spend the next few days being cosseted in their cosy cottage.

I slept in late and enjoyed the quiet of Number One Cobblers Row. The weather had settled into a run of softly warm June sunshine, the blue sky an open invitation to lazily savour sitting in the courtyard garden with a succession of coffees, inhaling the crisp, pungent scents of the herbs growing in the many pots.

Cake was also in great supply.

Mabel called round the morning after I had returned from visiting Mum, laden with a couple of tins. I was just making my second cup of coffee, not yet having had breakfast, and the doorbell rang.

"I heard you were back, love. Sandra's holding the fort for me this morning. I wanted to pop round and give you a little something." The friendly baker smiled at me with blue eyes alert, scanning over me in a manner that suggested she was searching for something more than physical.

Something within my soul perhaps? That was the feeling I had. But it was not intrusive. More in a protective way. I smiled back, genuinely pleased to have her company, and of course whatever was in the tins. "Come in. I was just making a brew would you like one?"

"Tea would be lovely, thank you." She followed me through the lounge, to the kitchen and deposited the two tins on the counter.

"I know chocolate brownies are your favourite; these have a little special extra added to them." She lifted the lid to show me the delightful contents and gave me a wink along with her smile.

"Added extra?"

"Purely medicinal. Good for you, and the baby."

I wondered what witchcraft she had been up to, because clearly along with the baking, there had been spell making too. But I was wise enough not to ask, and wise enough to trust her.

"They look delicious. And what's in the other one?"

"My special flapjacks."

"Special?" I raised an eyebrow at her and received another smile and wink. "Well in that case as I have not had breakfast yet, one each will be perfect. Will you join me?"

"No thank you, I have eaten already. Are we sitting outside, it's such a beautiful morning."

"Absolutely."

We settled ourselves at the little table and I made a start on the chocolate brownie. There was definitely a different flavour to it, slightly bitter, but pleasant all the same. After a couple of minutes whilst Mabel commented on the various herbs that Aunty Ruth grew, enlightening me as to their culinary or witchy benefits, she got round to the subject that had clearly brought her here, along with the brownies and flapjacks.

"It's a funny little place, Maypoleton. I am sure you will know by now that there was another skeleton that Eve discovered. Led to all sorts of things happening to her. She doesn't like to talk about it, and for that matter, neither do I, but I do want you to be careful, Fae."

I remembered what she had said previously and reassured her that everything would be perfectly alright. There was such a sense of love and warmth coming from her, that I felt compelled to add further.

"It's alright Mabel. I do know what can happen when things go wrong." The memory of spellcasting. The desire to overturn another's will. The death that followed. No one knew better than I the disastrous consequences of magic falsely created.

"Well, I just wanted to say, now that things are out in the open for you, in that respect as well as the baby, you are more than welcome to join our coven. We're such a friendly bunch and I am sure you would enjoy our meetings."

I finished the brownie, licked my fingers appreciatively and answered, before taking a bite of the flapjack. "Thank you. I am sure you are. I think I have probably met all your ladies by now in one way or another." I grinned at her. "I think I can tell who they are by the way they come up and talk to me. Quite different to some of the other folk here, I must say."

"In that case, our next meeting is tomorrow night, funnily enough. We meet at my flat over the bakery at seven thirty. No need to bring anything, just yourself."

I gave my head a little shake. "I think you misunderstood me. Thank you again for inviting me, but really, it is not my cup of tea." I may have blown my cover in respect of that side of me, but that did not mean to say I wanted to jump head long into the village witch scene.

"I am more of a lone wolf."

She cocked her head in that bird-like way she had, reminding me of a friendly, inquisitive robin. "I can see that. But with company comes protection."

"I don't need protection."

Mabel said nothing in response to that and gently changed the subject to the other main topic, in other words the baby. It was still a mind dazzling concept that me, Fae, erstwhile slut, man eater, Miss Independent, I don't need anyone in my life, thank you very much, Winters, had not only got myself in the ludicrous situation of falling in love with a man who did not want her, but was also going to be mother to his child! Every time someone mentioned the baby, I had to remind myself that they were asking after me!

Of course, there were the critics, the judgmental types, in a village this size and especially one with such a strong church going ethic. All of which clashed wonderfully with the equally strong and far more ancient witchy vibe. Mabel was clearly on my side, but Mrs Mannering had a strong influence in the community. It was apparent from the snippets of gossip I overheard whilst out and about, that she was still advocating that it would be far better if I were replaced in my duties of looking after Arthur.

Much better for example for a good hearted, pure of soul widow to take my place, and whilst doing so occupy the empty vacancy of the Vicar's wife. A lot can happen in a week, and it appeared that in my absence visiting my parents and taking some time to recover from the psychic overload of uncovering Eliza, the lovely Lucinda had made her presence well and truly felt both in the vicarage and the village in general.

Did I need any more to ruffle my feathers, to poke at my already bruised ego, to stab deeper into the bleeding mess that was my heart? No. I absolutely did not. But that was what came my way. It seemed that the gods were not going to allow me the comfort of nestling back within Aunty Ruth's loving home without spoiling it somewhat. It was as though the Universe was playing games with me.

Look, the gods were saying, aren't we benevolent? After all those years of purgatory when you were blaming yourself for Fliss's death and thinking that the role of mother was never going to be for you, here you are, pregnant. And look, after feeling so disconnected after all those years of denying who you truly are, a gifted and powerful witch, you are back where you belong, amongst your own kind, reunited with the spirit of your natural mother.

Aren't we benevolent?

Indeed.

And perhaps just a touch malevolent as well?

It felt that way to me.

As if the powers that be were pushing me, testing, me, demanding of me how far I would take their little games before I stepped forward and took action myself. Furthermore, what shape would that action take?

It was enough to make anyone's head, heart and soul, spin, without the added dose of hormonal energies that were coursing through me every day. I was all over the place and Aunty Ruth, who had not had children herself, was super protective of me. I made the most of feeling like a beloved child wrapped up in her care.

On the last morning of my week off, I woke up early in my usual manner for once, free of the grogginess that had assailed me for the last few weeks. Hearing the noises of Aunty Ruth bustling about downstairs, I realised I was awake in time to join her down at the stables. Tossing aside my duvet, I pulled on my running gear, which was the closet attire I had to jodhpurs, t-shirt and hoody, and went downstairs to join her, thinking I would shower later.

"Oh, hello love, did I wake you?"

"No. I woke up myself. I feel so much better this morning. More like me."

She smiled at me, and I could see relief in her eyes. "That is good to hear. I have been fretting over you. It's lovely news about the baby, but I could see it was making you feel proper poorly. Hormones can do strange things to women, as natural as pregnancy is."

We both avoided commenting on the other issue. The effects of digging up dead bodies. And of course, she had no idea at that moment of the biggest issue of all.

Him.

He who had rejected me.

He who had invaded my heart and soul and stolen both away, leaving me in an empty void.

A dangerously empty void.

Why dangerous?

Because voids will always find a way of being filled, be that with good or bad intentions.

"So everyone keeps telling me," I said with a smile. "Annie made it very clear that I could expect to feel peculiar at any given time." I thought with fondness of my friend who had loaded me up with magazines, and books to bring back with me. "And make sure you read them, Fae, I know what you are like," she had said with a rueful smile. Did she? Did she really know what I was like? No, she didn't bless her, nor did Aunty Ruth but it was better that they didn't.

"I thought I could come with you this morning if that's okay?"

"Course it is love. I was going to take Treacle for a hack as it's such a lovely day. Why don't you join me on Toffee?"

As reckless as I was, I did have to ask if this was a good idea. Fancy that, me, Fae Winters considering the risk factor of something. But feeling the fluttering in my belly, I knew that nothing was more important now that this little soul growing inside me. But Aunty Ruth, and the other women down at Farthing Hall Livery for that matter were all in agreement. A nice hack on the slow and steady Toffee, in the company of the equally slow and steady Treacle, ridden by my very accomplished Aunty Ruth, was just the thing. Especially on such a beautiful June morning.

Off we went, the first part of our hack taking us through the grounds of Farthing Hall, and passed the small cottage where Eve's father, Seth lived. I had met the old Romany gentleman a few times on my trips to the stables. A quietly observant man who truth to tell made me a little uneasy at times. I got the feeling that he could see into me, far more than even Mabel for all her witchyness.

His face was at the window as we passed, by, washing the pots in the kitchen sink by the look of it. Aunty Ruth waved to him. I kept both hands on the reins but nodded my head. I wasn't expecting him to come out, he was never much of a talker, but he did so.

"Mornin'" he greeted us, going immediately to both horses and placing a hand on their necks, so that he was stood between us. Treacle and Toffee leant into him, their lips softening and gentle noises of appreciation coming from them. I hated to admit it, but I rather envied them his touch. There was magic there that they felt. No need to be envious though, because it appeared today, I was also going to be blessed. He came round to my side and looked up at me, a deeply probing, but kind look in his eyes. They were unusual in colour, just like Eve's a mix of blue, green and brown.

"Eve tells me thee's wi' chil'" He had a strong accent and use of dialect and at times I struggled to understand him, but his meaning was clear today.

"I am."

He nodded thoughtfully and then without permission, but somehow, I didn't mind, he placed a hand on my belly. Then he murmured something completely unintelligible in a very quiet voice, as though he was talking to my unborn child. He smiled and nodded once more. Then he turned to look at me again.

"Aye, a daughter o' Samhain. Little lass'll be well. 'Tis thee wot needs mindin'." He heaved a big sigh and there was a well of compassion held within. "Ah lass, thee needs t' let go. No good'll cum of this battle. 'Tis time t' stop fighting lass. Can thee not see? 'Tis that fight within that harms thee?"

He had deliberately moved to be at my side, away from Aunty Ruth and spoke so quietly, whispering almost, so she would not be able to hear what he was saying. I said nothing in reply just a little shake of my head to silently say that I was not fighting anything. He smiled kindly.

Speaking louder now, he said, "Ah well lass, any time thee needs me, thee just asks." He placed his hand again on my belly and uttered a few more words in his own ancient language and then asked Aunty Ruth how my uncle was, before wishing us a good morning's ride.

As we made our way off the grounds and onto the country lane that led towards the village, I had his words ringing in my head. Aunty Ruth picked up on my thoughtful mood and allowed me to be quiet which I was thankful for.

What had he meant?
Stop fighting?
What battle?

I wasn't fighting anyone. I convinced myself of this as I let the rhythmic movements of the horse permeate into my body and mind, until I convinced myself that Seth had read me wrong. I was not fighting anyone, or anything. I almost said this out loud just to prove a point to the Universe but stopped in time as I realised this would disturb Aunty Ruth. But the Universe is always listening and likes nothing better at times than to show us mere mortals just how ridiculous we are.

A car was slowing down to pass us on the narrow country lane. Aunty Ruth was in front of me and waved in acknowledgement at the driver, before pulling Treacle to a halt which of course made Toffee stop.

"Morning Matt, are you not at the school today?" Aunty Ruth greeted the driver, his window down, head poking out to speak to her.

"It's lunch time," he said with an easy smile to her, and I was struck again how attractive he was in that rugged, blond-haired way, a touch of a Viking about him. I was also struck by how long it seemed since he and I had been in a bed together. Or on a kitchen table for that matter.

I felt a restless squirming inside me.

"Goodness is it that time already," Aunty Ruth laughed. "Time just disappears at the stables."

"Beautiful day for it though," he said. "I wish I could get out into the hills for a run. I'm heading into Lancaster for the afternoon, got a course to do, not my idea of fun. Never mind."

Then he allowed his car to creep ever so slowly so that he was alongside me, with Aunty Ruth ahead of him. "How are you, Fae?" His words were casual, but the look in his eyes was not. This was a man pre-occupied with one thought and one thought only.

Remembering how he had pitied me, rejected me, I chose to ignore the unspoken question.

"I am very well thank you."

"I hear congratulations are in order?"

A question definitely. He had heard the news. I was pregnant. I wondered that Laura had not mentioned what I had led her and Eve to believe, that I had had a broken relationship before coming to Maypoleton, and that the pregnancy was a result of that. By the disturbed look in his eyes, it appeared that although my new friends loved to gossip, it was between themselves.

"Yes. I am going to have a baby." I blasted him with my super wattage smile, enjoying seeing the fear shadow those hazel eyes, like a cloud passing over the sun.

He dropped his gaze to my belly, and I knew he was desperately trying to gauge the state of my pregnancy by my size. Considering how slim I was, and how little I was showing, this would not have reassured him. He could easily have been the father. I was happy to let him sweat, a petty revenge for the hurt he had caused me, the bruises to my ego. I felt that anger rise up within me.

How dare he pity me

How dare he reject me.

How dare he suggest I was so desperate for sex I was addicted.

Unfortunately, Aunty Ruth, shortened my little victory as she cheerfully told him, "Due at the end of October, so there will be a baby in our house for Christmas. Isn't that wonderful?"

Matt's head turned swiftly back to look at Aunty Ruth and just as quickly I saw the relief flash into his expression as the sums gave him the answer he was hoping for. He could not be the father.

"Yes. Yes, that is wonderful. Fabulous news!"

Aunty Ruth would only have heard how pleased he was in general at the news.

I heard something else entirely.

I heard that he was so fucking happy not to have been caught out.

I heard that he was thanking his lucky stars, he was not the father of my child.

I heard rejection.

"Well, I will let you get on with your ride, as I said, I must get to Lancaster Uni and sit in a stuffy conference room. I hope you feel sorry for me?" He ended this comment on a laugh, his gaze moving from Aunty Ruth's to me. I saw his eyes widen slightly and the smile dim from his face. What had I revealed in that look of mine? I was not quite sure, but it was enough to rattle him. It rattled me. I felt on edge and out of sorts, the simple joy in the morning spoilt by the encounter.

It was to get worse.

We approached the village, the main street the shops and pub on one side and the green and duck pond on the other, with of course the centuries old stocks and maypole from which the village had derived its name. Not a pole as such, but an old, old tree around which folk had danced and sung, celebrated and yes, created magic. It had also been where Eliza had been hung, after being dragged out of the vicarage by her hair, hauled across the green, brutally beaten until the lifeblood of her child drenched the grass.

"Are you alright love?" I heard Aunty Ruth's voice calling to me.

Toffee automatically followed Treacle, which was good because I had not been paying attention at all to what I was doing. I was not there. I was in the past. I was seeing, hearing, feeling, the past. A quick flash of it, perhaps no more than a few seconds, but enough to shake me to the core. So much hate. So much powerful energy. Powerful enough to cross the boundaries of time. Powerful enough to cross the boundaries from one person's soul to another.

"Yes, yes, I am fine." I gave myself a big enough shake that even the placid Toffee turned her head round to question me. I patted her reassuringly and focused on the present. It was a beautiful sunny June day in 2024. I was in the place of my birth, with my lovely aunt. There were friendly villagers enjoying the sunshine, sitting on the benches, admiring the view, the river, that flowed under the ancient stone bridge, the pond where the mums and young children gathered to feed the ducks. It was the most pleasant and tranquil of scenes.

We let the horses meander onto the green and loosed the reins to allow them to graze, exchanging a few pleasantries with people as we did so. What could possibly be nicer? I was telling myself this, and yet somehow it was not resonating with me. I was not feeling the happy vibe. I was still feeling the residue of fear, anger and hate. Perhaps it was not such a surprise then as to what happened next.

"Ooh I have just remembered, I have to pass a message on to Gawain, do you mind if we head over to the vicarage?"

"What? No of course not." Another inward shake to lose the feeling that was growing inside me.

"Isn't it lovely to think of him and Lucinda getting together," she said, picking up Treacle's reins once more and giving her a gentle nudge to move on.

"What?" I struggled to concentrate on what I was doing, but Toffee appeared able to follow Treacle, still with her head down munching on grass.

"She's been helping him, as you know, with Arthur this week and it seems that the two of them have been getting on really well. It will be so nice for him to have someone by his side. Ah look, you see what I mean? Morning Gawain, Lucinda."

We were close now to the entrance of the vicarage, back on the quiet road that ran past the old building and out of the village into the fells. The vicarage door had opened and standing there were Gawain and Lucinda.

Looking far too comfortable together.
Looking, like a couple.
Looking like everything I wanted and could not have.
"Good morning, Ruth, Fae, yes isn't it a beautiful day. Lucinda and I have just been putting together some ideas for the summer fayre."

"Oh wonderful, that's always such a lovely day. Now before I forget I must tell you what Beryl said to me down at the stables," and Aunty Ruth went on to relay the message from her friend.

Whilst she was doing so, Lucinda and I were looking at each other. No that is not quite correct. We were staring at each other in the manner of opponents. Enemies. The look in her eyes made it very clear that she considered she had the advantage. At one point as my aunt and Gawain talked, she slipped her hand into his and he appeared to accept this as normal.

I was rocked by how much this hurt.

Then he turned his gaze to me. A neutral, unreadable expression. No idea what my eyes were reflecting back at him. My insides were shaking and that awful churned up feeling was growing in my stomach.

"And how are you, Fae? I hope this weeks' rest has done you good."

"Honestly there is no need to come back to work, if you are struggling with your pregnancy," Lucinda chirped up, "you don't look good, if you don't mind me saying."

I do mind.

I mind ever so fucking much.

I mind more than you can possibly imagine.

She went on. "Arthur has been quite happy me looking after him, hasn't he Gawain?" She leant in closer to him, tilting her pretty face up to his.

His immediate response, to smile back at her, a warm, loving smile. Then he turned back to me. "Yes, he has, and you have been an absolute treasure this week. But to be fair to Fae, this is her job we are talking about."

"Oh yes of course. Yes, we must be fair to Fae."

Fair to Fae?

The twisting, churning, sickening feeling grew, and it had nothing to do with pregnancy. My eyes were drawn to the downstairs window. I could see Arthur waving. He had clearly heard our voices. Pulling myself back from the desire to get off Toffee and slap Lucinda, I waved back, glad that I could at least smile back genuinely for him.

"Well, we had best be off then." Aunty Ruth's voice cut into my thoughts.

The general round of goodbyes, and then Lucinda shot one more poisoned arrow in my direction. "Bye you two, lovely to see you back, Fae." Then reaching up to Gawain she kissed him on the cheek. "See you later."

His smile told me he was looking forward to it.

"Oh, it's so nice to see you two together. I was just saying so to Fae, wasn't I?" Aunty Ruth's voice was dim in my ears.

I couldn't speak. My eyes were drawn to another window of the vicarage. The upstairs one that I knew was Gawain's bedroom.

She was there.

Eliza.

Watching, me, watching them.

I felt her pain. I felt her hurt. I felt her rage.

"Fae?"

I heard Aunty Ruth. I heard Gawain. But I heard Eliza more clearly.

"I feel your pain. I share your pain. I will help you. I will ease your pain."

"Fae?"

"Sorry, miles away. Yes. Yes, you make a lovely couple. I am happy for you."

Lucinda smiled at me, satisfaction in her face. Gawain did not smile. He knew. Oh yes, he knew. But he did not know all. How could he? Because at that point, neither did I. As we retraced out steps to the stables, I was preoccupied with one thought only.

How was Eliza going to ease my pain?

CHAPTER THIRTY

"We shall make him jealous."
"I beg your pardon?"
"We shall make him jealous. It hurts so much does it not, this feeling inside. It twists, it turns so, it tears. It devours us does it not?"

Eliza's description of how she was feeling was identical to mine and I could only nod in agreement, no longer surprised to find myself having a conversation with a ghost. In the week since returning to work at the vicarage she had made her presence felt much more strongly. From shadowy glimpses, ethereal wisps of a figure, she had become almost as clear to me as the reflection in my mirror.

Perhaps that is what she was in many ways.

A reflection of all that I was experiencing in this time and place. To be so wildly, passionately, soulfully in love with the vicar of this village, to be carrying his child. To be so painfully rejected by him for the love of another woman. Was this why she had called me to find her grave? To set her free from the torture of lying there unloved and forgotten for centuries.

It had been torture, for her, she told me so.

To be a soul lost between worlds, in an agony of unrest.

I was in torture. I was in an agony of unrest.

Gawain and Lucinda were now being seen as a couple within the village. The wretched woman was constantly popping in and out of the vicarage with one excuse or another to speak to him, or Mrs Mannering, who was clearly her ally. Lovely, Lucinda with her sweet, ever so sweet smile, her tinkling laugh, the coy way she had of tilting her head to look up at him. Kindhearted, gentle, Sunday School teacher.

The perfect match for the vicar.

Everyone said so.

Apart that is, from Arthur.

He was the only one, who knew the real state of affairs. On my first morning back, he had looked at me sharply and patted my hand as I settled him into his wheelchair to go for our morning's walk round the village.

"She isn't right for him, you know."

"What do you mean?" I tried to be casual, but he was wise to the edge in my voice.

"Oh aye, on paper it's a perfect match, but real life isn't all about ticking the right boxes and having everything all neat and tidy. Real love isn't like that either. Real love should be wild and brave, and fearsome." His blue eyes, a softer shade than his son's without the steely grey tone to them, went misty.

The emotion in his voice penetrated my armour. "Was that how you felt about Bessie?"

He stunned me then, wiping away a tear from his eye and clearing his throat with a cough. "No Fae. Don't get me wrong, I loved my Bessie, as good a woman as there ever walked this earth. But she was not the fire in my heart. She was not the passion that lit my soul. Bloody fool that I was, I let that one go."

We had got to one of the benches on the green and I paused in pushing his chair so that I could sit alongside him. He seemed content to talk, his gaze not meeting mine, but looking into the past, sadness and regret turning his voice to a husky whisper.

"Oh, she was a wild one, my Edith. As bold as brass folk would say. Bold in her speech, the way she dressed, the way she laughed. Oh, the way she laughed. She could brighten the darkest of days with her laugh. And as for the way she loved………Well. Only a damn fool would throw that away. And a damn fool I was. Edith Smith. Love of my bloody life only I was too damned scared to see it. Status. It was all about status you see. I was set on building my business, becoming a successful man, mixing in all the right places."

A pause and one which had him swallowing away the tears and my eyes filling at the same time. I dug in my pockets and reached out a tissue for us both.

"Thank you,' he went on. "She didn't fit you see. I was a respectable middle-class man, with his eye on moving up the ladder. Ambitious, aye I am not too proud to admit it. Ambitious bloody idiot. Edith Smith came from the back streets. Swore like a trooper........."

I had the feeling he was going to say, "fucked like a whore," instead after another pause, he went on. "Aye. Not the sort of woman I could introduce to the guild. And that was my aim you see. To become mayor. Which I did. And Bessie Longworth, well she was just right for the role. And don't get me wrong, Fae, I loved my Bessie, I did that. And I was faithful to her from the moment I asked her to marry me. But Edith Smith, oh Fae, she took a part of my heart and soul that could never, ever belong to another."

"Fucking hell, Arthur." Tears were streaming down my face now and I had to sniff noisily as my nose was dripping too. My tissue was soaked. I reached for his hand and held it tightly. "Thank you for sharing that with me."

"Aye, you swear like Edith." He turned his head then and looked at me through eyes that although dim with age, and swimming with tears, were sharp enough to see the reflection of his own story in my gaze. "And I would like to bet that you love like she did too. Heart, body and soul and not a scrap of you held back. And that is how you feel about my boy isn't it?"

I could not speak, only nod my head and look him honestly in the eyes. I respected him far too much to attempt to lie. I realised as well that I loved him, as another father figure in my life. A father who could see me for who I was, and still perhaps like, maybe even love for all of that.

"Oh Fae. Who was it said, 'Love makes fools of us all, big and small'? No, I don't know either. But damn them they were right." He gave my hand a gentle squeeze. "Please do not feel you have to answer this question. It is not my right to know."

"Yes." I said before he could even ask it. "I am carrying Gawain's child."

"Does he know?"

I nodded and he swore in a manner I had not heard him before. Then he grunted. "Damn fool boy! If I could do so I would box his bloody ears and shake him by the throat until he could see what is right in front of him." His anger was at least some comfort, and I felt my heart lift a little at the knowledge that I had someone on my side. "I do hope he is at least going to make sure you are financially taken care of, I will not stand by and see you struggle, Fae. If it takes the last breath in my body, I will not do that."

I wiped my tears, blew my nose with another tissue and gave him a reassuring smile. "He has. And please do not fret on my account. I am a tough cookie."

"That's as may be. Even so, Fae, I am disappointed in him. How can he not see what is right in front of him?" He gave a harsh bark of a laugh. "Ah but then who am I to talk hey? What have I just told you about my Edith? I hope he comes to his senses about Lucinda. Oh, flaming bloody hell, speak of the devil, here she comes."

Drifting across the village green towards the vicarage and the bench we were sitting on, in a floaty floral summer dress, so different to the ripped jeans and tie-dyed t-shirt I was wearing, came my nemesis.

"Morning Arthur. Fae. Oh goodness Fae, you don't look too well today. Have you been crying? Nothing wrong with the baby I hope?"

"All is well thank you, Lucinda. Fae here suffers badly from hay fever and I do believe the pollen is quite high at the moment." Arthur stepped in neatly with his reply.

"Oh. I see. Well, I must get on. Gawain and I have lots to do this morning. He is so glad of my help organising the summer fayre, it's going to be the best ever this year."

Arthur and I merely nodded at her but once she had walked out of hearing range, he turned to me with a wicked look in his eye. "Are you going to say it, or shall I?"

"Fuck off Lucinda."

He patted my hand. "That's the spirit. Don't let it get you down girl. You are far too good for that."

Therein lay the problem.
I was not good.
I was bad.
Very bad.

So, when a few days later, Eliza appeared in the garden with her suggestion of making Gawain jealous, I was all too ready to listen. Arthur was having a nap and as I usually did during these times, I made myself a coffee, helped myself to a slice of cake that Mrs Mannering had made and left out to cool, knowing how much this would annoy her, and went down to the bottom of the garden.

To Eliza's forgotten resting place. Only of course she was forgotten no longer, and neither was she resting. She was right here beside me, chatting as easily as though she were a real person.

"He needs to feel your pain. He must be made to feel what we feel."

"We?"

She touched me then, as much as a ghost can touch a person. Lighter than a feather, icy cold, fingers that I could see through linking with mine.

"I share your pain. Remember that, Fae. I share your pain. I was not loved. My baby was not wanted. I was rejected. I share your pain."

Of course, she did, and she had suffered so much more besides. As that ghostly hand held onto mine, I saw, felt, experienced once more in all its brutal savagery, the way her child had been beaten out of her body and those last gasping breaths as the noose took her life.

I started to choke, and she released my hand.

"Too much. I am sorry."

"You have nothing to be sorry for." I cleared my throat, rubbing at my neck as I did so. It was all so terrifying real. I needed a touch of modern life to bring me back into focus. "I am going back into the kitchen; I need another coffee." A bloody strong one as well.

She followed me in, my invisible friend, only me able to see and hear her. I set about brewing more coffee, the pungent aroma the perfect antidote to centuries old trauma. With the devil in me roused I cut another large slice of cake. Mrs Mannering would have a fit when she came back from the shops but what the hell. I checked my watch and reckoned I had about another twenty minutes before Arthur would be waking from his nap.

"So then, you agree. He is to be made jealous."

"What?"

"The Vicar, he is to be made jealous. Then he will understand our, your pain. Then he will see clearly."

Hateful though it was, I rather liked the idea of inflicting some measure of pain on Gawain. I definitely applauded the notion that he may come to see clearly. After all wasn't that what his father was hoping.

She read my mind. *"His father wishes him to see you clearly."*

I conveniently dumped into a large bucket of sand, the perhaps worrying thought that she could see into me so deeply. I much preferred to listen to what she was saying that making Gawain jealous would be a good thing. I wanted him to feel as I was feeling. I wanted him to understand just how much I loved him.

Do as thou will and harm none.

The wiccan creed.

I conveniently dumped that into the sand bucket too.

"How do we do that then?"

Eliza gave that mischievous little smile that I was coming to know so well and shook her head as if to say wasn't it obvious. Which of course it was. There is not a woman alive who does not instinctively know how to make a man jealous.

You don't need to be a witch to do this.

You just need another man.

Matt.

I returned her smile as I thought of the ruggedly handsome schoolteacher with whom I had shared so many heated encounters. Vigorous, earthy sex which served as a release for two physically active, healthy people. Neither of whom loved each other. Both of whom loved someone else. Both of whom were invisible to the person they loved.

As these thoughts were flowing into my mind, Eliza's smile widened and she began to laugh that soft, whispery, ghostly laugh. I did sometimes wonder how deep into my mind and subconscious she could delve, dimly aware that this was not a good thing. Her cobwebby touch, her ghostly hand on mine, blew the thought away.

"It is good is it not. It is a perfectly balanced notion. He loves Laura, she loves another. You love Gawain. He loves another."

She began to move around the kitchen whilst I remained sitting at the table, drinking the last few mouthfuls of my coffee.

"Matt loves Laura, she loves another, Fae loves Gawain, he loves another, tis a perfectly balanced notion, time now then to brew the perfect potion!"

With this, she giggled and then the movements became a swirling dance around the table, as she repeated this refrain in the sing song voice of a child with a nursery rhyme. Only this was no child singing about Jack and Jill going up a hill, or Humpty Dumpty on a wall. This was a centuries old ghost of a witch dancing round the table in the vicarage and creating a dizzying psychic energy as she did so.

I was caught up in the cyclone and the next moment I was dancing with her, holding as much as it was possible, her ghostly hands and following her lead in both movements and words, only mine were slightly different.

"Matt loves Laura, she loves another. I love Gawain he loves another, tis a perfectly balanced notion, all we need is to make the perfect potion."

Time underwent a fractured shift.

I was no longer a thirty year old woman, I was younger, much younger, I was closer to the age Eliza was, I was that raw, untutored witch, that hormonally charged teenager, with all her hopes and dreams ahead of her, I was that girl who was so desperately afraid of losing the love of her life, that she sent her twin sister out to meet him in her place when she was forbidden to go out.

The emotions and feelings came roaring back, bursting through the barrier of time, surging into the room with a super charged energy. It mingled, blended, synergised with the raw, painful emotions of the here and the now. A long-lost reservoir of feelings, emotions, held back for far too long, and suddenly released now, to be used, utilised, brought into play. The dam had burst and there was no holding it back.

More than that, Eliza's life came rushing to the fore.

In the blink of an eye, it seemed that I was in two eras at once. Aware I was in the here and now, that was my coffee cup on the table. That was my plate with the cake crumbs on it. That was the beast of the aga that Mrs Mannering cooked on. Only those were not the sleek and shiny modern pans hanging up on the hooks overhead. Those were much older copper pans.

There was no dishwasher, no microwave. I was dancing in the kitchen that had been here centuries ago. I was dancing with the vibrantly alive, rosy cheeked, pregnant young Eliza, with laughter in her bright blue eyes. All at the same time I was being swirled around the room by this ghostly version of her. The same place, different times.

We danced, we swirled, we chanted.
We danced, we swirled, we laughed.
We danced, we swirled, we created.

There was in actual fact no need for a potion. Of course, we could have brewed one up. No doubt we would, just to add to it. But the truth of the matter was, we were making magic, casting a spell purely by our thoughts, our words, our feelings, our energy, our intentions.

Intentions fuelled by centuries old pain, grief, rage.
Intentions fuelled by decades old pain, grief, loss.
Intentions fuelled by pain, heartbreak, jealousy in the here and the now.

Oh yes that was all it was going to take. I say all, there was nothing trivial about what was happening in that kitchen at that moment. This was powerful stuff. It came to an abrupt halt when Eliza released her ghostly grasp on my hands.

"It is done."
"It is?"

Never mind that the room had been spinning, and I had been shifting backwards and forwards hundreds of years with every swirl and twirl or so it seemed, I was dizzy suddenly at the thought of what I might be getting myself into.

Do as thou will and harm none.

"Trust me. You do trust me, don't you. I share your pain. We are the same. We are soul sisters."

As I sat, or rather stumbled into a chair, the room coming sharply back into focus, just as Eliza herself, faded back into the barely visible ghostly presence, it was all I could do to dumbly nod my head. Then I had to promptly switch into another gear as I heard the bell that was connected from Arthur's room to the kitchen ring.

I checked my watch as saw that yes, it was about the time he usually woke from his afternoon nap. I quickly slurped the last mouthful of now very cold coffee, flicked some cake crumbs from the table to the floor which I knew would incense Mrs Mannering further, and rose somewhat unsteadily from the chair.

"You alright?" Arthur greeted me with a querying look as I went back into his room with what I hoped to be a brightly breezy air about me.

Clearly, I had failed. "I'm fine," I lied as truth be told I felt very sick.

"You don't look it," he harrumphed as I helped him out of bed and into his wheel chair, in fact you look like you are going to....."

I was, and I did.

I had to leave him at a rather uncomfortable angle in his chair, and rush past into the ensuite wet room that Gawain had had fitted for his father. I retched horribly for a few minutes, sweat forming on my brow and a sudden bout of chills wracking my body.

Sick bug, no.

Pregnancy, no.

Psychic energy reaction, absolutely.

The worst I had ever experienced, and I could only put it down to the intensity of what had just happened. I reassured Arthur as he called through to me that I was fine, and staggered up from clutching the toilet bowl, to rinse my mouth out and splash cold water onto my face. I didn't look fine; I looked dreadful. Arthur echoed my thoughts when I went back into the bedroom and helped him into a more comfortable position.

"You look dreadful." Concern flickered in his gentle blue eyes. "Do you need to see Doctor Jay?"

"Thanks," I stuck my tongue out at him and rolled my eyes, "cos every woman really likes to hear she looks like shit."

He laughed. "You're ok then."

"I am," I said, to hastily reassure him. "My friend Annie told me that some women do get these weird bouts of morning sickness that are not just in the morning."

"Oh. Isn't that usually just in the first three months? You're past that aren't you."

"Usually yes." I then managed to grin properly at him as the nausea began to recede. "But then I am not your usual woman, Arthur, am I?"

He chuckled at that. "No missy you certainly are not. Let me see, you have been accused of murder, you've discovered a skeleton in the garden, you've rattled the dragon more than anyone I have ever come across." He paused and looked at me then with a dash more solemnity in his eyes as his gaze flitted over my stomach. Unspoken were the words, "and you are carrying my grandchild."

What he did say, reaching over to pat my hand, was, "I am very glad you are here, Fae, I am very glad you are here. You put a fair sparkle into my life, you really do. Yes, you're like a sparkling fairy." He gave another small chuckle then. "Maybe even a fairy witch hey?"

The witch word never sat easily with me. I wrinkled my nose at him. "I like the thought of a sparkling fairy." Fairies never harmed anyone.

He nodded as if appreciating my reluctance to be associated with the craft in the way that numerous women in Maypoleton were so overtly. "How about a dose of Drummond to bring us down to earth hey?"

"Bloody good idea. I think we only have a couple of chapters to go with this one." I went over to the shelf where the book I had read to Mr Carlisle was propped up next to a bird spotting guide. I settled myself comfortably in a chair, opposite Arthur and began to read. Bulldog Drummond and his crew, thwarting the ever-scheming Carl Peterson and his beautiful but dangerous wife Irma. A perfect antidote for wild witchcraft. A short while later, I closed the book and we both gave a satisfied sigh.

"So, is that it then?" Arthur said thoughtfully. "Is that the last we see of Carl and Irma? Doesn't seem likely that they can come back after that one?"

I smiled at him because I knew there were more books in the series. "Oh no there's more."

"What's the next one then?"

I tilted my head to smile wickedly at him. "The Female Of The Species."

"More deadly than the male."

"Exactly."

Our book discussion was then cut short as voices became audible in the hallway. Two male voices. My senses pinged into hyper alertness, something I struggled to hide from Arthur's keen eyes.

"I'm fine lass, and it's about time you were going. Off you pootle now, I'll see you in the morning. And bring that book with you."

A look of understanding passed between us. He knew how I felt about his son. He knew that every moment I could spend in his company with him, regardless of whether he wanted me or not, was precious. He did not know about the whirling, swirling, weaving and spinning of spells that had been performed in the kitchen earlier. But it was once more in the forefront of my mind. I quickly stood up and pecked him on the cheek, my heart unfathomably racing as I went to open the door.

Oh, my gods, I love you.

That sledgehammer hit to my heart and soul each time I saw him. It was not getting any easier and I wondered if that was the pregnancy hormones, or something else. Gawain had been laughing with Matt, that rare sound that I loved to hear, and never did when he was just with me.

How I longed to have him laugh with me.

Love with me.

Be with me.

"Fae, good afternoon." The laughter stopped and that mask was quickly in place in those blue grey eyes. "How is my father today?"

"Good," I nodded with a bright smile on my face. I was holding the book I had just finished reading and he commented on it.

"He thoroughly enjoys you reading to him. Especially those books. I think they remind him of his own time in the army."

"Arthur was in the army?"

Gawain nodded and a deeper shadow entered his gaze. "During the war. He doesn't talk about it much."

I held his gaze, my mind back to that first night in bed with him. Those scars I had traced with my fingers. That story written across his body in pain and memories. The frightening manner in which he had laid low five men, so brutally easily. He knew what my eyes were saying to him, and I saw a tiny muscle twitch at the corner of his mouth.

"Matt and I have some details to thrash out for the charity races we are organising."

Brisk, business like.

Shutting me out.

Rejecting me.

"Matt loves Laura, she loves another. You love Gawain, he loves another."

I felt her energy and emotion mingling with mine, and a tiny push from within. I turned my gaze to Matt and when I spoke, I knew my voice held magic in its tones.

"Good to see you again, Matt."

For a second he stared at me and then blinked as though he had heard something whispered silently in his head.

Words unspoken.

Words whispered by a witch.

Words of dark magic.

"Good to see you too, Fae. You're looking really well. Blooming as they say, isn't she Gawain."

I hid my smile well as Gawain's expression grew even flintier. Thankfully Matt was so entranced he didn't notice his friends lack of response.

"We should go for a drink, Fae, or a meal maybe. In fact, I could cook one evening if you like? I make a mean Bolognese don't I mate?"

Gawain grunted in response.

"That would be lovely, Matt, yes let's do that soon." I beamed my super wattage smile at him and then turned the full blast onto Gawain. "Perhaps we could go out together, you, me, Matt and Lucinda?"

"Matt, shall we get on, we've lots to cover."

"What? Oh yeah, right, mate. Fae, I'll call you." Matt gave himself a little shake and moved to follow Gawain who so clearly wanted to end the conversation.

"See that you do," I dimpled my smile at him.

Gawain went to his study across the hallway and opened the door for Matt to go through. He turned to give me a long and very thoughtful look.

I heard Eliza laughing.

"The female of the species is more deadly than the male."

Gawain entered the study and shut the door.

"Well done. The seeds are sown."

As I left the vicarage and walked back to the cosiness of Cobblers Row, I wondered quite what I had planted.

CHAPTER THIRTY-ONE

"This wasn't supposed to be happening." Matt's voice was sleepy, slumbersome, passion filled and quizzical.

I let out a soft sigh and pressed a kiss gently on his brow. His eyes were closed. There was a light film of sweat on his skin, and mine for that matter. The duvet had been tossed aside long ago, the heat of the summer evening adding to the heat in our bodies. It was two days after Eliza, and I had danced around the vicarage kitchen creating that whirlwind of witchcraft.

Matt had phoned me the next morning inviting me round to his house the following evening for supper. Bolognese as promised. The meal was tasty, the setting in his garden, overlooking the fells, delightful, the atmosphere between us, energetically, magically charged.

Witchcraft at work.

"You know don't you that I love Laura?" He had said with a generous amount of spaghetti twirled around his fork. His hazel eyes had regarded me with an expression of puzzlement as though he couldn't quite believe that he was sitting there with me.

Could not quite believe that he was fighting down such a surge of attraction.

Could not quite believe that he was going to take me upstairs, peel off the short summer dress that I was wearing and fuck me long and hard.

Which he did remarkably well.

That sense of disbelief was still in his voice as I lay replete on top of him.

"I love Laura." He said it again, his hand absently stroking my hair, damp with sweat and tangled with passion.

"I know."

I knew as well that everything he had said to me previously, that we should stop being together like this, because of how he felt about someone else, was not going to withstand the effects of Eliza's magic. My magic, I thought with a shiver of guilt rippling down my spine and into the deep recesses of my soul.

"It's okay," I whispered to him softly because in truth I really liked Matt and I wished nothing more than to see him with Laura, instead of her revolting, abusive husband.

I told myself I was taking pity on him and remembered that sharp stab of pain and rejection when he had pitied me that time. How the tables were turning, I thought with no small amount of satisfaction. He had rejected me and that had stung. It was some balm to that wound to know that right now he was under my spell, and I could pretty much do as I pleased with him.

Which I proceeded to do, my turn now to lead the dance.

I moved my hips, raised myself up on my elbows, leant over him so my hair brushed across his face, teasing him with its soft silky strands. Then the hardened tips of my breasts, so much fuller and more sensitive now with pregnancy, brushing against his mouth, no option for him other than to greedily open his lips and take in one nipple, his hands clasping me to him as though he could not get enough.

Sucking and biting hard, it was bordering on painful, delightfully so, bolts of sensations shooting down to my core, still tender, still wet from before. He groaned as he felt my slick heat move teasingly across his now hard shaft.

"Christ Fae, I don't think I can," he gasped before taking the other nipple into his mouth to lavish the same attention upon it.

I smiled inwardly, glowing with that feminine knowledge that the male beneath her was straining, desperate to be invited in, enveloped deep into the core. Not yet, I thought with wanton pleasure as I took my time, sliding across him, raising up to tease the quivering tip of him, with the barest of wet touches, opening up to him a fraction, then pulling away.

"Fae, please," a whisper, a plea, his eyes open now, on mine as I hovered above him, rocking back slightly on my haunches, still agile, even though my belly was now swelling and my body far softer and rounded.

"You are so fucking beautiful," he said in the voice of a man entranced and so he was. No thoughts of Laura now in his mind. That magic was for now overruling all within him. His hands wandered over my body, fingers tracing the curves, the dips, coming to rest on my hips, pushing slightly, a silent demand that I lower myself onto him.

I did but not in that way.

His intake of breath was enough to tell me that he was unused to the woman taking the lead quite like this. A breath and then a groan of sharpened desire as I shifted a fraction more and invited him, no, insisted, by my actions that he taste me, suck me, lick me.

Bite me ever so, ever so gently.

An exquisite touch of pleasureful pain, painful pleasure.

My turn to groan and lose that shackle of control.

Greedily I writhed above him, needing more and that need within me, fed his own. His hands came to dig deep into the flesh of my buttocks pulling me down harder, clasping me to his mouth, his tongue plunging deep into my core.

My eyes were closed, my mind seeing another face beneath my hips. My heart beating in time to another. My soul reaching across the divide to merge, blend, become one, become whole. Heaven and hell in one moment. Physical delight. Mental, emotional, spiritual torture.

The wrong man.

The wrong heart.

The wrong soul.

Part of me recognised this, knew it, heeded it.

That other part of me, the part that Eliza had connected with so deeply, was blind to it. I had to make him jealous. I had to make him suffer. That rage within, fed by Eliza's loss and suffering, centuries apart from where I was now, had stirred up this brew of desire and entrancement, and nothing was going to stop it. The power of these feelings transmitted to Matt, a silent, command that he was unable to ignore.

His fingers dug deeper into my buttocks as did his tongue into my core. I screamed out loud, a fierce, primal scream of lust fulfilled. A cry from the heart, a soul bleeding in agony as though I were being ripped in two.

I felt I was. Half of me was here. Half of me had disappeared completely. Lost in the vast empty space of the universe, desperately searching for that other part of me and knowing it was beyond my reach. Rage and fury that it should be so. How dare the gods be so cruel. How dare the fates torture me so. How dare another woman steal what was rightfully mine.

My feelings or Eliza's?

I really wasn't sure.

I just knew that I was dangerously out of control.

So was Matt.

My body eased from the spasm that had rushed through me. I was breathing hard, close to crying and all I wanted to do was to curl up on my side and imagine that Gawain was there to hold me, spoon into me, comfort me as I wept. Instead, I was moved across the bed, flipped over and entered roughly from behind as Matt took his turn to find his own release.

There was anger in his movements, nothing playful at all in the way he slapped my backside a couple of times, as though he needed to beat something out of himself and the only way he could do that was to inflict pain on me. My tears fell silently onto the pillow.

This was not how it was meant to be.

This was not meant to be at all.

This was not love. It was not even friendship sex.

This was magic brewed out of hate and revenge.

This was witchcraft, dark alchemy at work.

He came violently, shuddering with a total loss of control. It was just in time too as I was suddenly swamped with the desperate urge to be sick. As fast as I could, I crawled out from beneath him, pushing away the now prone body that had collapsed in a sweating, heavily breathing heap on top of me. I just made it to the bathroom in time, falling to my knees to cradle the toilet with my hands and purge the poison.

Because it was poison.

Do as thou will and harm none.

Which meant, do not cast fucking spells to make people who do not love you, fuck you against their better wishes and desires. Do not cast fucking spells to manipulate the will of another. Do

not, under any fucking circumstances, Fae, play with fucking fire.
Which was precisely what I had done.
Was doing.
I groaned as I vomited harder.
"Christ Fae, I am so sorry. I don't know what came over me."
I could hear the anguish in his voice and my body wracked with another guilty spasm of vomiting in response. There was nothing more to come up and the dry retching was painful, but I welcomed the feeling as a worthy punishment.
"Do you need a doctor? Fae, I haven't hurt the baby, have I?"
I shook my head, clammy with sweat and shaking now. As I gingerly got to my feet I caught sight of my reflection in the mirror. He had every right to look worried.
"I'm fine."
"You don't look it. Please let me call the doctor."
"No honestly I am fine."
I did my best to throw off what I knew were the effects of the misguidedly brewed spell and gave him what I hoped was a reassuring look.
"Let me get you some water."
I shook my head. "Tea. I need a mug of tea. Three sugars. And biscuits. Yes, biscuits if you have them, or cake. Cake would be good."
He looked at me oddly and rightly so. How was he to know that the only way I was going to come round from this was to stuff sugary stuff into my mouth until the jitters went.
"I bought a raisin tart from Mabels for dessert?"
We had abandoned the meal he had so carefully prepared. The tasty Bolognese with the freshly cooked pasta, left discarded as Eliza's magic had taken over.
"Perfect," I nodded. "Cream?"
His turn to nod.
"Lots of it."
"Do you want a shower?"
The heavy scent of sex lingered in the air, over laid with the sour odour of vomit that clung to me. I nodded again and Matt went into the ensuite to get the shower running. He presented me with a clean fluffy towel, shower gel and shampoo.

"Do you need anything else?"

Only the return of my sanity. "No. Thank you." He turned to go and was at the door when I called to him. "Matt?"

"What?"

"You're a good man."

He looked at me over his shoulder and shrugged as if to say he was still wondering what the hell had just happened and who could blame him? I stood under the powerful jet of hot steamy water, generously lathering myself up with bubbles, enjoying the sharp tang of citrus, but knowing that no amount of washing could make me feel clean within my soul.

What the fuck had I just done?

Dancing around the kitchen with Eliza, the notion of a potion, as she had so gleefully put it, had been too enticing to turn away from. The thought of making Gawain suffer the pain of jealousy, far too appealing to ignore. I felt sick inside at how I had just used Matt. This was so far removed from those many other times when I had used him for sex, when we had used each other. Two healthy adults satisfying a need with an open and mutual consent.

Under bewitchment?

That turned it into something very different indeed and not something I cared to dwell on too deeply, if at all for that matter. I towelled myself dry and pulled on my rather crumpled summer dress from where I had tossed it so carelessly on the floor. Internal shivers were still coursing through my body, nothing to do with temperature, the after effects of magic.

Witchcraft.

Ghostly witchcraft.

Ghostly dark witchcraft.

Raisin tart and cream might fix the shakes, but not the consequences. For I knew down the line there would be a price to pay.

"I thought you might prefer to eat in here now," said Matt as I went down to the kitchen. "The sun will be out of the garden soon and it might get chilly. Would you like me to close the doors?"

"No. It's pleasant with the fresh air," I replied as I sat at the table where he had placed a bowl with a large slice of the tart and a very generous amount of cream. I proceeded to shovel it into my mouth with all the manners of a navvy.

Matt went to lean against the counter, his back to the window, arms folded across his chest as though to erect a barrier between us. "Fae, this isn't right. You do know this don't you?"

He had no idea how very not right it was, I thought soberly as I continued to eat. The first portion was quickly devoured but I was still hungry for more. Matt raised his eyebrows but made no comment as I pushed the empty bowl towards him.

"You know I love Laura, and I know that she is married to Mark."

"Muppet Mark, "I managed to mumble between mouthfuls as I started on the second portion.

The tiniest of smiles flitted across his face. "So, I know nothing can ever happen between us, but that isn't the point. I don't love you and I don't want to use you."

Oh, you lovely man do you not realise just how you have been used by me and a vengeful ghost? I wanted to reply but I couldn't. Not just because I was still greedily consuming excessive calories in a bid to counter the effects of potent magic, but because there were sounds of someone walking on the gravelled path in his garden and then the bulky figure of a man in the open doorway.

"Gawain?"

"Matt."

The two men looked at each other as though questioning the presence of each other.

"What are you doing here, mate?" Matt moved slightly away from the counter, hands reaching towards the kettle. "Fae's just finishing her tea. Would you like a coffee?"

"What? Coffee? Yeah, thanks, that would be good."

As Matt busied himself making coffee, Gawain stepped further into the room. Sea coloured eyes in a rare old storm of confusion as he stared hard at me. I felt a ripple of unease pass through me as I finished the last mouthful of cream-soaked tart and laid my spoon quietly into the bowl. He was under Eliza's enchantment. He had no idea why he had called round to Matt's house this evening. It was as clear to me as it was puzzling to him.

"Here," Matt handed a mug of coffee towards him. "Is everything alright?"

"Thanks." Gawain took the mug and unnervingly for me, pulled out a chair so that he could sit directly opposite me, and avoid looking at Matt. "I am not quite sure to be perfectly honest," he said as he began to drink the coffee. "I was on my way to visit Mrs Wentworth, who as you know lives in the other direction, but as I drove over the bridge to turn right, I had this overwhelming thought in my head that I had to come and see you."

Definitely Eliza's doing.

"How odd." Matt cast a quick look at me. "I had invited Fae round for a meal."

"So I see," said Gawain and then he looked at me in a different way as though seeing now through another lens.

I saw the moment when the effects of the magic wore off.

I saw the change in his eyes as he took note of my damp hair trailing across my shoulders, the lack of make up on a face freshly scrubbed, the soft poutiness of lips that have been kissed long and hard, the telltale signs of a woman who has not only been fed well but fucked well too.

I saw the varying emotions flash at lightning speed in those dark stormy eyes.

Anger.

Definitely anger, although I was not sure what right he had to be angry.

Jealousy?

Was that jealousy I saw in that deeply probing stare?

Whatever it was, I didn't like how it was making me feel and I had to control the impulse to childishly stick out my tongue. He always seemed to bring the worst out in me.

Instead, I smiled at him. "Would you like some of Mabel's raisin tart, it's really very good. And I don't think I have eaten all of it, have I Matt?"

"No." Was Gawain's clipped response.

"You sure mate, there is some left. Fae hasn't quite gobbled it all." Matt then gave me a serious look. "Fae, are you alright now?"

"Why wouldn't she be?" Gawain shot in like a bullet.

"Fae, er, wasn't feeling too good." Matt looked distinctly uncomfortable. However strong Eliza's spell had been to coerce him into inviting me over and going to bed with me, it had clearly now well and truly worn off.

"Is the baby alright?" A look of dark intensity in Gawain's eyes.

The baby.

Not my baby.

Not, our baby.

It writhed once more inside me, that dreadful serpent of pain, hurt, anger and resentment.

"My daughter is fine." I pushed my chair back sharply, its wooden legs grating on the tiled floor and stood up, hands lightly touching my belly. "I would never allow any harm to come to her. Matt, thank you for a lovely evening. The food was excellent, and your company......" I tilted my head to one side, my nearly dry hair falling softly over my face, a smile on my lips that had nothing to do with magic, only natural devilment, "Matt, your company is always pleasurable."

Only a fool could have missed the point, and neither were fools. Matt blushed and Gawain looked grimmer than ever.

He stood up abruptly, towering over me. "I'll drive you home."

"I am quite happy walking thank you."

"I'll drive you." The look in his eyes told me this was non-negotiable. For a moment I was back on the seaside promenade on that bitter cold night in January. The night he rescued me. The night he floored five men. The night our daughter was conceived.

All thoughts of trying to make him jealous, wanting to play games with him, needing to punish him, flew out of my mind, out of my heart, out of my soul. Who was I trying to kid? All I really wanted was to be with him. To be loved by him.

Eliza's magic had clearly worn off me too, and I couldn't prevent a tiny gasp of shock from escaping my lips as my true feelings hit me right in the solar plexus, a body blow of emotional pain.

"Fae?" He took my arm and instantly there was the connection between us.

"I'm okay," I said softly, vulnerable now and so quickly stripped of my defences.

"I am driving you home." Once more in that commanding tone, but the look in his eyes had changed.

I nodded and repeated my thanks to Matt, only this time with none of the mischief making. Gawain kept his hand on my arm as he steered me out of the kitchen, through the back garden and round to the front of the house where his car was parked in the driveway. He held the door open for me, quietly shut it and got in the driver's side. As soon as he had pulled out onto the road in the direction of the village, he turned his head and looked at me.

"What the fucking hell are you playing at, Fae?"

CHAPTER THIRTY-TWO

He repeated the question when I failed to answer him. I couldn't look at him directly, but out of the corner of my eye I could see that his hands on the steering wheel were gripping it tightly. Waves of energy were emanating from him, and in the confines of the car I was struggling to interpret them.

Overwhelmingly there was anger, but a part of me understood at some deep level that this was not directly purely at me. I closed my ears to the steely blade of accusation in his voice and shut my eyes to any glare of judgement that might be coming my way.

I could not however jam the lid tight on my feelings which were exploding through me like fireworks all going off at once. I didn't know how much of it was left over from Eliza's meddling magic, odd that I could phrase it that way in my mind now, meddling magic. Or was it simply a muddle of messed up hormonal emotions? An understandable state of confusion having got out of the bed of one man to be in close contact with the man I really loved and who was the father of my child.

Never mind my body feeling as though it was going to internally combust, or that my heart and soul were bleeding out into the universe, I began to fear that my mind was close to shattering. I didn't realise that I had begun to make a peculiar keening noise, my hands going to clasp my temples as though to hold on to my sanity, until his voice came through to me in another tone.

"Fae, what the hell is going on with you?"

I couldn't speak. My voice had shut down, throat blocked by an almighty lump of pain. This was not how it was supposed to be. This was not what I was supposed to be doing. This was not what Rowan wanted me to do.

I inhaled sharply, lifting my hands away from my head and turned to look at him. My vision was somewhat bleary as tears had pooled in my eyes, but that didn't matter. All that mattered was that I had to speak to my mother. I told him so.

"Ring her then." I could see the battle within him. The man at odds with his personal anger and the side of him that needed to care for a member of his community, however bloody frustrating they may be, in his role as vicar.

I shook my head. "No, I mean Rowan. I have to speak to Rowan."

Now I really was pushing his buttons. Mother to be of his child, who he has just discovered has been sleeping with his best mate, now tells him she needs to speak to a dead person.

A long, controlled expulsion of air.

We had just crossed over the bridge that took us onto the main street of Maypoleton. The turning into Cobblers Row was on the right-hand side. The road up to the vicarage and graveyard went straight on.

We went straight on.

He parked the car at the back of the vicarage, got out and came to open my door. His face was a mask of unreadable calm, but his eyes held an expression of such focused intensity that I had to look away. I felt like I was an enemy he had just got in his sights with a gun. One false move and that would be it. Surprisingly, his hand on my arm as we began to walk towards the graveyard was gentle and not the vice like grip, I imagined it would be.

The air was heavy and sweet, a hot summer evening fragrant with lavender, honeysuckle and other blossoms that I did not recognise. As my feet followed the path between the grassed areas with the headstones, I heard a buzzing in my ears that had nothing to do with any bees that might be about. Voices of the dead, calling to me. Tuning in to the heightened state of my emotions.

"Go way," I hissed under my breath.

"I am not leaving you."

"I wasn't talking to you," I said to Gawain, not daring to look at him.

His footsteps did not falter for a second and a small part of me could smile inwardly. Only Gawain could take that comment in his stride, quite literally. We carried on walking, and I tuned out those I did not wish to listen to, my eyes seeking out Rowan's headstone just in front of us.

There was a rumble in the sky overhead and briefly I glanced up. Were those storm clouds gathering suddenly in the distance? I paid little heed to the sudden change in atmosphere, but felt Gawain stiffen behind me, his gentle hold on my arm suddenly a little tighter. I smiled inwardly as I draw nearer to Rowan's grave. Whatever Gawain was feeling, for me there was a sense of being enveloped in love and warmth.

Releasing myself from his hold, I moved forwards and off the gravelled path to weave through a couple of graves until I was kneeling down in front of Rowan's headstone. I closed my eyes and traced my fingers over her name, feeling as I did so that immediate tingle and deepening heaviness in my head that told me I was connecting. I wanted to be alone with her.

"You can go now." I spoke the words softly, but Gawain was having none of it.

"I am not leaving you." Quiet, steely, determined, curious.

No. He would not leave me alone to do my witchy thing, of course he wouldn't. I heaved a sigh of frustration. The one time I didn't want him near me, he would insist on being present. Fucking typical. My frustration rose further as momentarily I felt the connection with Rowan loosen.

"I can't talk to her with you here," I hissed over my shoulder, impatience making me snappy.

"I am not leaving you."

I swear I growled then, and heaven only knows what expression was in my eyes as I whirled around to glare at him. There was too much energy here on top of the aftermath of Eliza's spell and the sex with Matt. I was wired, jangled, and desperate to clear myself of this tangled mess I had got myself into.

"I am not leaving you."

Spoken for a third time.

Three is the magic number.

As within so without.

The energy changed in that moment as our eyes met, mine no doubt reflecting a deep passionate fury, his in the first instance mirroring back to me. Then it changed. A fraction of a second, barely even there, but powerful enough to register. Powerful enough to break through those barriers. My breath caught in my throat, my heart paused in its beating, my soul shivered with joyful bliss.

"He is not leaving you."

There was laughter and joy in Rowan's voice. I heard it across time, across the eternal divide. My head whipped back to her gravestone, my hands once more on the stone. I clutched it as though I could clutch her.

"He is not leaving you."

I sank deeper into the connection.

She was with me.

Not here in this graveyard, not with me as a thirty-year-old pregnant woman, but with me in another dimension entirely. We shared a lifetime together in that alternative reality. We encountered those magical moments of infancy, childhood, adolescence, adulthood. I saw in this other reality my life as though it had happened to someone else.

It had.

But what Rowan was allowing me to see, was that nothing had ever broken that bond between us, no matter that she had died when I was two.

"He is not leaving you," for the third time, *"just as I have never left you. I have been by your side, always, my beloved daughter. Love never leaves. Love never dies."*

Tears were streaming down my face as I sank even deeper into this blissful cocoon of pure joy that I could happily stay in forever. My mother's loving embrace. A spiritual embrace. Not physical but maybe more powerful. I could not of course stay there forever. I had to return, back to the reality where turmoil in my heart and soul reigned supreme.

He doesn't love me; I told her silently.

Her laugher rippled softly back towards me. *"Daughter of mine, how can he not love you? You are one and the same."*

I don't understand.

"You will in time. Trust and surrender to your path. He shares your pain."

Rowan's words from beyond the grave puzzled me. For one thing they echoed those of Eliza. She had insisted that I shared her pain. The pain of loving the man who had fathered my child and being rejected by him, scorned for another. How could Gawain possibly share my pain? It didn't make sense.

"I cannot say my darling child," Rowan's words seem to hold a heavy note of regret as though she knew more but was not allowed to tell me. *"Stay in the light and all will be right."*

Another echo, a repeated phrase that stirred from somewhere in the back of my mind. Who had said that to me? I could not recall, but I knew as I knelt by Rowan's grave that this evening I had most definitely strayed from the light, wandered off the pathway. A rumble in the sky and a change in the atmosphere fitted perfectly with my thoughts. Allowing myself to fall in with Eliza's wishes for revenge was not in any way shape or form, in keeping with light work, light magic. I felt then a desperate longing to be with Rowan.

Not holding onto a cold slab of marble.

Not crouching on my knees in a graveyard.

Not wishing with every cell in my being that the past could be rewritten.

Such a powerful feeling, a longing, a yearning to not be here, not exist in this form, but to let go completely and surrender into the deep void of eternity where Rowan's spirit, Rowan's energy shone so brilliantly. Not just Rowan's but Fliss too.

Oh God Fliss, the other part of my self.

Beloved twin who had died because of me.

Let me be part of you once more.

The call was so powerful I was willing myself to be drawn to the other side. But it was not to be. At the same time a shocking clap of thunder shattered the silence of the summer evening, a sudden surge of energy shot through me. Lightning followed the thunder, and I felt as though I had been hit by such a force as with an involuntary scream, deep, raw and primal from the depth of my soul, I was pushed back from the gravestone as though someone had physically hauled me backwards.

"Fae!"

He was there in an instant, lifting me to my feet as the heavens opened quite literally. Raindrops so large and dense they felt like hailstones hammered down upon us. Within seconds we were both drenched, my flimsy summer dress moulding to my body like a second skin.

"Fae what the hell happened just then?" Gawain had his hands on my shoulders, lightly and with a care that belied his earlier anger. "You were blasted back as though you had been hit by the lightning.

Are you alright?" His eyes dropped to my belly; the evidence of his child now visible as the wet cotton clung to my pregnant form.

Concern in his eyes, and something else maybe.

Something I dared to hope might be love?

Trust and surrender, Rowan had said. Stay in the light and all with be right.

Then along with the sudden storm, another darker energy in the graveyard.

"Do not be fooled. He does not love you. He will never love you. He loves another. He has already abandoned you as he abandoned me."

I clamped my hands to my head. "Go away."

"I am not leaving you." Again, those words, how ironic

"I don't mean you." I shook my head, water shaking from the sodden strands of my hair. I meant Eliza. I could see her ghostly form on the edge of the graveyard, feel her animosity towards Gawain. Standing there in the pouring rain, shivering now with more than physical chills, it was all too much. The longing to rewrite my past. The yearning to be reunited with Rowan and Fliss. The magnetic pull I felt towards Gawain. The empathy I had for Eliza.

Where the hell was I in the middle of all this?

"Leave me alone." Was I directing this at him or Eliza? Truthfully, I wasn't sure. I just wanted the peace that I had momentarily felt with Rowan. Maybe it was the tone of my voice that held such longing, or maybe it was something else. Perhaps Rowan was bringing her gentle energy through in order to combat the spiky hostility of Eliza, either way something changed.

"I will not leave you alone. Not like this, Fae. Come." It was a command but issued softly.

Helpless to do anything else, I allowed him to lead me out of the graveyard and towards the vicarage. It was still torrenting with rain and we were both utterly soaked by the time we got into the kitchen, large drops of water falling from my hair to the floor, making patterns on the stone flags.

Despite the warmth of the evening, and the cosiness of the kitchen, I was shivering uncontrollably now. A double dose of psychic energy from Eliza's spell and the connection with Rowan. I hoped to high hell that my ghostly acquaintance would keep her distance for a little while. I couldn't cope with anymore tonight. All I wanted to do was to fall asleep. I knew I was swaying on my feet.

"Here, sit down, before you fall down." He pulled out a chair and ushered me into it. "Don't move."

As if I could! My legs had gone to jelly, and my head just wanted to be cradled onto my arms. I gave a soft grunt of agreement in reply. I heard him leave the room and then a couple of minutes later return.

"Here, you need to get out of that dress. You're soaked and shivering." He passed me a large bath towel and an oversized robe. My hands went to the towel but refused to cooperate further. He gave a sigh, and it was hard to tell it was exasperation or something else. The latter I think as his voice was unbearably gentle when he spoke.

"Let me help you, Fae." A world of meaning in his words. Let me help you. Not just to get dried and changed. Let me help you. I heard something in his voice that had me whipping my head up to meet his gaze. There was an understanding there that went beyond my comprehension. As though he was looking into my soul and feeling every bit of pain.

"He shares your pain."

So, Rowan had told me. What did she mean?

I was too numb to ask. All I could do was to allow him to help me stand, towel me dry and peel my sodden dress from my shivering body. Even my underwear was soaked. A feather light, unintrusive touch as his hands went first to remove my bra and then wriggle down my pants until they fell to my ankles. He avoided my eyes now. They had traced every curve of my body, the newness of my pregnant form, the curve of my belly where his daughter lay.

Once I was dry, he draped the towel over the back of a chair and was about to reach for the robe. Freed from my numbness, driven by a deep female instinct, I grasped hold of his hands and placed them both on my belly.

"Fae!" A sharp intake of breath, a flash of emotion in his eyes that met mine.

Anger?

Frustration?

Wonder?

Most definitely wonder as our daughter chose that moment to move and flutter within me. I no longer felt cold and shivery. I was glowing from an internal source of energy that seemed to wrap itself around me and him as we stood for that precious moment, connected by the child we shared.

"She knows you," I whispered softly.

"Don't say that." His voice was husky, a tone I had never heard before.

"She knows you," I repeated, moving his hands slightly as I felt her move.

"This can't be, Fae." He was now the one in turmoil and my heart opened even more to him.

"Why not?" Genuinely I did not understand why not.

"I can't......." For the first time since I had met him, he appeared to be at a loss for words. He pulled his hands away and reached for the robe, enveloping me in it with swift, practical movements, tying the belt as quickly as he could. "I'll go and get you sweater and some jogging pants of mine. They'll be ludicrously large on you, but your dress is soaked. I need to change too. Wait there."

As if I was going anywhere else.

"You can't what?" I asked him a few minutes later when he came back into the room. He had changed out of his vicar's attire into jeans and a plain silver-grey t-shirt which made his eyes more that colour than the normal stormy grey-blue. It also fitted snugly to his torso, well-muscled in the way not commonly associated with a man of the church.

"I beg your pardon?" He asked as he handed me some clothes which were indeed laughably too big, but dry and cosy and just what I needed to take the chill from me.

"You can't what?" I said insistently, shrugging off the robe, holding his gaze and daring him with my eyes to not turn around whilst I dressed.

He didn't and I had the satisfaction of seeing his pupils dilate slightly. Mine must have been reacting in the same way as beyond the reach of my question, my thoughts were on what that body had felt like next to my naked skin. I remembered the feel of the scars that rippled over his back and chest, and even in parts on his thighs. I wondered then briefly if Lucinda had felt the same passion with him.

That shocking jealousy sharpened my tone. "You can't what?" I repeated harshly. "You can't admit to your flock that you had a one-night stand with a woman you thought was a prostitute. You can't admit to anyone that you got me pregnant. You can't lose your reputation as a pillar of the church by hooking up with a witch?"

"I thought you said you weren't a witch?" He matched the harshness of my tone.

Instantly I regretted my outburst. I shrugged my shoulders carelessly as if it didn't matter, which of course it did. "Maybe I am. Maybe I am not."

"Don't play games with me Fae."

I flashed him a look of anger then. "I am not the one playing games. You are. You know I love you. You know I want to be with you. You know you feel something for me."

He was rattled. That icy calm was turning to fire. "Stop it, Fae."

"Stop what? Saying it as it is? What are you frightened of?"

"Frightened?" He snorted and gave a shake of his head. "I am not frightened of anything Fae."

"I think you are," I said softly and as I spoke the words; I had that deep sense of *knowing* that told me I was right.

Fear was behind his reactions towards me.

Fear.

Fear of what? Or whom? Himself? Or me?

The knowledge that had come to me from nowhere, or maybe Rowan had had a hand in it, flipped a switch inside me. The anger dissolved in an instant and I was overwhelmed by a surge of compassionate love. I wanted to reach for him, hold him, find my way through the barriers that he had built up around his heart. Barriers that I knew now were something to do with those physical scars.

I took a step towards him.

Instantly he retreated. "I need to get you home."

As if to conspire with him and against me, his phone rang then. He looked at the screen and swore before answering it, calm vicar mode fully turned on.

"I do apologise Mrs Wentworth. No. I had not forgotten. I had to make a detour. There was an incident on my way to you. No, nobody is hurt. But it has delayed me. I am on my way now. Yes, do please put the kettle on and of course I would love one of your home-made scones. And jam, yes, yes of course. Goodbye Mrs Wentworth, I will be there shortly." He finished the phone call with a frown on his face. "I was on my way over there when I felt that strange urge to go to Matt's. Never felt anything like it before?"

Of course he hadn't.

Eliza's magic to make him jealous.

My magic to make him jealous.

I didn't like the way he was looking at me now. "How long have you been having sex with Matt?"

"None of your business." Judging by his tone I don't think the spell had had the desired effect. If anything, I was feeling more contempt from him than wounded male pride.

"It is if you are meddling with magic Fae, I won't have it. Not in my parish, and not, certainly not with one of my best mates."

I am my own worst enemy.

I really am.

Unbelievably stupid.

"It wasn't magic," I lied. "It was just sex. We just fucked. And it was fucking good too."

He shook his head, and I knew that I had just given him exactly what he wanted. There was silence between us on the two-minute drive from the vicarage from Cobblers Row. He insisted on getting out and speaking briefly to Aunty Ruth, explaining oh so smoothly how I had got caught in the down pour in the graveyard, hence the odd attire.

As gently as I could, I rebuffed my aunt's loving fussing and excused myself to have an early night. I crawled into bed, still wearing his clothes, hugging my arms around my body as though he were holding me himself and allowed silent tears to fall. Just as sleep began to weave its way into my mind and body, I heard Rowan's soft voice in my head once more.

"He shares your pain. He will never leave you. You are one and the same."

There was comfort there, but mystery too.

What had Rowan meant?

And if I figured it out, would it possibly mean that he might love me?

CHAPTER THIRTY-THREE

The next morning, I woke with the mother of all psychic hangovers. My body felt as though it had been pummelled from head to toe and even though I had consumed no alcohol at Matt's, my senses had that whirly swirly feeling as though I was drunk. Thankful that Aunty Ruth and Uncle Eric were already out of the house when I gingerly made my way downstairs, I tried my best to block out the insistent thought that I had spectacularly messed up.

Eliza's idea to make Gawain jealous had backfired stupendously. All I had done was to push him even further away. It crucified me how much this hurt. Where the hell had the Fae who didn't give a damn about any man and what they thought, disappeared to? And I knew I could not blame this addictive obsession on pregnancy hormones because I had felt this way from the moment, I had met him.

My feet were reluctant to say the least as they trudged the short distance from Cobblers Row to the vicarage. As much as I was desperate to see him, I was dreading him being the one to open the door to me.

Which of course he did. "Good morning, Fae." Cool grey blue eyes scanned my face sharply, narrowing slightly as they did so. "Are you ill?"

Great. I must have looked as bad as I felt. "I bought your clothes back."

He took the bag and repeated the question. "Are you ill? You look dreadful. Is the baby ok?"

The baby.

Not just the baby.

His daughter.

"She's fine," I snapped, "and so am I. Here. Your clothes. Thanks for the loan of them."

"You don't look fine," came the snide tones of Mrs Mannering who appeared in the hallway, carrying a tray with a tea pot, and two cups. "We don't want you passing any nasty germs on to Arthur. You'd best go home if you've got a sick bug. I'm sure Lucinda would be happy to come and look after your father today, Gawain."
Over my dead body. "I've not got a sick bug," I snarled across the hallway and pushed past Gawain before he could decide to shut the door on me.
He caught hold of me by the arm, his grip tight, the look in his eyes unreadable. At the same time, he said ever so smoothly to Mrs Mannering, "Thank you, Margaret. Just put the tray in my study. My nine o'clock appointment will be here soon."
"As you like."
In an undertone to me, he added warningly. "I am not in the mood for games, Fae. We haven't finished our conversation from yesterday. We still have much to discuss on that subject."
I smiled sweetly at him, making a promise to myself that I would do no such thing. "Arthur will be waiting for me."
Releasing myself from his grasp I crossed over the hallway, knocked gently on the bedroom door profoundly grateful for the down to earth tasks required in looking after his father. I had grown genuinely fond of the old man. His lively wit and humour were always a breath of fresh air. Today though, he appeared rather melancholic and absent. I waited until he was showered, dressed and sitting comfortably in his chair by the window before commenting.
"Out with it, Arthur. You're a million miles away." I sat on a chair across from him, leaning in close to gently place my hand over his.
"Sorry." His gnarled hand squeezed back tightly. "One of those painful days."
Immediately my own woes left me. He never complained about his condition, so for him to comment, it must be bad. "Do you need me to call Dr Jay?"
"Not that sort of pain my lovely." His chin wobbled and his eyes slid away from mine to gaze out of the window but not before I had seen the mist of tears.

"How about a bit of fresh air? It's a beautiful day. We can go and buy some of Mabel's brownies and sit and eat them by the duck pond. Or, if you like I can take you for a drive. We've never done that. Would you like to go out somewhere for a change? I'm sure Gawain wouldn't mind," although as I said this, I wasn't sure. The object of my obsession appeared to be in an even grumpier mood than normal.

"A cake."

"Yeah, that's fine. We can buy cakes instead."

"A birthday cake," he said taking me by surprise. "One I can put candles on."

"Yes of course." I said, standing up and beginning to gather my bag and the blanket which I always took for Arthur, even on warm days. "Who's birthday is it?"

He gave me a very odd look then but didn't answer. "It would be nice to see the sea. I miss the sea."

Of course, Gawain, like me, had moved here from the south coast. The fells and moors surrounding Maypoleton were lovely, but the sea had a special kind of magic that I understood. I remembered days out with Aunty Ruth and Uncle Eric when Fliss and I used to stay with them in the long summer holidays. A trip to the seaside was always on the agenda.

"It's about an hour," I said to him, checking on my phone how long it would take to get to the beach I remembered. "Would you be ok with that in my car?"

He nodded and for the first time that morning there was a touch of the Arthur I knew returning. "I will. But can we go and buy a cake first from Mabel's before all the best ones sell out. One of those triple layered chocolate ones she does, covered in icing. And some candles from the shop."

"Shall I nip and get those for you? Then we can go for the drive."

"I want to come if you don't mind. I want to pick some cards too."

"Of course I don't mind. We've got all day. We can please ourselves. Birthday cake, candles and cards first, and then a drive to the sea."

He smiled at me. "You're a good girl, Fae."

Oh, but I am not. "Let's get you ready then," I said breezily. A short while later, we were outside Mabel's bakery. "Are you ok if I leave you here for a moment, it's very busy in there."

He nodded and I made sure the brake was on the wheelchair and that I was not blocking the pavement for others then nipped in to the bakery. The queue had lessened by this time which was good. Not so good, however was that standing right in front of me, with her pre-school toddler, was Lucinda, Gawain's love, my nemesis. She was talking to Mabel about the forthcoming birthday party arrangements for Toby, soon to be four.

"And Gawain has promised to take us all out for the day," she said in her light breathy voice that irritated the shit out of me, "and then we are going to have a lovely party in the vicarage gardens. He's even said we can have a bouncy castle. It's going to be such fun. So of course I want you to bake the cake, a Thomas the tank engine cake, you can do that can't you?"

Standing behind her, I had to fight the impulse to not turn tail and make a sharp exit. Bloody Lucinda. Bloody little Toby, innocent in all of this, but still a thorn twisting in my side. My hands had gone to my belly, and I thought of my daughter, Gawain's child who he was refusing to acknowledge, publicly at least.

Would she ever have a birthday party with her father present? Or her grandfather? Arthur, who so clearly wanted to join in with the birthday celebrations for Toby by buying a cake as well as Lucinda, my daughter's grandfather, would be there too, enjoying the day, the sense of family time together.

Jealousy and bitterness, those twisted twin serpents writhed within me. I was fighting the urge to pull Lucinda round by the shoulders and confront her with the truth. I felt a churning in my stomach and a horrible buzzing sensation in my head. The inside of shop seemed to change suddenly as if I was in two places at once. Still there but somewhere else. Or some time else?

Another woman in front of me.

Different clothes, different hair, different voice.

The same feelings of jealousy, bitterness but someone else's hatred.

Whirling, spinning, weaving, distorting the present moment into an echo of the past.

"Fae, Fae, love what can I get for you?"

Mabel's voice, bright, loud, clear, cut through the misty mirage and brought me back to the present. I saw with a shock that Lucinda had turned to stare at me, wrinkling her nose in that smug little way she had.

"Oh, it's you. Dear me, Fae, are you really sure you should still be looking after Arthur? Pregnancy does not appear to be suiting you at all, does it Mabel?"

"Your cake will ready to collect the day before the party," Mabel said to Lucinda with a brisk nod before she then bustled her out of the shop.

Ramming my hands in my pockets in order to not lash out as she brushed past me, I was horrified by the feelings of rage that were pulsing through me.

This was not me.

This vengeful bitch full of hatred was not me.

Or was she?

"Fae?" Mabel's voice was loud and clear in my ears and her bright blue eyes, pierced into mine, bringing me back from wherever the hell I had been. "Cathy fetch a glass of water from the back," she said to her assistant. "Here, sit down, before you fall down." Gently she ushered me onto a small stool in the corner of the shop. "Drink that and tell me what you came in for. I'll get it whilst you recover."

I told her of Arthur's wishes for a chocolate birthday cake, doing my best to not let that horrific feeling of jealousy swamp me again. As I sipped the water, and watched as Cathy served the other customers and Mabel busied herself with boxing a cake for Arthur, I felt intense shame at my emotions.

What the hell was happening to me?

"You're under a spell lovey," Mabel's voice drifted back to me as she leant in close with the cake box and spoke so quietly that no one else could hear. "And not a good one, either by the look of it. What's going on Fae?"

I was under a spell?

No, she was wrong about that.

Eliza and I had woven a spell for Matt to want me again to make Gawain jealous, but I was not under a spell.

I shook my head. "Don't be daft," I said lightly. For one thing I did not want her to know anything about Eliza and how present she was in my life. For another, I was recoiling from the idea that I was also bewitched.

Surely not?

"It's this pregnancy," I said, relieved to have such an excuse for any odd behaviour.

The look in her eyes told me she did not believe me for a second, but there was nothing she could do about it. I thanked her for the cake, and the glass of water and made as hasty an exit as I could. Arthur was happy to hold the cake box on his lap and then we went to the general store at the end of the main street so he could buy a card.

My mind was still on bloody Lucinda and her son's bloody birthday party as Arthur was perusing the selection of cards neatly arranged in order in the shop, so I wasn't paying attention to what he was choosing until I got to the till. Or rather it was the shop assistant who brought my mind sharply into focus.

"You do know he's picked two cards exactly the same, don't you?" She whispered to me, with a sympathetic glance at Arthur who again appeared lost in another world, really not his usual self.

"Let me see?" I spoke quietly as well, mindful not to upset him.

She held out the two cards. Both were "To My Wonderful Son". Both were clearly for adults, pictures of sailing boats on them. Identical. I frowned and looked back at the assistant who shrugged her shoulders at me.

Gently, I touched him on the shoulders. "Arthur, have you got the right card here? Is this meant to be for Toby?"

"What? Toby? What would I be wanting to buy Toby a birthday card for? No, no, not Toby."

My heart did a leap.

His wonderful son.

Gawain.

"It's Gawain's birthday?"

He answered with a grunt.

"It's alright," I said to the assistant, "the cards must have got stuck together. Shall I go and put one of them back for you?"

"No!" Arthur's voice was strident and fierce. "Two of them."

"Two?"

"Yes two. And no, I am not going potty. Two sons. Two cards. Just pay for them Fae, please if you would."

I don't know what stunned me more. The content of what he was saying, or how he was saying it. I had never heard such pain in his voice before. And the thought that he had two sons, that Gawain had a brother. More than that, their birthdays were on the same day possibly and therefore, twins.

Like me.

Like I had been.

With Fliss.

Rowan's words from beyond the grave floated back to me. *"He shares your pain. You are one and the same."*

My mind was reeling as I paid for the cards and then proceeded to wheel Arthur back along the high street towards the vicarage. "I think it's best if we put the cake in the fridge before we go out on our drive."

Arthur remained untalkative as we set off out of the village. Silence never bothered me. It was a skill I had acquired in many years of caring for the elderly. I could be still and at ease without feeling the need to fill the void with endless chatter. It was also partly how I had been given the nickname of Angel.

As well as my fragile, ethereal looks, long ash blonde hair and turquoise blue eyes, I had what one lady described as, "A lightness of spirit my dear, otherworldly in nature." I recalled her words now as I drove through the winding country lanes, across moors and fells, and then on towards the Lancashire coast. Otherworldly maybe. My connection with Eliza was most certainly that. Angelic and light in spirit?

I felt a long way from that.

Last night with Matt.

Today in the shop with Lucinda.

Mabel's words banging away at the back of my head.

Arthur's declaration that he had two sons.

Muddled, messed up, and in a maze of mayhem was where I was at right now. So, it was pleasant to be quiet next to Arthur and let my eyes take in the changing scenery and concentrate on the directions my sat nav was giving. Eventually we got to

Morecambe and the memories of playing on the beach with Fliss and swimming in the sea came rushing back. I held in my breath and wondered if this had been a good idea.

"What a lovely spot and a wonderful view. My word you can see right across to the Lake District. How delightful. Ooh look Fae, a café. They sell ice creams."

"They do indeed," I said smiling as his pleasure eased my pain. "Would you like one now, or after we have had a little walk?"

"Walk first. Sea air. I've missed it." He sniffed the air like a dog, eyes closed, a smile of appreciation on his face.

"Me too." I said, although my mind had now flown back to that cold dark night in January. That careless walk on that promenade in the early hours of the morning.

Careless?

Or fated?

My turn to be quiet and reflective now as we walked a short distance before turning round to buy an ice cream. We found a place to sit and enjoy people watching, both on the beach and passing us by on the promenade. I was desperate to ask Arthur about the birthday cards, about Gawain having a brother, and to know if indeed he was a twin. But I knew if I probed, I might lose some of that special friendship there was between us. I finished my ice cream and sat with my hands cradling my belly, enjoying feeling the gentle movements of my daughter.

"He'll come round."

"I beg your pardon?"

Arthur looked at me with the clarity in his gaze that had been missing before. "Gawain. He will come round. Oh, I know he thinks Lucinda is the woman for him. She ticks all the boxes as they say. But I know he loves you really. And you are carrying his child. That will be too much for him to ignore in the end. You just have to be patient my dear." He reached out a hand to hold mine.

"He hates me, Arthur. He hates everything about me." It may be driven by a fear I didn't understand but the end result was the same. I repeated it, unable to keep the sadness from my voice. "He hates me."

"No, my dear. He does not. He hates himself."

"I don't understand. Why does he hate himself? And what on earth has that got to do with him not wanting to be with me?"

Arthur sighed then, a deep and heavy sigh that spoke of unbearable pain that somehow had in fact been borne. But not without a price. A burden he carried and was weary of. I knew that feeling well.

"It might help to talk?" I said softly.

"It's not my tale to tell."

"Isn't it?" I said, thinking of the two birthday cards. "Gawain is your son. You're his father. You say you have two sons? So that must be Gawain's brother. Where is he? Why doesn't Gawain talk about him? Why don't you for that matter?"

So much for not probing, but it seemed the right thing to do at that moment.

He battled with himself. "Gawain does not like it speaking of."

"Gawain is not here. And I will not tell a soul. I can keep a secret. Believe me on that."

Wise, sad old eyes stared into mine. "Yes Fae, I believe you on that. I believe you keep more secrets than just the baby you are carrying. And maybe in time you will trust me with yours. And maybe for now, it is time to trust you with mine. Or rather Gawain's."

"I would never do anything to hurt him," I said truthfully. "I couldn't. I can't explain it, but he's part of me. I have never felt like this about anyone before in my life. If I hurt him, I hurt myself." As I said this, I realised with a shock it was true. What the hell had I been thinking of colluding with Eliza to make Gawain jealous in order to feel my pain, share my pain.

Again, Rowan's words, *"He shares your pain. You are one and the same. He can never leave you."*

"Yes, I see that," said Arthur. "Very well. It's quite a tale. But the short version of it is this. Gawain had a brother. A twin. Lance."

A shiver went down my spine and I felt sick. Without Arthur telling me I knew what had happened. The only way Gawain could possibly share my pain, my guilt was if he had been responsible for the death of his twin, as I had with mine.

"It's alright," I said, desperate to stop the words falling from his lips, "You don't have to tell me. I think I know."

"Yes, somehow Fae, I think you do. But I will say it anyway because it needs to be said. It needs to be heard. I had two sons and one of them sent the other one to his death."

A sorrow beyond bearing, but one that must be borne nevertheless.

I closed my eyes and thought of Gawain. That night in my flat. The battle within himself. The way he had looked at the photo of Fliss and me. The way he had then made love to me with such passion, such pain. A passion and pain in which our daughter had been conceived.

I had sent my twin to her death.

Gawain had sent his twin to his death.

Not a co-incidence surely?

CHAPTER THIRTY-FOUR

"They were both in the army," Arthur began to talk softly, his eyes on the bay and the Lake district beyond. "Green berets the pair of them. Could not have been prouder. Still am. Both served multiple tours of duty."

He paused and I gave his hand a gentle squeeze. "You don't have to tell me if it's too painful."

"It's too painful keeping it inside at times, Fae, and it seems to get worse the older I get. You would have thought time would lessen the pain, that's what everyone says."

"Everyone is wrong," I said softly.

His eyes turned away from the distant hills to look at me. "You know, don't you?"

I nodded and let him continue with the tale.

"The last time Lance was away, Gawain had been at home, recuperating from wounds." A long lengthy pause, and then. "I often wonder if he had not taken that bullet, which he did, by the way to save one of his lads, if things would have turned out differently. Or would it still all have happened. Maybe it was one of those situations that was always going to implode."

"What do you mean?"

"Lance, Gawain, and Jemma."

"Jemma?"

"Lance's wife. But she was Gawain's girlfriend first. They had all been at school together, then the lads went into the army. As I said, both green berets but Gawain was always the one with the leadership qualities and held a higher rank. Lance had more fun about him. On one of the times Gawain was away, Lance and Jemma got together. She broke it off with Gawain by sending him a text."

"Ouch."

"Very ouch. Doubly so that they married so quickly and did so in Gawain's absence. Things were never quite the same between the boys then as you can imagine."

"Absolutely," I murmured, thinking how devastated Gawain must have been to find his girlfriend married to his brother. Had he felt then the twisted jealously that consumed me now? Part of me hoped he had. Part of me hoped he had not. "What happened?" I prompted Arthur who had fallen silent. I needed to know.

"They remained civil and got on with their lives, both lads continuing in the army. Until that time Gawain was home on leave and Lance was away. It was coming up to Christmas. Out of the blue Lance arrived home on a surprise visit. Only the poor boy got more of a shock than a surprise."

"Oh no." I think I knew where this was going. It would explain a lot.

"Yes. Too much wine, the Christmas spirit, Jemma missing Lance, Gawain still in love with her, and Lance comes home to find them in bed together."

"Oh hell." I could just picture the scene.

"There was a huge fight, as you can imagine. Lance stormed off in his car. Fatal accident. One other person killed, a young father on his way home, car loaded up with presents."

"Oh God!" What a tragedy. "Arthur I am so sorry. That is so awful. For all of you."

He wiped away the tears from his eyes and shivered, despite the warm sunshine. I tucked the blanket more snugly around his knees and started to wheel his chair.

"Come on," I think you need a hot cup of tea now. Let's go to the café."

He didn't demur and was quiet until we had walked the short distance to the café, settled ourselves at a table where we could still see the sea, and had a steaming pot of tea in front of us, with a large, buttered scone each.

"Gawain was never the same after that. Jemma moved abroad which I was glad about to be honest. I don't think either of us could have coped if she had stayed. Gawain continued with his tours, taking more and more risks, accepting the most dangerous assignments he could, searching for atonement, until he nearly got himself well and truly blown up."

I closed my eyes, remembering the scars on his body and now understanding a little more about the scars in his mind. He couldn't forgive himself, just as I had never been able to forgive myself over Fliss.

"They gave him an honourable discharge in the end. He had more medals to his name than any other soldier in his regiment, but he was on a suicide mission, that was clear for all to see."

"And that's when he went into the church?"

Arthur nodded. "He was still relatively young. It was the army chaplain who visited him when he was in hospital who inspired him. And thank God he did, because I don't think my boy would still be with us, without him. He set Gawain on a path that meant he could feel he was giving something back and atoning in some small way. The path to forgiveness."

"He hasn't though, has he?" I finished the last mouthful of my scone and looked Arthur directly in the eye. "He has not forgiven himself for Lance, not really. It's still there inside him."

"Which is why my dear Fae, I know you are the woman for him, and Lucinda, as lovely as she appears to be, is not. You see him. You see all of him. Even without me telling you his story, you see all of him, don't you my dear."

"Is it that bloody obvious," I said with a sigh.

"Only to me. And I see in your eyes, that same haunted look I see in his."

My turn to talk then, which required a second cup of tea and another scone. We were really loading up on the sugar today, but sometimes that was what was required.

"It seems to me, dear Fae, that you two are meant to be together." This was Arthur's pronouncement when I had finished telling him about Fliss.

"You think?"

"Don't you?"

"I know I have never felt this way before about anyone. It's a real physical pain deep inside me; to be around him and know he doesn't want me."

Arthur snorted then. "He wants you, Fae. He wants you too much. That's the problem. You have lit the fire inside him that he has done his best to quell for such a long time. Since Lance died. He hasn't allowed himself to have any fun of any kind. No women, that I know of anyway."

I thought of Gawain's icy self-control the night we me. I thought of the outpouring of fiery passion when that control finally shattered. My heart leapt in the knowledge that I had been the one to break through that wall of resistance. Then I reminded myself how things were now.

"What about Lucinda then?" I asked as I gritted my teeth thinking my rival.

"Oh Fae. So young, and so blind. My dear child, he doesn't love Lucinda. I don't even think he is really attracted to her. Not like he is to you."

"So why the fuck is he with her then?" I thumped the steering wheel in frustration.

Arthur laughed quietly. "Why is he with her? That's simple."

"Really? Cos it feels fucking confusing to me."

"She's his shield. His armour. His protection."

"From what?"

"You, of course. She was buzzing around him for months before you arrived in Maypoleton. He never gave her a second look. Then up you popped and hey presto he's in need of defence. And what better form of defence then the perfect example of a would-be vicar's wife." He sounded rather pleased with himself as though he had just solved an extraordinarily difficult puzzle.

"You make it sound as though I am attacking him," I muttered, feeling my prickles coming out like an angry hedgehog.

"You are attacking his heart," replied Arthur sagely. "You have blown a bloody great hole in the defences he has built up over years. He is far more attracted to you, drawn to you than he ever will be to Lucinda, and I bloody hope he realises it before he is stupid enough to marry her. As much as anything, that would not be fair on her. I know you can't stand her, but really it is not her fault, she is innocent in this."

"Hhm." I grudgingly had to allow him that. "He's got a funny way of showing it."

"He employed you as my companion, didn't he?" Arthur gave a sly chuckle. "He couldn't help himself. He won't admit it, but he needs you just as much as you need him."

The idea that Gawain might need me in any way was as mind shattering as the rest of the story Arthur had just regaled. We were both quiet on the walk back to the car. As I helped Arthur with his seat belt, I felt the impulse to lean in and gently kiss him on the cheek. In silent response he reached for my hand to offer a light squeeze.

"Would you like some music to listen to?" I don't think either of us had any more words to say at this point.

He nodded. "A little classical might be nice."

Not my cup of tea but that was irrelevant. I scrolled through the radio until he nodded his approval. Within minutes of setting off, his eyes were closed and the soft sounds of snoring blended with the music. I was glad. It gave me chance to try and make sense of my thoughts and feelings. The closer we got to Maypoleton, the clearer it became to me. I could not carry on as I had been doing.

I felt sick inside at the twisted game that Eliza had pushed me into playing. Appalled at myself for resorting once more in my life to use magic for ill purposes. Memories of that night when the police knocked on door with the dreadful news of Fliss's death flooded back.

The guilt.
The pain
The loss.
The agonising heartbreak that had never truly healed.

Images of what Arthur had told me came in alongside these memories, superimposing themselves on my storyline until it felt as though Gawain's agony was my own, and mine was somehow his. My heart began to pound, a pain in my chest as though there was simply too much emotion, to contain.

Too much love.
And that was the point.

If I loved him, truly loved him, what the holy fuck was I doing trying to hurt him? As I said to Arthur, it felt as though I was hurting myself. I simply could not do this anymore. I had no freaking idea what I was going to do, other than I could not action another thought that would inflict more pain on him than he was already suffering.

Part of me even considered moving back down south, or somewhere else for that matter. Anywhere where I would not be tortured by living alongside him as he created his life with Lucinda. A life which I now understood would be as much as a lie for him as the last fifteen years for me had been.

Not something I wished on anybody.

But as I parked my car in the village, I knew that this was not going to happen. I was rooted here. Born here, brought back here, and here I was meant to stay. Maybe, I thought to myself as I helped a sleepy Arthur into his wheelchair, this was my penance. My own path to atonement. Gawain had chosen to go into the church. I had chosen to work in care. The fates had brought us together, and I desperately hoped that it was to bring us both to a place of peace.

I would stay.

But no more magic.

No more games.

Fae Winters was walking a new path from this moment on.

I bravely told myself this as I pushed Arthur back into the vicarage, and later I said the same thing to Eliza. Arthur and I had passed the rest of the day quietly in his room. His nap on the way home had refreshed him and he seemed in lighter spirits all round. Possibly the sea air and being away from the vicarage for a while, possibly the indulgence of ice cream followed by tea and scones, but I thought more likely he was feeling the lessening of the burden he had been carrying.

He wanted to play chess, which we did for a while, and then unusually for Arthur, he rather bossily told Mrs Mannering, that he did not wish to eat the salmon quiche she had prepared for tea, along with a healthy green salad, he wanted a plateful of cheese and pickle sandwiches. On white bread. Not the homemade cobby loaf she had baked yesterday, plain, white bread, from the general store.

It entertained me no end to witness the exchange between the pair of them, but the housekeeper had no choice other than to hike herself off to the shop before it closed, returning with a face like thunder to make the requested sandwiches.

He then asked me to wheel him out into the garden, where we ate the simple tea which he told me had been Lance's favourite as a boy. Accompanied of course, with the chocolate cake. I arranged the candles, lit them, and sitting next to his chair, we quietly sang happy birthday, to Gawain and Lance. I had a lump in my throat as we did so, and his voice cracked at the end, but we did it.

Thankfully there was no sight nor sound of Gawain. Mrs Mannering had told us that he had disappeared with instructions that he would not be back until late. Arthur looked impassive at this news, and I guessed that this was his sons' way of dealing with the day. I totally got it. Finally, when Arthur was once more settled in his room for the evening, and Mrs Mannering had also left, I chose to make myself a cup of tea before heading back to Cobblers Row.

I had to speak to Eliza.

Up to this point, she had only ever appeared at her instigation. I was in two minds as to the wisdom in trying to summon her presence myself, but after the revelations of today it seemed imperative that I did so. I went back out into the garden, long and narrow, surrounded by an ivy clad wall, well established and well cared for plants and flowers, it was the archetypal English country garden.

With a ghost waiting at the far end.

No need to summon her then.

She was standing by the newly created bed which now covered the previously neglected corner where she had been buried, lying forgotten and unloved for all those years. I felt for her, I truly did. The images of what she had suffered which I had experienced through the time lapses which had occurred, were utterly horrific. The notion that her spirit had been left lingering in turmoil by her brutal end and the callous way her body had been buried in that unmarked grave was something that disturbed me deeply.

I wanted to help her as much as I wanted to help myself. A sense of kinship that maybe stemmed from being related through blood, centuries down the line. Not only that but the bond of a woman in love, a woman carrying a child, a woman rejected in that love. It was easy to see how that connection had been made.

Maybe, in coming to some form of peace with Gawain, it would bring peace to Eliza. I hoped so. She however, did not see it quite that way.

"He is jealous then?" Hopeful, gleeful, the tone of her words betrayed her emotions as much as the eagerness on her face. As I drew close to her, it struck me that she was clearer than ever. So very real I could almost see the coarse weave of threads in the clothes she was wearing, the varying shades of light blonde hair, so similar to mine.

I cradled the hot mug of tea in my hands. The air not surprisingly was now supernaturally chilly. I shivered a little, wishing I had brought my hoody out with me, despite the warmth of the evening.

"He was angry," I said cautiously as I sat down on one of the garden chairs.

"Good. But was he also jealous?" In an unseen movement she was there sitting at the table with me. She cradled her face in her hands, as I was cradling my mug, her young face so close to mine I could for the first time make out the oddity of her eyes. One brown, one blue. One so dark and unreadable, the other so bright and piercing. No wonder she had been taken for a witch in her time. I pondered my reply. Had Gawain actually been jealous? His anger had been easy to read, but I was stumped slightly as to whether or not he had been jealous.

"I'm not sure."

"He must feel jealous. He must. It burns so, this feeling inside. It twists and torments me so it does."

I closed my eyes for a second, partly to remove myself from the intensity of her stare, partly to acknowledge that I had also felt what she had described. Second to the heart shattering pain of losing Fliss, it was the worst feeling I had ever experienced in my life. A truly vile feeling and intensely powerful. Powerful enough to hold Eliza captive in her lonely grave for centuries.

I wanted to set her free.
I wanted to set myself free.
I wanted to set Gawain free.

"I know it does Eliza. It has burnt and twisted inside me too." I opened my eyes to see her smiling at me. She hadn't appeared to notice that I had used the past tense.

"So, you understand, he must feel this pain. It is the only way I will be free."

I shook my head, convinced now that we were on the wrong path. Hideously so. "No. He mustn't. He already feels enough pain." I told her what had happened to his brother, and that he must already have experienced a similar level of jealousy in the first place when Lance married Jemma. Eliza seemed unmoved by this.

"'Tis of no consequence. That was before he came here. Before he was the vicar of this parish."

I wasn't sure what disturbed me the most, her emotionless disregard for Gawain's story, or the idea that it could be any man who was the vicar here and she would still have attached the idea of revenge upon him. Because that was what we were talking about ultimately.

Revenge.

Do as thou will and harm none.

Revenge was all about harming.

I felt even chillier as I sat opposite her. "It doesn't matter Eliza. He has suffered. Surely that is enough."

Clearly not.

Her pretty face, so ethereal and delicate turned nasty. *"How can it be enough? It will never be enough."*

"This is not going to bring you peace. Or me for that matter. And I am the one living here remember." I tried to rationalise with her. Can you be rational with a ghost?

Clearly not.

"I do not wish for peace! I wish for revenge. And why should you have peace? You have your life, you have more than I have. You do not lie cold and lonely in your grave. You do not lie forgotten."

I didn't think it wise at that point to comment that she was no longer in her grave, she was not longer forgotten. Maybe this was worse for her, this lingering state where she could be present in this form and witness what was happening in this lifetime. I felt sorry for her which was a big mistake only I didn't realise it then.

"I am sorry Eliza for the pain you suffered. I really am. But this is not the way."

"It is!" Another hiss, accompanied by the grasping of my hand in hers which felt alarmingly far too real, icy as it was.

I shook my head and pulled my hand away. "It may be your way, Eliza, but it is not mine."

"I think you will find that it is," she said slyly.

I had had enough. I stood up. "No. It may have been. But not anymore. I have to do things differently now." As I said this, I realised that this did not just apply to Gawain. It applied to the rest of my life. "My way is no longer yours. I am sorry Eliza, but that is just the way it must be." I braced myself to look once more into her eyes, determining that this was the last time I would connect with her.

One dark and unreadable.

One light and piercing.

Spellbinding.

I gave myself a little shake and turned away, walking back up the path, Mabel's words and those of Rowan's coming back to me. Stay in the light, and all will be right. It scared me to think how close I had tiptoed into the dark. But no more. I was back in the light. I closed my ears to the ghostly laughter that drifted up on the breeze as I walked back into the vicarage.

CHAPTER THIRTY-FIVE

I shut the kitchen door firmly behind me, even going so far as to slide the heavy bolt across. Why I was doing this made no sense at all. A bolted door would not stop Eliza following me if she so wished. A ghost had no need for open doors. They only had need for open minds. And open souls. Or maybe disturbed souls. Souls in a similar vibration perhaps?

For the first time since I had been drawn to Eliza's grave, and in doing so, set her free, I felt a sense of unease ripple through me. My body began the usual reaction to the energetic connection I had just experienced, shaky and nauseous. Instantly I was craving sugar, and about to reach for more of the chocolate birthday cake, but my belly then rippled with something other than unease. My daughter. I placed my hands protectively over my tummy and smiled.

My child was growing livelier and as she kicked from within, I gave myself a kick up the backside too. All I had eaten today was mostly sugar. Ice cream, scones, and chocolate cake, the only meal closely resembling proper food was that cheese sandwich. Never mind that I was still lithe and slim with only my belly proclaiming the six months of pregnancy, never mind that I was shaking from my ghostly communications, my daughter was telling me she needed real food. Home then to Cobblers Row for tea with Aunty Ruth. But as I thought this, and put the chocolate cake back, something held me in place.

Something, or someone.

Gawain.

His birthday, spent without his twin.

A hellish day for him and one I empathised with all too well. There was a desperate need to see him. A longing to share that pain with him, to love him better, to heal him and in doing so, heal myself. What a turn around a day could make, I thought as I reflected on the last twenty-four hours. This time yesterday evening

I was having spaghetti Bolognese at Matt's before seducing him under the effects of Eliza's magic.

A wave of nausea washed over me at the thought and I closed my eyes against the images in my head. I couldn't go home to Cobblers Row just yet. I opened the fridge door and reached for the plate of food that Mrs Mannering had prepared for Arthur. A healthy salmon quiche with a vibrant green salad. My daughter would approve. I told myself I was suiting her needs as I sat down at the table to eat. It had nothing whatsoever to do with the fact that I was yearning to see Gawain. Nothing at all.

Lying again, Fae.

I was staying there because I wanted, needed to see him. I sent a text to my aunt saying I was staying a little longer and not to fret. Quite how long I intended to sit there I wasn't sure.

I ate the quiche.

The sun faded from the room.

He wasn't coming home.

My body was stiff from sitting at the table for so long. My tummy sloshed with the numerous cups of tea I had consumed. My heart stabbed once more with that hideous blade of jealousy and pain. He was with her.

That was all I could think. He had gone round to Lucinda's, stayed for tea with her and the children. Enjoyed the family routine of bath and bedtime stories. Would now perhaps be cuddled up on the sofa, maybe watching a film. Did he even watch television I wondered as my mind ran its self-sabotaging route? Or had they just waited until the children were fast asleep before quietly going hand in hand upstairs?

Stop right now, Fae!

Disgusted with myself, I pushed the chair back from the table so hard it screeched against the stone flagged floor. This was doing no good at all. Hadn't I said a few hours ago to Eliza that this was not my path anymore. I was damn well going to stick to what I said. Time to go. I let myself out of the vicarage and walked across the green. In a moment of beautiful synchronicity, I saw two women on the other side of the road, just about to go into the Maypoleton Arms.

One of whom was Lucinda, dressed up more than usual and laughing with her friend, clearly having an evening away from the children. And far more meaningful to me, not with him. My heart gave another leap now. One of hope. Ridiculous maybe but I clung to it, nevertheless. It meant that I could greet my aunt and uncle in a lighter mood and have a pleasant chat with them before heading upstairs to bed.

I awoke with a sudden jolt and so much light in the room I thought at first it must be morning. But no, it wasn't sunlight, it was the brilliance of the full moon with all its power and magic pouring through the gap in the curtains. I needed the loo and a glass of water and got out of bed to see to both. There was a compulsion inside me to go outside, drink my water and stand barefoot in the garden, grounding myself on the patio flags, connecting with mother earth, the same time I was dazzled by the light of the moon.

The air was soft and gentle, and I felt it caressing my face like a lover's touch. If only for that lovers' touch, I thought wistfully and dared for a second to imagine what it might feel like to have him touch my cheek with a gentle hand, to look in my eyes with a smiling gaze. A tear slid silently down my cheek. I could never see that happening. The best I could hope for now, after my behaviour with Matt, was to win back some level of respect and possible friendship so that at least moving forwards with our daughter we could behave amicable together.

How I wished for more.

I poured my heart out to the moon.

Oh, to be loved as I so wished to love.

Oh, to be at peace in my soul.

Oh, to feel joy in my life.

I closed my eyes and tried to imagine how this might feel. I felt the energy from the ground I was standing on, the power of the moon, the softness of the air, the beating of my heart within. For a gifted second, a glimpse of peace. I let out a gentle sigh and eased into the feeling. This was lovely. Then I felt something else.

Pain and sorrow.

Guilt and grief.

Anguish and despair.

Not my feelings, his.

My eyes flew open, my senses on overdrive. I was not thinking now, simply responding to the call of my soul, a voice that was too strong to ignore. It didn't matter that it made no sense at all, it didn't matter that I was probably going to walk into another mess. It didn't matter that this was no doubt going to rebound on me, wounding me even deeper. There was nothing else I could do.

Quickly, silently I went back upstairs and dressed, not bothering with underwear, just a pair of leggings and a hoody. I slipped my feet into my sandals neatly lined up by the front door of the cottage and let myself out. There were few streetlamps in Maypoleton, but that hardly mattered. The moon was like a floodlight, and even if that was not so, I could have walked there blindfolded.

I had my set of keys for the vicarage in my pocket. As quiet as a thief I let myself in. If my instincts were wrong, and I found him sleeping peacefully, then I would just as peacefully retrace my steps. I took the stairs slowly, to avoid making them creak underfoot. The only noise I could hear was the insistent drumming of my heart, growing louder in my chest with each footstep closer to his bedroom door.

I didn't pause as I reached for the handle, I merely prayed that the door would open as silently as I had crept in. If he was asleep, I had no wish to wake him. I knew though that he would not be asleep. How could he be with that heavy weight of sorrow and guilt drowning him, the pain that I knew, understood and shared. No, he would not be asleep.

He wasn't.

He was sitting in a chair, his head in his hands, dressed just in pyjama bottoms. Next to him on the dressing table was an opened biscuit tin, not full of shortbread, but photos. Memories to haunt and wound. Oh God I knew how that felt. My heart bled out for him, and I knew that whatever happened, I had been right to come.

"Gawain." Softly, lightly, a mere whisper.

His body stiffened in its pose, then he turned his head.

"Fae? What in God's name are you doing here?" No anger which surprised me, or maybe it shouldn't have.

"I have come to share your pain."

I dared to walk a little closer.

As I did so, I saw once more the scars that criss-crossed over his body, deeply traumatic wounds, but nowhere near as painful as those held within the mind, heart and soul.

I dared to place a hand upon his shoulder.

"Dad told you." A look of comprehension in his eyes. "I saw the cake and candles. Lance's card." He choked back a sob, closing his eyes.

I dared to lean in, to crouch down, to kiss him gently on the forehead. "Let me help you."

"Nobody can help me. Not even God."

To hear him say such words horrified me as much as the note of utter despair in his voice. He had turned to his faith for atonement, so his Arthur had told me. And it was failing him. I saw in my mind that night back in January, the anniversary of Fliss's death, the cold walk on the sea front, the attack, the rescue. He needed rescuing now. He was under attack. Not from five men hell bent on assault, but from the demons in his mind.

He may not love me.

That did not matter.

I loved him.

Besides, I was still searching for atonement myself. Maybe if I could heal his heart, I could heal my own. "I can help you," I whispered softly to him.

"How?"

As if he needed to ask.

I moved to stand behind him, to fold my body around his shoulders and back, to rest my head gently upon the back of his, to let my arms wrap around him, like angel's wings. That thought flew instantly into my mind as I did so, and a smile crept onto my lips.

The witch imagining herself as an angel.

Fancy that.

But hey, if angels could help him now, then welcome winged ones.

I felt a heat spreading over my back as I wrapped myself around his, a sensation I had never felt before. It was not unpleasant. I felt my daughter moving inside me as I pressed closer and wondered if he could feel her too. Our daughter, created in that night of grief and loss. I knew then for certainty that we were mean to be together.

She was to be our atonement.

Part of me, part of him.

A perfect union of souls.

More of that heat flooding across my back in response to these feelings and thoughts, and then a flooding of love so powerful it felt of though my heart was going to burst. Could he feel it too? I sensed a softening in his back, that hard rigidity of his muscles lessening slightly. I eased into that feeling. Surrendered to it, willing him to surrender too.

Don't fight me.
Don't hate me.
Just love me, as I love you.

I pulled back a little but only so that I could press kisses upon the top of his head, run my hands gently up and down his arms, pausing to lightly hold his shoulders. It's okay, I have got you. You are safe, with me. I will hold you. I will hold your pain. Could he read my mind, could he hear those unspoken words?

He answered with a sigh or was it perhaps the touch of my lips in that vulnerable spot at the base of his neck, gently up the side of his throat and then down across his back. So many scars, brutal and ugly, but a beautiful part of him. They were as healed now as they ever would be, pale and silvery in colour, I could do no more for them. But I was determined to heal the scars he held within.

"Fae."

Another answer, a mere whisper but enough. My fingers and lips explored those scars, every line, every knot, every ridge. I poured my love for him, into every touch. As I did so I felt a peace rising in my soul. A peace that was new to me.

Gentled me.

And with this feeling, with this contact of flesh upon flesh, my hands and mouth upon his back, there flooded in the rush of desire, the physical yearning for more, for deeper connection. Was he feeling it too? Was his despair turning into desire?

"Fae."

Another answer and this time, a moan, a plea. For more, or for me to stop? I brought my hands round to the front of his body. Curved around him more, leaning over slightly so my long hair fell across him, knowing that the soft silky touch of it would caress him as much as my hands. There were more scars on his chest, but they were hidden and softened somewhat by the hairs that ran down his tummy and lower. I pressed more kisses into the fold of his neck, down on to his chest, whilst my hands explored further, until I felt him vibrant and hard beneath the cotton of his pyjamas. Was his mind going to deny what his body was saying?

"Fae."

The answer that I wanted. My hands reached to cup, to enfold, over the cotton of this pyjamas, lightly, no pressure. Just the presence of my hands, the promise of more. His body wanted more, regardless of whatever his mind, heart or soul might tell him. He quivered and pulsed, grew beneath me. I moved from behind him, knelt now in front of him, placing my hands for a moment on his thighs.

Our eyes met.

Keenly I searched for the darkness I was used to seeing there, the anger, the hostility that was normally reflected at me. It wasn't there. There was darkness, I could see that clearly but stemming from another source.

Desire.

Pain.

Loneliness.

I knew those feelings well. They matched those emotions that overwhelmed me when I was in his presence and when he pushed me away from him. Tonight, it appeared there would be no pushing away. Tonight, it appeared there would be welcome, there would be an easing of that desire, that pain, that loneliness.

Tempting then, just to slide my hands beneath the cotton, to touch and hold him, to open my mouth and take him in. I wanted to, and I sensed he wanted me to do as well. But I had done that before, and whilst in the giving there was pleasure, tonight this had to be equal. Tonight, I had to know, to experience that depth of emotion and passion returned to me.

A gentle stroke and a promise, and then I stood up, daring to take his hands in mine, softly confident that he would not refuse my plea to follow. He didn't. A few short steps to the bed where the covers were already rumpled. I pulled the hoody over my head and let it fall carelessly to the floor. In a matter of seconds my leggings had followed suit along with his pants. Six months pregnant now and my body was not that of the woman he had first slept with. For one brief moment I felt a shadow of fear. Would he still desire me?

"Christ, Fae." Deep, throaty, guttural. Two words that told me yes. He still desired me, maybe even more.

CHAPTER THIRTY -SIX

An unsure look in his eyes though, a hesitancy in his touch as he reached towards me, hands lightly resting on my belly. Desire and something else.

"You are so beautiful, so fucking beautiful."

I wasn't expecting that, the raw honesty in his voice. It sent a shiver of delight through my body, deep into my bones, melting them, as I was melting at my core.

Our mouths met then, in the first kiss of many, me on tip toes, him bending his neck down. Fierce, urgent, greedy. The shock of the contact I think almost too much for us. We pulled apart with a little gasp, our breath mingling as we did so, the intensity of our reaction reflected in our eyes. Then once more drawn back in, two drowning souls in need of air and suddenly discovering that lifeline.

He scooped me up in one easy movement, just as he had done that night in January. Different though, the way he now gently, reverently laid me on the bed, not tossed down in anger as he had done then. It had been my intention to be the one who led, who loved, who healed. It seemed I was going to be wrong about that as I was so many things when it came to him. Supporting his weight slightly so he wasn't pressing down on my belly, he began his loving assault on my body.

Hands cupped my breasts, so much fuller and more tender now. Moans from both of us at the wonder of sensations. A cry torn from my lips as he teased one nipple with his mouth, his tongue circling and licking, and then mouth fully engaged in sucking. Straight to my core, a bolt of lust so intense I cried out more. Heat pooled deep inside, and I would happily have taken him in me there and then.

But despite the passion which I felt from him, it appeared he was not in any rush. The opposite in fact. A man starved he was not going to rush this feast. As he suckled on one breast, his hand toyed with the other. Then swapped. And again. More lavish attention, until I was writhing beneath him, my hips apart, the softness of my body wet against the hard muscle of his thigh.

"Please, I need you."

His answer was to kiss me, hard and deep. His tongue probed against mine, his teeth lightly grazed against my lips. Still supporting his weight by propping himself up on his elbows, he brought his chest lower to mine, careful not to press against my belly, legs tangling up with my limbs, the full heavy length of him in contact with me, but not where I needed him to be.

It didn't matter.

To feel the need rising within me was pleasure enough.

To soften and melt into that need was pleasure enough.

To allow my unquiet mind to enjoy the stillness of that need was enough.

For now.

For now, I was home. I was exactly where I needed to be. Lovingly held in the arms of the man I loved. And there was love there on his side, I could feel it. The way he kissed me so deeply, that edge of harshness gentled with a tender touch, featherlight at times all over my face, the vulnerable crook of my neck, round to my ear lobes, a moment of playful nibbling and then a return to devouring the depths of my mouth with his tongue, just as I knew he would do with the rest of his body, deep into mine.

But not yet.

This, my slumbersome, sensually delighted mind told me, was making love. This was a wonderful new gift that I had never experienced before in my life. Ever. Sex with many men, yes. Passion with him, yes. Angry lustful desire with him, yes. Desperate, tortured need with him, but never this. As we explored our body's, I felt the wetness of tears on my face, in echo of the wetness of my core. If my veins could have bled out then, I think they would have done.

My heart was full to bursting.

My body both heavy as earth and light as air at the same time.

My soul ready to soar.

But not yet.

Why would I want to rush this bliss? Why would I want to hurry past this new joy of kissing him back in return. Why would I want to not savour the feel of him beneath my hands and lips? Solid muscle, rough and ragged scars, smooth skin on his buttocks, abrasive hairs a delightful friction against my skin, his hardness such a contrast with the blossoming softness of my curves, a six pack and a belly with our baby nestling within.

I swear she knew her father's touch as his hands lingered and played softly over my bump. She was moving with us, a soul in perfect synchronicity with her parents. I felt his tears now, as he softly, so very softly, reverently, pressed his mouth to me, to her.

A lover's touch, a father's caress.

A moment of perfect peace and harmony.

My hands stroked his head as he kissed my belly, tenderness from me to him, wonder in his eyes as he shifted to look at me.

The world stopped then I think.

In that moment, all that had been, and that was, no longer existed. There was magic present in that room, born not of a desire for revenge or hatred, born instead from the miracle that was cradled between us. The innocence of our daughter's soul far more potent that any brew, potion, or spell a witch could create, be she alive in the present or risen from her grave.

Healing magic.

I had never seen him look this way before, vulnerable and yet powerful. Something had changed within him. He was not the same man he had been when I had entered the room. I sent a silent prayer up to the gods I had believed to be so cruel up to now and welcomed him into my body.

"Are you sure?" Quiet, respectful, caring. "I don't want to hurt you, or it."

"Her," I said with a feeling of sleek contentedness seeping through every pore, every cell. "You won't. She wants to feel her father's love."

"Christ Fae, I think she has it already." His voice was not the one I recognised. He pressed another lingering kiss on my belly, and then with the slowest, most careful of moves, he entered me.

So connected, so utterly right.

I breathed out a sigh, an exhalation of wonder. How had I lived my whole life until now, without this feeling in my life? I slid my hands down to his forearms, and up along the strength of his biceps.

"Come closer to me. You won't hurt her or me. " He was still a little unsure, until I began to move my hips against his, taunting and teasing, beckoning deeper, drawing him in, with each subtle rise and fall of my body, my back catlike in its arching, my belly nudging up towards him.

Skin on skin.

From deep within.

Sweat on sweat.

A slick, silken dance of yin and yang, soft and hard, masculine, feminine. Binding us together, weaving those threads tighter, our daughter. The silence of the room was broken by the sighs and moans that came unbidden from our lips. Our breath grew heavy, words of passion, of heat, desire, whispered against each other, let fly into the night air, arrows of wonder piercing the battle worn armour we each had built around our hearts and souls.

"I love you so much! I love you so much it hurts." The words I could no longer shackle inside of me. "I need you to love me. Please love me. Please love me, please love me."

"God Fae, don't you know that I do. I fucking love you, you beautiful, crazy, gorgeous, sexy, fucking, witch of a woman." Untamed words let loose from his mouth as his body went into spasms and poured into mine. Perfectly in tune I arched up from the bed, my legs wrapping around his waist, my hands on his back, pulling him closer still towards me.

A moment of utter soulful harmony.

A moment of pure physical pleasure.

A moment of truth, that could no longer be denied.

Words once spoken that could not be taken back.

They hung in the air between us, as the raging passion that had swept through us gradually released its' heady hold and awareness returned. Two bodies entwined, damp with sweat, breathing just about normal, clarity surging through. Words spoken in the heat of passion, in that instant of complete connection.

Would they be denied?

My heart was pounding in a state of delirious delight, and total terror. Would he take them back now? Would he retreat, back behind that impenetrable armour, retract within that cloister of

coldness? Still close to me, his head lying on my breast, my hands, tenderly stroking his shoulders and back, I felt him shake slightly.
Was he crying?
No. He was laughing.
Softly, quietly, but laughing. Not what I expected.
"Men plan whilst God laughs," he said in a voice that sounded somewhat dazed. "I vowed I would never love any woman again. I made a promise to myself, to Lance, to that poor wretched father who died in that crash, that I would never love again. I made a promise to God. I would love only him, serve only him."

My heart nearly stopped in hope as I listened to him talk in a tone of voice I had never heard before. I didn't dare speak or utter any sound in case I interrupted the flow.

"How could I possibly love another woman again after what I had done? How could I deserve to feel that way, to have that joy, that passion, that light in my life? Not after what I had done. Two innocent people dead because of me, because of my love for Jemma, my lust, my desire. My jealousy that she had chosen my brother over me."

"I was so jealous. It ate me up inside. It tore at my soul. It fucking devoured me. And all the time I had to pretend that I was happy for them. It twisted my every waking thought. It was never too bad when I was away on tour. I could lose myself then in the job. But every time I came home it was there. Always there."

"And the worst of it, I was glad when he caught us together. That's the ugly fucking truth of it. Glad. Happy in that second when I saw it in his eyes that he knew. One second. One moment. And then a living hell there on after. I've been in purgatory ever since. Devoting my life to God, to the faith that pulled me back from the brink, that death wish to join my brother. I made a promise that I would do as much good as I possibly could, and then maybe one day I would no longer have to live with the guilt."

A long, warm sigh against my breast and a shudder as he let it all go.

"I made a promise that I would never love another woman again," he repeated.

I lay there, not daring to move, hardly daring to breathe.

"And then one night, trying to clear my head on the sea front, I came across a woman about to be raped by a gang of men. I came across a woman who begged me to stay with her, sleep with her, not just for sex, but because she felt the same pain I did. I knew it, felt it when I saw a photo of her and her twin, when she told me she had died. I told myself the next morning it was just sex for me. I left money for that woman telling myself it was a business transaction, nothing more. I left that woman determined that I would not think of her again."

"But I did. Most days, and every night. Another form of torture and I told myself that this was simply one more way in which I was to atone. To have this feeling inside of being incomplete, of having a glimpse of something that could be, may be, but knowing I would not be allowed it."

I was crying now, silently. Melting into him as he shared his pain, my pain, the soul deep connection that made us one.

"I know," I whispered against his head. "I felt the same."

He pressed a tender kiss against my breast. "Then you turned up here that day in church with your aunt." He laughed then, a lightness entering the mood, a lifting of the spirit. "I couldn't believe my eyes. I have no idea if any of my sermon made sense after that point. I could have been talking a foreign language for all I knew. All I could think was, '*She's here.*' And then you fainted at the altar for crying out loud! Talk about making your presence known."

"You know why I fainted now though," I said with a gentle note of laughter. in my voice.

"Our daughter. How do you know she is a she? You have not had a scan?"

"I know. Rowan told me."

"Rowan. Your mother beyond the grave." He gave a funny sort of laugh and sigh combined. "And there it was, the irony, the joke that I felt God was playing on me. You had come into my life, this beautiful, wild, fucked up soul, and yes, Fae you were as royally fucked up as I was, and turned out to be a fucking witch!"

I giggled then myself, and in a moment of joy we were bound together in sheer playfulness, a new feeling I think for both of us.

"The vicar and the witch," I said feeling happier than I ever could remember.

"Hmm. The vicar and the witch. I am not quite sure what the villagers will make of it, or the bishop for that matter."

Back to being a shade more serious. I swallowed hard, doubt creeping in once more. "I thought you hated me," I said with my heart still not daring to believe the opposite. "You were so cold."

"My defence."

I grew a little braver. "Lucinda."

He sighed heavily and rolled away from me to lie on his back, eyes now on the ceiling. I couldn't breathe until he spoke again. "My defence. There had always been a subtle pressure from the bishop and the villagers that it may be better if I was married."

"But not to a witch?"

He laughed then, a wonderful sound. "No. Most definitely not to a witch. I knew that Lucinda was interested in me. She had made that quite clear from the moment she had moved here. A young widow, two small children. A perfect solution. And if I began a relationship with her, then........."

"Then what?"

"Then it would protect me from you."

"Protect?"

"Don't you know how dangerous you are, Fae?"

"I'm not dangerous!"

He laughed again. "Oh, but you are. Deadly dangerous. You blasted your way through my defences with all the subtlety of a wrecking ball. An absolute wrecking ball."

I snuggled against him, smiling to myself, rather liking the notion. "But I am not going to hurt you. I have no wish to wreck you. I only want to love you."

"I only want to love you too, Fae."

Magical words that required no spell at all. We turned to each other once more, defences abandoned, and let love in, a night of coming home to where we belonged, wrapped in each other's arms.

Safe from the nightmares of the past.

Safe from the tortures of guilt.

Safe from any more wrecking balls.

Safe to believe that Fae Winters maybe was going to get that fairy tale happy ever ending after all. I allowed this image to play in my mind as I snuggled closer to Gawain, ignoring for now the doubt that raised a question mark at the end of this.

CHAPTER THIRTY-SEVEN

Usually an early riser, I woke with the awareness that bright sunlight was pouring into the room and that languorous feeling in my body as though I had just been enveloped in the most delicious of dreams. A dream in which I was being made love to, tenderly and beautifully, by Gawain, the man who had stolen my heart and my soul. I purred in blissful satisfaction as the remnants of the dream filtered through my consciousness. The purring became more of a saddened moan at the fragment of thought that told me I was dreaming that this was not real.

"I didn't want to wake you." His voice sounded too clear to be a dream.

The clouds of sleep disappeared in an instant. I sat bolt upright in bed. His bed, not mine. Duvet crumpled; two pillows dented.

"It wasn't a dream."

He was standing by the bed with a mug in his hands. "I didn't know if you preferred tea or coffee first thing in the morning." A boyish smile flitted across his face which took years off him and melted my heart even more. "Then I thought how many times Margaret complains about the mess you create when you make hot chocolate. So, I wondered if you would like one?"

"Now this is a dream," I said, taking the mug from him and feeling absurdly shy as he sat on the bed beside me. He was dressed already, but not in his work clothes for now, just jeans and a blue sweater. Less of the vicar, more of the man. I wondered if this was significant.

"Are you ok?" Oddly tentative, a side of him I had not expected.

"I am. Are you?"

Was this where he was going to let me down gently? Tell me that last night was a mistake after all. A moment of weakness born out of the vulnerability of his pain. I sipped my hot chocolate, my eyes meeting his over the rim of my cup.

A broader smile. "I am, Fae. I feel as though I am for the first time, since……." So many emotions flew across his face then, like watching the sky rapidly change from sunshine to dark clouds, then lighting up with a rainbow. "I am at peace. With you. Last night, last night was……."

I placed my cup on the bedside table and took hold of his hands. "I know. You don't have to say anymore."

Confident now that I was not going to be rejected, I shifted closer to him letting the duvet fall away. Natural then to lean in to kiss, to hold, to feel the warmth of him. No dream at all. A wonderful glow warmed me, and this time it was not merely that first flow of desire. There was so much more to this feeling. The sheer contentment of surrender.

For both of us.

The battle was won.

The fighting done.

I heard him laugh gently at the back of this throat, even as he kissed me deeper and deeper. "Oh Fae, do you know what you do to me. Much more of this and I will need a cold shower."

I bit at his mouth teasingly. "And where's the harm in that? I could scrub your back."

"Maybe tonight."

My eyes grew wide as I stared at him. "Tonight?"

He nodded. "I want you with me Fae, from now on. I want our daughter with me."

I was stunned. This was beyond my wildest dreams. Of course I had fantasised about being with him, of having him make love to me as he had last night, but somehow in my imaginings I had not gone so far as to what happened next. Maybe because I had never dared believe it could possibly be? Now here he was, sitting so close to me, tenderly stroking my belly and calmly telling me he wanted me to be with him.

An utterly glorious what the fuck moment!

"What will you say to everyone?"

"You care what people think?"

I had clearly astonished him. I had astonished myself. "No. Yes. No. I mean, I don't care about that for myself. But you,

you're the vicar. Everyone knows you've been seeing Lucinda, what are you going to say to everyone? To her?"

He gave a big sigh. "The truth. That I am human like everyone else, and I have been blind to what has been right in front of me. That I am in love with the most incredible, beautiful, ever so slightly mad woman, who is going to be the mother of my child."

Maybe I was actually dreaming?

He carried on. "Lucinda will be disappointed I know. But we were taking things very slowly. I had made no deep commitment to her as yet."

I had to ask, couldn't stop myself. "Have you slept with her?"

He gave me a wry look at that. "Really Fae? If you must know, the answer is no."

I hope I hid my triumph, but I doubted it from the way he looked at me. I shrugged my shoulders as though to say, hey I am only human too. His answering smile was enough to tell me he understood.

"Now, I have got to get going, but you take your time. Help yourself to anything in the bathroom. I've made Dad's breakfast and helped him shower."

"Oh, hell what time is it?" I suddenly remembered I actually had a life outside of this dream state that required me to show up for other people.

Another smile. Oh, my goodness I could fall even deeper in love with this version of him.

"It's okay. He's all sorted. And anyway, it's your Saturday off this week. But I am sure he would love a coffee or hot chocolate with you before you go. Unless of course you have things to do?"

"Bloody hell that's a relief."

I looked at my phone and realised it was already ten o'clock. I panicked for a second then about Aunty Ruth fretting over my absence but realised that her normal routine was to be up early and down at the stables with Uncle Eric on a Saturday morning, out before I would be up.

I then thought of Arthur. "Have you told your dad?"

His turn to shrug. "He knew something had happened as soon as he saw me this morning. I told him that you had stayed over last night. He already knew didn't he, about the baby. Our baby."

"He guessed. He could see how I felt about you."

"He's delighted; in case you were wondering. So maybe a coffee and chat might be nice?"

I could think of no pleasanter way to spend my Saturday morning. "Absolutely."

"Good. Well in that case then, I had best be off. I have a meeting with the bishop at eleven."

"The bishop?" He didn't look as though he was dressed to see the bishop.

For a moment that old serious look came back into his eyes. He stood up and wandered over to the window, his back to me for a second. Then he turned round, and I could see that whatever he was thinking about it was not detrimental to me.

"I emailed him first thing this morning and asked to see him as soon as possible."

"Is everything ok?" It struck me that some kind of emergency had occurred for the bishop to respond so promptly.

"Yes. But he needs to know before I announce it in church tomorrow what my plans are."

My voice croaked a little. "And they are?"

He looked at me oddly. "To marry you of course."

"Marry me?" Was there a touch of uncertainty in his eyes now? Surely not.

"That's if you want to, of course. I am sorry, I am being presumptive. I thought with the baby, not that that needs to be the reason."

I was momentarily too overjoyed to speak. Was this really happening? Was I going to get the happy ever after?

"I've not put that the right way, have? Damn. I'm not good with this kind of thing, Fae. I thought you would realise from last night, how I was with you. I love you, Fae Winters. I bloody love you so much it hurts at times. Will you marry me? Not just for our child, but because I can't bear the thought of living without you, not now."

Seriously, pinch me now because this cannot be real.

"Fae?"

"Yes. Yes of course I will marry you. I love you so much it hurts at times. It feels like I have always loved you, as though I have been waiting for you all my life, maybe even before Fliss...."

He looked thoughtful then but didn't dispute what I was saying. "I had better get going. Are you sure you are going to be alright? And the baby, our daughter, everything is ok, I mean after..."

How utterly adorable. "Yes, to all of those. Now go and do your bishopy thing. I hope it goes alright for you. I don't want to be the cause of any problems." I knew I was frowning as I continued, "I know I am not exactly suitable Vicar's wife material."

Our eyes met then and wonderfully we exploded into laughter at the same time.

"No. You most certainly are not. But then, Maypoleton is not exactly the most normal of villages so perhaps there is a certain synchronicity to it all. Either way, Fae, I am going to marry you."

I experienced a thrill of feminine delight in the way he said those words. He came to kiss me quickly, but hard on the lips and then picking up a jacket from the back of a chair, he left the room. I fairly danced around the ensuite as I showered and washed my hair. There was no dryer to be found, but it didn't matter, it was summer, and my hair would soon dry naturally. Pulling on the clothes I had quickly dressed in last night, no underwear but that didn't bother me, I went downstairs with a light step and a song in my heart.

Crossing over the hallway, I caught sight of my reflection in the mirror by the door. A different Fae looked back at me. A happy Fae. A Fae who loved and was loved in return. I blew her a kiss. Then I went to knock on Arthur's door.

"Come in my dear, I was hoping you would pop in." Arthur was sitting in his chair by the window that overlooked the green. He smiled warmly at me, and it seemed that much of the sorrow of yesterday had lifted from him. "Gawain has told me the happy news. May I be the first to congratulate you. I cannot think of a nicer daughter-in-law."

"Oh wow, I'd not thought of that." Truth be told I was still in a head spin with all that had happened. "You'll be my father-in-law. Oh my God I am getting married. He wants to marry me. He bloody well wants to marry me!"

"Well of course he does my dear. He loves you and you are having his child. He just couldn't see it that's all. Now why don't we go and make a hot chocolate and sit in the garden. We have a wedding to plan!"

In a total contrast to the energy of yesterday, Arthur began to manoeuvre his chair towards me. I opened the door, and we went through to the kitchen. My stomach began to rumble as we did so.

"Do you want any breakfast?"

"Gawain has already sorted that for me whilst you were sleeping. But it sounds like you do. It sounds like my grandchild does. Oh Fae, I cannot tell you how happy I am! A baby to look forward to, and Gawain finally able to forgive himself and move on. You've worked miracles my dear, miracles." He reached for my hand and gave it a squeeze.

I felt a sudden chill in the room, just a moment, but it was there. "I am not sure about any miracles," I said with a light laugh that hid the prickle of unease that had crept in. I had worked a spell in this room that was for certain.

Arthur would have nothing less said. "No, it's the miracle that I have been praying for. Ever since Lance died and that other wretched soul in the car crash, I have been terrified I was going to lose Gawain as well. He did his best whilst he was still in the army to get himself blown up and as you know he damn well near succeeded. And thankfully, the army chaplain stepped in and gave him his new direction. Do you know my dear I think I will have a boiled egg too if that's what you are making for yourself."

"Just one?"

"Please, with soldiers."

"Of course." I smiled at him and popped another egg in the pan along with the two for myself.

"But even though he was better once he was in the church, and I felt safe that he wasn't going to do anything.......you know, I still felt that I had lost him. He had gone. The Gawain that I had watched grow up, that brave, confident young man with so much promise and leadership, had disappeared. Oh, he still inspired others, you could see every Sunday as he stood in church. He gave off that same magnetic quality, that quiet inner strength that makes everyone want to follow him, be they parishioners or soldiers, Gawain would speak, and they would listen. It's a gift he has always had. Even as a child. He would draw people to him."

I set my timer for the eggs and laid the table as I continued to listen.

"But he was not there inside. Not all of him. No-one else saw that of course. But I knew. I knew he was lost in some godforsaken purgatory. And then you came to Maypoleton. He was different from that moment, but I didn't realise at first what it was. Oh, thank you my dear, this looks lovely. What a perfectly boiled egg, there's nothing better."

We ate our eggs in companionable silence and knowing that Mrs Mannering would not be in today, I for once washed up, not wanting to leave a mess for Gawain to come back to. Every other second my heart seemed to explode in a whizzy whirl of happiness.

Gawain loved me.

He wanted to marry me.

I was to be his wife.

What Arthur had said before rang around in my head. It did feel like a miracle. I made us both a hot chocolate and placed the mugs on a tray for Arthur to hold and then opened the back door to wheel him into the garden. It was alive with summertime. Colours, scents, sounds, flowers, herbs, birds, butterflies, bees. A perfect morning to sit in the sunshine, Arthur protected somewhat under the leafy shade of a tree.

"We will need a swing," he said with a thoughtful look around the garden. "And the pond will have to have wire mesh over it."

He was way ahead of me, but I quickly caught up. Another rainbow of delight to consider. My daughter taking her first steps here. Playing here. Would she have a brother or a sister? Now I really was racing ahead, but why not? I felt like a child on Christmas morning discovering the stocking at the end of the bed, full of wonderfully wrapped gifts, each one a surprise waiting to be opened.

I felt drunk on happiness.

Arthur picked up on my energy and we spent the next hour enjoying a merry conversation of 'won't it be nice if,' weaving the thread of a future that had until yesterday seemed utterly impossible and way beyond my imagination.

"Of course, it's going to go down like a lead balloon with you know who," he said after a while, nodding his head in the direction of the house. Then he started to chuckle and roar with laughter. "You must let me be there, Fae, when you tell her."

"Mrs Mannering? The she dragon." I began to laugh with him, picturing the housekeeper's face when she realised that I would be marrying Gawain. "I imagine it won't be me who tells her. I think Gawain will be the one to do that."

"Unless you get in first," he suggested with a wink.

"Stop it." I playfully tapped his hand. "You're getting as naughty as me. I've been a bad influence on you."

"Quite the reverse my dear Fae. You have been the best thing to happen in my life since you moved to Maypoleton. Life has been so much more entertaining! For one thing," he said now pointing in the opposite direction towards the end of the garden, "We would never have known there was a body buried down there if you hadn't come along. Blow me that was the weirdest day I can recall!"

His words seemed to bring a chill in the air. Or was it just me that sensed that?

"Did you ever find out who she was? I remember Gawain saying he was going to look into it in order that she could be given a decent Christian burial." He gave a shudder, and it echoed through my body. "Poor lass. Whoever she was, she didn't deserve to lie there with no one to think about her all that time. "

My voice had developed a bit of a croak when I tried to speak. I coughed and began again. "I don't think there were any records to be found. I have no idea who she was." The lie caught in my throat and suddenly I was coughing in earnest.

"You know who I am. Tell him! Tell him I am Eliza Pendleby and I do not wish a decent Christian burial, I wish for my revenge. I wish the vicar to suffer as I suffered. Tell him!"

"Are you alright?" Arthur looked concerned.

I nodded and gave one more guttural clearing of my throat. "I'm fine. I think we had better go in though. My aunt will be back from the stables soon."

"Yes of course and you have such good news to tell her!" He looked delighted at the prospect for me.

"I think I will wait until I can tell her with Gawain."

I placed the mugs back on the tray and handed it to him. Even as I said the words I still had to pinch myself mentally.

Was this really happening?

Was I going to marry Gawain?

Was I going to have the fairy tale ending?

I felt a blast of cold air swoop up from the end of the garden. Arthur felt it too. "Goodness me, it's gone chilly all of a sudden. The forecast didn't mention a change in the weather today."

"Just a cloud passing over the sun behind us," I lied, eager to get him back into his room. I wanted to come back and talk to Eliza. Things had changed and she needed to know. It was only fair. However, ten minutes later, I began to realise that ghosts do not have the same sense of fairness that we do.

She appeared the instant I stood at the spot where she had been buried. Clearer than ever before, she seemed more real than the trees, flowers and shrubs around us, as though the reality of life had somehow faded, and her presence was superimposed upon it.

"This has to stop Eliza. It's different now. He loves me. Don't you see that. We're going to be married. There is no need to make him jealous or make him suffer."

"No! This cannot be. I will not have it." She shook her head, corn blonde hair framing her face, dainty features scrunched into an ugly scowl.

"We are getting married," I said again. "It is over Eliza. There is no need for you to linger here anymore. You can be at peace."

"There is no peace for me. Not until he suffers as I did. Not until he feels my pain." She took a step towards me. Unnerved I stepped back.

"Eliza he is not your vicar. He is not the man who denied your love. He is not the man you rejected you."

"Tis of no consequence. He is the vicar here now. He is a man as he was."

"No Eliza, this is wrong! I won't have it. I love him. He is a good man and deserves to be happy. I deserve to be happy!"

She frightened me then.

"Do you? I was not happy? Why should you be happy? I did not get to marry the man I loved? Why should you?"

I tried to quell the sick feeling in my stomach. "Eliza this ends now."

"It ends when I say it ends."

"Eliza?"

She had gone.

CHAPTER THIRTY-EIGHT

Eliza's vehement reaction to my news disturbed me but it was not enough to overshadow my joy at how events had so swiftly turned around in my favour. As I let myself back into the kitchen, it struck me that this would become my home. A girlish giggle escaped me as I pictured myself, not Mrs Mannering, cooking a homely tea for Gawain, our daughter sitting in a highchair at the table. Fae Winters, domestic goddess, wife and mother. How was this even possible?

I would have to tell Annie this incredible news. I grinned even wider at the thought of how she would react. Then of course my parents. They would be relieved to know I was getting married and maybe Mum would even be impressed that I had managed to land the catch of the village, because in her eyes, marrying the vicar would be precisely that.

First though I had to go home and hide my present state of excitement from my aunt and uncle. I clearly failed. I was in such a tizzy of delirious delight that Aunty Ruth pestered me to tell her what I was so excited about. Of course I didn't dare say at this point. What if Gawain returned from his visit to the bishop with a negative response. What if, in me blurting out my news, I somehow jinxed myself. I was jittery enough as it was with Eliza's nasty reaction.

It was such a relief when late afternoon there was a knock on the door, Gawain standing there, a look of calm composure on his face. Shrieks of congratulations bounced around the small terraced cottage when Gawain pulled me close to him, kissed me in front of them, and produced a velvet ring box.

"It may of course need altering, but the jeweller assured me that would not be a problem."

My aunt and uncle quietly and unobtrusively slipped into the kitchen as I took the tiny box with shaking hands and opened it.

I couldn't contain my gasp. Stunningly simple, but then what would I expect from Gawain, stunningly huge, which had my eyes widening as I looked from the ring to the man.

"It's, it's….." It was the mother of all engagement rings. A beautifully cut diamond solitaire.

"Will it fit?"

Gawain took the box back from me. My hands were shaking at this point. He was about to slide the ring onto my finger, when he paused. I was stunned when I heard a note of uncertainty in his voice, "Will you marry me, Fae?"

My yes was a whisper, and then a most definite, "Yes, yes I will marry you."

The ring fitted perfectly as though I had been in the shop to try it on. He pulled me close then, kissing me deep and tenderly, cradling my face tenderly in his hands. It was a novel and wonderful experience to feel so cherished.

"You can come back in now," he said in a carrying voice to my aunt and uncle who were no doubt waiting behind the kitchen door.

They emerged with a bottle of Uncle Eric's homemade sloe gin and Aunty Ruth's best glasses, only brought out for special occasions.

"Of course there will be champagne later," said Uncle Eric as he opened the bottle. "Although I suppose, Fae should I get you some elderflower cordial?"

"I don't think one glass will do any harm," said Gawain with a smile. "It will be nice for our daughter to share in the celebrations too."

"Aye well that's another cause for celebration," said Eric handing me a glass with a small measure poured, "I was never completely happy that our Fae here was going to have to go it alone as a mother. Oh, I know it's common these days and there's no stigma, but still it would have been hard. And credit to you Gawain, not many a man would be so happy as to being up another man's child."

Gawain gave me a quick look. "You haven't told them?"

"How could I?" I said quietly.

He gave my hand that he was holding a reassuring squeeze. "The baby is mine. Fae and I perhaps did not get off to the best of beginnings…….."

Uncle Eric in his straight-talking way said that it never mattered how things began, all that counted was how they ended, and then most unlike him, quoted Voltaire, "All is for the best in this the best of all possible worlds."

"I'll drink to that," Gawain said, clinking his glass against Eric's.

Aunty Ruth, having finally mopped up her tears, raised the same point that Mrs Mannering had, only in a much kinder way. "Of course this is going to cause some ripples," she said with a fond look at me. "Our Fae, isn't exactly your typical vicar's wife material. She's very like her mother. You do realise that, don't you?"

"If you are trying to tell me that I am marrying a witch, then yes, I know." Gawain had stunned everyone then, including me with the boldness of his statement.

I had to ask him then. "What did the bishop say about that?"

His reply was guarded. "We had a lengthy discussion. Ultimately what is best for me is best for the parish."

Which meant that the bishop had not been happy but had given way. Understandable that this news was going to disturb more than a few people on both a professional and personal level, his housekeeper of course being one of them. He told her early on the Sunday morning before the main service of the day.

Mrs Mannering collapsed in a chair, hand to her heart, protesting palpitations and a hasty phone call to Doctor Jay was made. Whilst the housekeeper struggled to contain her shock, horror and utter dismay at the 'brutal news' she had just been given, the senior doctor in the village practice struggled to contain her delight.

"Fae, Gawain, this is wonderful news!" She exclaimed, stethoscope around her neck and a beaming smile on her face. "I am so happy for you both."

"How can it possibly be wonderful news?" The dragon could now speak, having been told quite firmly by Doctor Jay that she was not on the verge of dying. "I am sorry Gawain, it grieves me to say this, but I speak not just for your own good, but for the good of your parish. It is not right that a man of the cloth be married to one of the 'other'. It is unfortunate that you have fallen victim to her charms, but you are a man, and I suppose this is God's way of testing you. There may be a child but that is no reason, no reason at all, to throw away your life of service to the Lord for this, this………"

"Heathen witch?" I dimpled merrily at her, making an elaborate gesture with my left hand which now sported the flashing diamond ring.

"Fae do behave darling," said my newly besotted fiancé to the increased dismay of the housekeeper. To Mrs Mannering, he went on with that steely look in his eyes and clipped tone of voice that I had previously been on the receiving end. "I have the bishops' agreement and that should be enough. We haven't had any conversations as yet regarding your forthcoming retirement, but perhaps in light of your reaction today, now would be a good time to consider this. Your opinion, Doctor Jay?"

The doctor had closed up her bag having finished making her notes but had made no other moves to leave the kitchen where we were all gathered around the table. Arthur, who had been most insistent that he was not going to miss out on all the fun when his son broke the news to Mrs Mannering, had made sure that he was settled in place with a mug of coffee and a plate of biscuits. He flashed a quick, conspiratorial look at Doctor Jay.

A lively, efficient woman, Doctor Jay had been aware of the battles that Arthur had faced with the housekeeper, notably the repeated suggestions that he would be better cared for in a home. She tilted her head to one side and looked as though she was giving this careful consideration.

"Well, there will be so much more to do with a baby in the house, and you know how you like your routine to remain constant, there is your blood pressure to think about after all. It does seem like the ideal time for you to think how much more you could enjoy your life without the weight of responsibility lying so heavily on your shoulders."

"Exactly!" Arthur was triumphant.

Mrs Mannering looked as though she was going to have a heart attack for real at this point, until Gawain went on to say ever so smoothly, "Didn't I hear you talking on the phone to your sister that you had always wanted to join her on one of her cruises? I am sure I can sort that out for you as a retirement gift. Thank you, Doctor Jay, you have been most helpful."

I almost felt sorry for the housekeeper. Her world had just turned on its axis and she had no clue how to respond. I watched a similar reaction over the next few days as the news spread quicker than wildfire around the village. Half the population were delighted, half were horrified. The congregation in the church appeared to be in themselves divided. I sat with Aunty Ruth that morning, and even Uncle Eric who normally preferred to have a solitary run on a Sunday, had insisted he came. Underneath his serious demeanour, I knew there lurked a sense of mischief.

"I'm not going to miss out on the fun," he said to me with a wink when I questioned his appearance by raising my eyebrows at him. Like me, he was no church goer.

"Do you know if Lucinda knows yet?" Aunty Ruth asked me, quietly as the pews began to fill up.

"Gawain told her yesterday evening."

He had left my aunt's cottage to go and speak directly to the woman who thought she was going to be his wife, to 'let her down gently,' as he put it. I felt sorry for her momentarily and then I told myself that she could not possibly have the same bond with Gawain that I did and as attractive as she was, no doubt she would soon find another man.

Callous perhaps? Maybe, but in my loved-up state, I didn't want any cloud to dim the sunshine that had suddenly burst forth into my life. I was so used to living in the shadows of depression and despair, I was high on this euphoria and selfishly determined to protect it at all costs.

"How did she take it?" Aunty Ruth asked what no doubt many others would want to know.

"Gawain didn't say."

Of course I had asked, and of course he had given me one of those looks. A 'Really Fae?' look, only now there was a tolerant amusement in his eyes instead of cold disapproval. He had asked me to go round to the vicarage that evening and in a state of newfound contentment I had stayed with him. We were starting our honeymoon early. There was a feverish quality to our lovemaking that night as though neither of us could quite believe the other was there, and that the barriers between us had completely collapsed.

"Will she be here this morning?" Aunty Ruth whispered in the final moments before Gawain began the service.

I shrugged. "I have no idea."

And then the universal powers, or maybe the angels, given that we were in their house, stepped in and prodded me on the shoulder. I jumped to see the woman in question standing there at the end of the pew. She was wearing a brightly coloured floral dress, her glossy chestnut brown hair falling softly around her pretty face, perfectly made up and cleverly concealing any signs of crying, if indeed she had been driven to that.

"I must offer you my congratulations," she said in a voice that I thought was a shade too loud. People were swift to turn their heads in our direction. "I am glad for you that Gawain is doing the decent thing. When he told me about the baby, I immediately felt uncomfortable about our situation. Gawain, I said to him, you must do the honourable thing. You cannot let poor Fae bring your daughter up without her father by her side, it just wouldn't be right. I am so glad that he took it well when I ended it with him."

I had to admire her bravado and how well she had played her hand. A look flashed between us and there was perhaps a hint of respect on both sides. Hearing the sudden rush of gasps, and exclamations that rose like a tidal wave from our pew to those in front and behind, I thought it wiser to remain silent and merely nod my head at her. If I knew Gawain as I thought I did, he would not be altogether happy that she had stolen his thunder.

Lucinda took her place in a pew diagonally across from us, and then as the whispers had grown to a clamour of confused conversations, there came the sound of the choir singing which was the prelude to them entering the church with Gawain. For once the hymn could not be heard.

He was angry.

I knew it, even if the rest of the congregation did not.

With that inscrutable mask in place, he began the service leaving everyone hanging on in anticipation until he got to the sermon. Then with the rapier sharp deliver I had come to expect from him, which perhaps took the rest of the villagers by surprise, he made his announcement.

If a silence could become more so, it did.

The same air of ruthlessness that I had witnessed the night our daughter had been conceived was in evidence now. With a beautiful sparsity of words, he made it abundantly clear that this was not to be a subject for debate, gossip, or speculation.

He was marrying me.

We were having a baby together.

End of.

He then announced the next hymn to the stunned congregation. "Let us now stand and sing together, 'All things bright and beautiful.'"

When the service was over Lucinda made a hasty exit, announcing to all who cared to listen that she was in a hurry to pick her children up from Sunday school to go and visit her mother. As I trundled down the aisle with my and uncle, I received a kaleidoscope of looks and the odd quietly spoken congratulations. Regardless of what folk might actually think, few would dare to now speak against me and run the risk of falling out of favour with Gawain.

He was there outside the church, saying his usual farewells and spending those minutes enquiring after the wellbeing of his parishioners. As soon as he spotted me, he reached out a hand to draw me close. I was still unused to being on the receiving end of the supersonic smile. I felt myself blushing absurdly as I stood there next to him, Fae Winters, fiancé of the village vicar.

Fae Winters wife of the village vicar?

Really?

Witch turned vicar's wife?

"I have to speak to my mother," I said to him quietly but insistently when finally, all had departed, including Aunty Ruth and Uncle Eric.

"As in Rowan?" He had changed his outer garments from those he had worn during the service, less of a vicar now, more the man, black trousers and his shirt without the collar, open at the neck.

I nodded, wondering if he would now gainsay me speaking to Rowan beyond the grave. Would that count as unacceptable behaviour for a vicar's wife? Was this where we would have our first row as a couple? Would it end as quickly as it had begun? I hadn't realised I was holding my breath as I waited for his answer. I hadn't realised that if he had said no, I would have been unable to go ahead and marry him. I hadn't realised that I could no longer live a lie about any aspect of my life until this point.

No more living in the shadows.

I couldn't breathe that way.

I couldn't live that way.

He pulled me close, brushed a stray strand of hair away from my face and looked deep into my eyes. "I could no more ask that of you, than I could walk away from my path here. I love you for who you are. God knows I have tried not to!" He laughed and shook his head. "And I mean that literally. I have prayed for guidance and sanity over you, Fae Winters, more than you will ever know. You're wild, reckless, shameless even. You are everything a vicar's wife should not be. You're a witch. You denied it before, and I know how much it destroys a soul to deny who and what they are. I will not ask that of you."

"Thank you," I replied softly and reached up on my tip toes to kiss him.

"So go and talk with Rowan," he said when we pulled apart, long moments later. "Just promise me one thing, Fae, no more sleeping with other men. I can accept who you are in all aspects, other than that. I cannot bear the thought of you with another man now."

I lowered my eyes so that he would not see the shame in them. Then, annoyed at myself for this cowardice, looked him straight at him. "I wanted to make you jealous."

The arms that were holding me tightened. "You did, Fae. You did." A silent promise was made then with another long, deep, kiss, one that held maybe a touch of desperation as if there was a tiny, dangerous dart of doubt embedded still in our hearts and souls.

We walked out of the church hand in hand, but then he took the path to the vicarage whilst my feet wandered through the gateway that led to the graveyard. Rowan was happy for me. I could tell that as soon as I knelt by her headstone. Even without tracing my fingers along the carving of her name, I felt the surge of energy washing over me, that connected from mother to child, from the spirit world to the here and now.

I could hear her clearer than ever, maybe because I was so buoyed up with the heightened emotion of love. Love that for the first time in my life was being returned fully and equally to me. A heady power. The headiest of all.

Rowan agreed. *"There is no greater power my child. My darling daughter you are loved beyond measure. You always have been. You just could not see it."*

"I see it now. I see it now. He loves me."

A beautiful merry laughter. *"Yes, he does love you. You are his twin flame."*

"Twin flame? Oh, you mean because we were both twins. Because of that and what happened ….. to Fliss, and to Lance?"

More laughter. *"That and more. You are his twin soul. One soul, split into two."*

I rocked back on my heels, trying to absorb what Rowan was saying. "Wow."

"It is destiny my daughter. It is your path, and it is his. Two parts of the same soul. Mirror opposites, drawn together to heal, to complete the other."

In that moment I felt a wave of peace wash over me that rippled right through my heart, soul, every cell in my body, to that of my daughter. I placed my hands over my belly and breathed a sigh of utter contentment. It was as though everything I had been through in my life up until this point had been merely a stepping stone, an obstacle, heart shatteringly painful at times, but now all of a sudden, wonderingly necessary.

Nothing would ever bring Fliss or Lance back.

But maybe in Gawain and I coming together and bringing up our daughter, there would be some kind of peace for them across the divide. I bade a silent farewell to Rowan and made my way back to Cobblers Row where I knew Aunty Ruth would be eagerly waiting to discuss wedding plans.

CHAPTER THIRTY-NINE

After the announcement in church there followed a whirlwind of activity.

Gawain insisted that we make a flying visit down south to see my parents, not wanting such a big announcement to be given over the phone. My neighbour Eve, had been one of the first to offer her congratulations as soon as she heard the news and when she knew that Gawain wanted to come with me to tell my parents, immediately stepped in to help with Arthur.

"I am guessing that the lovely Lucinda will not be doing that for him now," she had said with one of her mischievous grins.

I spent the long drive in a jumbled state of anxiety and excitement wondering how they would both react. However, it appeared that Gawain held two magicians tricks up his sleeves. Not only the magnetic attraction he seemed to hold for women of all ages, but the fact that he was a vicar.

Mum greeted him suspiciously at first until she realised this fact. Then it was as though the sun had just come out after a particularly heavy burst of rain. In that one moment my previous sins were to be forgiven.

Dad was delighted, insisting on giving Gawain a manly hug, then vigorously shaking his hand. "We'll be up to visit you both as soon as the baby is born," he said with a somewhat wistful expression on his face as he pulled me close. I knew he was thinking of Rowan.

"You do realise you have just worked a bloody miracle, don't you?" I whispered to him as we lay close together in bed that night, our lovemaking quiet, deliciously secretive beneath the duvet, Gawain hushing my moans with kisses that held laughter within them.

"That's my remit," he answered in reply, his hands working a miracle of their own on my body, "to work miracles, to follow that example."

"I work spells," I had replied with a husky giggle as I opened my legs to welcome him.

"Spells of this nature, I am happy to fall under," he closed my mouth with a never-ending kiss and pulled the duvet further over our heads.

My friend Annie and her husband Shane were of course delighted. We compared sizes of bumps and due dates. Annie was overflowing with excitement that our children would be born just a couple of months apart. "It's just shame though that you now live so far away." She said over the brim of her mug of tea, with a slightly down cast look at Gawain.

The shadows on her face soon drifted away when he smiled in her direction. "The vicarage has plenty of spare rooms. You will always be welcome to come and stay."

I hid my own smile, watching her fall under his spell as most women were wont to do. It was still all ridiculously new, this being a couple. I felt as though I was a child playing at make believe. All very enjoyable, but very unreal.

"I knew Fae would find romance in Maypoleton," she said with a knowing smile at me and a nod to her husband. "I said so didn't I."

"You did make a few comments of the sort," he grinned at me, and I could imagine the conversations Annie would have had, spinning her fairy tale vision of what she wanted for me. He then excused himself as he had to go to work. "It's so good to see you looking so well," he said giving me a lovely hug. "And it's not just the impending motherhood Fae. You're different."

"She's in love," said the voice of cupid in Annie form.

We made our farewells soon after, declining the offer to stay for something to eat. There was the long drive ahead of us and I knew that Gawain had had to shift around his weekly schedule to accommodate this unplanned trip. Nevertheless, he wanted to take a walk on the promenade first.

"Are you sure we have time?"

We left the car parked at Annie's and began the short walk to the sea front. It was the middle of July, but the schools had not broken up for the holidays yet, so it was not too crowded.

"We won't be long." He held my hand as we walked and once more, I had to pinch myself to believe this was my reality. I received a warm smile from an older lady who passed us, hand in hand with a gentleman I presumed to be her husband. A wave of emotion washed over me. Would that be us in the future? Would we be coming here to visit, reminiscing on where we met? Maybe we would, because that was Gawain seemed to have in mind right now.

It looked so very different on a sunny July afternoon. A welcoming place to sit and admire the view, shaded from the hot sun, not a place of dark concealment where a foolish woman with a death wish had nearly been raped and maybe even murdered. The place where we had met.

"You remembered the spot?"

He laughed. "As if I could forget?" Then he went on, serious now. "That was a bad night for me Fae." He sat down on the bench, eyes looking far out to sea. I was still holding his hand, and I squeezed it tightly.

"It's okay. You don't have to tell me if you don't want to."

"No secrets, Fae. Never between us. Secrets destroy. Secrets kill."

And he had seen too much of death, I realised that. I had not, however, realised quite the depths of despair to which he had sunk.

"That night in January, I had come back here to see the army chaplain who saved me after I stepped in the path of that mine, walked that route, knowing it was the one most likely to get me blown up. Derek was the only one who really saw me underneath the armour, the only one who knew how fucking close I was to never coming back. He had retired from working officially but he put more bloody hours in helping at the shelter where I used to act as chaplain, than the paid staff."

"He sounds a wonderful man. I can't wait to meet him. He will be coming to the wedding, won't he?"

"No. He had a massive heart attack the day before I had chance to visit him."

"Oh Gawain."

Another loss. Maybe a natural one, and not tragic if he had been elderly, but still, another river of grief to navigate. From Gawain's next words, it appeared that he had been close to drowning, in more ways than one.

"I was devastated. I needed him so much that night. Not just because of Lance and the other man who died, but because my faith was dying. I had lost it Fae. I couldn't see where the hell I was going anymore. Nothing seemed to matter. What difference was I making? It all seemed so bloody pointless. I just needed to see Derek, I knew that if I saw him, if I could sit with him, share a beer with him, he would somehow dig me out of the pit that was sucking me down into hell. I was so close that night Fae. So, fucking close."

I looked out at the calm sea, remembering how wild it had been in contrast that dark January night, how high the waves, how deep the swell. I shivered in the warm sunlight, imagining how deathly cold it would have been. One minute would have been all that was needed.

"There are people within the church who consider suicide the most grievous of sins. Unforgiveable. It would not have mattered Fae. I was ready that night. That's why when I heard about your mother, Rowan, I mean, that there had been a question over her death, I could never have condemned her, or any other for taking the step that I had come so close to. Twice in fact. The mine didn't kill me, but when I heard that Derek had died, that was it. I had lost my faith, and I had lost the man who I believed could bring me back to my path. Bring me back to the light. Because it all felt so fucking dark Fae, darker than I had ever known it. I can't describe it other than that. But I think you know what I mean?"

Remembering the desolation of that night I answered him softly. "I do."

"So, I walked down here, at two o'clock in the morning, or whatever bloody time it was, telling myself it would be easy and quick and then I would be free of the pain. Only it didn't quite work out like that." He laughed then, and it was a wonderful sound as though something had just lit up his soul.

It had.

"Oh, my Lord of course! I see it now."

"What?"

"Derek. The canny old bastard saved me after all."

"What do you mean?"

"I was walking the other way. Not in this direction. Engrossed with my thoughts. Oblivious to all else other than I could no longer continue. Then I heard him. Derek. Clear as a bell in my head."

I understood this completely. "What did he say?"

Gawain turned then and looked at me, an odd smile on his face. "Turn around." He kept saying it. "Turn around. I thought he meant turn around from the notion of killing myself. But I know now, it wasn't that. It was you, Fae. He meant turn around to walk to you. To find you."

We both felt it then.

The charge of energy between us.

The connection of souls, divided for so long.

"Wow," I said, incapable of uttering anything else.

"Wow," he agreed, his grey-blue eyes searching mine. "I was intent on killing myself that night, Fae, and then the next thing I knew I was battering five men, hell bent on raping you." Another ironic laugh. "I was so fucking angry with you. With them! And then you begged me to stay with you. Christ Fae have you any idea what you did to me that night?"

"No more than you did to me," I said softly, prompting another long soulful look which turned into a deep, heartachingly beautiful kiss.

"And you left me money like a bloody prostitute!" I slapped him playfully on the arm when we finally pulled away.

"I am sorry about that. It was my way of detaching from how much you had affected me."

"I spent the money on baby things for Annie."

"And now we have our baby, because of that night. Our baby and a whole new future ahead of us. Thank you, Derek," he said loudly to the air around us.

"Yes. Thank you, Derek." I added with a silent blessing of my own.

We made our way then back to Annie's to say another quick goodbye before setting off home to Maypoleton. I must have nodded off because one moment we were on the motorway and the next thing I knew we were taking the winding country roads deep into the beautiful Lancashire countryside.

"I got off roaded by a sheep on my first trip up here," I said with a laugh, remembering the confrontation that had ended up with me hitting a pothole and bursting my tyre. "Matt came along to help."

A quick look from him. "You and him?"

I shook my head. "It was nothing. Two people…..two people in love with someone else."

"In love with someone else?"

"I was already in love with you. I could think of no one else. So bloody annoying let me tell you."

"And Matt? Who is Matt in love with? I'm his closest mate and he's never said anything to me."

"Yes, well that's because you are both blokes, and you don't talk like we women do. And besides, he couldn't tell you."

"Why not?"

"Because he's in love with Laura."

"Laura?"

"Exactly. And she's married to muppet Mark."

"Muppet Mark? Yes, that does rather sum him up. Even so, he is her husband."

"He cheats on her."

"How do you know?"

"It's obvious, he's that kind of man. Besides, Will thinks he is."

I told him that Laura's oldest son had confided in me on one of the Wednesday nights I had looked after him, his brother and his two sisters. I didn't tell him of the frequent occasions that Mark had made more than obvious hints to me that he would be happy to get to know me better.

"Does she know?"

"About Matt or Mark?"

"Mark."

"I think she maybe suspects, but she doesn't want to know. Eve knows though. We both agree that Matt would be so much better for her."

"It's not for either of you to think or comment on that Fae."

Was this Gawain the man speaking or Gawain the vicar? I sent him a look which told him that however much I had fallen deeply in love with him, I could still actually think for myself. Some of the time at least!

"I mean it Fae," he said as he took the last turn in the road that led onto the main street of Maypoleton. "Eve is a lovely woman, but she is also one of Mabel's bunch and renowned for being something of a mischief maker. I know you are who you are, and I am not going to try and change you. But and this is a big but Fae, as my wife I cannot have you meddling in parishioner's affairs. Laura is a very good woman and a regular member of my flock. Her marriage and what goes on in it is her affair. Unless of course she is in any harm and then, well, I wouldn't be able to stand by and see anyone hurt of course not."

"There are other ways of being hurt," I said. "Just thinking she is being cheated on could be having a terrible effect on her."

I saw his mouth tighten and wondered if I had pushed the wrong button. After all, hadn't he been the one who his sister-in-law had cheated with, and look what that had led to. I cursed myself for my clumsy comment.

"Leave it Fae. If I think Laura needs someone to talk to, or some guidance, then I will play my part. Until then, no interfering."

I didn't like the feeling that I was being told what to do, or how to behave. Looking at the diamond on my finger, I wondered for a moment if I would find myself having to toe the line to fit with the role of being the vicar's wife. Or perhaps was that just to fit in with Gawain? Either way it sat uneasy with me.

"Do you want me to drop you off at your aunt's or are you coming home with me?"

Home with him.

To the vicarage.

A dream come true.

Mentally I gave myself a kick up the backside. Really what was I doing having any doubts? I was getting exactly what I had longed for, ever since that night in January. My daughter gave me a kick of her own and I smiled in delight. I was getting so much more than I ever dreamt possible. What did it matter if Gawain had strong views on certain things. We were going to be a family. He loved me. He loved our daughter. Nothing else mattered.

"Home with you of course."

He parked the car at the back of the vicarage, it being an older house there was no garage but there was a space adjacent to the graveyard that was his spot. A couple of villagers, regular church goers were walking in our direction, one of them holding a bunch of flowers in her hands.

"Evening Vicar." A slight pause and then, "Fae."

"Good evening, Charlotte, Agatha. Another beautiful one isn't it. Let's hope this weather holds until we have the summer fayre."

The one with the flowers, Charlotte nodded her head "Oh yes, I do hope so. I am helping Laura organise the children's dancing. It was such a shame last year they were all ready to perform and then the heavens opened. And not in a good way, Vicar!" She sent him one of those flirtatious looks I was so used to seeing from his elderly female parishioners.

"Well, I shall do my best to put in a good word for sunshine," he answered with a laugh.

"And shall you be helping out at all Fae?" It was Agatha who posed this question.

Oh fuck! Silently I could not prevent the words from pinging round my head. Fae Winters, vicar's wife, helping out at the village summer fayre? It was testing moment. Three pairs of eyes were upon me, two with curiosity, one with an expression that held love but also something of a warning.

I chose to ignore the warning. "Palm reading maybe?"

Definitely a flash of something there in his eyes.

I chose to look instead at the two ladies. They looked at each other first, then at Gawain, and then at me.

"We've never had palm readings before, have we, Charlotte?"

"Nor are we going to this year," said Gawain smoothly. "Perhaps Fae you could help Charlotte with the cake stall by baking for her?"

"Not unless you want the village to suffer chronic indigestion. I am totally crap at baking. I bring a whole new meaning to rock scones."

Yes, I was pushing him, but it seemed imperative that from the start I did not lose myself in another false identity. I had lived a lie for so long, pretending to be someone else to atone for Fliss. Never mind what I had thought a few minutes ago, I couldn't do it anymore.

Not even for him.

I smiled sweetly at Charlotte and Agatha and shrugged my shoulders at Gawain. "And please don't ask me to help Laura with the school dance because I have two left feet. I am pretty good at whacking things with a hammer though so maybe if you need any marquees putting up, I could bash away at the pegs?"

"I don't think that will be necessary," my fiancé said with a look that told me we were going to have words.

I answered his look then with one of my own and saw the light in his eyes change.

"Well, I for one would quite like to have my palm read." Agatha then surprised me. "I went to a fayre last year where my sister lives in Yorkshire. They had a palm reader there, longest queue ever. I wanted to have a turn but my sister had to get back to cook the tea, so we didn't have time. I reckon that stall made a lot of money. Something to think about Vicar. Isn't the fayre trying to raise money to repair the roof on the school hall?"

"I am quite sure our efforts will raise sufficient funds without any palm readings," Gawain replied smoothly.

"Oh well never mind. Maybe this year my sister will be better organised, and I will manage to have one done when I visit again."

"I am sure Mabel could help you there if you asked her?"

Another conspiratorial look between the women and a quick one towards Gawain who by now was giving me one of those, 'seriously Fae we need to talk', looks.

He managed to hold it off until later that night. We said good evening to Charlotte and Agatha and went inside the vicarage, Gawain insisting that he carried my overnight bag. Mrs Mannering, despite her eruption at the weekend had stoically announced that she was not ready to face retirement just yet and had left a steak and kidney pie in the oven.

Arthur joined us at the table, eager to hear how our mini trip down south had been. Talk turned naturally to the wedding, and he asked us if we had thought about a date.

"No, to be honest we haven't." I looked at Gawain.

Truthfully, I had not explored that avenue in my mind. It was enough to know that he loved me and wanted to marry me. The date in some respects was immaterial.

"I would like our daughter to be born with us married," Gawain said quietly but for once there was none of the steely sense of an order being issued. "But I will not go against your wishes on this one Fae."

I was torn and really didn't know. "Can I think about it?"

"Of course you can. But without wishing to add any pressure you don't have too much time."

I placed my hands over my belly. "I know. I think I just need some female guidance with this if you don't mind?"

He looked at me as to if to question would this be from the other side of the grave or more of an earthly nature.

"I'd like to ask Aunty Ruth what she thinks," I reassured him, although of course I would be asking Rowan. "And maybe Eve and Laura too."

He nodded. "Good idea."

In the bedroom later, he made it very clear what he considered the opposite of a good idea and that was the thought of his future wife offering palm readings.

"There are lines Fae that cannot be crossed. Roles that need to be adhered to."

I nodded at him as though listening to every word in complete agreement. At the same time, I was undressing, my eyes fixed on his face. I let my clothes fall to the floor. I tilted my head and let my long hair fall softly over my full breasts and belly. I let myself walk towards him, a sway in my hips, a promise in my eyes.

"Fae, I am being serious."

My hands went to the buttons on his shirt. My lips pressed kisses down his chest.

"Fae, I really am being serious."

The zip of his trousers now.

"So am I." Kisses pressed even lower. "We both have roles to perform."

"We do, Fae, oh fuck!" His hands were now in my hair, guiding, holding.

I teased him with my tongue, gently nibbling along the length of him, my fingers stroking and teasing him all the while. A light flickering touch at the now quivering tip and a promise of so much more to come.

"And this is mine," I whispered to him before taking that full, throbbing shaft deep into my mouth.

"Oh fucking hell, Fae." He gave himself up to my loving attention with a laugh that told me this conversation would not be held again. "I swear you are going to be the death of me."

We fell asleep much later, wrapped in each other's arms. But somehow my sleep was fitful and disturbed. His words kept ringing in my head. "You'll be the death of me."

I heard something else.

Malicious laughter.

Eliza's laughter.

CHAPTER FORTY

"When is it to be then? Before or after?"

Eve and Laura pinned me down with speculative stares. My friends had been wildly excited to hear the news and were full of questions. Eve had suggested we meet in the pub, but Laura had thought it better to spend a rare free Saturday afternoon enjoying the peace and quiet of her garden and the continuing sunshine.

Eve was already there when I arrived, comfortably seated on one of the expensive loungers that looked good enough to be used for inside furniture. She was wearing the skimpiest of shorts and vest top, clearly determined to maximise her tan. Huge sunglasses were lowered so she could look at me with those beautiful swirly coloured eyes of hers.

"I am guessing Gawain wants it to be before," said Laura, standing on the patio with a tray of iced cold drinks, Elderberry cordial for me and a spritzer for them.

"Bloody hell I hope not," interjected Eve as she took the proffered glass and a large swallow. "God that's good. You do make the best spritzer's Laura. Surely you want to show off that stunning figure of yours in a fitted dress, not looking like you have a rugby ball hiding underneath."

I laughed at her description. That was precisely how I felt and looked. "Thanks, Laura," I said, sitting on one of the loungers and making myself comfortable with my sandals off, feet up and light cotton dress hitched up high. "I don't know. I've never felt so indecisive about anything to be honest. Normally I just plunge right on in, head first."

Eve nodded. "You're like me in that respect."

"Hm." I thought of what else we had in common. Like discovering long buried skeletons. Eliza had been making her presence felt strongly these last few days and not in a good way.

She was careful not to appear when anyone else was around, but the subject of our conversations was always the same.

"*Why should you be happy? Why should you marry your love when I could not? Why should your baby be born when mine was not?*"

Disturbing thoughts, questions, energy. It was having a draining effect on me and at a time when I should be floating around on a cloud of euphoria, I was beginning to feel on edge and rattled. Especially every time the wedding was mentioned.

"So where are the kids? It's unusually quiet?"

"She's trying to change the subject," said Eve astutely as Laura began to explain that Mark had taken the two sets of twins over to visit his sister in Kendal.

"We don't get on," she said with a shake of her head. "Bethany has always thought that Mark married beneath him. A mere teacher, he could have had at the very least a lawyer or doctor."

"Er head teacher," I replied. "And what the fuck does it matter anyway?"

"Off subject girlies," Eve was not to be deterred. "Before or after? And by the way, you still owe us all the gory details of how this all happened in the first place. You told us it was just a one-night stand, and he paid you off like a prostitute!"

"Shhh"

Laura's garden was large and private with a high fence all the way round, but it was still in the middle of a housing estate surrounded by others and on a day like today most people would want to be outside. Another look without the sunglasses told me Eve would not give up until she had the full story.

Which of course had them entranced, and why wouldn't it? It sounded like something out of a novel or a rom com as Laura commented with a sigh, before reverting back to the original question.

"We can toss a coin if you like?" Eve suggested lightly when I struggled to answer.

"You aren't having doubts, are you?" Laura, although lacking Eve's psychic abilities was perhaps more in tune with my hesitancy, but not for any reason she might think of. "I remember when Mark asked me to marry him, I'd just gone through a horrible relationship before him, and I didn't dare believe my good luck that I had finally found a man who wasn't going to cheat on me!"

It was fortunate that Eve and I were wearing our sunglasses at that point, hiding our expressions to a degree. Eve then turned to me. "Are you having doubts?"

"No. No of course not." I said, mentally shoving away the insistent thought that somehow if I went ahead with the wedding, I would be jinxing everything.

The sunglasses came off. "You are, it's obvious. Why?" The direct question was what I had come to expect from Eve.

I shrugged. "I don't know. It's stupid, but I just have this feeling that if I go ahead and plan the wedding, it will somehow jinx things. Spoil the relationship."

"I suppose that's sort of natural," said Laura sympathetically. "And really, you haven't had chance to actually have a relationship as such until now. It's all been very cloak and dagger, hasn't it."

I jumped on this as a reasonable excuse. "Exactly! It's like there's been no, no, what's the word.....?"

"Courtship?" Laura supplied with a nod of her head and an understanding smile. "You haven't been romanced, Fae. That's the sticking point isn't it."

That had never occurred to me, but it seemed to hit the spot with Laura, so I agreed enthusiastically. It was better than the truth; that I was scared of provoking Eliza.

"Yes, that's it. Now that you mention it, I've not been romanced. You know we haven't even been on a proper date!"

"Well, that makes all the difference," said Eve dryly as though she didn't believe a word I was saying.

"You need to let him know that you would like some of the hearts and flowers, the wining and dining, that sort of thing, as well as planning for the wedding," Laura said leaning forward to pat my hand. "I am sure then it will all flow perfectly."

"Hm. Not really sure that Gawain is the hearts and flowers kind of man," I said with a wry laugh.

"What man is?" Eve rolled her eyes. "I mean I love the very bones of Craig; I really do. But romance?"

"True," agreed Laura with a conspiratorial smile. "I don't think there is a man alive who is naturally romantic."

We raised our glasses to each other and took a sip.

Eve then surprised me with what she said next, "Not alive, no." So much sadness in her voice I turned to stare. This was not the Eve I had got to know.

"Oh lovey, you still miss him, don't you?" Laura leant forward to lightly touch her hand.

I was stunned to see tears rolling silently down Eve's cheeks. She wiped them away with a careless hand. "Oh, never mind me," she said with a bright smile. "It wasn't real anyway."

I couldn't stop myself from questioning her with a look.

"I lost my heart and soul to someone...someone... I never thought it was possible to love so much, so deeply, so blindly!"

"Thank goodness you have Craig now," said Laura with that reassuring motherly air she had, practical and down to earth.

I was itching to ask Eve more, but Laura went back to the subject in hand. We hadn't really got anywhere before being interrupted by the sound of a car pulling up at the house and a cacophony of voices spilling out into the quiet Saturday afternoon. Laura's face froze and took on an expression I didn't like to see on any woman's face.

"I think you had better go," she said, hastily standing up to clear away our glasses.

"Jesus Christ, Laura, why the fuck didn't you tell me there's been a sick bug going round the school?"

The garden gate was virtually kicked open. Laura's husband burst through, a woebegone looking daughter holding onto each hand. The ten-year-old twins were struggling hard not to cry. Behind them, fourteen-year-old Will and Dan shuffled along with that awkward too large for their bodies gait that strapping teenage lads could have.

Mark was looking less than his usual best. The super white designer shirt he had chosen to set off his dark blue jeans was not exactly pristine. Rather it was vomit stained to the degree that it was clearly ruined. Eve and I shared a quick glance, stifling the urge to laugh as his temper was not something to provoke further.

"Oh God I am sorry. I thought they would be alright. They were both fine this morning." Laura knocked over one of the glasses on the tray in her hurry to get up.

"Clearly not! We had only just got to Bethany's when this one puked all over her new rug. It's totally ruined! As is this shirt."

"I'm sorry, I really am sorry."

"Then this one, couldn't hold it in for me to stop on the way back, and threw up all over the back seat. My car stinks Laura, fucking stinks!" He released the hold he had on his daughters, and they ran to Laura.

"Here, I'll take that," Eve jumped up and relieved Laura of the tray before she dropped it.

"Sorry isn't going to replace Bethany's new rug is it, or this shirt, or clean my fucking car!"

"For fuck's sake Dad, it's only puke!" Will, the oldest twin and the one who had confided in me that he thought his dad was playing away, glared at his father.

"Mind your fucking, language!" Mark swirled round to his son with the physical energy of someone about to hit another person. His anger was barely contained, held back perhaps by the presence of Eve and me, or maybe the sudden realisation that his son, captain of the rugby team, was as tall as him, stocky with it, and returning his look with a quiet fury of his own.

"Would you like to come over to mine for a little while lads? Craig's got a new computer game you might like?" Eve interjected smoothly as though a volcano was not about to erupt in the garden.

"Dad, can we?" Dan, the quieter twin, always the peace maker tried to stand ever so slightly between his twin and his father who were still glaring at each other.

"Mummy, I don't feel well," Tilly tugged at Laura's hand and Tammy, on the other side of her mother began to cry. "My tummy hurts," she said in the same miserable tone of voice as her twin.

"Oh Christ, get them cleaned up and tucked up in bed for fuck's sake, don't just stand there like a useless bloody garden ornament!"

Laura, looking white faced and teary eyed herself, fled indoors with her daughters.

"I'll wash these," Eve said with a glare at Mark as she followed Laura, the glasses rattling on the tray in her haste.

I had seen enough.

Probably not what the future vicar's wife should say, but hey, I wasn't married yet.

"I am really sorry boys," I said to Will and Dan, having walked over to where they were hovering uncertainly by the garden gate. Mark was unbuttoning his expensive white shirt, making a fuss over the cost of it before making an even bigger performance of tossing it in the wheely bin.

"What are you apologising to my sons for?" Mark stared hard at me. I could see he was torn between his anger at Laura and his attraction to me, even though I was pregnant. "Italian silk, finest thread and altered to fit especially. Fucking ruined."

"Mum shops at Primark," Will virtually spat the words out of his mouth as though they were bullets, with a look towards me, sensing he had back up.

He did.

"The only bloody useless ornament I can see around here," I said with one of my 'try it if you fucking dare', looks blazing from my eyes, "Is you. You are so fucking useless as a husband, you have no fucking appreciation of how fucking wonderful, talented, intelligent, and capable your lovely wife is. You really are an utter, fucking cockwombler! Sorry boys. It needed saying."

There was a moment of glorious, stunned silence.

Mark stared at me as though he could not quite believe what he had just heard. To the left of me Dan shuffled his feet and coughed. Will moved to stand next to me. I could feel from the energy in his body that he had somehow changed in that moment and taken on a new level of maturity.

"She's right. Mum is fucking wonderful, and you are a fucking cockwomble."

"Get inside now," Mark hissed at his son between gritted teeth. "I will deal with you later."

"No, you won't," I interjected, driven by a need to protect Will. "You will deal with yourself, grow a pair of balls and start acting like a real man. And if I find out that you've taken out your childish temper on either Laura, or your children again, you'll have me to contend with."

Another stunned silence. The air was weighty with anger, hostility and adrenaline. I felt it coursing through me, unnerved slightly as I recognised the spiky edge to it. Raw emotion, powerful intentions have the capacity to create a psychic pull. I tensed, and braced myself against it, but it was already too late. I willed Mark to back down now, go quietly inside, and let the force we had stirred up, dissipate.

He didn't.

He did the opposite.

He let rip.

"Just who the fucking hell do you think you are? Lounging around my garden, swanning up to me and speaking to me like that, in front of my sons, in my own fucking garden! How fucking dare, you? You fucking bitch!"

The last word was all that was needed. Or rather, the hatred that was infused into it.

"I'm not a fucking bitch. But I am a fucking witch!"

I heard Eliza's triumphant laughter coursing round the garden so loudly that I wondered they could not hear it too.

"As am I." Eve's cheerful voice was the rainbow that was needed to break through the storm clouds. Her arm linked through mine sent a shudder of relief through my body. An antidote to Eliza's sudden and unwanted energy.

"So, my lovely witchy friend, are you going to come back with me and the boys to have a go at this computer game?" She carried on talking to Mark as though nothing had happened. "I am sure you will be glad of some peace and quiet. And besides, don't you need to go and get your car valeted?"

It was almost possible, almost, but not quite, to feel sorry for him. Out manoeuvred in his own back garden. He stomped off inside, leaving Will and Dan looking at both of us with mixed expressions. Dan eagerly asked Eve about the computer game and she began chatting brightly to him as we made our way out of the garden.

Will on the other hand came over to me. In the quietest of voices, he said. "If you are a witch, can you do spells?"

"Maybe I shouldn't have said that."

Once my hot temper had had its chance to flare, I was beset with angst that I had overstepped the mark. Hugely. When this got back to Gawain which it would, he would not be at all happy. Laura's next-door neighbour was in their driveway, washing a car that looked immaculately clean. I could tell by the look I was given that he had heard everything.

"It is true though isn't it. I mean you found that skeleton. That was really cool. Eve found a skeleton too!" His voice rose slightly at this point.

"I did," she called back to us over her shoulder as we started to walk down the road and out of the estate where Laura lived. "And exciting as discovering skeletons might seem to you lads, trust me, it's not something you wish to happen to you. Is it, Fae?"

The village green came in sight on the other side of the river. As we began to walk over the stone bridge, my eyes were drawn to the stocks and the ancient tree that stood proudly in the centre. The stocks that Eliza had been locked into and pelted with missiles. The tree where she was hung after her baby had been brutally kicked to death inside her. My eyes then flew across to the vicarage. She was there in the bedroom window, watching us.

I shivered. "No. It's not."

"Are you coming back with us or going to the vicarage?" Eve asked me once we had crossed over the bridge and were walking across the green, past those wretched stocks.

I knew Gawain was busy and Arthur would most likely be having his afternoon nap. With Eliza's shadowy form still visible in the distance and the ripples of energy I felt coming towards me, I was not sure I wanted to be there right now. Equally I wasn't remotely interested in computer games.

"We can chat and have cake?" She linked her arm with me once more. In an undertone she added quietly. "We need to have a think what to do about our lovely friend."

She was right. We had left Laura with a real wasp's nest, one that I had perhaps unwisely kicked over. I was also wondering if I could possibly ask her about Eliza, without giving too much away.

"That sounds good," I nodded and once we were in the cosy comfort of her cottage, next door to Aunty Ruth's I knew I had made the right choice. My energy was hitting a slump as it seemed to do so frequently these days.

"Right then, tea, coffee, coke, lads what do you want? Cake all round I take it and then let's get you two sorted out upstairs in Craig's office and then Fae and I can talk weddings and boring girly stuff like that."

"Witchy stuff?" Dan surprised me by asking. He had been quiet most of the way here and was looking at the two of us with a thoughtful expression on his face.

Eve gave a light laugh. "Maybe. Nothing you need to worry about."

"Could you do a spell then?" Will asked more directly, an eager note in his voice.

"What sort of spell?" Eve asked softly, pausing in the act of filling the kettle with water. "Fae, sit down please you've gone very pale."

I pulled out a kitchen chair and sank into it gratefully.

"One to stop Dad being such a wanker." There was deep anger in Will's voice, and I kicked myself mentally. I had not helped the situation at all by shooting my mouth off at his dad.

"Sadly no," replied Eve.

"You mean there isn't a spell strong enough?" Will suggested with a snort. "Wouldn't surprise me. It would take some pretty powerful fucking magic to have any effect on him."

Eve opened a cake tin and began serving out slices. She was quiet as she answered him, and I thought, a little sad. "There is magic, and there is magic. And some of it, Will is very powerful indeed."

"So, you could do it then?"

"It's best we don't." She smiled and handed him a plate. "Here you go. Take that upstairs to Craig's office. I'll be up in a second to sort out his computer."

"Why not?" Will persisted.

"There are rules."

"Witches have rules?" It was Dan's turn to comment, his mouth half full of chocolate cake.

"Yes, rules," said Eve with the hint of motherly attitude I rarely associated with her, but I remembered she had grown up children of her own.

Will flashed a cheeky grin. "Yes, but rules are there to be broken."

"Not this one," she said firmly. "Now go on. Upstairs."

"Okay." Will shrugged and with his brother made his way to the door. Then he paused and turned round. "I bet you would break it though, Fae, wouldn't you?"

It was not so much a challenge in his eyes, more a direct plea. I couldn't answer.

Eve spoke for me. "No, she won't. Working a spell to manipulate another soul is way out of bounds. Whatever the reason, Will. Fae would never do that, would you?"

Remembering the cruel intent with which I had aided Eliza in her spell to make Gawain jealous by seducing Matt against his will, I lied once more. "No. I would never do that."

Twice in my life I had done. I made a promise to myself then, there would not be a third time. I blocked my ears to the sound of Eliza's mocking laughter which seemed to follow me so closely these days.

CHAPTER FORTY-ONE

"Is there something you're not telling me?" Gawain held me close, his legs entwined with mine, one hand lying gently over the growing swell of my tummy.

I turned my face into his chest, pressing soft kisses against the hardness of his muscles. This post lovemaking closeness was a new gift that I treasured. More so on the lazy Saturday mornings, when there was not quite the same rush to get up, and I could savour this delicious knowledge that I was exactly where I wanted to be.

In the warmth of Gawain's bed.
In the warmth of Gawain's arms.
In the warmth of Gawain's love.

I had been out in the cold for so long, since Fliss died that I was loathe to let any thoughts creep in and spoil these cherished moments. Here I was completely safe, whole, who I was meant to be. It felt utterly wonderful beyond words. So, I ignored his question and continued my sleepy, satiated enjoyment of his body next to mine.

"Fae, talk to me."

"Hhm?" My hands were about to trail lower, greedy for more.

"You were restless all last night, I heard you talking in your sleep, but I couldn't make out what you were saying exactly. But you were arguing with someone. Yourself maybe."

The beautiful moment was slipping away and the serpent within the garden of Eden crept back in.

Eliza.

That was how I had begun to see her.

Gawain moved so he could cradle my face in his hands, something I adored him to do, and kissed me. "I am beginning to know you, Fae, and I know you are worrying about something."

He got out of bed and walked over to the window, drawing back the curtain to let in the morning sunlight along with the sound of the birds. It was still early, but it looked as though it was going to be a beautiful day.

"Perfect weather for the fayre," I said with a yawn and a stretch. I felt like going back to sleep. Gawain was right. I had been disturbed with dreams. Well perhaps not dreams as such, that would be too normal a word. Visitations was maybe more accurate. Eliza was stalking me, both during the day and whilst I slept. In no way was she happy that Gawain and I were happy.

"Talk to me, Fae." Gawain walked back to sit on the edge of the bed.

I felt desire rising within me as I looked at his body, muscled, scarred, strong, masculine. Mine. A feminine feeling of power flowed through me, and I smiled lazily at him, inviting him back to bed with a languorous look in my eyes.

"No, you don't my beautiful witch." A quiet loved filled laugh that flooded my heart with joy. "For one reason I really do have to get up. It's going to be a very busy day. But I do want to know, Fae, what is bothering you?"

"Nothing."

He frowned then and rightly so because he knew I was lying. "Is it the wedding? Are you having doubts? You haven't said yes to a date."

I sat up reluctantly, childishly chewing on the skin around my thumbnail, a habit of mine when I was disturbed. He took hold of my hand.

"Fae if you don't want to marry me, just say. I would rather know."

"I do! Oh, believe me I do."

"Are you sure. It sounded like you were saying, 'I can't do it' in your sleep. What can't you do, Fae?"

My turn to frown then. The recollection of last night's disturbance was hazy, but not a conversation I had had with Eliza earlier on during the day. She had made it quite clear that she did not want me to marry Gawain. Her hostility and ripening thirst for vengeance was beginning to frighten me. She had intimated that if I went ahead with the wedding then something terrible would happen to Gawain. She had also intimated that if I did not do as she wished in other ways, the same thing may happen to me. I was beginning to feel like a puppet in the hands of a cruel master.

"*A witch shalt not waste her gift!*" She had argued scornfully with me last week when I had returned from Eve's after spending the afternoon with Laura's boys. "*You have been asked to craft a spell, and a spell you must craft!*"

In other words, to somehow expose Laura's husband for what he was, a lying, bullying, cheat. Tempting though it was, it was not my place to do so, and certainly not with any witchcraft involved. From my moment of refusal, she had plagued me day and night, whispering in my ears, appearing suddenly before me when no one else was around, invading my life, invading my sleep.

"Talk to me Fae. If we are to be married, if we are to be together, then we must be able to talk."

He was right. Here we were, in the sanctuary of the bedroom, still naked the pair of us, nothing between us, other than that secret that I was keeping, that the ghost of the skeleton we had dug up and reburied weeks ago, was frighteningly alive in many ways.

"It's nothing to do with getting married."

"But there is something worrying you?"

"It's……." I got no further. "It's……."

"Fae, trust me, there is nothing you can tell me now, that will shock me."

It wasn't that I feared shocking him.

I couldn't speak.

Literally.

I tried again.

"It's……." Once more that sensation of my throat tightening, not being able to breathe.

Behind Gawain I saw her. A horrific version of her dying self, rope around her neck, the life painfully squeezed out of her. I knew then that she would never allow me to tell him.

"Fae, are you alright? Do you need some water? Here, swallow, gently now." The concern in his voice was all apparent and the fear in his eyes must have been reflected in mine. I thought I was choking. I had felt as though the air was being squeezed from my lungs, that invisible rope around my neck.

"I'm fine," I reassured him, after taking a mouthful of water, although my voice was raspy, fragile.

He gave me a searching look that once would have held cold distance in his eyes. Now I felt myself melting beneath the warmth that he no longer tried to hide. Eliza be dammed; I would not let her come between us.

"Just hormones," I said softly to him, placing the glass of water on the bedside table. "And maybe the fact that I can't quite believe my luck. Do you know how much I love you? Really love you?"

I reached towards him and pulled him closer to kiss him slowly, lingeringly full on the mouth, gently teasing his lips apart so I could entwine my tongue with his. He echoed my movements and groaned.

"Fae, I am supposed to be getting up."

"Oh, but you are," I laughed as I felt him stir against me. "I need you. Hold me. Love me."

I felt an urgency then to have him within me, to lose myself in that sudden blinding rush of passion, where nothing existed other than the completeness of my body and soul joining with his. I needed to block out Eliza and her growing hostility, her venom and rage. My hands roamed down his body, his back, thighs, bottom, fingers digging in, clawing gently, pulling persuasively.

"Oh Fae, what do you do to me?"

His mouth was at my throat, the base of my neck, my breasts, in a feverish flurry of caresses. He was as urgent as I was now. Back fully on the bed, my hair flowing once more over the crumpled pillows, my legs eagerly opening for him, in seconds we were back in that flow.

Would I ever tire of this thrill? The shocking pleasure I felt when he pushed deep inside for the first time, his flesh making that most intimate of connections with mine.

I doubted it.

I could have a lifetime of this and never tire.

I could have an eternity of this and still crave more.

"Fae, I love you so much, so fucking much it terrifies me." His words were interspersed with deep, hard kisses that matched his thrusts.

My heart melted, my soul soared, my body fed the fire.

I raised my hips, my legs snaking lithely around his waist, clamping his back to drive him in further. Always careful of my belly, he kept the bulk of his weight from pressing completely against me, but there was no holding back from that need to drive in deeper and harder. Quick, urgent, raw, primal desire and heart whole love. A furnace of heated feelings, body, mind and soul. I could feel myself coming and let my throat open to lose the earthy sounds of pleasure that matched the spasms rippling through my body.

"I fucking love fucking you, my lovely, fucking witch."

My smile must have been one of sleek satisfaction, as he added. "And you know it, don't you. You fucking knew it that very first night."

His words more gasps now, as shifting himself into a kneeling position, he lifted my hips even closer to his.

"I knew it," I answered on a cry as yet another rolling orgasm began to rise within me. "Oh, don't stop, don't ever stop."

A bold and sexy grin then, so unvicar like it was a turn on in itself. "If God himself walked in right now I couldn't stop." His actions proved his words. His body was not his own now, it belonged to the master of desire, and I was the mistress who was driving it. Fully deep, nearly out, fully deep. An uncontrollable pace that had us both breathless and panting, sweat once more slick between us. It was only a good few minutes later, after the last few torn moans, and for my part wildly shrieked screams of pleasure, did we realise that the window was wide open.

"Fae, what the hell are you doing to me?" He said with a playful slap on my thigh as he got off the now very rumpled bed and attempted to get up for the second time. "If the Misses Tweed heard that, they'll never come to church again!"

"Sorry," I lied with a yawn, deliciously sleepy and slumbersome even though the sunlight was pouring fully into the room now.

"No, you're not," he said over his shoulder as he disappeared into the ensuite shower room. "You're a wild witch Fae Winters, and I love you for it."

I smiled to myself and stretched out luxuriously on the bed.

"I'm your wild witch," I murmured happily, "and your twin flame, the other half of your soul, as you are mine."

"Whatever you call it," he said a short while later as he dressed in front of me, "I am committed to becoming your husband and father to our child. It would be good Fae, if we could announce a date for our wedding at the end of today?"

In our second round of passion, I had momentarily forgotten that it was the summer fayre. From what I had been told it was one of the biggest days in Maypoleton's calendar. The village green would be crammed with stalls, entertainments and competitions, complete with a barbeque and prize giving. I could see how it would be the perfect time for such an announcement to be made. The whole village would be there.

Reluctantly I sat up, yawned and tried to shake off the sleepiness. "I suppose so."

"Well then?" Gawain, after all, was still Gawain. I may have softened the edges with love and passion, but the hard ruthless killer turned vicar was still the man in front of me. "I want us to be married before she is born." He placed his hands on the swell of my belly, and I felt our daughter respond to his touch. It was as though she was saying yes to him.

I nodded. "Okay. You pick a date. I am happy whenever you want."

It was the right answer. His eyes brightened and that boyish smile that entranced me lit up his face. "Perfect. It's going to make everyone so happy, Fae. Me most of all."

I lay there safely, snugly, smugly wrapped in my cocoon of blissful love, blowing him a kiss as he left the room, and allowed myself a few moments to sensuously indulge in this feeling of loved up contentment. It was a whole new world for me, and I was determined to make the most of it.

I took my time showering then dressed, regarding my reflection in the mirror with amusement. What would Annie say if she could see me now? Where were the ripped jeans or shorts, I would normally be wearing on a day like today? What had happened to the close-fitting skimpy summer tops that I would normally flaunt my body in with no need for a bra, and what about the casual canvas pumps so often favoured in the past?

Where and what indeed?

The version of Fae Winters I now took a photo of to send to my friend, was prettily attired in a knee length summer frock, blue flowers in a dainty pattern, tan leather sandals on her feet. And was that really a white knitted cardigan I was considering taking with me, not my faded, worn, torn, old faithful denim jacket? The version of Fae Winters who smiled at me so happily, was the woman I had never thought I would, or could become.

A woman at peace with herself.

A woman who was going to marry the man she loved.
A woman who was going to become a mother.
"I had no peace. He stole that from me."
The rosy glow with which I was viewing myself and my life, dimmed immediately with Eliza's harsh words in my ears.
"I did not marry the man I loved. She stole him from me."
The sun disappeared out of the room and dark shadows filled every corner as her reflection appeared in the mirror behind me.
"I did not become a mother. They stole that from me."
I whirled around to face her in person, so close, so real.
"I am real. You have made me so."
"No. Eliza, you are a ghost. You are not real," I said with a shaking voice, horrified at the fear that had gripped my insides and was spreading like icy dread through my veins and the cells in my body.
"My power is real. You have made it so."
I couldn't step back as the mirror was behind me. I moved sideways instead, inching away from her toxic presence, inching instead of running because my feet would not move any faster. Every cell in my being was screaming at me. Get the fuck out of there now! But as in a nightmare my legs would not obey that command. It was as though there was a magnetic pull between us, an invisible cord, one which she was tightly holding.
"Whatever I may have made, it is done and over. It should not have been made in the first place!"
"What is done cannot be undone! What has been done must be finished! What has been taken must be avenged."
Each sentence a powerful proclamation.
Each sentence a deadly desire.
Each sentence a malevolent manifestation.
Eliza had no need of herbs and potions, she had no need to be alive in flesh and blood, she had no need to touch and feel in bodily form. She had no need for any of these things and she knew I understood as she laughed at the horror I must have shown on my face.
I tried though. I had to. Surely somewhere in this ghastly presentation of Eliza, there remained a fragment of her former self, that original soul, once filled with love and innocence. Surely the playful, sweet natured Eliza who had loved so freely and happily,

was in there somewhere. Surely that love that she once had given from her heart, might be enough to bring her back from this dark place and into the light.

With a blinding flash of clarity, I remembered far too late, Mabel's words to me. "Stay in the light and all will be right."

I hadn't and neither had Eliza, both in real life and in this one. Jealously, fear, hatred, the need for revenge had pushed her to dreadful deeds and ultimately her own horrific death. There was a gut twisting sickness inside me as I faced the knowledge that I had walked her path, followed her steps in more ways than one.

Jealousy had enticed me.

Fear had encouraged me.

Hatred had hauled me along.

Off the path of my atonement for Fliss's death, derailed spectacularly onto Eliza's path of revenge, so willingly yet unwittingly, heartbroken and hurt as I was. The scales had fallen from my eyes now and I could see it all so clearly. A perfect storm of emotions brewed up at the right time, in the right place, with the right people. I had no need of anyone else to tell me that this had been a disaster in the making from start from finish.

But finish it must, and it could not be Eliza's way.

"Oh, but it will." Her voice was softer now, calmer, but oddly far more worrying for that.

"Let it go Eliza. Please for the love of ……." I paused then because really what could I say at this point.

"For the love of whom?" A cold, evil light in her eyes, one blue, one brown, always unnerving in that oddity.

"For the love of yourself," I tried to appeal to her. For the love of your soul. Let it go Eliza, I am begging you, let it go."

"I begged him to love me. I begged them not to harm my child. I begged them not to kill me." She reached for my hands then. A manacle grip of ghostly ice. It bound me to her. Centuries ago, battered, bleeding out her child, breathing her last.

I was there with her.

Reliving it with her.

Until I became her.

CHAPTER FORTY-TWO

Maypoleton was at her finest. A Lancashire village in all her summer glory. Masses of flowers in bloom along the high street, half oak barrels and hanging baskets overflowing with colour. Bunting strung between the old-fashioned wrought iron streetlamps fluttering softly in the breeze. The village green, a wonderful jumble of stalls, and tents, more bunting, more colour.

A delight for the eyes and treat for the stomach. A tempting array of food on offer, a sizzling hog roast, savoury pies, sweet pastries and cakes and locally made ice cream. And to wash this all down, the various teas and cordials lovingly prepared by two members of Mabels coven, or hearty ales from the local artisan brewers.

The weather looked set to behave itself, a few white fluffy clouds in the otherwise blue sky, but no threat of rain. Even the river, often as unpredictable as some of the villagers, was in a mellow mood. The ducks on the pond were friendly and fat and about to become more so, bread and cakes easy offerings today.

At the far end of the green Aunty Ruth was with Sally from Farthing Hall, Treacle and Toffee saddled up and ready to give children a safe and gentle ride around the village. They spotted me and waved. I raised my hand in a return greeting and let my eyes taken in more of the scene. Uncle Ron had volunteered to help in the beer tent so there was no sign on him just yet.

A group of children, dressed as I remember children dressing were being shepherded along by Laura and Matt. Laura looked stunning in a bright yellow dress that offset her glossy dark hair and eyes, but her expression was strained, the laughter I heard carried on the breeze, false to my ears. I felt a moments sympathy for her. She too had been betrayed by her man.

Beside her Matt was doing his best to keep the rowdy, excited children in some kind of order and not have his tongue hanging out over Laura at the same time. I made him look at me. So easy to do.

His eyes fixed on my face, and I watched with a smile as his expression changed. Men, I thought with a grimace of distaste, they were all the same.

Liars.

Deceivers.

Betrayers.

I watched his face go pale under the power of my stare. I let my smile deepen and then my attention was caught by Laura.

"Fae, wow you look gorgeous in that dress, doesn't she Matt?" He of course did not comment as she went on. "Are you looking forward to watching the performances later on? We are just going to have a quick last-minute rehearsal now. Benjamin, stop poking at Samantha, that is not nice behaviour! The children have a wonderful play to perform. First though, we dance around the maypole, which of course is the tree, even though it's not May now, we still love to do it when we get the chance. Did you know that the villagers have danced around this tree for hundreds of years? We love our tree don't we children?"

My eyes moved to the ancient tree.

A tree that had stood for hundreds of years.

A tree used to celebrate pagan rites and magic.

A tree used for execution and death.

"It's a hanging tree," I said coldly.

"I beg your pardon?" Laura stopped her excited chatter to stare at me open mouthed.

"It's hanging tree." I repeated, louder this time so that that children could all hear.

"I really don't think……" Matt's voice was interrupted by one of the children.

"What's a hanging tree?"

"I really don't think…."

This time I interrupted Matt "It's a tree they hang witches from."

Gasps of ghoulish delight from the children, shock and horror from Laura and Matt.

"Fae, really," they tried to speak at once and I cut them short.

Let them feel for a second the tightness of the noose. The words choked in their throats just as the air had choked in mine.

I returned my attention to the children. "It's where they hang witches with a heavy thick rope. They put a noose around the neck, stand them on a barrel and then kick the barrel away. The witch dangles and wriggles, her hands claw at her throat, her nails cut into her skin, cutting and bleeding, she cannot breathe, she gasps, she chokes, her lungs burn, her eyes bulge, her world goes black, she is dead!"

They are silent now.

Apart from those who begin to cry.

I have frightened them.

"I don't want to dance around the tree!" A wide-eyed little girl exclaims, swiftly followed by two, then three more, until there is a chorus of cries and shrieks, some of them suddenly wanting their mothers. Satisfied, I release Laura and Matt from their choke hold. They stare at me oddly as well they might, but they are too busy trying to calm the children to remonstrate with me, other than with their reproving glances.

I went on my merry way.

The cake stall looked so pretty. Daintily decorated and temptingly enticing, I wanted to try so many of them. But Mabel from the bakery was there, watching over the stall and watching over me. One of my kind, but for now, not on my side. Alas I would have like to have talked to her, to share with her my feelings, but I know she walks her pathway in a different manner to mine. But the woman selling pies was another matter. I had nothing to fear from her. My stomach grumbled and I followed the urge to satisfy my hunger.

"Do you want me to put it in a box for later, or are you going to eat it now?" She asked as I handed over the money. My stomach rumbled again, and she laughed. "Now I am guessing?"

"Now is good," I said and nodded at her, eager to enjoy the rich pastry and juicy meat of the pie. It was tasty, incredibly so. I don't think I had ever tasted anything so good in my life. Or was it just so long that I could not remember. "Another please."

"Another? Well, that little one inside you is certainly making you hungry. It must be a boy. I was always hungriest when I carried my boys."

I devoured a second pie and shook my head. "My child is a girl. Another witch for Maypoleton."

Her face fell at that point. She crossed the line from friend to foe. "But you are marrying the vicar. You cannot be a witch, nor can your child, be that boy or girl, be a witch. Your child must be brought up in the church."

Oh yes, a foe. I recognised her now. "Am I marrying the vicar? Is my daughter to be born?"

"What in God's name are you saying? The vicar has told everyone you are to be married, despite your background, and that just shows him for the saint he is."

"God has nothing to do with it. Nor does he. I decide this time what the fates decree! Will I marry him, will I not? Will my child be born, will it not? Will I live this time, will I not?"

"You are talking in riddles! Witch filled riddles!

"Witches do not talk in riddles. Witches converse in spells. Your pies are very good." I smiled sweetly at her. "You have cancer. You will die horribly in pain. Soon."

"Oh!" Tears from her then and more of those shocked gasps and comments from those who overheard.

I smiled at them all as I threaded my way through the crowd. I was enjoying myself and this was only the beginning. Puppets on a string I thought as I watched the ripples of reaction ebb and flow through the villagers. Dancing now to my tune. As I had danced to the tune of death, dangling and hanging from the tree.

Where to now among the melee of mayhem I wished to create?

To where it had begun on that night.

The stocks were another focal point today.

I saw that Craig was off duty today. A handsome, strong man, looking more so in his jeans and t-shirt, but even without his uniform he was still the village policeman. He was manning the stocks, an appropriate task for a man such as he. Villagers were queueing up eagerly to await their turn to be placed in the stocks and have wet sponges thrown at them.

Wet sponges!

Not clumps of hard earth and soil.

Not rotten food and putrid waste.

Not rocks and stones brought up from the river.

Wet sponges!

Contempt coiled in my belly; a serpent ready to rise.

They felt my anger; these stupid people who parted now to let me pass. Many stopped to comment on my pregnancy, or to ask that question, when was the wedding to be? I swatted away their comments as though they were wasps, irritating and unwanted. Their faces and mutterings reflected their surprise, shock even. Was that the correct way for the future vicar's wife to respond?

Future vicar's wife be damned.

There would be no wedding.

There would be baby.

"I would ask if you would like a turn," Craig said to me as he helped one sodden, but laughing gentleman out of the stocks, but I don't think you would be very comfortable."

"I rather thought that was the whole point," said the gentleman, "A couple of minutes in there was long enough for me, heck of a crick in my neck."

"Which is why," said Craig jovially, "We have Melissa right over there with her massage table, ready to give folks a quick neck and shoulder rub, ease their stiff muscles. Three pounds for ten minutes, absolute bargain."

"Crafty, but aye, I'll give it a go," said the gentleman and then turned to his wife, "but you're paying for that."

"Only fair, I suppose," she answered him with a smile and then turned to me, "You look lovely, but I think Craig is right, it wouldn't be suitable for you in your condition. Far too uncomfortable."

"What would you know?" I snapped at her. Stupid woman. Ignoring her gasp and husbands stuffy remark, my eyes went to the stocks.

"Fae?" Craig's voice was crisp with curiosity and concern. "Fae really, it's not a good idea."

The people next in line for their turn were more disgruntled that I had pushed them out of the way.

"Well, that's charming I must say," one tutted and I sent him such a look that he fell silent.

I knelt down, heedless that the hem of my dress now trailed in the grass, wet and slightly muddy because of the water and repeated footsteps in the spot. Never mind the mud, there had been so much mud before. It had been raining then, not dry and sunny as today. And into that wet mud, the blood and life of my daughter, my child. I reached out to touch the wood of the stocks. My hands shaking as I felt round the neck and hand holes.

"Fae, what's going on?" Craig had squatted down on the other side of the stocks.

I felt his eyes on me, but I had no desire to look at him. Some more talking behind and around me, and in the background the many different noises of the fayre, laughter, chatting, music, merriment. There had been no music or merriment that night. There had been a cacophony of noise of a much different nature. Cruel jeering, shouting, screaming.

"Fae, talk to me."

My accuser.

My enemy.

My executioner.

How would he feel to be locked up and helpless? Unable to move, to defend himself? A big strong man, brought to his knees by a witch of a woman. I could not get him in the stocks, but I could lock him in place. I could do that. I raised my eyes to look at him.

"Jesus Christ Fae, what's happened to your eyes?"

He stopped talking then. He stopped moving too. Only the flickering of his eyes and the breath rising and falling in his chest gave the clue that he was still alive. More exclamations, calls for help, a rush and a push through the crowd. Was an ambulance needed, had he had a stroke, a heart attack? I got to my knees and began to walk away.

His wife, Eve, one of my kind rushed to his side. "Craig, oh the gods bless me, Craig what's happened. Fae, what happened?"

I shrugged and went on my merry way, hearing behind me the many voices in a muddle of suggestions and accusations, the panic and then the laughing relief as I released Craig from the bind. I could have held him there for longer. Much longer. He deserved it.

Had he not locked me in those stocks and passed stones for the villagers to throw at me? Had he not ignored my pleas to be released as the pains began to gripe in my belly? Had he not laughed as my daughters' lifeless body, was trampled underfoot in front of me, blood and fragile bones crushed into the sodden earth? He had done all that and more and suffer he should. Alas though, as powerful as I was, I must not waste all my energy on him.

I scanned the crowd noticing now the odd looks cast in my direction. Over in the distance he was easy to spot as he stood much taller than the others. I would come to him last of course but there were others I wished to attend to first. Only I needed to make haste. The ripples of my actions were spreading through the village green.

Where was she?

"Fae, Fae, can I talk to you?"

I couldn't see her. Damn the bitch she must be here somewhere.

"Fae, can I ask you to do it for me?"

She must suffer most of all, and him of course.

"Fae, I know you aren't supposed to, rules and all that. But I don't think you give a shit about rules, do you?"

Who was this, disturbing my mission?

"Fae, please, I know you could if you wanted to. Make a spell I mean. To stop Dad being such a wanker. He's having an affair and it's not the first, I know. Mum just refuses to see it cos she's scared of him, I know she is. He puts her down all the time, just like he puts down Dan and the girls. He tries to do it with me, but I won't let him. Fae please?"

Will, of course! Laura's eldest boy. Sweet lad with a crush on me and a thirst for revenge against his bully of a father. "Forgive me, Dan I was distracted in my thoughts. A spell to work on your father? A spell to make others see him as he is? This is your wish?"

The boy nodded at me, a flush to his cheeks, of anger and youthful infatuation.

How could I refuse? It was only what a good witch would do. "Where is he?"

"Dunno. He was in the beer tent earlier getting pissed. That's when he's always worse. He'll take it out on Mum tonight I know he will. But no one sees that."

"They will," I assured him. "Trust me, they will."

He looked at me eagerly. "You can do it then?"

I laughed. "I can and I will. Off you go now. Find your brother and enjoy yourself."

"Thanks Fae. You're awesome."

Charming boy, I thought as I watched him disappear into the crowd. No doubt he would grow up into another lying, betraying man, but for now he was innocent and sweet with that. I would do as he asked. I spotted his father a few minutes later, coming out of the beer tent, with that careful walk a man has when he is drunk but trying not to show it.

Excellent. He would be even easier to manipulate.

I followed him through the crowd, a few feet behind. He was heading towards a pretty young woman in a red dress. I saw as the woman caught sight of Mark, she flashed him a warning look with a shake of the head and a nod in the direction of an older man, also coming towards her and carrying two ice creams. So that was the lay of the land. How utterly perfect. How easy he had just made it for me.

This was going to be fun!

I watched as the woman smiled prettily at the older man and took one of the ice creams. She turned her back on Mark as she did so. The gentleman, tall and very well built bent to kiss her on the cheek. Both showed surprise when Mark approached them, calling out the woman's name, loudly for all around to hear.

"So, you're giving me the cold shoulder are you now, Tania. That's not very friendly, is it?"

The woman froze. The man looked over her to Mark, and then back at her. A frown replacing his smiling expression.

"Oh, hello Mark, I am sorry. I didn't see you there." With a high-pitched laugh and toss of her bright blonde hair, Tania turned slightly so she could glare at him warningly without her companion seeing.

"You bloody did, you whore!"

What a delightful sound, the shocked gasp from bystanders.

"Who the fuck are you calling a whore?" From the man, who was waving his ice cream about as though it were a weapon. Rather funny I thought, and I laughed, momentarily bringing his attention to me. I smiled at him, and he looked shaken. Mark's next words drew his anger once more.

"The whore standing by your side, you gormless prick. Sorry, you gormless, little prick! Wee willy winky as she calls it, more a cocktail sausage than a real man's cock."

Now there was laughter, of the horrified kind amongst some of the crowd, coupled with a growing feeling of unease as clearly there was going to be a fight.

Gormless Prick crushed the cone of his ice cream. I don't think he meant to, I think he was just becoming so angry his grip tightened, maybe imagining his hand around Mark's throat. Either way it was even more amusing to see the mess splatter down the front of his shirt.

"What….did….you…..just….call…..me?"

How odd, I thought, angrier at the insult to his manhood than the suggestion that his woman had been unfaithful.

"Gormless prick," repeated Mark, swaying nearer to Tania whose fair skin was now the colour of her dress. "You like mine much better don't you darling, can't get enough of it can you, and why wouldn't she? I mean, it's so much bigger and better for fucking you with, isn't it?"

"You bitch!" Gormless Prick was almost the same shade of red as Tania, perhaps a touch more purple.

This was so much fun. A little more, I thought.

"Do you want to see it?" Mark then addressed not only Gormless Prick but also the growing group of people who had edged closer to watch this drama unfold. Some even had their phones out.

"Oy get this on video, it'll be class," I heard someone say.

In the corner of my eye, I saw Laura, lovely, sweet Laura, pushing her way towards her husband. Word had swiftly reached her, and she was there to witness the grand finale.

Her husband had no idea his wife was close. "Here, have a good look everyone," Mark unzipped his trousers to the mixed delight and horror of the crowd. "Do you want to see what a real man's cock looks like?"

Sadly, he did not get to show everyone. Gormless Prick had had enough. Shoving aside the now crying Tania, wilted with embarrassment and shame, he launched towards Mark. One punch was all it took. Laura's husband dropped like a stone. There was a hushed silence. Into the void, Gormless Prick addressed Tania in a voice thick with disgust.

"How long? How long have you been shagging him?"

Laura, my beautiful friend Laura, who deserved so much more, asked in a voice somewhat shaky but with an underlying strength I admired.

"Yes Tania, how long has my husband been shagging you?"

Tania did not answer.

"How fucking long?" Roared Gormless Prick.

Tania was caught between the red-hot fury of her man and the icy cold rage of the village head teacher. "Six months," she said in a whisper.

"So not just a one off then?" Laura directed the next question. "Only I would like to be clear on the details when I file for divorce."

I saw then that Matt had come to stand by her side. His eyes caught mine, went wide with a shocked look of understanding. I smiled at him. See, I wasn't all bad.

"I am waiting?" Laura spoke to Tania as if she was one of her pupils.

"Not just a one off. I am sorry," Tania then burst into noisy tears and fled the scene of her shame.

"I am sorry too." Gormless Prick approached Laura. "Not for hitting him," he cast a look at Mark who was now beginning to stir, "but that you had to find out like that."

Laura's poise was beginning to crumble. She nodded and it was easy to see the tears were soon going to fall.

"Come on," said Matt, let's get you a cup of tea, or something stronger."

"Something stronger," I heard her say, then, "What about the children, what if they hear of this?"

"Would you like me to look after them?" I asked, surprised I have to say when they both looked at me oddly.

"It's alright Mum, Dan's taken the girls over to Ruth and Sally for a ride on the horses. I've told him to keep them out of the way for now." Will appeared with a bucket of water which he proceeded to toss over his father, growing more in my estimation. Maybe he would be a man to admire in the future after all? "Get up dad. Time you got your shit together and leave us to get on with ours." Then he turned to look at me. "Thanks Fae."

Laura and Matt turned to look at me, as did rather a few others.

"What do you mean, thanks Fae?" It was Matt, wiser perhaps than Laura who asked the question.

"I asked Fae to work a spell. I wanted everyone to see what Dad's really like. Sorry Mum, but he's been hurting you for too long."

Matt and Laura both stared at me and spoke in unison. "A spell."

I smiled and shrugged my shoulders. "I am a witch. It's what we do."

CHAPTER FORTY- THREE

"Fae, what the hell are you playing at?"

My fiancé it seemed, had reverted to type. How dreary. I covered my eyes with my sunglasses before turning to look at him.

He had an expression of confusion and cold anger on his face as he spoke in that cold clipped manner I hated. "I am hearing all manner of accusations flying around, from parents of children you have upset, to Mrs Forshaw who has been crying her eyes out declaring that you told her she was going to die horribly of cancer, not only that but you must have cast a spell on her and cursed her! Craig had some sort of fit whilst you stood there laughing, and now apparently you put a spell on Mark that has exposed his adultery to all and sunder!"

"It wasn't all he was about to expose," I giggled, thinking again what a shame it was that Gormless Prick had knocked Mark out before he could do that.

"Fae this is not funny, and I am not laughing."

"I can see that," I scowled at him.

"Have you been drinking?" he asked suddenly as if this could possibly be an explanation for my odd behaviour.

"No. Just entertaining myself. Livening things up a little. Besides, all of it is true. Mrs Forshaw does have cancer, and Muppet Mark is an adulterating cheat, and Laura would be so much better off with Matt, you know that as well as I do. And besides Will asked me to do that for him, how could I refuse?"

"My God, listen to yourself Fae! How can you say such things, behave like this?"

I almost pitied him then. I could see the battle within. Confusion, love, desire, disgust. I wasn't ready yet to show my hand fully. Let him think for a moment that I was contrite. "Forgive me my love. It is the crush of all these people, the weight of their expectations upon me. I wish to be the vicar's wife, truly I do."

He heaved a sigh. "We have a lot of repair work to do, but I am sure we will put things to right. But Fae, there must be no more spells. Of any kind! Ever!"

"Of course, darling, whatever you say."

Was he suspicious then, I wondered at my easy compliance? There was no time though for more talk as the schedule of events was pressing.

"We will talk about this later. For now, I must gather everyone to watch the children's performance, which is still going ahead, no thanks to you I must say."

With that he strode off, smile in place for the villagers who were eager to press further comments and complaints onto his attention. A short while later I heard his voice, clear, strong, authoritative, over the microphone.

"Ladies and gentleman, boys and girls, your attention for a few moments, please." He was awarded the hush he required, and all eyes, including mine turned in his direction. "Thank you all for attending today and making the most of this beautiful sunshine as well as the wonderful array of stalls Maypoleton's finest has to offer. Whilst I am reluctant to tear you away from enjoying spending your money," a pleasant roll of laughter through the crowd at this point, "and do please carry on as you know that the school will benefit from the roof repairs, assemblies with the rain leaking in are not much fun in the winter I can tell you."

More laughter. "But I would ask you all to pause in your activities and gather round the maypole in order to support our wonderful head teacher Laura, our fabulous deputy head Matt and of course most importantly the children as they perform their summer play."

Obediently, his flock began to gather most of them taking advantage of the seating that had been arranged around the temporary deck that served as a stage, close to the tree. My eyes scanned the crowd. I still had not found her and my frustration was growing as my energy was fading.

Where was she?

"Are you alright Fae, folk have been having a bit of a gossip about you?"

Distracted once more I turned to see Arthur being pushed along in his wheelchair by one of his friends who came regularly to the vicarage to play chess with him.

"Oh, hello Arthur, George. Lovely afternoon isn't it. Are you going to watch the play?"

"Just wheeling him over there now," said George with a beaming smile. I knew he liked me. Most of the men in the village did. "Would you like us to save you a seat?"

I shook my head. "I am just looking for someone."

"More spells to cast, hey, Fae," whispered Arthur in an undertone with a merry glint in his eye. "I heard about Mark getting his wotsit out!" He laughed and patted my hand playfully. "Just mind you don't get your fingers burnt. Gawain won't stand for too much nonsense, however much he loves you."

"Don't worry," I smiled at him. "I have no intention of getting burnt."

Others maybe, but not me.

And then as though I had conjured her up, which of course I must have done, she was there in my view, close by with the she dragon in the form of Mrs Mannering. The pair of them glared at me their disapproval evident on their faces.

Naturally I smiled and began to walk towards them.

"Mrs Mannering, Lucinda, how lovely to see you. Where are your children?"

Lucinda failed to hide her hatred of me. Without Gawain to witness, her loathing and hurt that he had rejected her for me, was clear to see and in Mrs Mannering she had a staunch ally.

"Toby is with my mother for the weekend and Susie is with the other children getting ready for the play."

"Good."

"What do you mean good?"

I meant that I was pleased her children were not present to see what was about to happen. I was not that heartless! I ignored her comment and walked in closer to her. They had no option either of them but to take a few steps back. Perfect. Just where I needed them to be.

"Fancy a burger ladies? Hot dog maybe?" The barbeque was sizzling a few feet away, delicious meaty smells mouthwatering and tempting. But not as tempting as the taste of revenge.

I looked at the woman who had stolen him from me. The woman he loved more than me. The woman he was going to marry instead of me. I looked at Lucinda and I saw Cressida. I saw the woman I had poisoned and whose death had brought about my own. My death had been far more painful, of that, I was sure.

My death had taken me to a cold lonely grave for centuries.

But now I was free to take my revenge to make others suffer as I had. Finally, then, I knew I would have peace. Not much more to do now.

First her, and then him.

Fire destroys, fire cleanses.

They would be destroyed.

The past would be cleansed.

I would be free.

Another step towards her.

Mrs Mannering spoke sharply. "Be careful Lucinda, the barbeque is right behind you."

A sentiment echoed by the man in charge of it. Careful ladies, you don't want to get to close. Don't want any fat to splatter those lovely dresses."

There would be no fat splatter a dress. But flames suddenly reaching out of nowhere to ignite the flimsy cotton. Oh yes there would be that.

And there was.

Shouts of alarm and astonishment as the barbeque became a furnace out of control. One little move of my hand, a flick of the wrist, a pointing of my finger, and Lucinda stumbled backwards.

Screams.

Flames.

Chaos.

I laughed and walked away, but first my eyes went to those of Gawain.

He stared at me in utter horror.

I smiled back at him.

He would be next.

And so would the love of his life.

Twin Flames.

And together they would burn.

CHAPTER FORTY-FOUR

"Gawain," I said groggily, fighting my way through a dense blanket of weighty darkness.

My eyelids felt as though they had been glued together, I struggled to open them, but when I did, I saw that I was still in the bedroom at the vicarage. How odd? I thought I had got up to go to the village fayre. But now, here I was lying on the bed, fully dressed. Had I had a funny turn? My head was certainly spinning and there was that growing feeling of nausea that had me moving quickly to get to the bathroom.

I couldn't make it.

My legs were like jelly. Weak as a newborn kitten and just about as clumsy, I fell to my knees on the floor, crying out as I did so. "Gawain?"

"He can't hear you."

I heard her voice close by, but my vision was blurred, my head too dizzy to focus on anything.

"Gawain!" I tried again and got no further as violent bouts of vomiting had me in a vice like grip for what seemed the longest time. When I had finished, I slumped on the floor, my body shivering and shaking, icy cold yet burning hot at the same time.

I had never felt so ill in my life. "I need a doctor," I whispered, although I wasn't quite sure who I was speaking to as my fiancé was obviously not here.

She was though.

Eliza.

She came to kneel beside me, that ghostly touch caressing my face as a mother would a child. But there was no love in this touch, and I shuddered beneath it.

"No doctors."

"What's wrong with me? My baby? Is my baby ill? Am I losing my child?" That fear overrode all other thoughts.

"Not yet. But soon, yes soon, you will lose your child. As I did."

"What do you mean?" Terror gave me some strength to force myself up into a sitting position. I could see her now. Crouched on the floor beside me, a cold, cruel oh so cruel look on her face.

"You betrayed me."

"I betrayed you? How? How did I betray you?" Absurd to be having this conversation when I really needed a doctor, and I really needed Gawain! What must he be thinking? I should be at the fayre by now, not being struck down by goodness knows what ailment Eliza had manifested for me. And why for that matter? None of it made sense. Neither did her explanation when it came. Only that it was that of a mind twisted with pure insanity.

"You turned against me! You wished him to not suffer!"

"I didn't turn against you! I just love him that's all as he loves me, and our child. How is that turning against you?"

"I thought you were my friend."

"I was. I mean I am. Eliza this has to stop, this desire for revenge."

"You see! You betray me with these words. Have I not lain lost and alone for all these years? Abandoned. Forgotten. It is my chance now to make them see what they have done. Let them know what I have become! Let them see my power! Let them feel my rage!"

I shuddered at the knowledge of what she had become, and my part in that. A powerful, evil presence. I cried inside as I listened to her spew forth her venom, regaling with delight her activities at the fayre.

"They all think it is you who have done these things. I have killed his love for you, just as I have killed the woman who dared to think she could take my place."

"No! No Eliza, no. Tell me you have not done these things?"

I wept out loud now as I pictured Lucinda burning, an image too horrific to contemplate, the knowledge that the man I loved thought I was responsible.

"I told you. Not I, but you! Or so they all think." More horrible laughter and then she went on. *"And now your turn to suffer for your betrayal."*

My mouth was almost too dry to utter the words. "I never meant to betray you. I am sorry, I really am." I didn't know what else to say.

She sighed. *"It's too late. Far, far, far too late. You betrayed me with your love for him."* Her face twisted into a nasty smile. *"You call him your twin flame, and indeed I feel he is, the other half of your soul, as my lover was to me! And in the flames so shall you both perish, and your child with you!"*

As she spoke, I became aware of the smell of smoke close by and an unusual heat building in the room.

"I shall burn this house down with you in it. And when he sees the flames, he will come running. For although I have killed his love for you, I shall bid him run. I shall bid him enter. I shall bid him die with you in the flames."

"Eliza no, please, I am begging you. Don't do this!"

It was no use.

I was speaking to an empty room.

An empty room that was rapidly filling with smoke. Where was it coming from? Was there any chance I could get out of the house before it was too late? I tried to stand. Couldn't. Coughed and choked, my eyes beginning to smart with the thickening black cloud.

So hot now, a furnace gathering around me. I could see the deadly bright glow of the flames beneath the door, licking at the woodwork, fiery hot tendrils flickering through, slowly at first, just a hint of what was to come, and then with a far greedier hand, devouring the door, as it blackened and scorched beneath the heat.

Was there any way I could get out of the window? Climb down, or even jump? Not something I wished to do with my baby to consider, but if I stayed there would be no baby. I managed to drag myself to the window. I saw the mass of people hurrying now away from the fayre towards the vicarage.

I saw Gawain, running the fastest, coming to save me as he had done on that night. I thought of her words. How she wanted him to burn with me. Her power sufficient to draw him in. I reached for the catch on the window, my fingers clumsy, my movements stupid, my head swimming, my lungs struggling to breathe.

It jammed.

Stuck fast.

Helplessly I banged on the glass.

"Don't come in! I screamed with a dry throat, a useless attempt as he would not be able to hear. "Don't come in. She wants you to die too."

He reached the vicarage, others close behind, his face a mask of horror and fear.

Tears streamed down my face now, with the smoke, the grief, the loss. For I knew I was going to die, and my child too. But not him. I could not bear it if he died also.

I thought of that night when we had met. Two tortured souls in desperate need of forgiveness and salvation. Seeking a way out. Looking to end the suffering. Ironic that now that desire to leave life behind, was being granted, and in such a way.

"Don't come in!" I mouthed silently against the now hot glass. "I love you. I love you. I love you."

He disappeared from view. I heard his name being shouted. Knew that others would have tried to pull him back. But who or what could possibly be strong enough to withstand the ghostly power of a witch gone mad? Or perhaps, the power of deep soul love?

Twin Flame love.

"Fae!"

Through the angry roar of the flames, the splintering of wood, the shattering of glass as windows blew out with the heat, I heard his voice.

"Fae!"

The flames were coming into the room now. Even if he could climb the stairs, he would not be able to save me.

But he could save himself, there was still time. He did not have to die too.

"Go back! It's too late!" I screamed, sobbed, or tried to. My voice was too choked with smoke.

I heard a terrible creaking, cracking, crashing, as though the very timbers of the old house were collapsing under the force of the fire. I heard screams and shouts from outside. I heard his voice once more, faintly this time, lost in the ferocity of the furnace that rampaged hideously closer with every second.

"Go back!" I tried once more, feebly this time as the smoke filled my throat and lungs, my last words to him choked out on a cough, "I love you. I will always love you."

He would never hear me, and I knew him too well that he would not turn back. No matter if he hated me, no matter if he thought me capable of the foul deeds that Eliza had created, he would not turn back. He was that kind of man.

He was the man I had been waiting for all my life.

He was the man I loved.

He was my twin flame.

And in the fire of Eliza's revenge, we would perish together.

CHAPTER FORTY-FIVE

Rowan greeted me with a mother's loving embrace. *"My darling child do not cry so. There is nothing to fear."*

She looked so beautiful, radiant and glowing. This was not the shadowy, exhausted version of my mother I had seen when I connected with her spirit. This was a light filled, serene Rowan, tall, strong, powerful.

Powerful?

Had I ever envisaged my mother as powerful?

Her laughter was a joy to behold. *"Yes, my child I am powerful. As are you and as will your daughter be."* I could feel the energy emanating from her. It seemed to enfold me in its golden glow, as though I was in a light filled bubble where nothing could hurt or harm me anymore. I had never felt protected, sheltered, and safe in my life. I had never felt more loved.

"Am I dead?"

"Do you wish to be?"

I wished to stay with her in this blissful bubble for all eternity. I wished to breathe in this joy. I wished to embrace the peace I had been searching for, for so long.

She shook her head gently. *"This does not have to be your time. Your daughter is waiting to be born."* Her hands went to my belly. A surge of love so intense it took my breath away rippled through me, from her touch to my child, my daughter. She nodded. *"Your daughter wishes to be born. Your daughter has her life to live."*

Tears swam in my eyes. I was so torn. To stay with her or go back to life.

To a life where my daughter would be born.

To a life where her father would be dead.

"I don't know if I am brave enough."

Rowan looked at me, an enigmatic expression in her eyes. All knowing. All loving. *"You may stay if you wish."*

I could stay? I could have this choice? I could have what I had been seeking for so long, a way out of the life that caused me so much pain. I could finally be free of the guilt over Fliss's death.

My mind went back to that night in January when I had met him, when he and I had both been on that edge, that brink of despair and desolation. Our daughter had been conceived that night. Her father may well have perished in Eliza's wicked revenge, but my daughter, his daughter did not have to lose her life even before it had begun. I placed my hands on my belly, my eyes lowering to the swell beneath my breasts.

My gaze lifted to meet Rowan's, and she smiled as she saw the answer in my eyes. *"It is the right choice."*

"I don't want to leave you."

"You are not leaving me, just as I never left you. I told you, love never dies. Love cannot die. Love always is."

"Fliss?"

"Is at peace as I am. Now it is your time to be at peace. Amongst the living."

CHAPTER FORTY-SIX

I was falling.
Such a long way.
Falling, drifting, floating, ever downwards.
Never ending.
Gently at first, softly, fluidly.
Then with more of a tug, a pull, a drag, a harder force.
Uncomfortable, awkward, a rigid resistance.
Not pleasant now the feelings surging through me. Where was that sense of light in every cell? What had happened to the feather like sensations that had fluttered so beautifully within me? As though I had been a mere wisp of air, a fluff of a cloud carried on a warm summer's breeze.
Such beautiful feelings.
Such bliss.
Such peace.
Where had it gone?
This was painful, hard, this was dense, heavy.
This was leaden, lumpy, this was jolting, jarring.
This was gasping, choking, this was coughing, breathing.
This was being alive.
"Oh, sweet Christ Fae, I thought I'd lost you!"
If I had died and been in heaven, then I must now be in hell. My senses screamed at the contrast. Raging heat, noise, voices, a thundering roar from somewhere, cracking, shattering sounds. And pain the like of which I had never felt before. In every cell, every particle of my being.
I had to be in hell.
But if I was in hell, then so too was Gawain.
As my eyes shot open, I looked into his.
Blue-grey eyes, the colour of a stormy sea, bloodshot and teary in a blackened face.

Eyes so very close to mine.

"I've got you, Fae, I've got you. You're safe now. You're safe now."

I gasped another choking, coughing breath. I was not dead. I was neither in heaven, nor hell. I was alive and being carried by Gawain, out of the vicarage, out of the fire, out of the flames and away from Eliza's revenge. Into the crowd of people, the whole village it seemed who had rushed to watch the vicarage burn to the ground.

"I thought you were dead," a fractured whisper all I could manage. "I thought you were dead.

"I thought you were dead," tears spilt down his blistered cheeks. "I thought we both were." A look that I will never forget.

We knew.

We had both died.

We had been brought back.

Eliza's witchcraft was dark and powerful. Magic woven from hatred and a desire for revenge. Powerful enough to reach across the boundaries of time and reality. Powerful enough to kill.

But a mother's love is more powerful.

The desire for forgiveness is more powerful.

The intention to heal is more powerful.

It was too much to take in right now. All I could do was cry with the enormity of it. "She wanted to kill you. She wanted to kill us both, and the baby. Oh God our baby!"

"I know, I saw her Fae, I saw her. Eliza. She taunted me with all she had done and all she was about to do. To kill us both and our child, to perish in the flames of her revenge." Gawain's voice was as croaky as mine, his eyes bewildered yet at the same time shining with a brilliance I had never seen in them before. As if he had been lit up from within.

He had.

"And then I saw you, walking towards me through the flames, untouched by them. Only it wasn't you. It was your sister. It was Fliss."

"Oh God, Fliss?"

Tears streamed down his face now, so close to mine. "She came to save me. She told me I was meant to live. That we both were. That we had purpose together."

I couldn't hold back the tears then, they came in harsh, wild sobs torn from the very depths of my soul. Cries of relief, release, and the heart-healing knowing that all was forgiven.

"Shush, don't cry, it's going to be alright, I swear to you it's going to be alright. Everything's going to be alright, darling, just rest easy now."

I clung tighter to him as I wept at the wonder of it.

And then memory came smacking me across the face. "Lucinda....oh God Lucinda!" I moaned in horror at what I had done. "How can it possibly be alright? I killed Lucinda!"

"No, you did not, hush now child, all is well. Light has prevailed."

Another voice now, close by. Was that Mabel I could hear? Gawain had brought us both safely away from the vicarage now and into the throng of people gathered around. It was all so chaotic and noisy it was hard to think, to feel, to understand.

"Here Gawain, let me take her, you look fit to drop. Alright everyone, just move away and give us some space."

Easy to recognise Craig's voice, strong, clear, full of authority. The air began to feel cooler, fresher as I was carried now by Craig further away from the intensity of the furnace that was the vicarage.

Another cocoon now of an earthly kind. Surrounded by people who I knew loved me. Aunty Ruth and Uncle Eric shock and fear in their eyes. Mabel and Eve, compassion and wisdom in their looks. Craig, the solid, dependable neighbour and policeman with surprising sympathy emanating from him as he gently laid me on the ground. Matt and Laura, standing close together. He had his arm around her, and I remembered with another shock what I had done to Laura's husband, that cruel exposure of his adultery. I gasped with the inner pain of it, and then gasped some more as my lungs protested the damage from the smoke.

"Laura, I'm so sorry. It wasn't me. It was her. It was.... oh God has she gone? Please tell me she's gone?" I tried to sit up desperately seeking reassurance from someone that Eliza's malignant influence had gone. I was terrified that maybe even now she was exerting her power over me, and this was all some cruel hoax, an illusion and that any second now the people I loved would disappear in a cloud of smoke, like the black billowing mass that was now filling the sky above the vicarage.

And I would be lost, alone, and in the dark.

Without my lover, without my child.

Just as she had been.

I felt a pull, a silent scream, a wave of nausea so strong it had me vomiting onto the grass. Gentle hands, Laura's I think supporting me as I painfully wretched, voices in unison, Mabel, Eve and Seth. Seth? What was he doing here? They were chanting something I couldn't make out.

"Gawain?" I called for him, needed him. Where was he?

"He's fine, Doctor Jay is with him." Craig's voice, calm, strong, steady.

"So tired," the spasms in my stomach had passed but I was sinking now into another deep cocoon. Scared though to enter into this numbing void for fear of what may linger there. I had felt Eliza's desperation, the knowledge that she had failed. I had felt her last final attempt to call me to her.

Dare I close my eyes and sleep?

Dare I rest and recover?

Dare I believe it was all over?

The need for atonement, the quest for forgiveness, the desperate searching to be made whole again, granted in a love that was returned, as the other half of my soul came to me as one.

Dare I believe in magic of that enormity?

Dare I possibly believe in a miracle of that magnitude?

Dare I possibly believe in a fairy tale ending?

Soft gentle laughter, and a blessing from beyond the grave.

"Dare to believe my child, for it is done.

The magic is worked, the miracle granted.

Twin Flames united and a child born enchanted."

I heard Rowan's voice on the wind, I felt her kiss on my brow, I closed my eyes, and I slept.

EPILOGUE

The vicarage was gutted.

Eliza's wrathful revenge burnt through the building and destroyed what she did not manage to do between Gawain and me.

Love, true love, pure love can never be destroyed.

Love, true love, pure love has the power to cross all boundaries and create magic and miracles that cannot be imagined.

And in the weeks and months that followed the fire, it took some magic and working of miracles to bring peace and some kind of order back into the village. Despite the constant reassurances from Mabel, Eve and Seth that I was not responsible for the damage, it was hard for me to shut out the knowledge of what I had done whilst bewitched.

Lucinda had escaped with superficial burns thanks to the quick actions of the man in charge of the barbeque, and Mabel who alerted by Eve that I was under the influence of malignant magic had come to the rescue. So too had Seth, Eve's father who by all accounts had also helped send Eliza's spirit over to the light as she had battled that last final time to pull me back to her.

But there were fractures, of course there were.

Laura began divorce proceedings with Mark, and although she was soon allowing herself to be wooed by Matt, our friendship needed careful handling.

The bishop was inundated with complaints about me, and it was a close call as to whether Gawain remained in the church. But Fliss won that battle. Or rather Gawain's unshakeable stance that a miracle had granted him life, and that his life was to be spent with me. So, he either remained in the church to inspire others to believe in miracles, with me by his side, or he walked.

The bishop wisely nodded and said he would be happy to preside over our wedding.

The healing began then as the village came together to celebrate with us. I walked down the aisle a few short weeks before my daughter was due to be born, Dad proudly giving me away, and Mum wearing the most ridiculous hat ever, wiping away what I hoped were tears of joy and finally some pride.

As Gawain's wife, the vicar's wife, I moved into our temporary home in Maypoleton, a house we were renting whilst the shell of the vicarage was demolished, and rebuilding could begin. And in this home, this new start for us both, on 31st October, Samhain, under the light and power of the full moon, our child was born.

Gawain was with me throughout, and once the midwife was happy that all was well after an easy birth, we were alone for the first time with our daughter.

"She is beautiful," Gawain whispered as he cradled her between us on the bed. "She is the most perfect miracle I have ever seen." His voice was full of wonder and love, his eyes shining with tearful adoration.

"She is magically perfect," I whispered back to him, my heart bursting with love as tiny, incredible fingers closed around mine.

"A magical miracle," Gawain agreed and leant forward to kiss me, and then our daughter. "Fae Temple, I love you with every particle of my soul, that I do. And you my darling daughter, I love you with every particle of my soul, that I do."

With my free hand I reached for his. "Gawain Temple, I love you with every particle of my soul, that I do. And you my darling daughter, I love you with every particle of my soul, that I do."

"She is special," my husband said as he continued to gaze in awe at our child.

"She is," I agreed, and I knew that this was more than the usual new mother's notion. Rowan had told me how special our daughter was going to be.

"A child of light, a child of love, a child of healing. A child with magic and miracles flowing in her veins."

With the merriest of gurgles as though she could hear my silent thoughts, our daughter opened her eyes.

Unusual eyes.

One brown.
One blue.
Eliza's eyes.

And in that moment, I knew that she was blessed with a guardian angel who would watch over her, every step of the way.

A guardian angel in the guise of a once troubled, lost and lonely witch, now finally at peace.

If you enjoyed reading about Fae, and would like to discover Eve's story, this is told in A Secret Love For Eve – Magic of Maypoleton Book One.

www.ingramcontent.com/pod-product-compliance
Ingram Content Group UK Ltd.
Pitfield, Milton Keynes, MK11 3LW, UK
UKHW022021310325
456929UK00006B/472